The Sleeping Life

by Andrea K Höst

All characters in this publication
are fictitious and any resemblance
to real persons, living or dead,
is purely coincidental.

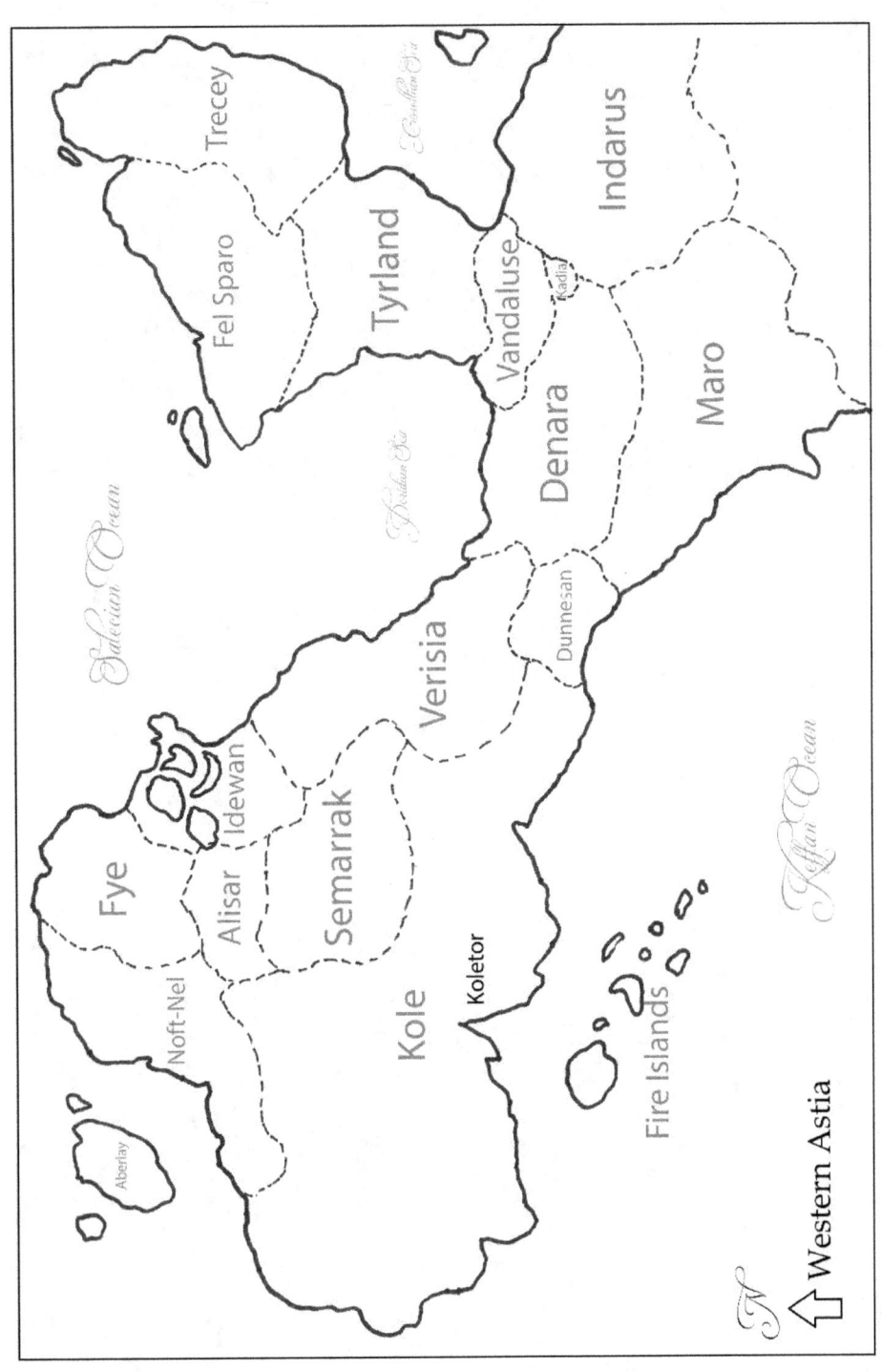

Western Astia

Chapter One

Even ignoring his nightmare predicament, Fallon DeVries would be glad to get back to the Arkathan and away from the ritual of saying goodnight to an idealised statue of his mother and sister. Every evening, as his father pressed lips to a marble forehead, Fallon's heart crawled into his stomach and writhed.

"You're looking well today, my dears," Vannan DeVries said. He reached down to pat the head of the smaller of the two figures, then glanced expectantly at Fallon.

"Goodnight Mother," Fallon said, obediently. "'Night Auri."

"You must be sure to visit on rest day, Fallon," his father said. "The house will be quiet with only we three."

"You're forgetting Mrs Pardons."

"Indeed. Though I regret to say this evening's offering will not easily slip my mind." Fallon's father tugged at his short, brown-blond beard. "Perhaps she would do better with an assistant. We burden our old helpmate too much."

"It's just because I've been home." The words had come too fast, too strong, and Fallon bit his lip, then forced a lighter tone. "I've eaten out the pantry. Besides, Mrs Pardons would be hurt if she thought we were angling to replace her."

"Oh, she could not think that." Distressed, Fallon's father held a hand out toward the smiling, seated figure of his wife. "My dear, I had best go speak to her. Goodnight, lad."

Fallon let himself relax, knowing that Mrs Pardons would take in stride sudden reassurances that she was too valued a friend to be replaced, and nip in the bud any further ideas of new staff. Her cooking wasn't likely to improve, but if Fallon's plan succeeded she would be able to go back to providing meals delivered by her granddaughter. Father would never know.

"But he's getting worse," Fallon said—to himself, not the statue.

The two figures smiled on: his stone mother relaxed in a stone chair, head turned attentively toward the library door, while stone Aurienne leaned against her knees, lips curved enigmatically. Even Auri admitted that the marble version of herself was a good deal prettier than it should be—and laughed at the thought of herself ever sitting devotedly at their mother's feet—but still this remembrance of the dead was a triumph of their father's skill. Mother had always had that complacent expression, that expectation of an audience. And Auri looked properly herself: restless and eager all at once.

Fallon went and ate jam tarts. They sat uneasily on the burnt grease Mrs Pardons had produced that evening, but were necessary energy. While his stomach settled he did the household accounts, refusing to let himself factor in any hope that his father would begin to work again, and make their financial situation less precarious. Then he prepared his room, setting a glow above a new book in the page-turner Sigillic, and weighting the corners of the latest collection of newssheets before settling with his head under a pillow to escape the light and dream his sister.

Though she neither ate nor drank, Auri had aged during the three years of the Dream, and now appeared fourteen to his sixteen. Even so, she was already inches taller, since Fallon took after their mother's blond delicacy, while his twin had their father's lanky frame. She read through the newssheets before crossing to the bed to take Fallon's hand and draw him fully into the dream state that was now the whole of her existence.

"Can you think of anything to hobble Uncle?" Auri asked. "You'll never get anywhere with Rennyn Claire if he keeps up this campaign against her husband."

"He was here today." Because he didn't want to notice how frayed Auri was looking, Fallon glanced down at himself, shifting uneasily in the bed. "Banging on at Father about the need to counter the Kellian threat. Perhaps, if the first approach doesn't work, I can offer Lady Rennyn inside information."

"Was Father very upset?" Auri asked, her voice sharpening as she crossed to the door. "Why can't Uncle leave him be?"

Fallon followed his sister through the cold soapiness of the wooden door. "If anything, Uncle's visits do Father good," he said, rubbing his goose-nabbed upper arms. "He gets annoyed and that makes him less vague and more in tune with the real world. But he—he is talking to them more."

Without replying, Auri stepped through the door of their father's room, and again Fallon trailed her through slippery chill, finding her standing by their father, who was sitting up before his fire leafing through one of their mother's books of verses.

"It might be too much for him," she said, stroking the oblivious man's shoulder. "If you manage to get me back, he might be even more convinced Mama's still alive. Or—"

She stopped, and moved to warm her hands over the fire, growing visibly more solid. Warmth was important to Auri, and while Fallon had learned to make sure there were always heatstones nearby, she preferred fires. Fallon didn't go too close—fires in the Dream always made him feel floaty and less real.

"Father won't blame you. You did something stupid, but Mother's the one who made your disappearance all about her. She spent more time picking out becoming mourning clothes than crying. And wandering weeping in the rain was a scene right out of the last novel she'd read."

"She still wouldn't have fallen ill if not for me," Auri said, bluntly. "And Father wouldn't have—wouldn't be this way if she were still alive. Me coming back isn't going to make him better, is it?"

"It's not like Father's the only reason to fix this," Fallon said, moving away from the fire. He knew Auri's mood was due to tomorrow's return to the Arkathan, where Fallon would have to share a room with five others, and could not set the page-turning Sigillic without prompting questions impossible to answer. She'd been desperately bored during Fallon's first term: unable to travel far from Fallon's side, and finding little entertainment in a dormitory of sleeping students—beyond the things people did in their beds when they thought everyone asleep, which was hardly what Fallon wanted her watching.

"At least there'll be plenty of food," Auri said, her thoughts obviously following—nearly—similar lines. "You look liable to snap in half. We'd do better to see if we can get any use out of Lady Rennyn before risking more experiments."

"This will be the last we can do for an age," Fallon pointed out. "And you promised not to wriggle out. Don't be weak."

He pushed out through the door, knowing any suggestion of cowardice would bring her to the point. But, while Auri followed into the corridor, she passed him and stopped, blocking the way.

"*I'm* not the problem," Auri said. "You are. You kept putting this off until you were sure you had the right

Sigillic, and now you're all thin and worn looking. Do you want Father to carve a third family member?"

Fallon flinched, but would only concede a partial point. "I know I'm run down. But this is just a divination. And *you* know we can't pin our hopes to one solution. No matter how clever and powerful a mage Lady Rennyn might be, if she isn't told the problem she won't be looking for a solution. It's not as if I can explain anything."

"Bah. If she's truly as good as the Elder Mages were, then she should know all at first glance, have an answer after a second. And why you'd argue against this I don't know—admit it, there's nothing you'd love more than to be the student of someone like that and burble on all day about the structure and nature of magic."

"I'm not arguing. But even without Uncle the chances of me convincing Lady Rennyn she wants another student are slim at best. We need to—"

"We need the best. And to have a better strategy than 'I'll show her how much I love magic'. Be clever about this, instead of falling into your usual trick of getting caught up in whatever you're thinking and letting your mouth run on by itself. How I ever thought you'd keep a secret—"

"Well I have," Fallon pointed out.

"Exactly! Well, with the help of a little choking, but you obviously can think without your tongue slipping the leash *sometimes*."

"Nothing other than discussing you has me blue-faced and fainting," Fallon said. "And you're one to talk about minding your words given it was your note that caused the problem. 'Keep this a secret or I'll kill you' indeed."

"It was just a note. I still can't see how I went wrong. I had the Sigillic perfect, and it all was going as described and—Fel, I wish Lady Rennyn would come back to the city!" Auri whirled and dashed back through Fallon's door.

Thinking too deeply about the miscasting always unsettled her, and Fallon knew better than to try to talk his sister into joining him. Rubbing his arms in hopes of warming them, he made himself turn the opposite way. The door of Auri's room was different to all others: was like treacle or spider web, clinging and catching. All of the walls were like that too, but the floor was the worst, and Fallon still couldn't bear to think about the time he'd tried to go down through it and almost been trapped.

In the waking world the room felt heavy and cold. The door stuck in a warped frame, the beams of the ceiling bowed, the walls leaned. The floorboards spiralled to a point in the very centre of the room. On the night Auri had complained of a headache and refused to go to the theatre, they'd returned to find every piece of her bedroom furniture clumped in the centre of the room, bent and distorted into a single mass. But no blood, no body.

Hand investigators concluded that she'd been trying to summon a mage's focus—six years before legally permitted—and paid for her over-eagerness with her life. The note Fallon had found in his room had confirmed that, though he couldn't show his parents or the investigators, since the slip of paper had crumpled into nothing as he read it, and when he'd tried to talk about it hands seemed to close about his throat.

Standing in the centre of the warped and nearly empty room, Fallon wrestled with that memory, with the suffocating weight of Auri's half-life. It was unsustainable. Wherever it was she was trapped, she drew on his strength to come into the Dream. If she did nothing but read the books he set out, he did not feel the impact too greatly, though there had not been a morning since Auri's death that he had not woken feeling tired. But it was Auri's boredom that was liable to kill them both.

The very first night of the Dream, she had found that the world was not entirely soap bubble permeable. If she tried hard enough, she could touch, move, even cast if a Sigillic had been set written and waiting for her. But the energy this cost Fallon was ruinous, not only forcing him to sleep more and more, but bringing him to the very verge of over-commitment, the most common cause of any caster's death. If a mage commenced a casting that they did not have the strength to sustain, something had to fail: either the casting, or the mage's heart.

They had found a balance. The page-turner, a Sigillic Fallon would activate before he slept, would allow Auri to read without touching. He would set out newssheets, leave notes. On nights he was better rested, she would draw him into the Dream, and they would talk. But most of Auri's existence was cold silence while the world slept, and Fallon desperately needed to understand what had gone wrong with her casting so he could fetch her back to the physical world. Focus-summoning required a trip to the dangerous shadow world of the Eferum, but Fallon was certain she was no longer there. Instead, she seemed to have found some place between the two worlds, less dangerous, but also less tangible.

Since it was essential for him to excel as a mage to figure out this puzzle, he attended the Arkathan, the most prestigious of the schools, but the cost took up most of their Mother's annuity, leaving too little for household expenses. Fallon had hit on the idea of becoming a private student even before Rennyn Claire had surfaced that summer and shown Tyrland the kind of casting that hadn't been seen since the Elder Mages had walked—and nearly destroyed—the world.

But how was he to win her interest when he couldn't explain how important it was? He loved magic, but he had hardly set the Arkathan ablaze with his brilliance.

"Get to know her other students." Auri, tense but resolute, stood at his elbow. She crossed to examine the Sigillic he had chalked earlier that day, adding: "Not her brother, but those other two: that villager and the Kellian girl. Work out why she decided to teach them, and maybe you can catch her notice the same way. Or get them to recommend you."

Moving carefully, so she didn't push through it, Auri settled into one of the few pieces of furniture that had not been distorted beyond recognition: a heavy and ornate chair that had been left with a permanent forward bow, embracing its occupant.

"I'll think about it," Fallon said, though he suspected those reasons would involve being a Kellian or having his home destroyed, neither of which were practical options. "I'm trying this divination because I think the floor in here might be distorting the ones I've used before. This should just make any magical emanations visible."

"Did you try it waking?" Auri asked, propping her chin on her hand.

"Yes. Just the usual miscast. The distortion in the physical world is fading a little, I think, but it still makes it too difficult for me to cast there."

Fallon frowned at the sigils he'd chalked down the length of one curving board. Why was it worse in the physical world than Auri's Dream? And where was the Dream, if it was neither the physical world, nor the Eferum, the dimension that was the source of all magic? There were so many experiments he could try, and it was maddening to never have the energy to attempt them, or the freedom to discuss them with someone more interested in theory than his sister. She'd always found the *why* of magic boring, and had been so naturally talented that she felt she could skip plodding lesson plans and all the theory that went with the practice. If Auri had cared about theory they wouldn't be in this situation in the first place.

"I swear, if you meet Lady Rennyn and spend an hour standing there thinking about what you *might* say to her instead of just going ahead and *doing*, I will—"

"Haunt me?" Fallon swallowed a giggle he knew would sound wrong. It wasn't funny, not at all, and if he was half the mage he wanted to be he'd be neither slow nor rash, but simply sure. The kind of mage Lady Rennyn was said to be.

Sigillic casting was easy—so long as it was written correctly, was a true and tested formulation, all that was necessary was to feed power and let it work. He'd researched a divination that seemed perfect for his purposes: simple, and robust, showing only lingering traces of worked Efera. Fallon could cast it in his sleep—and almost stopped feeding power, thinking about how true that was. But neither distraction nor the strange environment prevented the Sigillic from obediently completing.

Pastel blue shading. It made the cold worse somehow, but it had done exactly what Fallon had wanted, and he let his breath out, pleased. That the entire room still carried the imprint of Auri's miscasting was obvious to anyone who entered it, but what Fallon had wanted was the impression of the sigils she had used, the Sigillic form that had dictated the magical result. Sigils written with ink or chalk were usually consumed during a casting, but a strong Sigillic could at times leave a physical or Efera imprint, and Fallon's divination was one used by the Hand to uncover the terms of Sigillics which had burned away or been erased.

"I didn't write them like that," Auri said, staring down at the circle of glowing, snowflake shapes.

Fallon, spirits sinking, didn't doubt it. Just like the floorboards they were written upon, the sigils had been twisted into spirals by the miscasting. The light would have made them hard enough to read: the distortion made it near-impossible.

"If I could trace them out, I suppose," he said, trying to puzzle out the nearest sigil. Three spokes, so it would be an action...

"Don't be stupid." Auri, avoiding the Sigillic, crossed to tug on his arm. "You can't maintain a casting like this nearly—" She broke off, and went back to her chair, kneeling down to peer underneath it.

"What?"

"Come see."

Her cheek was shining blue, reflecting a strong light source beneath the chair. Fallon hurried to poke his nose around the other side of the chair's leg, and found that the light was coming from the base of the chair, from a sphere embedded into the wood.

"I did it after all," Auri said, reaching out to stroke the curve before Fallon could object. "It's warm."

"I don't think that's a focus," Fallon said. "It looks dark, not clear."

"What else could it be? I read that Lady Rennyn's focus is black. Maybe I accidentally summoned the way she did." She smiled, and poked the sphere again. "It feels good."

Resting back on his heels, Fallon murmured the cut-off for the detect Sigillic. "I guess this is progress. I'll dig it out in the morning."

"And then go find out what you can about Lady Rennyn's students."

"That too, for all the good it'll do me. None of them are in the city."

"They'll have to come back for her annunciation as Duchess. You can do it, Fallon."

He'd have to. Without being able to read the structure of Auri's Sigillic, he had little chance of understanding just what had gone wrong. And even if he stumbled upon a solution, his ability to cast was greatly limited by the strain Auri constantly placed on him. Nor would it be sufficient to somehow enlist the help of his teachers, or the Hand mages, or even the Grand Magister. He needed an expert in the Eferum, and there was only one mage considered so brilliant, so revolutionary, so sheerly powerful, that she would have any hope of saving a girl trapped in a dream he couldn't admit to.

If Auri was ever to find her way back to this world, they needed Rennyn Claire.

Chapter Two

Kendall Stockton returned to Captain Faille's quarters to discover her so-called teacher standing daydreaming on a footstool while a pair of dressmakers scuffled around her feet fooling with her hem. Really, there were times Rennyn Claire acted almost as silly as she'd pretended to be when Kendall had met her.

Not bothering to point out the obvious to someone who couldn't be trusted with stairs and frequently came over dizzy and had to sit down, Kendall instead looked over the dress.

"It's not as fancy as I expected," she said, considering the floaty, dark blue sleeves and the tiny silver flowers embroidered on the broad black waistband. Not bad, though it failed hide that Rennyn was still too thin, and it was cut low enough to show neck and shoulders. Rennyn didn't exactly try to hide her throat, but she rarely wore anything that gave a good look at the scar left by her demon uncle. "Wasn't it supposed to be green?"

"This is just for today's audience." Rennyn glanced down at her dress as if she hadn't really thought about it yet. She was the type who would wear exactly the same thing every day, if no-one poked at her.

This dress was a good deal more like what a nearly-Duchess would wear than the plain skirt, blouse and jacket Rennyn usually went about in, but she still didn't look as expensive as most of the ladies Kendall had glimpsed flitting through the palace. Her teacher's long black hair was caught back from the sides with a dark ribbon and the rest hung down her back same as always—she never tried to do anything with it. If

Kendall had hair so nice and straight, instead of a mop of dirty blonde curls, she wasn't sure she would bind it up in braids either. Though it was probably just that all the braiding the Court ladies liked was too much effort for Rennyn at the moment.

"How long have you been standing on that?" Kendall asked, handing Rennyn the newssheet she'd been carrying.

"Not long. For this dress." Rennyn's smile was totally unconvincing. She glanced down at the newssheet and added: "Why does everyone draw me so short?"

While Rennyn wasn't as unnecessarily tall as her husband, she definitely wasn't small, so the most likely reason was the people making the newssheet didn't care. The picture was nothing new: a drawing of a black-haired, dark-eyed woman dangling from puppet-strings held by a shadowy figure with claws, his arms and legs all long and spidery. Rennyn and her Kellian husband Captain Faille. While the picture properly got across the idea that Captain Faille was a scary man, anyone who thought Rennyn the least bit like a puppet really didn't have a clue.

Kendall didn't know why her teacher even bothered to read the sheets, though she did privately feel Rennyn had been out of her head, or at least not thinking things through, when she'd insisted on marrying Captain Faille before she'd even been able to get out of her sick bed. People had already distrusted the Kellian for being descended from magical constructs called golems, and not properly human. When the Black Queen—who had centuries ago created the first Kellian—had taken control of their descendants during her attempted return, every suspicion seemed confirmed, for all that the Kellian had had no choice in the matter. A ridiculously powerful mage like Rennyn Claire up and marrying one—in an evening ceremony in the infirmary with the bride propped into a sitting position, her face still black with bruises—well, of course people would say she'd been taken advantage of and start making a fuss. Rennyn was too used to acting like the Boss of the World to imagine anyone would think she could be bullied into getting married.

Kendall noticed the blue sleeves had acquired a distinct tilt. "You need to sit down now."

Rennyn straightened. Kendall just caught her change of expression, but as usual her teacher immediately tried to hide how upset not being able to do anything much made her. "Can you finish it with me sitting down?" she asked the dressmakers.

"Of course, Your Grace. I've pinned the level."

Rennyn needed help stepping down off the stool, and blinked and swayed a bit more while Kendall kept her upright. Knowing the looks she'd get if she let Her High and Mightiness fall over, Kendall made sure to keep hold of her elbow until she'd settled in one of the chairs by the window.

"It won't be much longer, Your Grace," said one of the dressmakers: the older, less-snooty one who looked like a pigeon stuffed into ruby silk. No-one was supposed to call Rennyn 'Your Grace' yet—not officially—but a lot of people did anyway. The huge amount Rennyn was spending on too many clothes—not just for herself but for her brother and husband, and for Kendall and her fellow student Sukata as well—made the dressmaker extra keen to please. Rennyn probably didn't even notice, since she had her eyes closed and was taking long, deep breaths. She was supposed to be having an audience with the Queen that morning, and should have known better than to tire herself out before she even reached the Old Palace.

After a while she opened her eyes and began annoying herself with the newssheet again, carefully reading all of a long playbill for something called "The Black Queen". How a bunch of players could hope to 'Reveal All about the Return of Queen Solace' Kendall didn't know, and wondered if there was any way she could sneak off to see them try.

"There you are, Your Grace," said the plump dressmaker, clambering to her feet with just enough effort to show that scuffling about on her knees had been an especial favour. "I will make the adjustments to the other dresses, and have them to you soonest. Are you certain in regards to the decoration of the Court Gown?"

Kendall knew Rennyn's main interest in the gown she was going to wear to be made Duchess was that it wasn't heavy. Green and white for the Surclere colours and no and no and no again to all the other things the dressmakers said formal Court dresses had to have. While they were occupied, Kendall spotted a long jacket which she guessed was meant to be hers, and swapped it for her coat, checking that it would fasten up the front with the black wood oblongs that passed through little loops. Very spick, fitting exactly over the new trousers and crisp shirt that were already on the list of all the things Kendall planned to pay Rennyn for after she started earning.

Before the dressmakers could do more than notice, Kendall had it unfastened and off, and then made herself scarce until the pair staggered out under their load of pricey cloth. She had no wish to have them tut over her again with all their comments about how adorable she'd look in a dress and what a shame it was she didn't grow her hair long. They could take their dainty and shove it up their petite.

Rennyn had made almost as many faces as Kendall while the dressmakers had been saying that, trying not to laugh. But right now she was expressionless, sitting staring out the window, one of her hands closed on the skirt of her new dress, creasing it. Kendall wondered if she could be nervous about her audience with the Queen, or just fretting because Captain Faille wasn't with her.

"Are you going to be able to go to this meeting?"

"Sitting down and drinking tea?   I think I can manage that."

Kendall's shrug was an unspoken "don't say I didn't warn you", but she bent to help Rennyn with her shoes anyway. Rennyn's broken ribs hadn't healed properly, and she still had problems with bending and twisting. And laughing and sneezing and coughing and a surprising number of things. At least when she stood up she was steadier on her feet. No swaying as she turned, smoothing the line of her skirt.

"Tell me when you get done preening," Kendall said. "I'm sure Queen Astranelle won't mind the wait."

"You're planning on coming along?"

"There's a pair of guards hanging about to march you up there, but I'll go as far as the Old Palace with you." Been ordered to, more like. Whenever Captain Faille couldn't sit around watching Rennyn, he made everyone take turns following her about. Not that Kendall wouldn't have thought of it anyway. Rennyn would hate fainting somewhere on the way to see the Queen, and not having anyone she knew around.

"Is Seb still at the library?" Rennyn asked, making a snail's business of the stairs down to the main hall of the Sentene barracks.

"Be there all year," Kendall replied shortly. She had no interest in the spellbooks Rennyn was gifting to the Houses of Magic, and no patience for the endless fuss over the mouldy old things. Except for a couple, Rennyn had said there wasn't much in them which hadn't already been done by someone else, and done better. It was stupid for everyone in the Houses to get so excited just because Rennyn's family had had the only copies.

As they crossed the main hall, she searched again for some sign of life in the barracks. "Where is everyone? Sukata said she had to go to a big meeting."

"It wasn't a Sentene meeting," Rennyn replied, but then closed her mouth tight as they met up with the two black and gold-clad guards come to escort her to the Queen.

A Kellian meeting then. Kendall closed her own mouth as well, and kept it that way. She could guess well enough why the Kellian were meeting. People were really and truly afraid of them right now, and not just because the Black Queen had been able to control them so totally. They were a lot stronger and faster than normal people, and the pointy fingernails were harder to overlook now that a few people in Court had seen how easily they could be used to cut through flesh. The newssheets and people in the Council had turned into braying asses about the risk the Kellian posed, and totally ignored the fact that the people they wanted to get rid of were busy saving their lives. It was because they were strong and fast that they were so good at hunting down the monsters out of the Hells— the place the mages called the Eferum. And they hadn't done anything wrong by choice, had been totally under the control of the Black Queen, hadn't even hurt anyone except Rennyn. But it was as if this was the first time the majority of Tyrland had really noticed the Kellian, even though they'd been around working as Sentene for ages. So there was all this talk about whether the Kellian counted as real people when the first ones had been things called golems, made by the Black Queen. Whether they could be trusted. Whether they should be killed.

Whether Rennyn owned them.

None of the Kellian had been happy to learn descendants of the Black Queen existed, and though they put a good face on it, they still hadn't recovered from discovering that Rennyn had inherited an ability to command them. Most of them avoided coming near her.

Sukata, who had more to do with Rennyn because she was a rare Kellian mage, said they hated what she represented about themselves. And Sukata wouldn't even talk about what it had been like to be taken over by the Black Queen, but she'd had nightmares most every night she and Kendall had shared a room at Rennyn's old house, and the memory surely made Rennyn's lesser control harder to bear.

No-one had told Kendall it was a secret Kellian meeting. Probably Sukata wasn't allowed to. Obviously they were going to talk over the choices they had when their ungrateful country wanted them gone, and no doubt what to do about Rennyn and Sebastian and the Claires' evil uncle as well. Kendall was nobody who would get invited to that kind of thing, or told what was decided.

Frowning, Kendall checked Rennyn's colour. She was walking slower, and it would probably be best if she sat down and rested somewhere before going on. Villemar Palace wasn't a single building, but a mismatched clunch of them sitting on top of the central hill of Asentyr, with a big wall all around. The part called the Houses of Magic wasn't that far from the Old Palace, where the royal family lived, but Rennyn was useless at any kind of distance. Kendall had known ancient grandmothers who had more stamina.

Since they were running a little late, Kendall bet Rennyn didn't want to stop like any sensible person would, so she caught at the woman's hand and arranged it on her shoulder. The way the thin fingers tightened told Kendall just how well Rennyn was managing, but she'd stick to it anyway. After being so powerful she could pretty much do whatever she liked, Rennyn was just too stubborn to accept being so weak she couldn't get from one building to the next without help.

Kendall had only been intending to go as far as the entrance, but kept on until Rennyn was safely stowed in a flower-striped chair in a flower-striped room looking dubiously at the delicate flowery cups neatly laid out for tea. Kendall knew her teacher would be thinking of all the problems she'd had dropping things. Not often recently, but her hands still shook when she tired. Fortunately there was no sign of the Queen.

"Have you done your practice today?" Rennyn asked abruptly.

"Not yet," Kendall replied, annoyed. "The bowls aren't going anywhere." For a whole month now she'd been doing the same thing, and though it was far more than Kendall had ever expected to do, it was achingly dull and pointless. Putting five wooden bowls in a row and lifting and turning them one after another was enough to kill anyone's enthusiasm for magic, and Kendall hadn't had much to start with. No-one would pay her for turning bowls over.

"I've a different exercise for you then," Rennyn said, in the extra-reasonable tone Kendall distrusted. "Seb brought a small chest up to Illidian's quarters. The contents are in poor condition since it wasn't under any form of preservation—there's cloth gone rotten and turning to powder. Take it out to the Sentene practice ground and try unpacking it without touching it. You can toss the rotted cloth, and sort the rest into colours."

Kendall shrugged, but decided this meant Rennyn was feeling better now she was sitting down. "Do I have to do it out in the practice ground?"

"Since there doesn't seem to be any way to unpack it without getting everything in the vicinity filthy, yes."

"All right."

Suppressing her irritation, Kendall headed out, wishing she hadn't decided to stick out playing student while Rennyn was still sick. When Sukata's mother, Captain Sarana, had withdrawn her daughter from Tyrland's best school of magic and made formal arrangements with Rennyn for Sukata to be her student, Kendall hadn't resisted the same arrangement being made for her because she thought she'd learn more than she had staying in the annoying and useless Arkathan. Huge mistake.

Rennyn and Sebastian were both totally in love with how magic worked, and kept trying to get Kendall to understand how to create original spells, when all Kendall wanted to do was learn how to cast the common ones she could get paid for, like how to create the protective Circles around settlements, and make light and heat and cold stones. She was the wrong sort of student for Rennyn and everyone knew it. And felt the need to tell her.

A mage like Rennyn Claire deserves the best students the Arkathan can offer. Don't you see, the time she spends teaching you the basics could be put to better use? Such a pity. Such a waste.

Those were just the outright rude, but most of the conversations she'd been having lately hadn't been any more fun. Kendall had had more than enough of mages telling her how lucky she was, and to be properly grateful, and never once minding their own business. Maybe worst of all was Sebastian trying to make her catch his enthusiasm for how things worked, so that she could be a fancy-pants 'true' mage instead of what he called a 'rote' mage.

Rennyn at least didn't do that. She just said that Kendall could decide what kind of mage she wanted to be after she had a command of the basics, and that memorising a bunch of spells someone else had made up wasn't the basics. But so far that had meant absolutely nothing but boring lifting exercises and lectures, and if Rennyn hadn't been so sick, Kendall wouldn't have stayed a day. She'd already made plans to find a better fit of teacher after Rennyn had recovered some more. She'd miss Sukata doing that, but Sukata would understand, and it's not like they wouldn't be able to meet up. No, it was the smart thing to do. Kendall would grit her teeth and put up with being a charity case until then.

Back in Captain Faille quarters she changed out of her best clothes. Finding the chest behind a chair, Kendall carried it down to the sandy triangle where the Kellian came and danced around each other with swords, and their supporting Ferumguard sharpened their musket skills. Fortunately no-one was about, since Kendall hated practicing with an audience. Not only because it had taken her so long to get the things she was trying to move to do what she wanted, but because everyone was all too interested. Rennyn was—or had been—the most powerful mage in centuries. And not only that, she and Sebastian did magic differently from everyone else, using three methods instead of just the one that was safest. It was hard to concentrate when people watched you as if you were about to give away some great big secret.

Sighing, Kendall sat down cross-legged in front of the chest. Thought Magic—Force Magic as most people called it—wasn't taught because students kept accidentally hurting themselves when they were trying to learn it. Yet the first thing Sebastian Claire had done when he'd met Kendall was give her a Thought Magic exercise to do, just because he couldn't imagine being a mage without it.

It was simple to explain, if not to do: you willed things to move about and they did. It had taken Kendall a month to be able to pick up a pebble, and now after more than two months she could move things about and turn them over so long as they were light. She had no idea why it was so hard to turn something over, or how this was going to end up making her like Rennyn, who could do all sorts of unlikely things without having to spend loads of time writing out sigils like the other mages.

Unpacking a chest should be simple, though Kendall knew she'd end up feeling almost as tired as Rennyn for the rest of the day. Magical strength was something you built up through practice, and Sebastian had told her to think of herself as a two year-old trying to move furniture.

The chest had a catch, not a lock, and it was easy enough to turn this and then lift the lid, letting out a stink of dust and rot. Inside were little bags, and rolls of velvet that had once been dark blue and now were a faded and mottled grey. Kendall realised she should have brought something to sort it out *into*, but figured the lid would do. Unpacking the chest was going to be a bit more involved than she'd expected, since getting stuff out of little bags was more than just lifting and turning.

The rolls of velvet looked easier, but even just picking one up was a surprise. It sagged. Kendall sat for a while trying different ways of holding a sausage of cloth that shed little fragments of itself at each attempt to make it sit flat and still. It was a *lot* harder than making a rock turn over, but before Kendall could puzzle out what to do she caught it somehow by a corner and the whole thing unravelled.

A waterfall of colour. Ruby. Emerald. Sapphire. Necklaces tumbling from the roll of cloth to lie winking in the mid-morning sun. Kendall stared, stunned, then snorted.

"Sort it into colours? Bet you thought *that* was funny."

An entire chest of the Black Queen's jewels. The Claires had spent less effort looking after it than the stupid books they were donating to the Houses of Magic, which at least had been under some sort of spell not to fall apart. But what would you expect from a pair who'd never had to earn a coin in their lives?

From the looks of their home, the Claires had lived modestly. They hadn't kept any servants, had maintained an ordinary three-bedroom house in a smallish town. Sebastian said they owned four other similar houses in Tyrland, and moved between them to keep from becoming too known in one place. Owning five houses seemed a lot to Kendall, but a Duchess was supposed to live in mansions and have crowds of servants and things. Rennyn wouldn't get that kind of money out of the Duchy she had inherited, since everyone knew Surclere was chicken-scratch poor. Kendall wasn't entirely certain how much a mansion cost compared to a chest full of jewels, but it looked like Rennyn'd at least be able to pay the dressmaker.

Most of the necklaces were ugly, clunky things: the metals tarnished to black and green. It was hard to picture Rennyn or even the Black Queen wearing them. It didn't seem likely they were fake though, and it was going to take a while for Kendall to decide how much she didn't appreciate Rennyn giving her a chest full of jewels to see what she'd do with them.

Still, it was better than bowls. Kendall was well into making piles of red and blue and green and yellow and white when the faint crunch of sand warned her of an onlooker.

The sprat standing before her was no-one Kendall knew, though his robe gave him away as a student of the Arkathan. He was maybe a little older than her, though not much taller, with pale blond hair, peach-fuzz cheeks, and a look like porcelain too fine to use. Peaky.

"Is it true you can't cast the simplest Sigillic?" he asked, with a glance down at the glittery mess Kendall had spread about.

Kendall sat back on her heels. If there was one thing she was sick to death of, it was rich noble brats. The Arkathan was full of them, and when Kendall had been stuck there they'd only stopped ignoring her when they were trying to squeeze gossip out of her, or making it real clear she didn't belong.

"I don't see that's any business of yours."

"Is it a secret? I was told you're from one of the villages destroyed by the Grand Summoning, that you don't have any connection to the Claires. No background in magery, haven't even passed the first rank of the Sigillic comprehension tests. Can you read?"

It would be interesting to see how much of a necklace would fit up this snot's nose. It could count as unpacking—or she could say he'd distracted her and it was an accident. Better to ignore him, though she didn't want to keep practicing while he was there. And it was annoying as spit that he was right, that she couldn't cast a single Sigillic, that Rennyn wouldn't let her try.

Lacking a response, the boy went on: "It would be tremendously ironic if an unlettered—"

"Unmannered?"

Sebastian Claire stood in the shadow of the nearest archway. He had the same colouring as his sister, but was nearly ten years younger, having turned sixteen just before the beginning of the Black Queen's return.

The thing to remember about Sebastian was that he lived and breathed magic, and thought everyone else should do the same. For all that, Kendall had seen him be sharp enough about the real world whenever he bothered to pull his head out of the Eferum.

"You must be Sebastian Claire," said the boy, sounding pleased. "I—"

"No, really, you'd do better to shut up," Sebastian said. "I've no time for people who are rude to my friends."

The boy looked startled, then flushed and glanced down at Kendall. "I suppose I was. My mouth ran on." He bowed, quick and deep from the waist. "Your pardon. I just wanted to know. Another time, Lord Sebastian." He nodded, bit his lip and left, sand crunching beneath his shoes.

Sebastian plopped down to one side of the chest and looked over Kendall's piles. "Garish stuff," he said. "I don't suppose Solace wore much of this, either. A couple of centuries of Surclere heirlooms."

"Did you know him?" Kendall asked, not willing to be so easily distracted.

"No. Probably another one wanting to be Ren's student. All week I've had people making bright suggestions, some more subtle than others, about putting in a good word for this or that promising mage."

"Has she said she wants more?" Kendall asked, warily.

"Everyone wants her to want more. They'd have her instructing classes at the Arkathan if they thought she'd agree. Ren hates the idea of people killing themselves trying to cast like she does, but she knows she can't personally tutor every would-be Thought Mage in Tyrland."

"It would be good for Tyrland though, right? Teaching as many mages as possible to cast like you and Rennyn?"

"You can't just teach people to cast like us. You can show them the path, but it's not like maths, where you add one and one and end up with two. We're not rote mages." He glanced down at the nearly empty chest. "How were you emptying these bags, for instance?

Kendall, with pleasing surety, reached with her thoughts and tugged open the top of one bag, lifted it and tipped it until a bunch of rings fell out into the sand.

"Like an extra pair of hands, right?" Sebastian's eyes narrowed and the last of the bags hefted itself. But instead of upending, it writhed briefly, and a dull gold bracelet slid out.

"How do you move the bracelet without seeing it?" Kendall asked, impressed.

"With fingers you have a sense of touch. You can tell weight, texture, temperature—all sorts of things. And Thought Magic is even more than fingers. There's a big leap beyond making things move, and I doubt many could even learn to do that reliably. Some just can't attain that sort of mental discipline—they stopped teaching it not simply because it's dangerous, but because it's hard."

"I just don't see how to move something I can't see."

"It's a leap," Sebastian said, agreeably. "But keep at it. Thought Magic isn't as dangerous as they make out—at least not during the extra-pair-of-hands stage—and you've more than enough sense to not do anything outside your exercises. It's the weak-minded and the impatient who kill themselves."

"Do they try and get you to take students too?"

"Not yet—they know I'm far behind Ren."

"The way people act about Rennyn's way of casting, I don't know if they'd give up just because she said no to more students."

He laughed, and pulled out a kerchief to pile all the smaller jewellery in. "Good luck getting Ren to do anything she doesn't want to, now that Solace is gone."

Two months ago Kendall would have agreed wholeheartedly. But the Rennyn who had lost all her massive magical strength, and who got too tired to stand up, was a different prospect. Especially now it was so important to her to protect the Kellian. The Rennyn Claire who pranced around doing whatever she wanted was a thing of the past.

Chapter Three

"Lady Rennyn."

Rennyn blinked, and realised she'd been asleep. This happened too frequently for her to be surprised, but it annoyed her to be caught unaware. Wondering how long the Queen had been in the room, she gathered herself to stand and curtsey, since it wouldn't do to start out being offensive.

"No, don't rise," said the Queen, holding out a belaying hand as she sat opposite. This was to be a private audience, ostensibly to discuss the Surclere Duchy, and while the Queen seemed withdrawn she at least wasn't going to stand on ceremony. Astranelle Montjuste was a blond woman of nearly seventy years, though of course she was able to afford an attendant mage to lengthen her life and preserve an appearance of youth. She looked delicate and sweet, and it was difficult to match her to her reputation of cold competence until you heard her unexpectedly resonant and commanding voice. "The healers have informed me that you have not recovered as you should."

"No," Rennyn agreed, with a wry thought for the visit she'd made to the Sentene's Senior Healer yesterday. Of course she would report to the Queen. "Your Majesty knows that my—Prince Helecho— attempted a Symbolic casting on me. It would have made me a slave of sorts, but he used the removal of my focus as a symbol of that casting, and because he had not at that time discovered my true focus, the spell went awry."

Queen Astranelle nodded. She had witnessed the Eferum-Get prince, Rennyn's very distant relative, attempting the casting, and would have felt the power warping away from the original intent. "So it slows, but does not prevent your recovery?"

"Yes and no. The focus was a symbol of my strength, and instead of subsuming my will, the miscasting sapped my physical resilience. Bones that should have been whole by now are only partially knit." And still made their presence felt when she coughed or laughed or lay on her side. "They will heal eventually, just as the bruises went, and the wound. But...the spell is still there, and like most Symbolic castings, is not going to be easy to shift. So I have little endurance, I'm at great risk of disease, and the toll casting places on me..." Rennyn shrugged. "There is a measure of physical exertion in casting, and it exhausts me quickly."

The Queen considered this while a swarm of servants swept in to lay out spiced tea and a collection of intriguing little cakes. Rennyn liked trying new sweets, and wondered if she could take one of each without looking more interested in eating than talking. Having staved off a private audience this long, it would probably set the wrong tone.

Queen Astranelle had too many reasons not to like Rennyn as it was. Although Rennyn's ancestor, King Tiandel, had abdicated his throne three hundred years ago, there were some in Tyrland who had suggested that Rennyn was Tyrland's true Queen. Fomenting mischief. It wouldn't lead anywhere, but it was an annoyance to a Queen already less than impressed by Rennyn's failure to keep her informed about anything during the crisis of Solace's attempted return. Secrecy had been necessary, but she could have at least attempted not to act like Queen Astranelle was entirely irrelevant to proceedings. Perhaps worse, she had most inconveniently married a Kellian without letting anyone official know first, and if the Queen guessed at the reasons for the haste it would almost amount to a direct insult.

"Lady Weston tells me that, as yet, she sees no way of removing this casting from you."

The Grand Magister had barely been able to detect it. "It may not be possible," Rennyn said baldly. "It doesn't respond to dispels, and trying to pull it from me by force, even if we could get a hold on it, would probably kill me."

"You are very matter-of-fact," the Queen commented. "Will you accept such a limited life?" The strong do not enjoy being weak, her cool gaze added, and Rennyn had been very strong.

"No. I am going to hunt my Wicked Uncle down and kill him." Rennyn took a sip of spiced tea, recalling the Grand Magister's advice that she should request permission to leave Tyrland, and ask for support. But she found she'd rather simply explain and see how the Queen reacted. "He cast the spell, and he later took my true focus. Killing him will drastically increase my chances of overcoming this spell. Particularly since the symbology was one of him controlling me."

The Queen sat back in her chair. "The best Tyrland can muster has yet to find the creature calling itself Helecho. It has likely left the country. Even if it can be found, you yourself named it one of the most dangerous of the creatures born of the Eferum. The abilities of a mage, the form of a human, and the command of other Hells-spawned creatures."

"I don't have a great deal of choice," Rennyn said, bluntly. "Other than the broken bones finishing their healing, I am not going to recover further physically. And while it might be possible to accept living in this fashion, I'm simply too vulnerable to infection. A harsh winter would finish me without the constant care of a healer. Besides, regardless of my own problems, he needs to die."

"That I do not dispute." Rennyn's Wicked Uncle had been quite despicable all around. "How, then, do you propose to locate it?"

"He has my focus. Even were I not ill, the distances involved would be too great for me to track it properly. But my brother has created a very general directional spell using me as a subject. Nothing more than 'over there'," she gestured vaguely to the west, "but it can be recast as we get closer."

"And when you find it?" The Queen didn't bother pointing out Rennyn's frailties, but then she made a gesture as if to put aside the discussion so far. "We are prevaricating. Even if it is not currently among us, this creature is a threat—not simply to Tyrland but to any that Hells-spawn would feed upon. It is not a matter for you alone. Nor do I imagine you so short-sighted as to expose both yourself and your brother to this creature, given the consequences of your deaths."

Her Wicked Uncle inheriting the ability to control the Kellian would be a disaster, and Rennyn didn't bother pretending that she hadn't seen this, or wanted Seb anywhere near Prince Helecho. "You will assist?" she asked simply.

"The Sentene's role is to hunt the monsters from the Eferum. They will hunt this one, with your assistance. The difficulty lies in taking a military force outside Tyrland's borders. Even in those lands inclined to cooperate with us, it would cause alarm."

This was not an aspect that had occurred to Rennyn, but it made sense. "A large group would be too noticeable to him, anyway. But there's no reason I can't travel as a private individual—there's a property in Kole that has been left abandoned since the last of that branch of my family died. It would not be remarkable for me to be accompanied while I attended to removing anything of worth and selling the house. And if a second small group travelled separately, and joined me there, then they are simply mages with their own personal guard. I don't know if he's in the Kolan Empire, of course, but it's a good starting point, and in the right direction."

"The Emperor's intelligencers are not to be underestimated. But, on the balancing hand, Corusar is no fool, and it might be possible to apply to him— even in relation to your health. At the moment he is no doubt more than usually inclined toward an exchange of assistance."

The Emperor of Kole had had a formidable reputation as a healer-mage before he'd taken his throne. But that had been nearly three hundred years ago, and he most certainly no longer practiced those arts. Still, there were other scholar-mages in Kole that Rennyn intended to consult.

"At the moment?" she repeated.

"You have not heard that Kole has misplaced Arugar, Keshkant—and quite a number of other mages?"

"Misplaced? Mages?"

"Gone without trace. It began a short time after Solace's attempted return, so perhaps their disappearances are related to the monster you seek. You hope to depart soon?"

Rennyn hadn't heard anything about missing mages, but then she had enough trouble with local news, and had not been paying attention to Kole. "Being ill has delayed me too long already."

The Queen nodded, sparing Rennyn the arguments the healers had insisted on boring her with and instead saying practically: "I will make a ship available to you. Avoiding the Vandalusian roads should keep the journey from being improbably arduous, and sidestep any chance of being caught in their mountains by early autumn rains."

This settled, the Queen turned the discussion to Surclere. The title had been left untenanted by agreement between Rennyn's ancestor Tiandel and the Montjuste in whose favour he had abdicated. The Duchy itself was small and now badly neglected. A mountainous part of the kingdom's north-west, it had never been a very rich area, and Rennyn was treated to a precise summary of what would be due to her, and required of her, when she became its Duchess.

Rennyn forced herself to concentrate. She couldn't become Surclere's Duchess and then ignore it, but the mountain of legal precedent and economics she would need to climb was daunting. Illidian would help, of course, but she would be ultimately responsible. Duty. It was a word she had thought to leave behind after Solace's defeat. Still, there was still a chance that before she formally became a Duchess the Kellian might decide their future was not in Tyrland, and that would change everything. Illidian might want to make a home in Surclere, but could Tyrland be their home when there was so much hatred for the Kellian as a people?

Sharp anxiety washed over her, but Rennyn pushed it back. She hated this unreasonable fear that would creep up on her whenever she wasn't entirely certain where Illidian was. Despite two months of recovery, a part of her remained convinced that he was dead, or in urgent danger, and she was always being overwhelmed by this need to see him, to make certain he breathed. And still chose not to hate her.

As if she had read Rennyn's mind, the Queen stopped talking about wool and said: "You make no representations on behalf of the Kellian, Lady Rennyn?"

"I don't speak for the Kellian," Rennyn said, trying not to sound wary. "I inherited the ability to control them, not authority over them."

"But you are naturally partisan."

"Very," Rennyn replied, wondering where this was going. The Queen had long treated the Kellian as a necessary evil, whether because they were a link to the old Montjuste-Surclere rule or because they were descendants of golems. The last few months had been the worst in Kellian history, and because Queen Astranelle had made no show of support, the anti-Kellian factions had been spurred to outright venom.

Rennyn found the whole situation endlessly frustrating. Her desire to protect and support Illidian warred with a disinclination to battle for public opinion. She had trained to manipulate magic, not people. She couldn't force Tyrians to value the Kellian, any more than she could make the Kellian come to terms with her family's ability to command them. And she doubted even Illidian would appreciate her taking it upon herself to fight Kellian battles anyway.

"I constantly receive representations *about* the Kellian," the Queen continued. "They have as many supporters as detractors. Yet never have they themselves put forward their case. Lady Weston tells me this is because the Kellian consider it impolite to try to influence the decisions of others. I would be curious to hear if this is your own view."

"It would be at least one of the reasons," Rennyn said, after thinking it over. "It's true enough that they place great weight on personal choice." She looked at the Queen. "I suspect that they also consider the situation self-evident. You will support them, or you won't."

"Do they presume to judge me? I have not countenanced the calls for punishment. This spate of talk will pass, and is only natural."

"I hope that you are right, Your Majesty," Rennyn said, putting her cup down. "It seems to me to grow louder and shriller every day, but I am oversensitive where my husband is concerned."

Further than this she would not be drawn. Perhaps Queen Astranelle was correct, and all this misplaced concern would die down. Rennyn was aware that her own reason for wanting the Kellian to decide to leave Tyrland was due to her anger with those who did not appreciate them. But it was not a good solution.

She had expected Illidian to be waiting for her, but instead found a man almost as wide as he was tall, his face permanently shadowed by a hint of reddish-brown beard. The all-enveloping black coat of the Sentene, with its brilliant phoenix blazon, seemed to double his size: a wall of a man.

"Don't look so disappointed," he said, with a rumbling chuckle. For a moment his gaze drifted, inevitably, to her throat, but he was too polite to stare openly.

"How are you, Captain Medan?"

"Passing fair. It's good to see you on your feet, Lady Rennyn." He made a shooing gesture at the two royal guards lining up as escort. "Faille asked me to see you back to quarters."

Only Kellian had been at the meeting, so Illidian must have returned to the Houses of Magic. "He's caught up?" she asked, taking the arm the Captain proffered, and trying not to lean too much.

"Senior Captains are always in demand. And most of us have been in the field almost constantly since the Grand Summoning. Tremendous amount of organising, signing off, catching up."

Rennyn waited, for she'd found Nikolar Medan to be forthright enough. His pace quickened for a few steps, then he let out a gusty breath.

"Most of the Sentene mages haven't seen Faille since you regained consciousness. Your marriage came as more than a shock. A bit of reassurance will go a long way."

"Do they really think the Kellian would let me live if I'd ordered Illidian into my bed?"

"It's not that, though I won't deny we worry. The idea of you commanding them fills us with horror, for all you've never given the least sign of wanting to. But hasty marriages are unprecedented, you know. Kellian are cautious taking human lovers, let alone establishing permanent bonds. Particularly ever-rare male Kellian. Too many people think them all very fine and exotic and noble, with a delightful dangerous frisson, and then can't bear that they never smile, that they forget to start conversations. Because they don't act human enough."

Rennyn wondered what colour her face had gone, but knew Medan was more messenger than accuser. "Is so little weight placed on Illidian's judgment?"

Captain Medan snorted. "Not to mention his much-vaunted instinct. It's not sensible—or anyone's business—but it's been a bad few months and we'd all heard of course that he cut short his nails. It will make them feel better to talk to Faille for a while, and see that he is happy."

This time his gaze dropped to her waist, since everyone knew Solace had used Illidian Faille to slash open Rennyn's side. The pointed Kellian nails were effective weapons: a facet of the race's overarching enchantments that hadn't been commonly known. But they were also part of the Kellian identity, a matter of pride, and Illidian had been one of the few who had kept both hands untrimmed.

Rennyn didn't answer his unspoken question, spotting a useful low wall holding back a drift of early autumn leaves. She'd made it almost halfway from the

Old Palace to the Houses, and needed her legs to stop feeling like jelly.

"You make quite a picture in that dress," Captain Medan offered.

This earned only a faint smile. "Sarana Illuma told me yesterday that even she finds herself avoiding me; that at times she has to force herself to go into a room if she knows I'm there. This embarrasses her, but she is too honest to pretend that being glad I saved them from a worse fate has reconciled the Kellian to my ability to control them. Illidian loves me, but he can't be immune to that instinctual aversion. And then, to twist everything further, Solace used him to injure me. Even though there's no logic in blaming himself for my injuries, he can't stand the thought of my blood beneath his nails. So he keeps them short."

She sighed. "And I can't say I've handled well not being able to stand up, let alone the limits on my casting. I'm a bad patient, and when I've been too weak even to read I've had to struggle not to hate everyone around me. But I am on the mend. My wounds were only physical, Captain. Illidian has yet to recover from his. He sleeps so little because of the nightmares, and I'm a tremendously difficult person for him to be with. There are so many things that we will have to work against, to not be pulled apart, but I've come to realise our marriage is practically the only thing he is happy about. And you're right—it's nobody's business."

That kept him silent all the way to the stair that led up to Illidian's quarters.

"If you think I'm going to watch you try to climb these, you sadly underestimate me."

"It's probably why he picked you to send," Rennyn said. Illidian had firm opinions on Rennyn and flights of stairs, and was uncharacteristically disinclined to restrain that view.

"Sweeping young ladies off their feet is a hobby of mine," Medan said, lifting her delicately. "Feel free to call on me for any minor hillock that comes your way."

Rennyn shifted, since he hadn't picked her up in a way that favoured her ribs. The healers had explained that what they called a callus had formed to join her broken bones, and this was slowly turning to bone itself. Until it had strengthened, she had to put up with twinges and avoid jarring or stressing her side. It had been a bad break, collapsing a lung, and even now she never felt like she could take a proper breath. Her ribs were her greatest annoyance, and she wondered what all these too-interested people would think if they knew how chaste those fractures had left her marriage.

"Do you know anything about plays, Captain?"

"I can quote the entire opening soliloquy from *Siana of Kole*. Or perhaps you'd like the victory speech of Lady Nidama?"

Regaining her feet, Rennyn shook her head as she led the way into Illidian's quarters. "That's all meaningless to me, I'm afraid. I've never been to a play. I was wondering if you could think of any way I could see this one." She handed him the newssheet, then tried to not be too obvious about her need to sit down.

"You really want to see this?" Medan asked, lifting heavy brows.

"Illidian said the other day that what was being printed in the 'sheets would be forgotten soon enough. That it was the stories people told that had the greatest impact. It seems the papers aren't going to change what they're saying—so I want to see what the stories that will be remembered will be."

"Hmn. Well, I haven't heard much about this piece. The playwright's an up-and-comer. Lucius Sandrey. I saw his last, and liked it. Bawdy and full-blooded and very, very funny."

Rennyn blinked, trying to think of anything involving 'Kellian' and 'bawdy'. "It's not likely to be a comedy."

"Not described like this, anyway." He handed her back the newssheet. "I do know someone with a private box at the Faranea and they may...well, I will let you know. If their box is available, then good timing and the most minor of illusions would make it an easy matter."

He bowed himself out and, left to herself, Rennyn abandoned the newssheet to gaze about the book-lined room. Shelves covered all available space in this and the spare bedroom, with only a patch left bare for a mounted selection of swords. Faintly daunting. It was not that Illidian read more than she did, but all her studies had been focused on magic, while her husband's collection ranged through every imaginable topic, and included extensive forays into poetry, novels and all the luxuries of the mind Rennyn had never allowed herself. There were moments when this ranked knowledge made her feel tremendously ignorant, but for the most part she found Illidian's quarters a comforting place.

Not least because Illidian was usually there with her. Determined to train herself to cope with his absences, she made certain to not look too relieved when, after five or ten minutes, he arrived. It would do neither of them any good if she acted like a baby every time he was out of her sight.

Sarana Illuma accompanied him, carrying a cloth-wrapped book, and Rennyn tried to guess from their posture how the meeting had gone. But they walked with their usual ease: that efficiency of movement which wasted no gesture. Both were well over six feet tall, lean muscle corded over a wide-shouldered frame. Only their cobweb-fine hair, so colourless it looked grey in most lights, provided a hint of softness. Their proportions were faintly wrong, elongated, and many found them uncomfortable to be around, especially because they did not fidget and never smiled, though Rennyn had not failed to notice how many of the Sentene mages became wholly devoted to their Kellian partners.

"Your audience with Queen Astranelle went as expected?" Illidian asked, moving a footstool up beside her while Sarana took the other seat. His voice was thin, as if strained from overuse—or lack of use. The original Kellian had been mute, for Solace had seen no reason for her construct guards to have voices, and that their descendants could speak at all had been a surprise to Rennyn's family. Almost every other facet of the spell that made them Kellian had been passed on unchanged.

"Nothing particularly surprising." Rennyn smiled as Illidian curled his hand over hers, then told them of the Queen's offer of a ship, and of the question asked about the Kellian. "Do you consider yourselves the leaders of the Kellian?" she asked when she was done.

Illidian lifted fine, straight brows, which for him was more than ordinary surprise. "At most, designated speakers."

"I did wonder if that was what was behind the question. No-one within the Kellian is an ultimate authority. If the Kellian consider that the individual must make their own choices, then the Queen cannot truly command you as a group."

"All who stay within Tyrland's borders acknowledge the authority of the monarch," Illidian said. "By remaining, we agree to obey Queen Astranelle in matters of duty."

"Exactly," Rennyn said, and after a moment he nodded.

"A distinction Her Majesty would not enjoy," Sarana agreed. "As for service itself, until this current wave of

Eferum-Get has been dealt with we cannot properly decide our future in Tyrland. Those few who are not actively serving with the Sentene have departed to the Ten. And that is something I have been asked to speak to you about."

The Kellian woman glanced down at the wrapped book, a thick and formidable block now resting in her lap. "First, we thank you for allowing us to study this. It has been...illuminating." She started to lift it, but Rennyn shook her head.

"That's the only original of Solace's work journals that will not be presented to the Houses." Because the method Solace had used to create the Kellian, and her subsequent study of them, was not knowledge Rennyn cared to share with the entire kingdom. "I can't think of more appropriate custodians than you and Sukata."

"Thank you," Sarana said, more softly than usual, her hands shifting around the bundle. Rennyn wasn't certain if this meant she was pleased, but Illidian tightened his grip and rubbed his thumb against Rennyn's palm, so she decided it had been the right thing to do.

"The terms of our existence," Sarana added, smoothing the cloth. "You said, that day, that we were part of a continuing enchantment, that to be Kellian was to be at the command of the Montjuste-Surcleres. This has led us to ask, if there were no Montjuste-Surcleres, would we be Kellian?"

Rennyn had discussed the same question with her father, many years ago. Back then it had only been an intellectual puzzle.

"Symbolic Magic is not given to hard and fast certainties," she said carefully. "Anything I say would be no more than a guess. But—yes—if Solace's line ended, it's possible that the spell that makes you Kellian would unwind." She glanced at Illidian, who as usual showed only intelligent attention. "I don't think that would kill you. But the magical aspects would be lost." The speed, the strength, long life, effects with light, the sense of awareness the Sentene called Kellian instinct. And... "I couldn't say how greatly your personalities would be affected."

"It would be interesting to know," Illidian said, perhaps less daunted by the prospect than Rennyn. Kellian were by no means identical, but they all shared a certain calm, a patience and a loyalty it was hard to picture them without.

"The need for the bloodline to continue was something we too guessed at," Sarana continued. "But I am less certain on another point. The Ten were the creation of the casting, not us. We are a side-effect, not covered in the structure, though you have...events have proven to us that we are constrained as the Ten are."

The original ten golems created by Solace Montjuste-Surclere were a difficult topic for all the Kellian. Not for the will-less years serving Solace, or even the devastating abandonment following her departure, when Solace's son Tiandel had ordered them to leave Tyrland and never return. They had survived, grown into something more than constructs, even found new purpose after a violent assault had unexpectedly shown them they could bear children. But as the years had stretched, they had lost the energy for daily activity, had retreated into a sleep far beyond any weariness of Rennyn's. In the three hundred years since their exile, one of the Ten had been killed, but the rest neither died nor truly lived.

"The question we have now is, if the Ten did not endure, would we remain as we are?"

Rennyn blinked at Sarana's calm grey eyes, then looked up at Illidian. She could always read his emotions best of any of the Kellian. Resolute. Worried, but determined.

"It doesn't make any difference what I answer, does it?"

"It will not decide our course," Sarana acknowledged.

"Again I can't rule out anything absolutely, but I would consider it unlikely that the spell would dissipate. What is it you want to ask of me?"

"That you visit the resting place of the Ten. And allow them to decide their own fates."

Rennyn looked up at Illidian again, aware that she'd gripped his hand very hard. "You want me to command them to wake?"

"If that is the only way," he said. "It is sometimes possible to wake them, and they did revive during Queen Solace's return."

Illidian's voice was even, but the vertical lines that bracketed his mouth had deepened. He was unhappy about this, not least because he knew how much she would hate it. Over sixty people were at her absolute command, and they had nightmares about her because of that fact. She had given Sarana a command to prove to them that she could, and Illidian a command because he had asked her to. Then promised herself, over and over, that she would never again give an order to any of the Kellian, not accidentally, not even in an emergency. And certainly not like this.

"You want me to give them leave to die."

Chapter Four

Going to see Rennyn be made a Duchess had never sounded like fun, but Kendall hadn't expected to do more than lurk behind the crowd gawping at the things nobles thought it proper to wear. The problem was the outfits Rennyn had bought them. They were based on the Surclere crest, which was a twisty green and white dragon on a black background. The Black Queen's crest had included the Montjuste phoenix as well, and technically Rennyn could use it as well, but she'd decided to stick with just Surclere. So as part of the revived Duchy they were all decked out in knee-length, moss-green coats fastened with a dozen ebony toggles, with a black under-layer which showed for a few inches at the hem and cuffs. The dragon was a tiny outline stitched in white on the right of their chests.

It wasn't that they didn't look good. Kendall hadn't recognised herself, and she thought Sukata had never looked better. But nobles at a Court Occasion were more impressive than Kendall had ever imagined. It was as if an undecorated bit of cloth was against the rules. All the women were wearing what looked like four skirts, with the front of the outer layers cut away so that you could show off all four at once. Great big sleeves with pictures embroidered on them hung down over all that, and there were criss-crossing ribbons above the elbows, with gold net and whatnot across the bodice. If that wasn't enough they'd added bracelets and necklaces and brooches, and things in their hair. The men were more top-heavy, with close-fitting jackets over crisp shirts: the shoulders so large they must be padded with something, and these funny little half-cloaks over the top which were all crests and battle-scenes, and better than tapestries.

Kendall had been around the palace for months, and hadn't seen anyone wearing anything even close to this. When the snooty dressmakers had talked about Court Dress as if it was in a league of its own, maybe Rennyn should have listened a bit harder. You could buy entire houses with what these people were wearing.

The main result was that everyone belonging to 'Surclere' looked totally out of place, like nicely-dressed servants, and there wasn't even a chance Kendall could avoid being noticed—unless perhaps she hid behind the dark wood of the currently empty throne. At least Sebastian was a useful shield. He was about to become heir to a Duchy, and was all very romantic and interesting after helping defeat the Black Queen, so every second noble was keen to slime up to him. No matter where they went in the over-sized throne room, people would circle them and ask prying questions disguised as congratulations. Sebastian was never lost for an answer, though Kendall was willing to bet he found the whole thing boring just because there wasn't any magic involved.

The buzz of chatter dropped abruptly as Captain Faille walked into the room. His coat was long and snug with no extra layers, all in black with mottled green panels at the front. In this crowd he looked like an executioner come to Court, especially given he was already the grimmest man in the world. Kendall would never understand why Rennyn had gone silly over him.

Talk started up again in hissed whispers, which was stupid since most of the people there had to know Kellian could hear better than a cat. Not that Captain Faille would react to what was being said. He scanned the area, like all Kellian did when they entered a room, then crossed to talk to the Grand Magister, Lady Weston.

There were a group of people over by the tall windows that marched up the left side of the room. Kendall hadn't paid much attention before, but noticed them now because everyone else was looking at them like they were expecting something to happen. They weren't dressed any more or less fancy than anyone else, but most of them seemed cross and impatient. Then one of them moved and Kendall spotted the smart-mouthed idiot from the practice ground, dressed in a tamer version of their colours. Anyone associated with him had to be rotten. Best bet was these were some of the nobles who said stupid things about Kellian, and Kendall wondered if they'd make a scene about Captain Faille being there. He'd be Lord Surclere after this ceremony, though it would be hard for Kendall to think of him as anything but Captain. The way some people acted, giving a title to a Kellian would be enough to make Fel rise from the shadows and turn the world upside down.

Horns sounded, loud enough to make anyone jump. Two boys in red and gold had planted themselves just inside the doors to the right of the room and were turning their faces cherry-plum puffing away. Everyone stopped milling about and backed away from the throne, leaving a big semi-circle. Handy of the Queen to give them all a warning that they were supposed to start bowing.

Queen Astranelle had had two sons, but they'd both died years back. Prince Justin and Princess Sera were her grandchildren, and it was really easy to see the shared blood when the three of them walked in together. A little golden family, very grand. The Montjustes had ruled Tyrland since forever, and though Kendall had seen all of these three before, this was the first time she'd really felt it. Royalty.

While everyone pointed noses to the ground the Queen sat herself on the throne, with Justin and Sera on either side. Then the tara-tara-ing changed and everyone straightened up in time for Rennyn to come in. She'd been given use of a little room not far from the throne room, and had been there half the morning, dozing most likely while Lieutenant Faral fixed her hair. Just as the ceremony had been redesigned to avoid Rennyn falling over in the middle, and the important thing about the dress was that it wasn't heavy, they'd made sure she'd have plenty of rest while getting ready.

Kendall hadn't seen Rennyn wearing the dress before. The bodice was white, covered with twisty dragons wrestling each other, but they were white too so it was hard to tell. A high tight collar went all the way to Rennyn's chin, close-fitting sleeves hid her palms, and there was a row of green stone buttons up her back to the nape of her neck. The skirt started low, down past her hips, and fell in a straight line of dark green to the floor, longer at the back to make a little train. For possibly the first time ever, Rennyn was wearing her hair up, smoothed into a heavy knot high at the back of her head, with no attempt at the fancy braiding the Court ladies liked. There was maybe a hint of a green flash in the depths, a pin or two, but no other jewels.

It should have made her look plain and poor, since the whole room was dressed to show off how wealthy they were, but instead everyone else just seemed overdressed. Being Rennyn, she walked into the room like she owned it, didn't even glance around, and crossed right to the centre where there was a pad of gold cloth on the floor a bit before the throne. There she stopped and curtsied, not even for a moment looking like bending down made black spots appear in front of her eyes.

The ceremony was simple and to the point. Rennyn knelt on the cloth and recited an oath to obey and protect the Queen. In return, Queen Astranelle produced a long strip of black cloth embroidered with red and gold phoenixes, which she laid around Rennyn's shoulders like a scarf, then sounded off a whole bunch more titles than just Duchess of Surclere.

That was over quick enough, but then they decided to introduce her to everyone in the room, one by one, which was about the most boring thing imaginable. It got worse when Princess Sera, who was a horrible brat, had another go at 'dear cousin-ing' Sebastian, trying to get one over on him. The only good part was that Rennyn had latched on to Captain Faille's arm to help stay upright, and was making sure everyone was introduced to him as well. Even this wasn't as entertaining as it could be, since the group of people who'd been with the snotty boy had snuck off rather than say hello to a Kellian.

"Shall we get out of here?" Sebastian asked Kendall and Sukata, as Rennyn was introduced to Noble Number Ten Thousand. "Ren won't last much longer, and I think I've spoken to everyone I know."

"Finally!" Kendall wasted no time heading for the door. "Do you think Rennyn will still want to do this thing after lunch? She's likely to fall asleep in the middle."

"That doesn't really matter," Sebastian said, shrugging. "All she has to do is sit in a circle while I make sure Lieutenant Meniar can cast the divination."

Kendall glanced back as they reached the big doors at the back of the room, and saw that the receiving line had broken up exactly as Sebastian had predicted. But—

"Sukata, do you know who that is talking to Rennyn?"

Sukata looked, said: "Fallon DeVries," and paused to watch, which told Kendall a good deal more than the name.

"Him again?" Sebastian said, sounding surprised, probably because Rennyn was talking to the scut like she knew him. "Can you tell me anything more about him?"

"He is a solid theorist," Sukata replied, in the extra-neutral tone Kendall was coming to recognise as Sukata saying far less than she could. "Though considered a tentative caster. His father is a sculptor with a reputation for eccentricity. His uncle is Earl Harkness."

"Ah." Sebastian turned on his heel and strode off, forcing Kendall to double-step to keep up with him. Earl Harkness seemed to be the main person who wanted Kellian to not exist at all, and his money was the reason most of the newssheets had nothing but bad to say about them. Sebastian was even-tempered about most things, but the fact that Earl Harkness could do this drove him wild.

"Do you really not mind having to stay in Tyrland?" Kendall asked, to distract him before he really started brooding. "You're going to just let her go without you?"

Sebastian gave her a suitably startled look. "Were you expecting me to have a tantrum and insist Ren took me along? I hate the idea of her chasing after our uncle without me—not only because I might never see her again, but because I know damn well I could help. But the risk to the Kellian is too great for me to argue against. It does annoy me rather a lot that she thinks it's fine for you and Sukata to go."

"Just until they get a hint of where he is, from the sounds of it. I doubt they're planning to let Rennyn anywhere near him either, and think Sukata and I make good babysitters."

"You could have taken the option of staying here and having me play tutor."

"I know why Rennyn finds that idea so funny, now."

"Pft."

"When you study you have no sense of time, Sebastian," Sukata said, sounding all grave, but with her eyes bright with the Kellian version of laughter. "We would spend our day making sure you are eating, and finding you the books you want."

"Well, at least you'd get to hear me rant about my latest theory," Sebastian said, with a quick look at Kendall, who had made a few pointed comments about said ranting. "Or you could help me look for this house I'm supposed to buy while everyone's gone. Not to mention liaise with the people she's sending up to Surclere to survey its condition. Do you know what room Rennyn wanted the divination set in?"

As usual, Sukata had paid far more attention to their instructions than anyone else, and at her direction they returned to their rooms to change to more everyday clothes, and then met in the rarely-used Sentene dining hall. Kendall had spent some time carefully putting away her fancy Court clothes, but still found only Sebastian when she arrived.

"Sukata's gone to find out about the meal," he said, hefting one end of a bench. Kendall pulled a face, but helped him move some of the furniture aside so there was room enough to chalk a circle on the floor. Thinking it would have been more sensible to have the Kellian-strong Sukata move the furniture while Kendall annoyed people in the kitchen, she sat down to watch Sebastian marking out sigils.

"Has Rennyn had an argument with Captain Faille?"

The glance he gave her wasn't pleased. Sebastian acted very easy-going, but as soon as you touched something he didn't want to talk about you'd hit a wall bigger than a mountain. This time, though, he went on to sigh and shake his head.

"Not Illidian. The Kellian as a group have asked her to visit the place they used to live before they returned to Tyrland. Aurai's Rest. She's not happy about something they've asked her to do there."

The set of his jaw told Kendall that he didn't want to talk about it, so she altered course. "You've gotten used to calling him Illidian."

"More or less. He is my brother by law, after all. It was a real adjustment at first, since it's been just Ren and me for so long, and we actively discouraged people from getting near us. It was like, as soon as we stopped hiding, Ren, ah—"

"Started collecting people?"

"Well, that too. But I was thinking in terms of her priorities changing. All of a sudden there was someone more important to her than me." He shrugged, and glanced over the last sigil he'd drawn. "I suppose you picked up on how subdued she's been the last couple of days?"

Kendall hid a smirk. The best way to get Sebastian to come across was to change the subject. That gave him the chance to think things over, and maybe decide to spill some more.

"She stopped noticing stuff," Kendall said. "When your sister's upset, the first thing she does is try to hide it. She sometimes manages that, but she broods, and pays less attention to what everyone else is doing. She stopped reading the newssheets. And though she still acts the same whenever Captain Faille comes into the room, sometimes she doesn't notice when he leaves."

"Hard to believe you've only been with us a couple of months." Sebastian tapped the chalk he was using on the floor. "Did you know she has nightmares about killing them? Not from the spell we cast, but accidentally. She has to watch everything she says, because a few careless words—she could tell Sukata 'wait here' and Sukata would. Forever. And they've *asked* her to give them an order, to—" He paused. "Well, she'll tell you soon enough. Will you do something for me?"

"What?" Kendall asked, warily. Sebastian didn't ask for anything, as a rule.

"Look after her."

He didn't say anything else, and Kendall didn't really need more. They'd have a whole bunch of dangerous people with them to keep monsters away, but it was herself that Rennyn needed protection from.

"Am I supposed to call him 'Lord Faille' now?" she asked, disliking the whole mess about Rennyn's health.

"'My lord'. Or 'Lord Surclere' if you're talking about him."

"Is Herself 'Duchess Rennyn', 'Duchess Surclere', or 'Duchess Claire'?"

"Not the last one. Technically, if you're talking about her it's 'Rennyn, Duchess of Surclere', but that's old-fashioned usage, so Duchess Surclere is what most people will use. Are you really planning on using her titles?"

"No," Kendall said firmly. "And if you think I'm 'my lording' you, try for another answer."

Sebastian just laughed, then looked up at an arrival.

"Here they are. Ah, and lunch." Lieutenant Meniar, tall, naturally tan and disturbingly cheerful, poked his nose in the door, his big, black Sentene cloak hanging open. All enthusiasm and energy, he crossed to meet Sukata as she arrived with an oversized platter. "There's more?" He disappeared toward the kitchens, followed by his Kellian partner, Lieutenant Faral.

Lieutenant Meniar was always like that, enjoying everything unnecessarily, but it was hard to be annoyed with him.

Other people started arriving, Sentene and Hand mages who could never resist news that one of the Claires was going to talk about magic. The quiet room filled with people chatting and eating and asking Sebastian questions. Eavesdropping on a conversation between two Hand mages snarking about Lieutenant Meniar being a 'no more than average' mage, Kendall almost didn't notice when Rennyn finally arrived.

She was in her sneaky bed clothes. Back when Rennyn had been stuck in the infirmary, with people constantly visiting her, Captain Faille had produced a collection of what he called Verisian lounging suits. They were knee-length fancy shirts paired with matching light trousers, comfortable enough to sleep in, but making Rennyn look like she was dressed for visits. It was the first thing that had made Kendall feel maybe Rennyn wasn't so wrong marrying Captain Faille, that he'd seen she didn't like talking to people while in a nightgown, and figured out how to fix it.

Rennyn usually didn't wander around in the lounging things, but often wore them during days when she wasn't going outside so she could comfortably go to bed without changing clothes. She'd probably not been expecting the horde crowding the dining hall, or that they would start applauding her once they saw her, but she just smiled and shrugged, said thank you, and went back to talking to the blond-haired scut, who was following her like he'd been invited.

"What's she thinking?" Kendall hissed to Sukata, who shook her head, eyes confused. But that was Rennyn all over—full of inexplicable whims.

Sebastian looked up and caught sight of the boy, but he wasn't one for scenes, so he just looked down again and finished the last few sigils. Like most complicated castings, it had been chalked in a big circle to strengthen and confine the purpose. The sigils were in a language called Efanian, which mages had made up so that their spells didn't get confused over words that had more than one meaning.

It was no surprise, since words were so important to them, that mages loved to talk about them. They could all read the spell, but by the time they'd done asking Sebastian why this word, why that word, how much power it would take to cast, what kind of range it could potentially reach, Kendall had managed to finish off two helpings of lunch, and had had to poke Rennyn awake when she started to fall asleep over her own plate. But that did give her the opportunity to point her chin to the blond boy in the crowd around the Lieutenant and say: "You know who his uncle is?"

Rennyn, of course, found the question funny. "He told me. Said it was one of the three good reasons I'd have to not take him on as a student. The second was that he'd made himself objectionable to my other students, and couldn't guarantee he wouldn't do so again since sometimes he means to be polite but simply forgets and asks about things he wants to know."

"A complete and total prat, in other words. What was the third reason?"

"He likes magic too much."

"That's a bad thing?"

"It could be."

"Tell me you didn't agree to teach him."

"I told him I'd think about it, but that I'm not looking for more students. Still, we had an interesting discussion on circle-turning and how magic was re-learnt after the Elder Mages had killed themselves off and left everyone else to deal with creatures spilling out of the Eferum. How was he objectionable?"

"He asked me if I could read."

"Oh? And which do you think he was being? Deliberately rude, or forgetful?"

Kendall gave her a sour look. "You like him."

"He reminds me of Seb. I don't know if the differences are positive ones, though." She paused, then smiled at someone over Kendall's shoulder, and there was no need to turn around to know it was Captain Faille. There was only one person who made Rennyn look like that.

He had the double-sized Sentene mage called Medan with him, and stopped to say something to Lieutenant Meniar that made Meniar's excited smile fade. Too much talking, not enough business.

Captain Medan came on toward Rennyn, and put something into her hand with a murmur of "Mission accomplished," but Kendall didn't get to see what that was about because Captain Faille was close on Medan's heels, helping Rennyn to her feet and giving her a hand into the centre of the circle.

"Like most spells of this sort, the aim here is to not kill the caster," she said, settling down cross-legged. "Since it's likely that my focus is a considerable distance away, we modified a standard location spell to give only the briefest and vaguest response. It's still a very tiring spell. Are you ready, Lieutenant?"

"As I'll ever be." Meniar began walking around Rennyn, pushing power into the sigils so that they glowed. Sigillic magic was totally different from the kind Kendall had been learning. There was no effort in controlling what was happening: you wrote down what you wanted, you put power into the words, and that was it.

Of course, if you'd worded the spell badly, or if you didn't have enough power, it could all turn out very nasty. People said Thought Magic was dangerous, but at least it didn't make your heart stop if you 'over-committed' yourself.

Kendall had seen Sebastian cast this spell before, so wasn't particularly surprised when the sigils on the western side flushed blue, just for a moment. That was the direction of Rennyn's focus, which is something she would really like to get back even if she wasn't looking for her monster uncle.

Most really good mages tried going into the Eferum—the place outside the world where magic and monsters came from—and using all their strength to make a thing called a focus, which was almost as much a part of you as a finger and made you a lot more powerful. You weren't supposed to try until you were at least nineteen, and a lot of mages never did at all. Rennyn's had been really special, and had been stolen by her horrid many-greats-uncle.

This wasn't a spell where Kendall could sort out what the magic was doing, unlike some that people cast where she could now tell what the spell was meant to do. It made it dull to watch, other than for the pasty grey shade Lieutenant Meniar turned.

"It's not even specific to variations like north-west or south-west," Sebastian said. "And until you get closer—in fact, until you're starting to return an indication of 'east' instead of 'west', I wouldn't risk altering to a more specific casting."

"We leave in three days," Captain Faille said. "Split in Port Enara and re-join in Koletor."

And then chase all over the western kingdoms for a monster who would probably like nothing more than to have Rennyn delivered to him. Sebastian wasn't the only one worried how things would turn out.

Chapter Five

"DeVries. Take that smug look off your face and sit down."

Fallon sat, wondering how his wary puzzlement translated to 'smug', then waited to find out why he was there. A summons to the House Master's office usually meant a lecture, and Fallon had already had two in the first part of the year, all about the need to balance study and practice with rest and resilience. Each time, they'd doubled his weekly exercise schedule.

That had helped, much to his surprise. For all he'd been taught that physical hardiness made casting safer, Fallon hadn't expected the ordeal of jogging around the palace's protective circle to reward him with less exhausted mornings. But he hadn't kept it up during the extended break following the attack on the Arkathan, and now didn't seem able to get ahead of his own weariness. Or perhaps simply the sense of defeat.

"I can see you already know why you're here," the House Master said. "I won't congratulate you, just offer a note of caution. The Teremic approach to casting became so prevalent because a good portion of those who didn't adopt it ended up dead. Not that this isn't an opportunity half the school would give their eye-teeth for, but, well, you surely know the consequences of getting ahead of yourself."

The faint discomfort told Fallon the House Master was referring to Auri's presumed death, but before Fallon could untangle the rest of the warning, the man added: "Your father is in the guest area. Be sure to hand in any school property before you go."

Cold shock kept Fallon's face frozen, and he wondered if he still looked smug as he carefully thanked the House Master, then made himself walk, not run, to the room tucked into the dormitories where guests were left to cool their heels. Father? Here? Father had barely left the house in years.

Had Fallon made some massive error in the household accounts? Was he being dropped from the Arkathan for lack of funds? But, no, the House Master had talked of opportunities. Could Fallon dare to hope that his approach to Duchess Surclere hadn't been such a complete disaster? That the combination of his idiot mouth and being Earl Harkness' nephew hadn't made his goal unachievable?

Only he could start out by alienating both the village girl and Duchess Surclere's brother. Auri had been livid when he'd explained that he'd heard so much about how the girl didn't know anything about casting, didn't even know the most basic sigils and standard forms, that when he finally stumbled across her he'd just asked if it was true.

But he'd thought of a way to counter that, had even managed to make use of it just as the Duchess was leaving the annunciation ceremony, and purely taken for itself that conversation had gone very well. He'd captured her attention, and held his own discussing the early development of casting. He might not be a daringly confident caster—the other students called him Slow-and-steady DeVries—but surely a solid base of theory was more interesting to a devising mage like Duchess Surclere?

Fallon had thought the Duchess had genuinely meant it when she said she'd think about his request, and had let himself hope. But then he'd learned that the talk of her illness wasn't exaggeration, and that she was on the verge of leaving the country, and knew it had all been for nothing. Yet here was the Duchess' husband, Lord Surclere, talking to—

"Father?"

If Vannan DeVries caught the note of incredulity, he did not show it as he turned and smiled. "My boy. The first time I have visited you here. Are you still having trouble sleeping?"

"Not too bad, Father," Fallon said, finding no answers in Lord Surclere's expression, and all too aware he was closely observed in return. "I didn't expect you."

"I did not expect myself," Fallon's father replied. He was in high good humour, eyes bright, which only confused Fallon more.

"I will leave you to your preparation," Lord Surclere said, his voice thin and unnatural. "Contact me if there are any issues."

"I will indeed, sir," Fallon's father said, and then disconcerted Fallon completely by clasping the Kellian man's hand in both of his and pumping it warmly. "And thank you again. I have enjoyed our discussion enormously."

"We will continue it in the spring," Lord Surclere said, glanced at Fallon, and departed.

"Why did you not tell me that you wanted to study with the Duchess of Surclere, lad?" Fallon's father asked. "You could not fear my disapproval, surely?"

"I didn't think she'd agree," Fallon said, sitting down to combat sudden dizziness. It had worked? There was a roaring in his ears, and he had to take deep breaths just to keep himself together. He'd done it.

"—remarkable man," his father was saying. "Did you know, he has travelled to see both the Casellian marbles and Ridena Tower? And he recognised that Tisian carving Geralt gave for a wedding gift—said it was most likely looted from one of their temples, that they're mounted in the windows as wards. That would be Geralt all over: too insensible to wonder where a piece might come from, what vandalism had been committed to obtain it."

"The—Lord Surclere was at the house?" Fallon felt sick.

"Yes, indeed. We had a long interview—perhaps longer than he intended, since it has been an age since I could chat with someone so knowledgeable. And then he brought me to meet the Duchess. Charming young woman, though sadly under the weather. You must be sure to support her as best you can."

Stomach twisting, Fallon gazed at his father helplessly. How to ask if he'd introduced Lord Surclere to a cold marble wife and daughter? Impossible to guess whether the Kellian man knew of his father's fixation, or what he might do about it.

And they were starting for Kole tomorrow.

"I'm not sure I can leave you," Fallon said, betrayed into a high, panicked note.

"My boy, what is this?"

"I—"

"If you are concerned about the creature they are hunting, don't be. Lord Surclere, while he acknowledged that no travel is without its dangers, has assured me that there is no intention of exposing the Duchess or her students. The Sentene are experts in these matters, and, upon my word, if ever I met a person I'd trust you with, it's Lord Surclere."

Fallon was entirely unequal to telling his father that it was his safety that was the problem: that Fallon didn't dare to leave him unprotected. Vannon DeVries' overwhelming grief and withdrawal from society made him an object of pity. But if it were known that he held affectionate conversations with two lumps of stone, sympathy would turn to derision—and consequences. Madness in even a minor mage was not taken lightly.

"You'd best not let Uncle hear you say things like that," Fallon said weakly. "He's always insisting Kellian bewitch people."

"Geralt!" Fallon's father snorted. "Would he have me meet a man of singular knowledge and competence, and not acknowledge the privilege? His private misfortunes need not colour my opinions."

"What do you mean?"

"Ah, well—" Fallon's father glanced toward the door, then gave Fallon an embarrassed smile. "We can discuss that on the way home. Shall we collect your things? I will look out my old travelling trunk and we'll see if it can manage everything you need. And, ah, I must give you a list of places to see in Koletor."

Fallon's father talked happily of friezes and columns all through the afternoon. It was the most like his proper self Fallon had seen him since Auri's miscasting, and he had to wonder at the transformation. One thing everyone said of Kellian was they hardly spoke, and it was difficult to imagine the taciturn Lord Surclere in lively conversation about art. But probably Fallon's father had done most of the talking.

It wasn't possible. The plan had never included leaving the city. Certainly hadn't envisaged a teacher as burdened as he, the power of her focus lost, her casting limited by a physical fragility which surpassed Fallon's own. And no plan could ever involve leaving Father at risk of exposure.

After achieving what he'd thought impossible, Fallon would have to give it up.

Chapter Six

Rennyn felt like a child sneaking a tart from the pantry, and realised that seeing *The Black Queen* was the first true indulgence she'd managed since being injured. Tomorrow they'd leave on the Uncle Hunt, but she felt she'd earned at least a night to pander to her curiosity.

It had gone very well so far. They had arrived nearly late, and walked unremarked through a rapidly emptying foyer. Rennyn was dressed in some of Seb's clothes, with her hair caught into a tail, and her brother had added the most minor of illusion spells to make her look more like a boy.

The door that belonged to Captain Medan's key was up only one flight of stairs, and the little cup-shaped balcony beyond was conveniently toward the back of the playhouse, away from the glow of the stage. Seated in the rear pair of the four chairs, they were in no danger of catching a casual eye and were comfortably out of the heaving press below.

The strange, tall room throbbed with excitement, rowdy but good-humoured, and Rennyn could not even regret that her first time at the theatre was to see a play that was sure to annoy. Her main concern was being able to hear anything, as a flushed man came onstage to welcome everyone only to be drowned out by jeers and cheers and the shout of someone objecting to a shower of peel tossed down from above. The man bowed and left to be replaced by the first two actors, and thankfully the hubbub dropped to a dull murmur when the pair began to speak.

Solace Montjuste-Surclere and her Eferum-born son Helecho, discussing their plans to escape the Eferum and claim Tyrland. Neither of the actors looked like their subjects and Rennyn was more interested when those two left and a bit of painted canvas moved aside to show a woman curtseying before another on a throne. Lady Weston bringing news of the Grand Summoning, and of a strange woman who had warned of an incursion in Asentyr. Rennyn thought it very clever that the canvas returned to hide the throne as the pretend Lady Weston crossed to the other side of the stage, moving to a different place and day. Someone behind the scenes was playing with mageglows, and everything became a lot darker as four more people stepped into the remaining pool of light.

The gold-worked insignia of a famous uniform blazed, the Montjuste phoenix appearing to move on its own, but then the four loosened their high, concealing collars and became Sentene preparing for battle. Two looked like they'd had a sack of flour dropped over them, which was a far from accurate way of illustrating the effect of light on Kellian, but Rennyn supposed it got the point across. One was meant to be Illidian, and the other Sarana Illuma, and it was disappointing that they hadn't even tried to reproduce the attenuated quality of a Kellian's voice, though the crisp discussion of preparations for an incursion of Eferum-Get inside the city's protective circle was very typical.

Beside her, Illidian straightened, and she looked up, trying to make out his expression in the gloom. Kellian were very difficult to see in dim light, but she could feel a tension in him.

"What's wrong?"

He didn't answer immediately, then sat back as all the people on stage ran off in response to a shout.

"Parts of that were word-for-word," he replied, not sounding pleased. "From the meeting we had earlier that day."

"Oh." This could grow complicated. "One of the Sentene helped write this?"

"Or the Ferumguard." He let out his breath, and then curled his fingers over her nearest hand. "More a breach of courtesy than of the rules that govern our service. I could wish that whoever it was had taught them to hold their swords less haphazardly."

Rennyn had no idea of the proper way to hold a sword, and so was more than content to lean against Illidian's arm and watch the actors pretending to fight shadows as the room filled with the sounds of musket shot, clashing metal, and a monstrous howling.

The whole attack had been a disaster. No preparation could have anticipated the hundreds of creatures that had escaped into the city. Rennyn had heard it called the Black Night, or the Night of Claws, and she felt in the hush that fell over the room her own dismay at the deluge. There had been no containing so many, and there were sure to be more than a few here who had lost those they knew and loved, or been attacked themselves. The crowd grew stiller and ever more silent as desperation crept into the Sentene's hard-pressed battle to save the city.

The woman who stalked out onto stage spoke some of the words Rennyn had said, and pulled the Eferum-Get back to be killed as Rennyn had done. The dress she wore revealed a lusher figure than Rennyn possessed, and she did not look particularly like a Surclere, but if she was trying to live up to the Surclere reputation for arrogance she succeeded. She was rude to simply everyone, particularly the Kellian. Especially Captain Faille.

"There's not very much of Solace in this."

"Cause, not subject."

Very true. The Black Queen might lie behind events, but the play was about an accomplished soldier whose world was turned upside-down. First by a woman he did not want to admire, and then by the denial of his people's humanity, and a threat to their very selves. Rennyn had been worried that parts of the play might upset Illidian, since they were sure to at least touch upon the injuries the Black Queen had inflicted. She had not imagined that her husband would be publicly dissected.

The story of a hero: not wholly inaccurate, and far from uncomplimentary. The audience had been raptly attentive since the battle in Asentyr, and Rennyn could feel their response to each setback. Whoever was behind this had a very real understanding of the Kellian, but a sympathetic portrayal did not leave Illidian any less exposed. He was a hard man to upset, but the muscles in his arm had not relaxed since she'd commented on the play's name, and she thoroughly regretted her indulgence even before the woman pretending to be her struck a pose and asked the crowd: "How can I in conscience want such a man?"

Rennyn was so focused on Illidian's feelings that her own reaction blindsided her. They had reached that final day of the Grand Summoning, and her Wicked Uncle had said: "Wake up, cousin" to bring her out of the sleep casting he'd used to subdue the city. Rennyn listened to the actor gloating, wondering if the audience would be confused by the way he called her cousin because it was easier than many-times great-niece. And then the woman who was not her was pretending to be bitten and suddenly Rennyn couldn't look, couldn't breathe. She turned her head and hid her eyes against Illidian's arm, blood pounding in her ears in response to remembered pain, the disgusting noise he had made as he drank, and a sense of being crushed, of being invaded by something trying to force her into a different shape, and then the wrench of power going awry, laying an extra level of sickness on top of hateful touch—

Shuddering, Rennyn realised she'd been moved, pulled into Illidian's lap so he could hold her to his chest and stroke her back. She could not catch her breath, could not hear over the roaring in her ears or even control her trembling, could only stare at the creature she'd become: so vulnerable and so weak.

It seemed a long time before she could hear, and then she listened to Illidian's heartbeat, ignoring the noises from the stage. When her shaking had gone as well, he stopped smoothing his hand down her back.

"Shall we leave now?"

"Yes." Her voice was very small, and she wondered if Illidian would ever tire of the work she involved.

Kellian strength made it easy for him to carry her to the landing outside, where she made an attempt at standing, and found that she could stay reasonably upright clinging to his arm. A muffled roar broke as they reached the entrance, and she realised it was applause. Then they were out on the street, with all the traffic of the Crossways to deal with, but Illidian signalled and the coach he'd arranged to collect them was fetched from around the corner.

The journey back to barracks escaped her entirely, but she opened her eyes again when Illidian put her down in his quarters. "Something warm to drink," he prescribed, and the idea was a reviving one. Feeling more like herself, she managed to get herself to the privy down the corridor, and even warmed a bowl of water so she could wash before dressing for bed. It was the only time she'd cast that day, and she thought about that until Illidian returned from the kitchens.

He'd found some syrupy Kolan kur, and even dosed it with a tiny amount of spirits, which was something she couldn't drink in any quantity. But they sat together and it warmed her.

She leaned against him again. "I didn't know I could fall apart like that."

"Reaction from the attack." He took her empty cup and put it on the floor. "At the time, you pushed it aside. And then you were injured, and when you at last had the time and energy to think, that was not something you wanted to dwell upon. You haven't had to face the memory until now."

He touched her cheek, then bent his head to kiss her properly for the first time since that one night they'd spent together two months ago. Rennyn was considerably startled, since Illidian had made clear that the thought of hurting her while making love wasn't something he could bear, and until her ribs had strengthened he'd not risk more than the lightest touch. But he did not draw back, and she was more than happy to keep going, to try not to breathe deeply while Illidian shook with the effort of being entirely slow and gentle. The whole thing was awkward, and probably not very satisfying for either of them, but she didn't care. She'd hated that they hadn't been able to consummate their marriage.

"What changed your mind?" she asked, when they had finally settled curled together, breathing unsteadily.

He kissed the top of her head, but took his time answering. "I hadn't realised how deeply his attack had wounded you," he said at last. "I've only been thinking of your physical injuries. And haven't trusted myself."

Rennyn curled a little closer, aware of both release and conflict in him. That first time they'd made love, it hadn't escaped her notice that he had struggled with emotions that had knotted his muscles. She never doubted that he loved her, that he was passionately attracted to her, but theirs was a relationship that would always be hopelessly complicated by the power she had over the Kellian, by the nightmare she represented. She was so glad they were at least moving past the constraints placed on them by her injuries.

"Do you think that play will be popular?"

"Very." He sounded resigned. "A number of the scenes are exceptional, and it captures the...distress Tyrians have suffered, that they needed to have spoken aloud."

"Is it better to have a very good play about you that everyone will see, or a very bad play that they will forget?"

"Neither? It makes our departure fortuitous. By the time we return it will be last season's sensation. To which point, it is past time you slept."

That made Rennyn laugh, and she was even more pleased when her ribs raised no protest. "Do you really think I'll last more than a few more sentences? Perhaps I should try one of those crowd-stirring speeches." She smiled, thinking of the way the actress pretending to be her had kept stopping in the middle of battles to have little debates with herself, or to be lofty and dismissive to the Sentene.

"So unlikely..." she murmured, blinked, and realised he had moved, had settled in the chair beside the bed to read, as he did every night after she fell asleep because he tried very hard to sleep as little as possible, because he dreamed of horrors and would not risk injuring her waking in fright. That, at least, was something no-one knew to put in a play: that her husband wouldn't sleep with her.

The evening's gloss dimmed, she drifted off again, wishing the good things between them could banish the nightmares.

Chapter Seven

Kendall hadn't been keen on this plan from the start. There was such a thing as weighing the risks. Not bumping over roads might make the trip a bit easier for Rennyn, but everyone knew people died on boats. Ships, as Captain Faille said these big ones were called. Did an easier journey balance out a more dangerous one?

Floating about in a creaky wooden tub couldn't be the best solution. Sleep outside the protection of a Circle? Sail onto the ocean, which was full of things that could swallow whole people for lunch? Even if nothing came and killed them, there were storms to toss you overboard, and then maybe you'd have a chance to drown before you were eaten.

Kendall had learned enough about magic to know the difference between the circles of protection that kept Night Roamers out of towns, and the wards you'd have to use on a room or a ship. Wards were expensive, requiring a lot more power. Unless you were going to sail right back into port before sunset, you'd need a mage or two to keep them up. And they weren't nearly as strong as a Circle, which meant if they were attacked there was a chance of the wards being overwhelmed.

Despite all this, and the fact that they'd had to go down before dawn to a cold, misty and stinking river, Kendall had to work at not gawping as she crossed the thick plank between dock and deck. People were busy moving everywhere, and the masts seemed immensely tall when you stood underneath them, and you could feel the weight in all that sailcloth. If it was not for one fly in the ointment, she'd let herself enjoy setting out.

The fly had turned up when they were crowding into carriages back at the Houses of Magic, and short of pushing him overboard, Kendall didn't see much hope of getting rid of him. She hadn't said anything back at the palace, since Rennyn had been saying goodbye to Sebastian and not looking too happy about it, but first chance she got, Kendall buttonholed her teacher for an explanation. As usual it was hardly worth the breath.

"Straightforward curiosity," Rennyn said, glancing around the room she'd been shown to, with its little table and the long padded seat beneath a bunch of leaded windows looking out the back of the ship. "I found him interesting, the same as I do you and Sukata. But if it will make you feel any better, you're free to treat him with just as much courtesy as he treats you."

"Bah," Kendall said, but left as Captain Faille arrived with luggage. She wouldn't get anywhere pointing out that 'interesting' was the wrong way to look at the nephew of the Kellian's worst enemy. You couldn't make Rennyn change her mind about things by repeating the same argument at her.

Rennyn's room was at the back of the ship, and was a lot bigger than the one Kendall had. That was down the corridor, where Sukata, Kendall and Lieutenant Faral were going to sleep in things called hammocks— nets strung from the walls. There was a curtain for the door, and Kendall almost pulled that off as she reached it because the floor decided to tilt.

"If it sways this much while it's tied up, how much are these things going to rock when it's actually moving?"

"Almost dangerous," Sukata said, eyes bright, and they picked which nets would be theirs.

There was a painting of Vella Wind-Eye on the back of the door. Kendall noticed lots of them scattered about—big and little ones—as she and Sukata clambered their way back on to the deck and found a place where they were allowed to stand and watch. No surprise that sailors were devout sorts—not that Kendall could ever make her mind whether the gods paid the least attention however much you waved your arms and tried to make them take notice. The Elder Mages were supposed to look after people on a day-to-day basis, but they'd killed themselves off centuries ago.

Sukata, typically, was straight-out enjoying the prospect of putting to sea. "I am trying very hard to remember this is a serious undertaking," she confessed, as the board they'd used to cross from the dock was dragged aboard and all the sailors started pulling things. "It's too much an adventure not to be excited."

"The serious part doesn't really start until we get there," Kendall pointed out, holding hard to the bit of railing they'd been told to stick at. "And even then we're just along to be nursemaids and entertainment."

"Would you say that Duchess Surclere enjoys teaching? Or do you mean we are someone to talk to?"

Kendall hadn't noticed the fly grubbing up behind them, and wished Sukata had warned her. It was tempting to ignore him, let him buzz, but a couple of weeks on a boat would make that hard and probably prompt Rennyn to do something annoying. Though Kendall wasn't about to let him get the idea that there was any "we" involved.

"So what does your uncle think about you becoming Rennyn's student?" she asked instead.

"I expect he'll be livid," the fly said, looking pleased, though maybe just to hide an edge of worry. "I wonder how long it will take him to realise I'm gone?"

"You ran away?"

He gave her an impatient look. "My uncle is not my guardian. My father does not like my uncle."

And they were supposed to just believe that. Kendall shook her head, and wouldn't have wasted any more attention on the pest, but Sukata had turned to him and said: "Do you know what is your uncle's reason for hating my people?"

The Pest didn't act at all embarrassed, looking straight at Sukata as if it was just an interesting discussion. "My uncle tells everyone the problem is the Kellian are loyal only to themselves, but my father told me it's because of Aunt Halla, Uncle's late wife. She liked one of the Kellian far more than my uncle. Apparently. She's been dead for years, so I don't remember her."

Sukata murmured: "I see," then glanced up at the sails. The mist around the dock was shifting, beginning to stream with a lifting wind, ready to pull them down the river past the marshes to the ocean. The whole ship creaked, which was less than comforting, and then the docks started moving away.

Wind was the reason they'd had to get themselves down here before dawn, and wind was the biggest thing Kendall couldn't work out. She could understand well enough that the sails belling above them could drag the ship along in the direction the wind was going, but from what Captain Faille had said about sailing, the mages weren't on board to make sure that the wind always went in the right direction, or to push the ship against the wind if it was blowing the wrong way. Rennyn was always going on about understanding how things worked before trying to get magic to do the same, and this was a puzzle Kendall wanted to know the answer to.

The ship's Captain didn't look like the sort of person you could ask. She was almost as grim as Captain

Faille, and Kendall never enjoyed asking Captain Faille questions, even though he always answered and would never even think of teasing her. The fly had trapped Sukata into being polite to him, so Kendall went and found Lieutenant Meniar, who was up the front of the ship watching the mad people who'd climbed up the masts.

"Sorry, not a clue," he said. "I expect we'll find out when the wind changes. How's the Duchess holding up?"

"Got out of bed too early, and busy pretending the idea of not seeing Sebastian for months hasn't upset her."

"Has she said anything about the play?" He looked quickly over at the few Sentene who had remained on deck, his face a mix of curiosity and concern. "I know you three were there. We saw you."

"I don't think Rennyn's likely to want to talk about that," Kendall said, shrugging. "Most of what happened was right, but Rennyn was wrong." And it had left Kendall and Sukata out altogether, which annoyed Kendall far more than she was going to admit.

"Keste said something like that. That it was the same story happening to different people. Fel, I'm most-ways sorry I went. The thought of the pair of them sitting there watching Roms Hightley in anguished soliloquy on whether you could trust a woman who could order you to do anything—we were squirming in our seats."

"Sukata said the person who told those players all that stuff won't be in trouble."

"There's nothing in the rules against it—and they probably thought they were helping. But I definitely wouldn't like to be in their shoes. The Kellian will consider it a breach of trust, you see, and if they find out who it was, well, they'll not do more than treat them with utmost courtesy in return and that's...not something you want."

Kendall tried to imagine Sukata or Captain Faille being really really polite to her, and agreed heartily. Sukata suspected the person helping the playwright was probably one of the Ferumguard, the support troop that assisted the Sentene, because Sentene pairs of Kellian and mage worked too close for them not to know if one of the mages had been responsible.

"Were the things they had the Sentene mages saying right?" she asked. "I thought you liked Rennyn."

"No. Or yes, but no. When she first appeared, we were all very excited. The Surclere reputation, and that incredible thing she cast during the Asentyr incursion, and, gods, the sheer power of the woman. We knew the Kellian weren't too pleased that any of the Montjuste-Surclere line survived, and stupidly we were a little annoyed that she seemed to want nothing to do with them, but for the most part we were all very admiring. And then she told us she owned them."

"She didn't actually say that," Kendall pointed out.

"I know. But that's what we heard. We—there are a few reasons people become Sentene mages. It's a dangerous job, not comparatively well paid. The ambitious know it to be a stepping stone into the Hand. Others want the variety of experience—it's a way to grow as a mage or to not be stuck turning out lightstones and heatstones. Some consider it honourable service to the kingdom. And the rest of us, well, who can resist prancing about in those coats?"

"Playing hero."

"That would be it. The reason people stay as Sentene mages is usually their partner. Kellian don't mix much outside the Sentene. If you attend the Arkathan you're sure to have glimpsed them a few times, but are very unlikely to have spoken to any.

And you hear stories. Most wrong, as it turns out. You soon learn the Kellian are the backbone of the Sentene, and their respect is very hard to earn. But they'll defend you with their lives no matter how worthless they think you are."

"They don't act like they think everyone's worthless," Kendall protested.

"No." He flushed, and lowered his voice, though with Kellian hearing it probably wouldn't make any difference if any of them really wanted to listen. "No, they're more neutral, with low expectations. That sounds a horrible thing to say, but they don't encounter many people who meet the standards they hold themselves to. They don't hold it against you for not measuring up, but, well, new Sentene mages often become wholly obsessed with knowing whether they're being tolerated, or if their partner thinks them worthwhile. It can be hard to tell the difference. And it's very common to grow protective of them, which is a bizarre way to behave toward such a deadly group of people, but that's just the way it is. If you survive your first few months in the Sentene without coming to hate the Kellian, you end up wanting to shield them."

Sweet on them, Kendall translated, though Lieutenant Meniar wouldn't admit he cared about Lieutenant Faral that way. Even Captain Faille's partner, Lieutenant Danress, had stopped being a Sentene mage abruptly when Rennyn had married him.

"Now, I like the Duchess," Lieutenant Meniar went on. "Unlike most of us, I'd at least had a glimpse of her quality before she made that announcement. And, no, I didn't say it would be convenient if she died killing the Black Queen, and I never heard anyone say that. I hope no-one put it into words. But I'm sure a few thought it. It's not even how she behaves—she did, after all, get herself badly injured saving everyone—it's how she makes them all feel. She might say that she has no authority over them, that all she inherited was the ability to control them, not their selves. But there's no escaping that the Kellian aren't what they thought they were. They can't help but see themselves as the continuation of a spell rather than a people, and that upsets Keste so much I can barely stand it."

He took a deep breath, and made a flicking motion with his hands. "That sounded dramatic enough for another play. Suffice to say the Sentene mages are upset. We'll adapt. And as Duchess Surclere's assigned mage-physician, let me assure you I have no intention of allowing her to die."

Kendall thought that was true. The Sentene were angry, but at the situation, not Rennyn. They didn't really want to hurt her. How any of them would stop the Black Queen's son from killing her was another question.

Chapter Eight

"You're sleeping in a net!"

"Hammock." Waking into the Dream felt particularly odd on the ship, not least because of the hammock.

"What's it like?" Auri asked, even as she reached eagerly through the ropes to touch the focus Fallon wore concealed in a special ankle-strap beneath the largest pair of bedrocks he could find.

"Awkward to get in and out of. But a lot more comfortable than I expected, so long as I keep a blanket under me to soften the rope."

Even in a wholly new place, Auri lingered to stroke the hidden focus. Despite its odd deep mahogany colour, the focus was most definitely Auri's: it made her feel warm, and since they'd found it she'd lost that disturbing frayed-about-the-edges appearance. Fallon felt he'd won them both a reprieve, even if he'd come no closer to restoring her.

Travelling was likely to help with her boredom as well, and Fallon suspected that it was this that pushed her past her own desire to stay near Father, ordering Fallon not to give up the chance he'd so unexpectedly won. There was certainly open excitement in her examination of the room, and of Lieutenant Meniar sitting on one of the storage benches that ran along the walls. New people to look at, new places to see.

"Is he a Sentene mage? Is he nice?"

"Lieutenant Meniar. He's the Duchess' personal physician for the trip. Very cheerful sort." He'd even greeted being roomed with Fallon with unimpaired good spirits, which was more than some of the other Sentene mages would have managed. A day of flat stares and puzzled frowns had made it obvious that few were happy with Duchess Surclere's latest choice for student.

"So where's the Duchess?" Auri didn't wait for an answer, plunging through the wall into the next room.

Fallon hurried after her, and narrowly avoided walking through Sukata, standing just beyond the wall. Walking through people was horrible, like a fog made of soup.

"Be careful of the hull—the outside wall of the ship," he said, joining Auri in watching Kendall swinging back and forth in her hammock. "The whole thing's warded."

"These are the other students?"

"Kendall and Sukata. And that's Lieutenant Faral, Lieutenant Meniar's partner."

"Kellian *are* very odd-looking, aren't they?" Auri said, peering into Sukata's face as she and Kendall discussed how much swinging the hammock could take. "Almost just people at first glance, a bit over-tall, but look at how her left hand is so much harder to see out of the light of the mageglow."

"The claws are odder, don't you think?"

"Anyone can file their nails to a point. Does she have a sore throat or does she always sound like that? Is she friendly?"

"Sukata?" Fallon hesitated, distracted by the way he could tell Sukata was laughing without even smiling. Her eyes were very bright and open, despite the grave line of her mouth. "Formally polite. No-one except Duchess Surclere is exactly friendly, but Sukata will answer questions and doesn't seem to hold Uncle against me. Kendall just glares, but I think that's her natural state." This was the first time he'd seen the village girl not wearing some level of black frown, and he was surprised by how pretty she could be.

"And the Duchess?" Auri asked, diverted back to her original course.

"Through here."

Fallon led the way out into the corridor and into the big room at the end, trying to control sudden nerves. His most logical course was to become a better mage so he could tackle their problem himself, but Auri was convinced Duchess Surclere would know she was there—would immediately see, and understand, and be able to fix them. Fallon really wanted the Duchess to be that brilliant as well, but he refused to let hope override common sense.

The room's mageglows had been covered and Duchess Surclere was curled up in one of the seats before the many-paned windows, looking out at a heavy moon striping the horizon. Auri marched straight up to her, leaning in close to peer into her face, her own expression very set and un-Auri-like.

"Help. Me."

Furious words, near to spat into the oblivious woman's face.

"Auri—"

"She doesn't know I'm here."

"No." Duchess Surclere hadn't even blinked.

"She's not going to be any use at all, is she?"

"I'm going to be of use," Fallon said firmly, stifling any hint of his own disappointment. "Duchess Surclere might have lost her strength, but she has the Surclere knowledge, and she's going to teach me. There's not a person in the whole of the world more expert on the Eferum. You just need to be—"

"Patient? What else have I been? She was supposed to see!"

Auri spun and would have run out of the room except that Lord Surclere had just come into it, and the moonlight set him alight, his hair glowing pale mist and eyes silver circles. Auri stopped dead, then stepped hastily out of the way as he reached Duchess Surclere.

"A great deal more comfortable than coaches," Duchess Surclere said, glancing back. "I have to admit it was very helpful."

"The Queen is a practical woman," Lord Surclere said, which didn't quite sound like a compliment. "She may be practical about Sebastian."

"He thought of that, too, but fortunately the girl's rather young and tying him to second-in-line really not a good idea. But he plans to be exasperatingly vague and bookish on the off-chance." She gazed back out the window and added unconvincingly: "He's well able to take care of himself."

Lord Surclere reached out and undid the thin black bow that held back Duchess Surclere's hair. Pulling it free, he wound it around his wrist.

"Are you going to appropriate all my ribbons?" Duchess Surclere asked, smiling up at him.

"Yes."

He slid one finger under a long lock of hair that had fallen over her cheek, letting it wind and slip. Duchess Surclere went pink, the change of colour visible even in the stark moonlight.

"Let's get out of here," Fallon said, alight with mortification. He grabbed Auri's hand, but she pulled free, and then both of them froze because Duchess Surclere had stopped looking pleased and shy, turning her head sharply toward them.

"What?" Lord Surclere pivoted on his heel.

"Some kind of scry," Duchess Surclere said. "Very finely done, but definitely an observation. Tch—it will have to be someone on the ship, given the distance and the wards."

Lord Surclere stood just a little straighter, and what could be made out of his expression in the vivid moon-glow did not change at all. And Fallon had never wanted more to be anywhere but where he was.

"Let's get out of here!" he said, pulling at his sister's arm as Lord Surclere turned and walked out of the room—not hurrying, but not slow either.

"Don't *quail*, Fal," Auri said. "If they find out the truth they're hardly going to be angry."

"All they'd find is that I'm spying on them," Fallon said. "I won't be able to explain more, and—"

"He'll only see that you're asleep," Auri pointed out. "No-one else has been able to tell you're in the Dream. And she can barely tell we're here. Calm down."

"Easy for you to say."

"Do you think we should push something over? Were you feeling well enough this morning?"

"Nothing out of the way," Fallon said. "I suppose she'd stop thinking we were a scry if we did. But—"

"But, but—you only ever think of objections, Fal."

"But what if she thought we were some sort of attack? She might try to dispel us."

"Where's her slate? We could write 'Help' on it."

"That—" Fallon shook his head. "You know what that will do to me." One or two quick actions, like triggering the page-turner or pushing something, would tire Fallon. Anything sustained, even only long enough to write a word, and he'd sleep half the next day.

"This time it might be worth it."

"So that they can question me when I wake up?"

"At least if you pass out they'll start investigating."

"You don't know what it's like, Auri. I can't—"

"I know what this is like!" Auri yelled. "Never touching, never eating, never doing! You don't care! Don't you want her to fix me?"

"I don't want her to kill us," Fallon said.

Duchess Surclere turned her head as if trying to hear them better, then looked to the door as Lieutenant Meniar strode in.

"Scries, eh?" he said, just a little round about the eyes, as if startled. "Probably one of the ship's mages being curious. Captain Faille told me to put an extra ward on the room."

"I suppose that's the simplest solution," Duchess Surclere said. "It's rare they'd find me doing anything but sleeping, but it's still annoying."

Fallon left, knowing Auri would follow rather than be trapped in the room by a ward. They'd encountered wards only occasionally since the Dream started, and they were painful and impossible to cross, no matter whether they were trying to exclude Eferum-Get or magical intrusions. At least the ship's wards formed a bubble over the masts, so Auri would be able to enjoy the view from the deck.

At the steep stair at the end of the passage Fallon concentrated on going up without slipping through, then headed toward the front of the ship. He hadn't quite reached it before experiencing that curious, stretchy sensation that told him he was at the limit of the distance he could go from his body, but almost all of the deck was within range.

"I'll take an afternoon nap tomorrow," he told Auri, when she finally joined him. "You definitely want to see what the sunset is like."

Subdued now, Auri eyed the nearest sailor fretfully. "Do you think Mrs Pardons will look after Father properly?"

"As she said, she's managed him well enough when I've been at school. What worries me is if Uncle decides to get back at him for letting me go off with Duchess Surclere, but Mrs Pardons said she just wouldn't let Uncle in if he gets too bad. She had all these plans for pretending the household had come down with Shaky Fever."

Auri didn't respond, just stood shoulder to shoulder with him and watched the moon inch higher. Her way of apologising. Fallon doubted he would be able to handle the long isolation much better, but the chance of Auri letting her temper ride her to disaster was another worry to add to Uncle and Father and spells gone wrong and a seriously angry Lord Surclere.

He was so tired.

Chapter Nine

Rennyn glanced out the window at grey, damp sky, then back to the warm cabin that had been home for the past two weeks. "Can you hear music?"

The range of expressions in return for her question clearly told her 'no', and were also a nice illustration of the different personalities before her. Sukata concentrated, even though Kellian hearing meant she would ordinarily have caught any sound before Rennyn. Fallon was analytical, searching for a double meaning to the question, while Aven Meniar's light smile gave way to a quick, professional survey, on the off-chance that she'd suddenly developed a fever. And Kendall was just suspicious, convinced as ever that half Rennyn's actions were for her own quixotic amusement.

"Guess not. Sorry for interrupting." She gestured for Meniar to continue, though the impression of notes too distant to be truly audible hadn't gone.

"For bone-work, caulding isn't a replacement for a splint," Meniar said, with a shrug. "For all kinds of reasons, you don't want to rely solely on magic to keep fractures in position. With a clean break, once the bone is set you don't truly need caulding at all after the splint is in place, but where the bones have been shattered, where there are many fragments, caulding might be the only thing to save a limb. And to cauld a bone you need to see the bone, which is what this casting is all about."

The Sigillic was straightforward, but Rennyn had found the lecture interesting for the new words that stood for all the different layers of people. She'd only ever learned the most basic of healing magics, because the study of how living creatures worked required many more years than she could devote. This trip had become a good opportunity to explore new avenues, and she and her students had enjoyed a round dozen of these lectures from Meniar and the other Sentene mages, as well as the specialist ship mages.

This Sigillic had been written in a circle around a flat bowl filled with water, and as Meniar began to activate, the liquid took on a silvery sheen while a faint glow appeared around his left hand.

"There are many variations of this casting, depending on just what it is you wish to look at," Meniar said, touching his left hand to the back of his right. "Term substitution is possible, but only useful for issues that can be diagnosed simply by looking."

Rennyn leaned so she could see the bowl more clearly, watching a collection of bones flex in time with Meniar's hand. It was an eerie sight.

"This isn't the spell everyone uses when they look at my ribs," she commented. "At least, not illusions in bowls."

"This version's mainly for when trying to set the bones," Meniar said. "When it's necessary to see the movement. Sukata, you give it a try."

The Kellian girl was a confident caster. Her Sigillics were always precisely written, and she didn't rush or hesitate, but had a nice surety. Rennyn enjoyed watching her, especially the pleasure in her eyes, for Sukata straightforwardly enjoyed magic. Fallon had said he liked it too much, but though he cast without effort she felt as always an underlying lack of certainty. Kendall usually pretended to be bored during Sigillic lessons, since she wasn't yet permitted to use them, but this was far too intriguing for her not to crane forward wide-eyed.

"Do you feel up to casting?" Meniar asked Rennyn.

She considered how much or little she wanted to peer through the faint mist of rain in hopes of an early glimpse of Port Avecna. They'd followed a cup-like course south, west, then north, making port frequently to take on supplies and trade cargo, and finally to part ways with most of the Sentene. It always seemed they would reach land while Rennyn was sleeping, and she'd been looking forward to Avecna, but knew she was more curious to see the ribs that had given her so much trouble.

Not bothering with the sigils, she touched one hand to her side and the other to the bowl, and considered the image in the water. Finding this too small to be satisfying, she lifted the illusion to the air before her and expanded it to cover all of her from the waist up. Much easier to examine.

"Is this blurring the calluses?" she asked, frowning at the faint dark cracks interrupting smooth bone.

"The part of them that has transmuted to bone," Meniar said, shaking his head at her variation of the spell. "Take a couple of deep breaths, will you?"

Wrinkling her nose, Rennyn obeyed. She'd had to do lots of breathing exercises the last couple of months, which she was told would stave off chest infections and help her lung not collapse again. It still hurt, but nothing like the knife of the first month.

Meniar circled the table for a better look, and nodded, pleased. "There's definite progression. Another month or so and it should be well knit."

"That's supposed to be encouraging, is it?" Rennyn asked, then laughed at the way the fleshless skull flapped its jaw. "This would be very interesting cast on a dancer. Or perhaps to use for a Death Day March." She wondered if Seb would be more interested in such pranks, now that they no longer had the pressure of the Black Queen's return hanging over them, and pushed away the immediate pang. She'd known she'd miss Seb. There was no point dwelling on his absence.

"Do you think you could translate whatever it is you're doing into a Sigillic?" Meniar asked. "It would be a valuable variation."

"I expect so," Rennyn said, and glanced at her three students. "As a first step to that, each of you can draft your suggestion for how the Sigillic should read. You can have three days. No peer consultation or actual casting attempts, please."

The door opened as she said this, and she smiled at Illidian, who had been on deck training with Keste Faral. He was thoroughly damp, since he didn't consider misting rain anything more than a useful extra challenge to a sparring session. Usually he returned from practice lightly energised, but Rennyn caught a hint of a frown before the sight of a moving skeleton in the middle of the table distracted him.

"The headland has been sighted," was all he said, wiping one of his duelling swords with a cloth before sliding it into its sheathe.

That was a signal to pack up. Rennyn dismissed the divination, and her small class cleared the table and moved it away from the window seat to where it could be bolted in place. They followed Illidian back through the door, and Rennyn glanced out the window again, but wasn't tempted to get wet and cold. For her, each day had two halves, and this was the end of the first.

"Your Grace."

Everyone except Kendall and Illidian was still very formal with her, and Rennyn had long since given up reminding her companions her name was Rennyn. Fallon, just like Kendall, was splendidly intractable. But while Kendall was a prickly ball of resistance, Fallon obliged on all but a few points.

"Questions?" she said, easing off her shoes.

"I would like a...an unsparing opinion on whether it is possible for any of us to reach your level of Thought Magic."

Rennyn considered the question then said: "Why would it be impossible?"

"It's obvious from your approach with Kendall that you feel it necessary to ground her in Thought before moving on to Sigillic. Centuries of mages who started with Sigillic never accomplished more than basic lifting with Thought, before it was abandoned altogether. Have we destroyed our chances of fully embracing Thought because we muddied the waters with Sigillic? Or...is it a Surclere trait? No-one outside your family is known to have achieved this."

"Given the reputation of the Elder Mages, I wouldn't say that's true."

"Your family and some near-mythic mages who are long dead, then."

Rennyn considered her family's past. "The Surcleres possess natural strength, but I don't believe the line is distinctive in other ways," she said. "There have been those in my family who never stepped beyond basic Thought manipulation, and I would put that down simply to it being difficult.

"Starting with Sigillic increases the probability of you inadvertently killing yourself, since you have more power to do damage, but it doesn't make it harder to gain control. I can't guarantee or guess as to how far you'll be able to progress, or whether any of you have the combination of discipline and...intuition that allows a mage to reliably Thought-cast. Both Sukata and Kendall are progressing well in physical manipulation, but it will be a long time before I ask them to do anything abstract."

"Will I be permitted to begin the exercises, once we leave the ship?"

She nodded. "The delay was only because of the danger to the ship. You'll make the very early attempts in a clear area so you're away from others, and if you achieve some measure of control will follow the same series of exercises as Sukata and Kendall. Increasingly complex physical manipulation. You will not attempt anything outside the exercises until I consider you ready."

"Do you—" He stopped, apparently changing his mind about the question. "Thank you, Your Grace." He gave her a slight, formal bow and left, passing Illidian, who had been waiting in the doorway.

Rennyn stripped off her thick woollen socks and wriggled her toes while her husband closed the door. He was even damper than before—he'd doused himself as a makeshift post-practice bath—and she watched him dry and dress himself with the spare efficiency that was so characteristic of him.

"Was that the first time you cast complex Thought Magic before DeVries?" he asked, tidying away his discarded clothing.

"Must be." During the trip, Rennyn had made a point of casting every day, but usually the most minor of things. "I hadn't seen anything like the reaction you noticed before now."

"He kept it from his face, but the intensity is palpable."

Rennyn nodded. Illidian had told her that Fallon had come close to fainting when she'd first agreed to speak to him. She'd only seen a boy with a clever stratagem to catch her interest, but hadn't doubted Illidian's ability to gauge reactions, and had taken the boy as a student at his request. Today she too had glimpsed an overmastering need behind Fallon's questions about Thought Magic. Desperation. She or Illidian would puzzle out the reason eventually, and hopefully be able to help him. Or stop him, if it was all some complex stratagem of his Uncle's, as a few had hinted.

"He does truly love magic, but he's frightened of it as well, which isn't surprising given the family history. At least that seems to have pushed him away from trying to work Thought out himself. Too many won't be so cautious, now they know what's possible."

Illidian drew her to her feet. "You can't take every would-be Thought Mage as a student."

"I know. Seb kept saying the same thing, and told me I should write a basic manual for the hordes." She leaned into his arms. "Just by being a Thought Mage I've started something that I can't control. The most I can do is be open about my methods and hope people will believe me about making an honest appraisal of a mage's abilities before any attempt to step beyond basic. Having taken the risk myself, I can hardly forbid them from trying to become..."

"A real mage?" Illidian asked when she hesitated.

"I'd rather not put it like that."

"Much as you've tried to qualify it, it's how you and Sebastian regard yourselves."

She sighed, and went to climb into the bed because she was starting to feel too tired to stand. "Full mages, perhaps. 'Real' is the wrong way to look at it, though there's no way I'm telling Kendall and Sukata that non-Thought Mages always seem so...half-made to me. I don't want anyone to consider Thought Magic a mandatory part of being a mage. So many shouldn't even make the attempt at basic manipulation: they're just not suited. To take the step beyond that really can be dangerous, and I can't even be sure that any of my three can manage it. Sukata may do it—she has that combination of confidence and intuition. And any of them could kill themselves in the process. And I will hate myself a little if that happens, and every time I hear that some child has died trying to be me. I'm working on not dwelling on it too much."

The impact of her family's casting techniques on mages in general was something she had not anticipated. Her life-long focus on killing Solace had left little thought to spare for what came after. A rise in Thought Magic should have been obvious—but she had not foreseen it any more than she had imagined that she would so completely link her future with the Kellian.

She was fortunate to have a husband who knew how useless it was to tell her not to feel guilty for existing. Better still that he chose to distract her with several long kisses. The time on the ship had shifted their relationship, the aspect of patient and nurse receding rapidly once Illidian had decided it was safe to touch her. That he chose to match his day to hers, to break it in half and stay with her when she went to bed after lunch, was something she appreciated so much she doubted she could put it into words. She was not good at enduring her complete lack of stamina, and the matter-of-fact way Illidian adapted to her limitations lessened her sense of being a dreary burden.

The limits of her physical health never went away, and when she was tired the hurdles in their immediate future seemed insurmountable. There was no guessing how much chasing about they would need to do to locate the Black Queen's son. And would these missing mages of the Emperor's be a clue or a distraction?

Looming large in the list of things Rennyn wished to be distracted from was the visit to Aurai's Rest, the settlement the Kellian had established in the massive forest north of Kole. Those who waited there troubled her even more than her apparent career killing her relatives: the Kellian descendants who chose not to serve in Tyrland, and the nine surviving originals. A different set of relatives.

"When was the last time you saw your mother?"

"Five years ago. Most of us will visit the Rest at least once every decade. Often more frequently."

Illidian had made clear that he doubted his mother would be enthusiastic about their marriage, and so the best approach to meeting her was exercising Rennyn's mind a good deal. "Does she ever come to Tyrland?"

"Never." Propping himself on an elbow, he traced a stray lock of her hair, a favourite gesture. "Mother feels we should manage our relationship with humans more strictly. That living as a minority among them will inevitably create a situation where we are driven out and hunted." His eyes were shuttered, grey as the clouds. "Events may yet prove her correct."

"What was worrying you when you came in?" she asked, abandoning the vexing issue of Darian Faille for the moment.

"A sense of unease with no focus. As if the future was overcast. Nothing useful." Illidian's voice was wry. The refined senses people called Kellian instinct were excellent for dealing with direct attacks, but tended to plague him when the threat they were responding to wasn't so easily defined. "Knowingly bringing you closer to Prince Helecho is not an easy matter."

"If he does still have my focus, it's probable he intends to lure me or hunt me at some point," Rennyn admitted. "Our best chance is to catch him unaware. Even then—" She paused. "We can only guess at how much strength he's gained while I've been recovering. He may have grown into a threat that will require armies to combat. And how we deal with that without looking like an official Tyrian expedition I can't guess."

"The hunting of Eferum-Get is something that should not, and usually does not care for borders. But this is a monster that could be a political tool, or pursue its own ambitions. Queen Astranelle would prefer him dealt with quietly. I—" Illidian shifted, the muscles in his back bunching. "I just wish him dead."

"Everyone does," Rennyn murmured, and hoped it could be done without her ever having to even see her Wicked Uncle again.

Chapter Ten

"It never ceases to amaze me how sitting on your rear all day is so tiring and leaves you feeling so grubby," Lieutenant Meniar said. "Since this Waystation is on Kole's border, I'm hoping it has Kolan style baths. And that they live up to their reputation."

"What are Kolan baths supposed to be like?" Kendall asked, sliding down the shutter of the coach window despite the damp wind outside.

The twitch at the corner of Lieutenant Meniar's mouth let Kendall know his answer was going to be entertaining, but not entirely true, so she turned her eyes to grey fields fading to blackness, and only half-listened to talk of naked people sitting around steamy pools together. They were travelling one of the Imperial Ways, so the coach ran smooth and straight, but a broken wheel had delayed the caravan and they weren't going to reach the next Waystation for at least another hour.

Lieutenant Faral leaned forward and touched her knee. "Faille would know and wake Her Grace if any life-stealers came close."

"I guess." Kendall shrugged, sharper than she'd meant to, but it wasn't as if she'd said anything about being worried.

"We're travelling too fast anyway," Lieutenant Meniar added. "Moving slower than walking pace is part of the reason life-stealers prey on the sleeping."

Kendall looked out the window again. She could see a few specks of light in the far distance, and supposed there was a farmhouse there. A few months ago, she'd never gone further than the nearest village, let alone swanned about in fancy carriages, and she'd always watched with envy as the mail coach passed. The Kolan Wayporters travelled in groups for safety, and sped at great speed along the roads they kept boasting about, and Kendall couldn't help but be pleased to have come along, despite certain unshiftable annoyances.

Wondering how much of the gab about the baths was true, she pulled the window shutter closed as the endless rain picked up again. At least there were plenty of light and heatstones to make wet autumn days bearable.

"Why don't life-stealers, or any of the Night Roamers, just hunt animals instead of people?" she asked. "No-one's ever been able to explain that to me."

"Possibly because no-one's ever been able to do more than guess," Lieutenant Meniar said. "Though I must remember to ask the Duchess what the Surclere view is."

"The most common theory ties to the popular idea for the origin of the Eferum-Get," the pest said, because the gods forbid a day went by when Fallon DeVries couldn't show off. "If Eferum-Get are created by our nightmares, then reciprocally we are what they need to feed upon."

"In parts of the west you will see depredation on animals," Lieutenant Meniar added. "The Empire doesn't manage Eferum-Get as efficiently as Tyrland. They rely on strong circles, often bolstered by walls, and periodically sweep regions. Eferum-Get who can't prey on humans usually die after a time, but some adapt. Their magical aspects fade, and so does their dependence on humans."

Kendall was willing to bet they wouldn't pass up anyone they could get their claws on, but settled back to deciding whether she was going to give Rennyn her attempt at the Sigillic divination or pretend she hadn't even tried. It wasn't that she had any trouble looking up words in the Sigillic dictionary, but writing precisely what you wanted to happen in sigils was harder than it sounded. There seemed to be a thin line between getting it just so, and having your head explode. And Rennyn wouldn't give her a 'form book' full of Sigillics that other people had already worked out, so Kendall could check how close she was to right.

She'd just about decided that it wasn't worth giving the Pest another chance to tell her how to do it right when Lieutenant Faral opened the door and climbed onto the roof. She moved with the total ease only a Kellian could manage, disappearing into the rain without even a pause. As the coach driver let out a startled oath, Sukata pulled the door shut, then slid down the shutter. Lieutenant Meniar tugged his slate book from the enormous inner pocket of his coat and flipped it open.

"You do numbers, Sukata. I'll do type."

Kendall reminded herself that Kellian instinct was all about approaching danger and that the Sentene used a lot of hand signals. At least the Pest looked just as astonished.

"We're very close to the Waystation," said Lieutenant Faral, her voice sounding spookily from the window just before the driver began clanging his warning bell to alert the rest of the caravan to danger. Kendall couldn't work out what else she said but by now Sukata had got through her casting, and the way her head moved back warned that it was bad.

"Dozens," Sukata said, with proper Sentene to-the-pointness. "Spread out ahead around a central cluster."

Lieutenant Meniar's eyes flickered, but he didn't falter in casting the second, more complex divination, despite the increasing jolting of the coach. The driver had whipped the horses to a mad dash, and even on an Imperial Way the coach bounced like a skipping stone. Kendall had a brief vision of the lead coach overturning and the rest of the caravan ploughing into it. They would be all tumbled and smashed and whatever was out there would have easy pickings.

"At this speed we should be able to break through," the Pest said, not sounding like he believed himself. "We only need to make the circle. If it's walled, the Waystation guards will get ready to open the gate when they hear the bell."

Not bothering to respond, Sukata slid Lieutenant Faral's sword out from under the seat and held it up out the window, then produced the long knife she kept strapped uncomfortably to one thigh.

"If we are stopped outside the circle, we must go directly to Her Grace," she said. "Stay close, on my left side."

That shouldn't be too far. Of the six coaches in the caravan, Rennyn had hired two. It gave them seats spare so Kendall, Sukata and the Pest could ride with Rennyn and Captain Faille in the mornings and the Lieutenants in the afternoons. Rennyn's coach was the next one up, third in line.

"Hells!" Lieutenant Meniar started out of his seat and stuck his head out the window. "Keste—it's a Kentatsuki in swarm. Can you see the Waystation?"

"Too close," Lieutenant Faral said as the coach lurched, slowing, and the driver stopped sounding his alarm. "Brace yourselves."

Lieutenant Meniar barely had time to throw himself back onto the seat before the coach lurched wildly, veering to the left. Sukata gripped Kendall's shoulder with her free hand, and the Pest managed to snatch at a strap as everything loose tumbled to one side. As the faint tingle of a circle's border made Kendall shiver she heard a huge bang outside. Wood groaned, then the coach thudded into a smoother course, lurched again, and stopped with an almighty judder and much clashing of hooves.

"Follow me. Now." Sukata had gone very commanding and in charge. She thrust open the coach's right door and hopped out into the rain. Kendall was slow to move, frozen by the noise: people shouting, pistols going off. Just ahead was a sound barely recognisable as a horse.

When Lieutenant Meniar slid out past her, Kendall managed to shift herself and follow, so busy trying to look in every direction at once she dropped straight into a puddle, drenching herself to the knees. There was a little light, and she could see that this Waystation was much the same as the one they'd stayed at yesterday. A vast wooden wall circled it all, with a big building to one side, four floors high, and a mash of stables and sheds around it. A third of the circle was left for a through-road and a place to unload coaches before they were drawn outside for the night.

The lead coach had clipped a wagon and overturned, the horses broken free except one lying tangled in the traces. There were horses everywhere, panicked and trampling. Kendall's coach had veered toward the main building and almost through the wide-open door, and there was a coach right behind them, the horses blocking the way to Rennyn's. The last two coaches had managed to pull up just outside the circle, and passengers were crowding out only to stop and fall over each other as they saw the same things Kendall didn't want to, scrabbling up on the first coach.

Bugs. About a third the size of a man, purple-pink and...fleshy. They had long wings, and legs that flexed and gripped like spiky arms. The heads...she struggled to think what they reminded her of. Dogs? And they were making a noise, a rasping scrape that bored into Kendall's skull.

There were more than the four trying to pull off the door of the fallen coach. There were flickers of movement everywhere, things darting forward, not bothered by the soft light of the Waystation's mageglows. They hopped more than flew, but they were quick, and the caravaneers trying to shoot them were far too spooked and clumsy, even without the rain dampening their powder. The lead coach had had an expensive rifle that used magic to spit its shot, but that must be lost under the tangle of spilled luggage.

Kendall's coach jerked as the driver struggled to control horses trying to back, and Lieutenant Faral jumped down from the roof as the Pest stumbled into Kendall. Sukata caught her elbow, and they all moved in a rush to find Captain Faille guarding the open door of Rennyn's coach.

He was holding the longest of his swords, the one nearly as tall as he was, and gave Sukata a smaller one as she arrived. Adding only a Sentene hand signal, he and Lieutenant Faral turned and were gone, blurring in two separate directions.

"Into the coach," Sukata ordered, and hustled Kendall and the Pest in before they could move on their own. Rennyn was sitting just inside the door, her face set. Lieutenant Meniar began casting something: a spell inscribed on a metal plate strapped to his wrist. He didn't even look up as Sukata, sword a blur, sent one of the bugs tumbling in pieces back the way it had come. Dozens, Sukata had said. Dozens.

"How did they get inside the circle?" the Pest asked, then started as something landed on the roof. As Sukata turned, a man dashed past her, two more bugs in close pursuit. The people crowded at the circle's entrance had started running in all directions, even out away from the Waystation.

It was too much for Rennyn. "Kendall, tell them to shield their eyes," she said, leaning forward.

For a second Kendall tried to snatch her back to safety, but then her brain woke up and she yelled with all her might: "Shield your eyes!" before half-covering her own. Through parted fingers she saw Rennyn glance up, which was the only warning before the sun came out.

No, brighter. Hot, white, piercing light, stabbing through Kendall's fingers. The thing on the roof made a noise like a clockwork cat being boiled: a shrieking, clattering hiss followed by a thump as it fell to the ground. Eyes slitted, Kendall felt rather than saw Rennyn start to tip forward, and grabbed at the back of her coat. Managing to catch hold before her teacher was more than halfway out, Kendall pulled back and ended with a damp armful already colder than she should be. Kendall hadn't figured out more than that before the glare through the coach door changed.

Light did weird things to Kellian. Sunlight turned them golden, their eyes yellow discs, their hair and nails pale flames. At full moon they were silver, and they even went a kind of rose during a painted dawn. Kendall had never seen one in light as strong as this, and for a moment couldn't even tell who it was, saw only a vaguely human shape of burning blue-white. Even the clothing was lit or lost in the glare.

But of course it was Captain Faille. One lightning-tipped hand found Rennyn's throat, touched her cheek, then he picked up a cloak from the seat opposite and laid it over them.

"Keep her warm. DeVries, assist Meniar."

Gone again. Kendall squinted into the glare, then tightened her grip on Rennyn.

"Is she—?" The Pest stopped trying to squeeze himself into the far corner of the coach and moved forward. "I suppose she must be. Fel, she can cast like that without a focus." He shook his head, grimaced, and then slid out into the blaze.

Frowning, Kendall slipped an arm under Rennyn's legs and struggled to move her limp figure away from the door. Stupidly tall woman. That she didn't stir at all during the heaving wasn't a good sign. Sliding into the gap by the door, Kendall tucked the cloak properly around her charge, then pulled one of the warm glowstones to her and set it in Rennyn's lap. She might still be breathing, but Kendall hadn't seen Rennyn so deeply unconscious since that first week after she nearly died.

But it was being wet that was the problem, and Kendall, still dripping herself, scuffled about trying to dry hair and skin and finding another of the glowstones. The demon prince's miscasting had stolen Rennyn's physical strength, so not only was she liable to catch colds, but Lieutenant Meniar had explained that even a minor sniffle could weaken Rennyn enough to make her more likely to catch another. And that would tire her more, so that she'd have a harder time fighting off the next. Even relatively little problems could lead to a deadly downward spiral.

With an arm around Rennyn's waist to make sure she stayed upright, Kendall squinted into the glare, trying to work out what was happening through the haze of rain and light. Less screaming now, more shouted questions but, since everyone except Kendall spoke Kolan or Verisian, this didn't tell her much. Over near the lead coach she could make out Lieutenant Meniar talking rapidly to the man who had run past, who was clutching his shoulder. Lieutenant Faral was a streak of lightning on top of the tumbled coach, helping someone climb out. The only caravaneers Kendall could see were trying to calm the horses of the next coach over. The Vanmaster, a grizzled and impatient type, came staggering up to Lieutenant Meniar, herded by Captain Faille. Collecting the injured, Kendall guessed.

Sukata and the Pest weren't anywhere Kendall could see. Even without the glare the coaches blocked at least half of what was going on. Two men came to help Lieutenant Faral lift injured people out of the fallen coach. Captain Faille carried another person up to Lieutenant Meniar, a woman with a stain down her stomach and skirt, who clung to him when he tried to put her down. The light made the colour all wrong, but Kendall knew the stain was blood.

Sukata ran up then and handed Lieutenant Meniar a slate, but raced straight away again, burning white. She and the pest must be in the other coach writing up Sigillics for him, in oil pastel to withstand the rain. Captain Faille went to one knee, talking to Meniar as he detached the woman's arm from around his neck. But he stayed holding her as Meniar began to cast.

Kendall was abruptly glad she wasn't any closer. Turning, she fussed with Rennyn's blankets, and wrapped her charge's icy hands around the glowstone, holding them in place. Out in the rain the woman had arched backward on Captain Faille's lap, and something had come out of her stomach. A little bug, hand-sized, shaking out its wings like a butterfly from a chrysalis in the few moments before the light made it sizzle and burn.

The woman was screaming. Screaming and screaming, and Kendall would probably do the same if a bug had come out of *her* stomach. The things had been stinging the people they were chasing, laying eggs in them. They'd grown so big, so quickly. Fel, it was no wonder Rennyn had cast, even knowing what it would do to her. It explained why Lieutenant Meniar was doing his healing out in the pouring rain, too. In the light.

Every time she glanced out, Captain Faille and Lieutenant Faral were in a different place. Collecting injured people, herding those who had run outward back into the Waystation's circle, organising for the wreckage to be moved, getting the final two coaches into the safety of the glare. Babysitting was the easiest job going. Not that Kendall was really doing more than stopping Rennyn from falling off the seat as the driver continued to struggle with the horses. But she'd been around the Kellian enough by now to know that having someone to sit with Rennyn made all the difference when they couldn't be with her themselves.

Even Lieutenant Meniar, who had more to do than any person could manage, came straight to check on Rennyn once he'd dealt with the people who'd been stung. Dripping all over Kendall, he didn't do much more than see how Rennyn was breathing, but he frowned all the time.

"It's not so much what she's done to herself by casting with all her strength, it's that when her system's shocked like this she's ridiculously vulnerable. If she grows at all responsive, try and give her a little honey and water. I'll send Sukata with a fortifier."

Rubbing a hand over his face, he hurried away, leaving Kendall to go through Rennyn and Captain Faille's belongings in the hopes of finding honey and water, or anything more useful than the squashed packet of honey cakes she discovered where she'd been sitting. She'd given up and was wetting Rennyn's lips with drops of rainwater when a blazing blue-white girl arrived, herding a crowd into the coach with a few words of Kolan.

Kendall needed a moment to recognise them as the people from the first coach, a family of Kolans who had ponced about in masks to show they were noble, and had both a maid and a manservant to send to tell people what to do. Only one of them, the extra-snotty oldest daughter, was still wearing a mask, and they all looked shaken and battered. They squeezed four across on the seat opposite Rennyn and Kendall's, both the father and the manservant missing.

"Move her a little closer," Sukata said, pulling out her slate. It helped when she spoke, because she looked like nothing in the world.

"Thought you didn't feel ready to try any healing magic," Kendall said, swapping sides with Rennyn again.

"A fortifier is straightforward. And one of the reasons we've been getting so many lectures on healing magic is so we can help in emergencies."

Those who were allowed to cast Sigillic Magic. Not that Kendall would want to try and mess with healing, but it was constantly annoying that Rennyn wouldn't even let her start with something simple. Sukata was a good caster though, and she didn't have any trouble with the spell, which would make it a little less likely Rennyn would get sick.

"We'll be heading out very soon," Sukata said, folding her slate. "You'll need to sit between Her Grace and I."

For a moment Kendall couldn't think why, but of course Sukata was completely soaked. "We're not going to stay here?"

"There's no way of knowing how long this light will last," Sukata explained. "Even if it burned long enough for us to fully clear the buildings, there are more outside the circle. We need to give warning, or this will be a plague across the region. There is a town an hour along the road, and if they reach there...."

"How did they cross the circle in the first place?"

One of the Kolans said something and Sukata paused, then replied in the careful Kolan she'd learned at the Arkathan.

"Kentatsuki are one of the most dangerous of the Eferum-Get," she went on in Tyrian. "Relatively easy to kill individually, but they can tolerate dull light, so roam on overcast days, or during dusk. And they implant their young in those they attack, without immediately killing them. The injured run for safety, and their bodies shield the Kentatsuki young when they cross the circle. Those who have been attacked rarely survive more than ten or twenty minutes, and the new Kentatsuki reaches full size within an hour."

"And when it starts stinging people inside the circle, some run *outside*," Kendall finished, shaking her head at the implications. "And you said there were dozens..."

But Sukata had turned away, looking back at the big main building. Without a word she walked off, catching Captain Faille as he strode past. Kendall watched them blankly, not used to Sukata being in any way impolite. Lieutenant Faral joined them, and the three Kellian stood studying the main building's entrance and ground floor windows.

One of the Kolans said something, a question, but Kendall could only shrug. The Kellian were obviously talking about going inside, but why they would suddenly want to do that was anyone's guess.

As usual, they didn't waste any time about it. Captain Faille took his shorter sword from Sukata and tucked the really long one on the roof of the nearest coach. He and Lieutenant Faral went through the open front door of the inn in one rush, and Sukata was a blur in their wake.

The Kolans broke into a spate of gabble, and the people the Kellian had been ordering about gathered in a confused clutch. Kendall strained to listen over the rain and chatter, and thought she heard something smashing. She didn't know whether to be worried or not: the Kellian moved faster than almost anything, but it had seemed like there were a lot of the bugs inside. Kendall had watched Sukata practice with Captain Faille, and knew she could easily kill almost anyone who attacked her. Still...

Rather than think about it, Kendall began inching Rennyn across to the far corner of the coach, since by now the inside of the open door was soaked. There still wasn't a speck of response from Rennyn, even with someone pulling and trying to lift her. Kendall propped her in the corner, tucking a small cushion behind her head and making sure she was as warmly wrapped as possible.

The Kolans had crowded around the open door and, when they gasped and began to point, Kendall let herself look and saw a lightning girl climbing out a window on the middle floor of the building. There was a shadow at her side, lost in her glare, and it was only when a second figure emerged with someone over their shoulder that Kendall realised that they were both carrying people.

The third lightning figure waited inside the building until the first two had reached the ground, then leapt down. Kendall knew this one was Captain Faille because he was taller, and stopped to collect his sword. The Kolans broke out in excited murmurs, then went mouse-quiet as the three headed straight for their coach. Sukata was first, and climbed inside to become herself again, except with a pearly radiance from the light streaming through the door. A little girl, four or five years old, clung to her side so tight Kendall couldn't see any of her face.

Lieutenant Faral handed another girl in: this one twelve or thirteen, eyes red from crying. She latched on to Sukata as well, while Lieutenant Faral turned away to say something to Captain Faille, and then start shooing people back to their coaches. Captain Faille gazed in at them—checking how Rennyn looked—then closed the door.

"How did you know they were in there?" Kendall asked, looking for anything she could give Sukata to dry herself on, since her friend was absolutely sopping.

"This one began crying," Sukata said, glancing to her left, then reaching to slide open the window. "They had locked themselves in a closet, but the door was weakening."

Captain Faille was standing in between the two rows of coaches. He signalled, and the driver of the coach ahead whipped up his horses. Kendall had only enough warning to put a restraining arm across Rennyn before their own coach jerked and moved forward. She stared back out the window, but couldn't see Captain Faille any more.

"Is he—?"

"Part of the swarm is outside the circle," Sukata said. "Once we are gone, they will disperse, searching for other hosts. Faille will remain, and attempt to hunt them."

Alone in the dark. Captain Faille might be the most dangerous non-mage around, but if he got stung, what could he do? Kendall glanced at Rennyn, slumped beside her, and pulled a face. What Rennyn would do didn't bear thinking about.

Chapter Eleven

Fallon tried not to eavesdrop on the Kolans sharing their carriage as they spoke in choked undertones. He only caught the occasional word. That was enough.

Cold, wet and fighting his own perennial weariness, Fallon struggled to put away horror, and think in purely practical terms. He would catch a chill. Worse, Duchess Surclere, though far less damp, really needed to be kept warm and quiet after casting such a powerful spell, not racketing along through the rain.

Such an incredible casting! Fallon had had barely a chance to consider it, but it hadn't resembled any of the standard light conjurations: there had been no container or point of focus. A twist of air, it seemed, burning white. Duchess Surclere cast so differently, with such complete assurance.

Reminded of the need to keep his teacher alive, Fallon debated the risk of another casting. Lieutenant Meniar, when his strength had run low, had had Fallon and Sukata cast the last few expulsions, since they could afford no delay. That had quickly brought Fallon near the limit of his casting capacity, but surely he could afford a standard warmth Sigillic, to dry them all out a little.

He slept immediately after, which was no escape since it only brought him the same scene in the Dream, with the added complication of Auri, confused and anxious. She stood in the middle of the carriage, unable to avoid the many knees, staring at the dripping, tightly-crammed occupants.

"Some kind of accident?" she asked, turning to Fallon. But she was at least able to gauge his state, and not attempt to bring him in all the way to talk to her. Vexed, she made an ungainly upward leap and swam through the ceiling of the carriage.

Fallon shifted restlessly, hoping in the vague way that the Dream brought to him that he would manage to catch up on sleep before Auri's impatience overcame her sense. Or at least listening to people within range would provide her with a little potted explanation in Tyrian. She could speak some Kolan, of course, but was years behind him now.

Beside Fallon, the older of the two girls the Kellian had brought out from the Waystation burrowed deeper into Sukata's side, kicking Fallon in the process. Neither of them had loosed their grip on the Kellian girl for a moment, even though she no longer burned like lightning.

Fallon didn't blame the girls—he'd been inordinately glad of Sukata himself—but clinginess did complicate matters when they arrived at the next safe place along the Imperial Way: a small town about an hour away.

Lieutenant Meniar, with officials crowding around him, became very firm on the subject of making sure Duchess Surclere was bedded down somewhere warm and quiet, and dealt with the girls by telling Sukata to just take them with her. Then he and Lieutenant Faral left.

Fallon played gatekeeper for a while, chasing off the curious, then retreated to one of the rooms they'd been allotted. He took time out to write a 'diary entry' he could prop open for Auri's benefit, then finally crawled under his blankets and stayed there.

oOo

Someone was making a lot of noise downstairs. None too pleased, Kendall cast a watchful eye over

Rennyn and Sukata. Rennyn stayed as she had been since they'd put her to bed the night before, but of course Sukata's eyes opened. Kendall hadn't been able to convince her friend she needn't stay up all night when they were in the safety of a circle, and had only won her point after she herself had slept and could take the next watch. Now, not even midday and there'd be no getting the Kellian girl back to sleep.

The noise was coming closer: at least a half-dozen people, gabbling away. Sukata sat up, carefully shifting the little leech she'd rescued from the Waystation. The other girl had been a local maid, and had been collected by her family the previous evening, but the younger was harder to get rid of. She spoke a mix of Verisian and Kolan, only seemed to know her first name, and had a fit whenever anyone tried to take her away from Sukata. Eventually Sukata had agreed to look after her overnight while the Kolan version of the Guard tried to find where she belonged.

Kendall guessed that they'd worked something out, since the leech's name was Maribe and that was about the only word Kendall recognised from the squawking and fussing outside. It woke the leech up, anyway. Sukata made a quick motion, but too late, as big blue eyes went wide and the little pink mouth opened.

"Nonna!"

The brat had a squeal like a needle. Rennyn sure jerked like she'd been stuck with one, then wrapped her arms over her head and cringed down under the blankets. Sukata froze for an instant, then crossed and opened the door, just as the leech barrelled toward it. She followed the girl through, and closed the door neatly behind.

It didn't seem like anything could stop the fuss outside, with excited gabble filling the hall, but then it lowered, heading downstairs. Sukata had drawn them off. No fun for her, since everyone in the town had heard about the 'lightning spirits' who had saved the caravan, and wanted nothing more than to gawp and ask questions.

The door opened again, but it was just the Pest, and Kendall waved him off, going to close the curtains and make sure the mageglows were most-ways covered. The Pest was sensible for once and went away, and when the door shut Rennyn uncurled enough to poke her head out from beneath the blanket.

Kendall helped her drink honey water and washed her face, and then Sukata was back to carry her into the so-fancy privy closet that Kolans actually built into the corner of their hostelry rooms. Rennyn was in bad shape, shaking, with her eyes slitted in pain. Sukata was worried enough about her to fret visibly about not staying in there to hold her upright.

They'd tucked her back in bed by the time the Pest showed up with hot soup, which Sukata tipped into a mug and held it for Rennyn to drink. Rennyn barely managed two swallows before she passed out again.

"There are city officials downstairs wanting to talk to her," the Pest whispered, after they'd all withdrawn to the door to discuss what to do next. "One of them speaks Tyrian, and doesn't plan to be fobbed off. They have a healer mage with them."

He'd no sooner told them then there was a brisk knock at the door. Sukata and the Pest slipped back into the corridor, but Kendall wasn't surprised when the door opened again and a skinny, grandfatherly sort bustled straight across to Rennyn. Sukata could stop anyone getting in if it was really necessary, but Lieutenant Meniar had told them not to make too much of a fuss.

A short, plump woman wearing a half-mask followed. In Kole, nobles, bureaucrats and people getting above themselves wore these masks to honour their creepy-sounding Emperor, who never took his off. The very plain masks covering the top half of the face seemed to be the style that meant 'official'. Despite the mask, Kendall could see the woman's dark eyes flicking left and right, checking out everything lying about the room.

Kendall left her to Sukata and the Pest, and went and stayed obstinately at the healer-mage's side. Lieutenant Meniar had given Rennyn a thorough examination and done what he could for her before he and Lieutenant Faral had headed out with a troop of the local soldiers to go bug hunting and find Captain Faille, and he'd said there wasn't much that could be done beyond keeping her warm and fed and casting the fortifier he'd taught Sukata. Fortunately the healer-mage just checked her over, and Sukata and the Pest had no problem with the official, who was more curious than suspicious. Their reason for visiting Kole was real enough—it was just the whole thing about hunting Rennyn's demon uncle down afterwards that they weren't broadcasting.

After they left, Sukata stayed by the door a little while, clearly listening, and finally said: "They are very interested because of the strength of the light casting, which is still active. The official has been specifically instructed to report directly to the Emperor's...to the palace intelligence network? Any incidents relating to mages, particularly mages of strength, is to be reported."

"The whole town is talking of nothing but lightning spirits and mages," the Pest said. "Though it's as much Lieutenant Meniar as the Duchess they've been discussing. He saved a lot of lives."

So much for keeping a low profile. If demon princes could read Kolan newssheets, then they'd just told him exactly where Rennyn was. Kendall didn't think that was much of a problem until the day stretched into the next, and they were still waiting around in the inn.

Rennyn never once asked where anyone was as she progressed to being able to sit in bed reading and napping, and tottering about for short distances. She'd glance around the room each time she woke, but that was all. She knew as well as any of them that Sentene were incapable of leaving something like a Kentatsuki out there, no matter what country they were in.

When Rennyn finally ran out of newssheets, she had them clear one corner of the room and spent her time dictating sigils for Sukata to write in a circle that curved across both walls and the floor.

From Kendall's careful consultation of the Sigillic dictionary, this circle had something to do with making sounds louder, which was an odd thing for someone with a persistent headache to be caring about. Sukata and the Pest couldn't work out much more than that either, and Rennyn wasn't in an explaining mood.

It was all very dull. Kendall longed to go exploring, but the Kolans' silly language and Rennyn's babysitting needs made a jaunt more trouble than it was worth. And the longer the day wore on, the harder it was not to fret about bugs.

One sting. That's all it would take.

oOo

The scent of rain, and oil on metal. Damp wool. Hints of sweat and horse and leather.

"Illidian."

As Rennyn climbed from her blankets into his lap, the cold knot in her stomach finally unwound. She'd spent the past day pointlessly angry at him, for not being with her, for being in danger. And yet she would have wanted him to do exactly as he had, should she have been conscious enough to have any choice in the matter. The damnable weakness made her selfish. On the bad days her hatred of being so incapable splashed over onto everyone and everything, and all she could do was bite her tongue and endure.

Illidian could say a great deal without speaking. An initial close embrace. A soft breath stirring the strands of hair on the crown of her head. Then slight shifts, as he inspected as much as he could see of her without relaxing his arms. One hand smoothed a short distance along her spine, and then he moved her so she was not so tightly held, lifted her effortlessly, and took her out and down to a steam-soaked room on the lowest floor of the inn.

In the short months of their marriage Illidian had quickly learned that one of the things she hated most was the sense of grime that came with being bedridden. That and the humiliating necessity of being carried to the privy—or collapsing trying to get there alone. They'd had several discussions about Kolan bathhouses, and it was typical of Illidian that once the Kentatsuki was out of the way he'd reverted to their original plan for enjoying the first one they came to. They were certainly more convenient than a beaten metal tub manually filled.

If only she could revert to the physical condition she'd been in two days ago. At least with Illidian there the probability of passing out in the bath was not so great an issue. And it was wonderful being very warm and slippery clean and able to see that he was completely uninjured, only a little worn and tired. She fell asleep, woke snug in bed, and watched him reading for the short time before Kellian senses alerted him to her gaze. With him safely under her eye she finally felt able to question what had happened.

"Could it have been coincidence?"

"I lean toward the view." Illidian glanced briefly at the nearest window, which showed only that it was still night outside. "The Kolan commander we worked with told me that this is not the first Eferum-Get of unusually high calibre they've encountered in the past month. They may be remnants of the incursions caused by the Grand Summoning, since the impact of that stretched well past Tyrland's borders. Merely bad fortune that we encounter a Kentatsuki. Yet, given Prince Helecho's abilities, not impossible that he could arrange such a thing. I could not find any trace of him, amongst the swarm."

"How far did it spread?" The length of his absence had already told her that containment hadn't been simple.

"Two of the nearby farmsteads were completely lost. Three more with some survivors. When we could no longer track any roaming Kentatsuki, the soldiery recalled the small bands searching the area. They will commit a very large force and sweep the entire region to ensure none escaped. It's a methodical approach, and they'll clear any other Eferum-Get in the area at the same time. And the settlements have been warned."

There was a hint of dissatisfaction in his thin voice. It was one thing to be unable to find any Kentatsuki in the immediate area, and another to be certain none had escaped.

"What was the Kolan attitude toward your involvement?"

"Relief, primarily. A little unease and surprise when witnessing our inhuman aspects, but the Sentene are not unknown outside Tyrland's borders, and of course the Grand Summoning has been widely discussed in many countries. The commander was also aware of the role we both played, and the recent debates regarding Kellian. Any hope we had of travelling unremarked is completely lost, but our reasons for journeying to Koletor are not openly doubted. They are unlikely to interfere with us, but will certainly keep us under observation. It is more the possibility that, trap or not, Prince Helecho will hear of our presence and come here. If that had been anything less than a Kentatsuki, I could not have risked leaving you so long with only Sukata as protection."

Her Wicked Uncle had already demonstrated that travelling via the Eferum made it easy for him to keep a step ahead of them, though the lack of Grand Summoning-related breaches from the Eferum might make that no longer so true.

"We leave at dawn, then?"

"Yes. A very large caravan, since this emergency has kept almost everyone from the roads. They were very careful to reserve space for us." His voice was dry, for Kellian were used to being seen as convenient. "What is it you're trying to hear?"

She shifted to look at the Sigillic barely visible in the muted light of the partially covered glows. "I don't know. Something magic-based, because if it was simply sound, it would be you, not me, trying to track it down. Three times now, since we approached port, there's been snatches of music too distant for me to properly hear. I've yet to construct something I would risk casting, since the subject is so vague to me, and I can barely stay conscious to concentrate. It is possible that it's simply area noise—part of the land's natural magic—but I don't like to ignore it."

The way Illidian's arms tightened told her that he didn't, either. She could only hope that the solution wouldn't be delayed too long by her interminable need to sleep.

Chapter Twelve

"Very different from the Little Mutching house," Sukata said, studying the building that would be their home for the next week.

After five long days on the road, Kendall was more interested in stretching than looking, but glanced up and nodded. "You'd not guess it belonged to the same family." The Claires' house in Little Mutching was bigger than Kendall's own family's had been, but of much the same type. This place was something else.

"We won't be short on room," Rennyn commented, critically eyeing four levels of windows, every one of them lit.

There was only a low bit of fence separating the straight-up rise of the house from the paved walkway, and the houses on either side were all the same type, with little in the way of gaps between them, so at first glance it all seemed to Kendall like a single endless building stretching down the street. There were other entry doors to show that wasn't true, but it was still a proper huge mansion, very near to the centre of Kole's capital, Koletor. The kind of place a Duchess might live in.

The shrivelled-up turtle of a man of business they'd collected continued his endless Kolan gabble, leading the way up the nearest short set of stairs. He'd been acting like Rennyn was some long-lost niece, but with just a touch of deference, and a lot of twittery excitement only dimmed when he noticed how very hard it was to see some of Rennyn's companions in the evening gloom.

"Mr Witteseer engaged servants after Her Grace's letter arrived," Sukata said, translating. "The house has been fully turned out, although some of the linens had decayed and needed to be replaced." She paused, struggling to understand, then added: "He is glad to see it open again after so many years."

"I'll be glad if he'd just get us inside," Kendall said, as the thin rain threatened to return. "Think these servants will have anything on hand to eat?"

"The agent said he engaged a household," the Pest said, coming up to them. "That will have included a cook." He was looking entertained. "Estimates of the remaining Surclere fortune have been over-modest. Do you suppose the library here is as extensive?"

"Probably," Kendall said shortly, though the Pest never could catch a hint.

Nor could he hide the avid note that crept into his voice whenever the Surclere libraries came up. Since one of the reasons Rennyn was here was to check this house for things she didn't want people to see, there was a good chance there would be some juicy magical secrets for him to poke his nose into. More fool Rennyn for giving him the chance.

The front door of the house opened almost as soon as the turtle put his hand on the shiny knocker, but Kendall hadn't a chance to do more than see how warm and welcoming the inside looked before Sukata abruptly moved to stand by Rennyn's carriage door. Captain Faille turned from where he was waiting at the turtle's elbow, and then came down the stair as a squad of uniformed people on horses clattered to a halt as close as the carriages would let them. A round dozen extra-fancy soldiers looked at them through masks of leather panels and loosely-swinging chain veils of black and silver. Their clothes were coloured the same, and even the horses were done up to show they were special and important.

More gabble, as one of the riders dismounted and came to talk to Captain Faille. It was unfair that everyone except Kendall could understand. Still, she could read tone and gesture well enough. Stern statement. Polite question. Uncompromising command. Glance at Rennyn. Request. Grudging agreement. The upshot of all that was that their luggage was quickly unloaded before they all had to pile back into the carriages, leaving the turtle behind to explain to the wide-eyed servants.

"Are we being arrested?" Kendall asked, as soon as the carriage door was safely shut.

"Summoned to audience," Rennyn said. "Having waited for us to reach Koletor after making ourselves so interesting, it seems the Emperor's of no mind to delay any longer."

"He doesn't sleep," the Pest put in, sounding more excited than anything else. "He conducts Court business at any time of the day or night."

"Must be really annoying to work for," Kendall said.

"There is a Day Court and a Night Court," Captain Faille said, his creepy, whispery voice unexpected just because he usually didn't pipe up in the middle of conversations. "Two Chancellors, two Masters of the Guard, two Lords of Ceremony. The Night Court is smaller, but a great deal happens there."

Only one Emperor, though: getting on toward three hundred years old and probably meaning them no good. Kendall glanced at Rennyn, who was gazing out the lowered window. Was this summons just because of them helping out at the border? Or because the Emperor had heard of Rennyn's power and current vulnerability? What would they do if he wouldn't let them get on with chasing Rennyn's nasty uncle about, but instead wanted to use her knowledge for himself?

Since it didn't look likely that Rennyn was going to try to avoid the meeting, Kendall resigned herself to an uncomfortable wait. It had been too many hours since their break for lunch, and even though Captain Faille said the palace wasn't very far from Rennyn's mansion, Kendall really wanted a privy, and a nice big meal. And she was willing to bet that, though she had slept much of the afternoon, Rennyn could do with a long lie down. All these days of coach travel had done her no good, especially since they'd started out before she'd properly recovered from casting. Even the restrained jouncing of a spelled coach on an Imperial Road kept giving her headaches.

Grumbling silently about the Emperor's lack of consideration, Kendall felt the presence of a strong circle as they crossed it, and glanced past Rennyn to see they were in a tunnel or long gate. And then more rain-shimmering streets reflecting light from grand buildings. Kendall lowered the shutter on her side, and peered out curiously, trying to decide if this was the Emperor's palace or just a fancier district of Koletor. And had her answer when the coaches slowed, and rumbled to a stop.

A woman in a mask that covered only the left side of her face appeared outside Kendall's door, and waited for the man with her to open it.

"Your Grace," the woman said, looking past Kendall straight at Rennyn. "My name is Kishida Dzay. I will conduct you to the Waiting Rooms."

Caught between pleasure at someone speaking proper words and outrage that they'd been hurried up only to sit about and wait, it took Kendall half the first corridor to realise that the woman not only spoke Tyrian, but could recognise Rennyn at a glance. The implications of that weren't exactly comfortable, and Kendall turned them over until it became impossible not to just gaze about her.

Kolan palaces were just like Tyrian Court costumes: not an inch left plain. The floors were red and honey-gold wood, locking together in tricky chains. The walls were a dusty moss green below waist height, with red panels bordered with black above. Not simple swatches of colour, but shot through with thin lines of gold in patterns which seemed to be floral from what Kendall could make out without stopping. The black was a very dark wood, with little designs at the corners. The doors they were passing were made of the same stuff, and cut full of diamond and flower-shaped holes so that you could see the rooms beyond: some empty, some with little groups of people. And there were tables with bowls of flowers, and great big vases taller than she was, and furniture that was all curving lines and cushions. It wasn't cluttered, but because just about everything was scribbled on or painted, it meant that everywhere you looked your eye was caught and overwhelmed.

"This room has been reserved for you, Your Grace," said the Kolan woman, pushing open one of the hole-filled doors. "You will be given priority in the audience schedule. Would you care for refreshments while you wait?"

"Very much so," Rennyn said, sounding more resigned than annoyed at being hauled off to the palace without notice.

Kendall forgot her own annoyance when Kishida Dzay pointed out several doors down where the corridor widened out, and she took herself quickly off to use a privy that was bigger, cleaner and even smelled nicer than many houses she'd visited. Along with a screen hiding a throne of a privy chair, there was a big mirror with a table and stool and a stone basin and towels. A low firm couch was set against the opposite wall, just in case you felt tired on the way to taking care of your business, and beside that an ornamental pillar with a big vase full of fresh flowers. Most unprivy-like.

Not one to pass up Kolan wetworks, which she'd found would deliver endless amounts of hot and cold water, Kendall gave herself a quick wash, straightened her travel-rumpled coat, and then sneered at herself for preening in front of the mirror. If what they looked like mattered to this Emperor, then he shouldn't have had them fetched the second they arrived.

Heading back, Kendall found that a new door in the long corridor had opened. She was sure that doorway hadn't been there when she'd gone past before, and cautiously poked her nose around the corner. But it was only a passage leading to the kitchens. A trolley laden with food was waiting, and Kendall was tempted to go nab something, but then a tall boy stepped into view and snaffled one of the plates himself. Pushing his mask up so it sat on top of his dark hair, he lifted something gooey and bit into it, eyes squeezing shut like it was the best thing he'd ever tasted.

A man came out from the kitchen to the left, holding two more plates. He drew himself up as if to say something sharp, but then paused and hastily shut his mouth. Putting the plates on the trolley, he turned and fetched another to add, keeping his head tucked down and his shoulders bent like a wary dog with its tail between its legs. The younger one just watched, and stuffed his face, then turned his head, and Kendall had to duck back or be spotted.

Not sure she'd escaped being caught staring, Kendall took herself back to their waiting room and peered innocently at the patterns and furnishings until Captain Faille brought Rennyn back from their own trip. Knowing how Rennyn hated being babied about privy visits, Kendall tried to decide if her teacher was closer to collapse than she'd thought, or if Captain Faille was worried about her being attacked. She did look tired, but greeted the arrival of their refreshments with considerable interest, and stuffed herself with almost as much obvious enjoyment as the boy in the passage. It was definitely a fine spread, with many new and sometimes-tempting Kolan dishes.

When it seemed that their audience wasn't going to happen immediately after food, Kendall sat back and said: "That lady's was the first mask I've seen that just did one side of the face. Do the different sorts have different meanings?"

"Very much so," Lieutenant Meniar replied. "One of the histories we brought along lists them out. Only the Emperor wears a full mask—a white one. Everyone in the service of the Emperor—all officials directly appointed to carry out his orders—wears a charcoal-grey mask marked with the sigil that represents Kole. That's not everyone who works in this palace or anything near as many—only what are known as 'delegates'—so anyone you see wearing that colour and symbol is carrying out the Emperor's will. They wear different masks when they're not representing the Emperor. And all masks break down into two groups. Those who have one side of their face covered are not of noble blood. Nobles cover both eyes, and differing amounts of their lower face depending on how important they are."

"And soldiers use those veil-masks," Kendall noted, trying to fit all the variations they'd seen into this system.

Meniar nodded. "Families have particular colours and wear their crests. There's some wonderful stories of deceptions played using masks, and Kolan mask farces don't lose much in the translation."

Before Kendall could ask what a mask farce was, their palace guide pushed open the door and said: "Please come this way to the Primary Waiting Room. His Excellence will have time for you shortly."

Just as if they'd been the ones wanting the meeting. Maybe the Kolan Emperor's wits were going, and they were being hauled before a *senile* Emperor. Better and better.

Their escort took them off through a pair of big doors with guards outside to show they were important, and enough magic inside to make Kendall want to sneeze. Lots of spells, too many to separate out.

Otherwise the throne room was boring: a white box without windows or any decoration. Nothing but a throne on a raised dais. And an Emperor.

oOo

After the riot of pattern outside, the blankness of the room was almost dizzying. Even the throne and the figure upon it lacked any colour. To non-mages that would give an impression of emptiness that must surely be deliberate, though Rennyn did not quite see what it was meant to symbolise. To the senses of a mage, however...

Old enchantment: thick, rich and deeply flavoured, filled every gleaming corner. A week ago the layers of it would have fascinated, but Rennyn was still not in any condition to enjoy magical puzzles, and only felt stifled. Her students reacted like dogs come to point, Kendall predictably rubbing her nose and squinting with irritation.

"Rennyn, Duchess of Surclere," announced their escort, then turned on her heel and left, the heavy doors closing behind her.

~Come forward.~

Absently analysing the enchantment structures that had produced the voice, Rennyn let her fingers brush Illidian's, then pushed aside growing weariness to walk the short length of the room so that she could see the figure on the throne properly. Her companions followed a step behind, silent and wary.

Yscaren Corusar. The Undying. Emperor of Kole for well over two hundred and fifty years. The precise details of what he'd done to himself had never been made public, but enough mages had visited this room over the centuries that Rennyn had a rough idea of the spell structure and methodology even before the shape of the enchantment came clear around her. Castings that allowed him to see, to hear, and to speak, while his body was preserved within a container of inscribed, enamelled armour, sustaining his life force but not allowing him to move, to eat, to breathe. Corusar had found a way to live indefinitely by ceasing to live at all.

He looked like a segmented statue, the limbs smooth, the joints subtle. The white faceplate merely hinted at human features, and there were the faintest ridges in the armour's smooth surface to suggest the possibility of clothing, of hair, of what the man within should look like. It would be interesting to know if the flesh had decayed beneath the casing.

All the white, without any hint of the Emperor's family crest or colours, reminded Rennyn strongly of Solace as she'd been after so many years in the Eferum—bleached and without human warmth. Corusar's reputation was of an impartial pragmatist, avoiding cruelty but not quick to give second chances. More Emperor than man. Even if his humanity had survived the preservation spell, it was unlikely they would succeed in achieving friendly terms with Kole's Emperor, or have him place anything above his Empire's interests.

Curtseying brought spots to dance before her eyes, but she kept any hint of asperity from her voice when she said: "You wished to see me, Your Excellence?"

~And your companions.~ The voice was directionless, without inflection, but gave her a definite impression of a *mind*, if not a personality. ~There have been many new reports of the people known as Kellian, and your activities on the border have caused considerable stir. The group you set down in Port Enara have not made such a loud impression, but their progress has not been without incident. They are expected to reach Koletor within four days.~

"Queen Astranelle mentioned the efficiency of Kole's intelligence network," Rennyn said, faintly amused. "Allow me to introduce, then, my husband, Illidian Faille, my students Kendall Stockton, Sukata Illuma and Fallon DeVries, and our escorts Lieutenants Aven Meniar and Keste Faral of the Tyrian Sentene."

Stepping back, Rennyn made herself one of the group—and conveniently within range of Illidian's arm. Her general stamina had dropped dramatically following that light casting, and she could only hope she made it through the audience without collapsing.

~There have been no confirmed reports of the one you hunt,~ the uninflected voice continued. ~A spate of unexplained deaths in Dunnesan five weeks previous, but no verification, and no further reports of killing of that type.~

Extremely efficient intelligencers. "Thank you. If we cannot gain his direction using our divinations, then that information may come in very useful."

~No pattern has been isolated that could be linked to the creature's ability to control the Eferum spawn. However, the number of current occurrences significantly outweighs the aftermath of the previous Grand Summoning.~

"The final iteration of the casting was considerably more powerful than the first," Rennyn said, finding the abrupt series of statements a little disjointed, perhaps because the figure on the throne was a frozen object, not reacting to her responses. At least their audience was likely to be quick, given how much the Emperor already knew.

~In addition, in the months since your defeat of Solace, twenty-two of Kole's strongest mages have vanished without trace. I cannot say whether he is responsible for this, or any of the instances of Eferum-Get outbreak, but Kole judges this Helecho Montjuste-Surclere a major threat. A resource has been assigned to coordinate action with you.~

The doors behind them opened, apparently indicating that their audience was over. Surprised by the number of missing mages—far more than generally discussed—Rennyn hesitated, then simply dropped into an abbreviated curtsey, and slid her arm through Illidian's as he rose from his bow. Ushering her collection of students before her, she found their escort, Kishida Dzay, waiting outside the throne room doors beside a slim man wearing a charcoal grey mask that left only his chin exposed.

"Our resource, I presume?"

"Your Grace, allow me to introduce Dezart Rhael Samarin," Kishida said, then bowed and smoothly effaced herself. Samarin, by contrast, inclined his head just a little.

"So what does a resource do?" Rennyn asked Samarin, puzzled by the multiple traces of casting she could sense about the man. The mask had a certification enchantment, but there was layer upon layer of something else...something distinctly out of the ordinary.

"Channel to you any supplies or manpower you might need," Samarin replied, his voice younger than she'd expected, but immensely self-assured. "Whisk you past checkpoints unchallenged, authorise access to restricted areas—or keep you out of them."

The mask made it nearly impossible to guess his expression, but she thought he smiled when he added: "Primarily I will save the Intelligence Service a great deal of following you about and watching what you do.

And serve to frighten off others wanting more than to watch."

"Perhaps you can tell us about the recent disappearance of mages while we return to the carriages," Illidian said, which told Rennyn she was leaning too heavily on his arm.

"Are you a mage, Dezart Samarin?" There was a recent casting about him, in addition to the enchantments on the mask. Healing magic?

"In theory," he said, ushering them toward the entry hall. "I haven't built strength with practice, or summoned a focus. I'm not chasing your techniques, if that matters to you, though we are seeing some impact of them: injuries from attempts to use Thought Magic. One death reported so far."

Rennyn bit her lip, but the guilt stabbed less than she'd expected. Ultimately, she couldn't control the actions of others.

"I really am going to have to release some kind of guide," she said. "Although there will still be accidents, and people totally unsuited to Thought Magic making the attempt, it will at least give them some idea of the safest way to go about it."

"That will lessen the number of deaths." Samarin's voice held just a hint of forbearance, as if she had apologised for an error. "As to the disappearances: the only firm similarity among the lost is their strength as mages. They were not taken in obvious order, and Mezuna and Keffar—considered the strongest in Kole—have not been taken, but all who have vanished are in the very upper tier in terms of unenhanced power.

"They've vanished at different times of day, but mostly at night. Two separate witnesses have claimed to have seen a mage literally vanish. Each assumed at the time it was a guise-shield, and only mentioned the incident when the mage was reported missing. That has led to a flood of reports of vanishing mages, who it eventuated *were* using guide-shields."

"Broken locks? Signs of struggle?" Illidian asked.

"None. Everything suggests voluntary departure. Multiple reports of a trace of strong magic a short distance from where the mage had been staying, but no clear sense of its intent. No reports of strangers— beyond the usual that follow any crime or event. Most mages have been taking precautions. Eslay Feralan, gone only five days, had hired guards and warded her rooms. The wards weren't tripped, and the guards saw nothing, but she left some time during the night."

"Do you know what wards she used?"

"Six Points Exclusion and the Non-named Alert."

Strong, fundamental castings. "A magic detect may have been more useful. Have any of the missing been young mages, strong but not yet having summoned a focus? Or were taken while not wearing their focus?"

"No very young mages. Details concerning their focuses I will find out." They'd reached the entrance to find their coaches waiting, the hired drivers goggling interestedly. A girl in livery was holding an over-tall horse, saddled and laden with bags. It was the kind of animal that jigged and danced about, but Samarin didn't seem to find this a bad thing, nodding approvingly and taking the reins. "Compiled dossiers are to be delivered in the morning. I will follow your coach."

Another servant set a long cloak around his shoulders and he mounted, apparently intending to ride despite the light rain. Rennyn obediently climbed into her coach, hoping that there would be no more interruptions to keep her from a bed that didn't bounce and rock. Her head was starting to throb, and she very much wanted quiet, so was glad when Meniar and Faral deftly channelled all her students into the second carriage.

"Samarin seems liable to organise us with ruthless efficiency if not checked," she said, curling against Illidian. "But is probably more useful than inconvenient. Hopefully."

"Did you believe his claim not to be a mage?"

"I don't see what he'd gain by lying. It's obvious he has a grounding in theory, as you do. Unusual for anyone with mage talent to study the art, but not to practice it though. There's a distinctly odd aura around him too, very subtle, and that mask is thick with enchantment. I'll have a better idea of what it's doing when I have a chance to study him away from so much background power. As he will study us. Would you be interested in working for the Kolan Emperor?"

"I would consider it." Illidian sounded almost surprised, and let out his breath slowly. "He has been a balanced ruler—and compassionate when compared to many of those who came before him. His long reign has given the Empire a stability it has never previously enjoyed, and what I know of his judgments I have agreed with. But Kole is not our home."

It was rare for him to allow himself to sound so tired. Rennyn curled her fingers through his, studying the blunted close-clipped tips, then held his hand to her cheek. Home to her was Illidian. Seb was nearly as important, but Illidian had become the single absolute. And she could do no more than support him as he struggled to heal, to find some measure of the equilibrium she and the Black Queen had destroyed.

Tucking herself against his shoulder, Rennyn wished she had the power to spare him nightmares.

Chapter Thirteen

"Who is the boy in the room next to yours?" Auri asked, after she had pulled Fallon into the Dream.

"An Imperial spy," Fallon said, and explained as he followed Auri through the wall to look the sleeping Rhael Samarin over. Without his mask, he did almost look a boy, though Fallon guessed he was eighteen or nineteen.

"Spy's the wrong word when they do it openly," Auri said. "Observer."

"Trouble," Fallon said. "Here to learn as much as he can on behalf of the Empire, and—"

"And what? What other secret is Duchess Surclere keeping? Does it matter if the Empire watches?"

"There's secrets and there's, well, uncomfortable attention. Still, not so bad to have someone along that they trust even less than me."

He trailed in Auri's wake, describing in more detail their unplanned detour to the Imperial palace, then regretting it when she sighed heavily and said:

"You get to do all the *fun* things."

"And I get to do all the dull things, too," he replied, since it was better to push back when this mood threatened Auri. "You'd have hated so many days cramped in coaches. Let's look for the secret library, since you've got me up."

"What secret library?"

"Where the Surclere research and histories were kept. Duchess Surclere knows there's a hidden room, but doesn't know where it is."

Auri brightened. "A proper hidden room?"

"Well, Duchess Surclere thinks it might be more of a cupboard. And it can't be a very big one, or the servants would surely have found it when they cleaned this place up."

They moved quickly, since there was a limit to how long Fallon could wander around in the Dream. He had carefully chosen a central room so that most of the building's five floors—from cellar to attic—were within reach his body's tether. The place was still too big for them to be able to explore completely, but they managed to reach the larger part. Auri, humming cheerfully, purposefully walked through any wall that looked a likely candidate for hiding a room or cupboard, and since they had headed down, rather than up, it was not too long before she discovered that she couldn't walk through the heavy stones of the cellar stairs.

"Some kind of ward?" she speculated, trying to poke a finger into the cracks. "I can tell when there's a ward, though."

"I wonder if there is a casting that would hide a ward?" Fallon said. "But it's been years since anyone's been here: can any ward have lasted so long?"

"Cast some divinations tomorrow," Auri ordered, turning to explore the rest of the cellar, which was large and high-ceilinged, and featured a central casting circle. Almost all the walls were out of her range, however, and so she shrugged and headed back upstairs to flit through the top two floors.

The attic was long and almost as clear as the cellar—perhaps again to offer a place for mages to cast—so there was little in reach to search.

"How long do we stay here?" Auri asked, singing to herself—ta ta TUM—while taking a few dancing steps on the long, bare floorboards.

"It was going to be a week, while Lady Claire reviewed the house contents. But we're running late, and the rest of the Sentene will arrive soon, so I don't know if we'll leave for the Forest of Semarrak on the expected date, or delay. After that, it depends on whether the divination to locate Prince Helecho ever stops pointing west. But no matter whether he's dealt with, or we can't find him, we're going to winter here to avoid the snows."

Auri's positive mood was fading, and she rubbed her arms in the doubled chill of the Dream and the attic. "Will Mrs Pardons really be able to take care of Father until spring?"

"I hope so. She'll at least have enough to feed him, presuming the Arkathan's fee refund went through. Having seen this place, I now understand why Duchess Surclere was so disinterested in charging for lessons, even though she could ask almost anything and people would pay it."

"Can you—"

Auri broke off. Someone had come up the attic stair, so quietly that Fallon hadn't even noticed until a man passed right through him.

"Who is this?" Auri asked.

"I don't know. Probably one of the servants Duchess Surclere's agent engaged? But that's..." Fallon frowned in the dim greyness of the attic. The man was carrying a small collection of books, and clearly attempting to move as quietly as possible.

"Do you think he found the secret library?" Auri trailed after the man.

"Is...I think that top book's one of the instruction texts Lieutenant Meniar brought along," Fallon said, blankly.

"Oh? It's a real spy?" Auri reached the limit of her tether and clicked her tongue in irritation.

The man walked into the gloomy far reaches of the attic, and knocked on the wall: a trio of double-beats.

After a tense moment there was a muffled clunk, and then the wall opened a crack. The man slipped hurriedly through, and the wall sealed shut behind him.

"Quickly!" Auri said, and they raced downstairs.

Fallon hurled himself back into his body, and woke with a start, then leapt out of bed, or tried to, landing on the floor with a thump. He staggered back to his feet and snatched open the door, then stopped.

What did he think he was going to do? Rouse the house and lead them in a charge on an empty attic?

Don't tell anyone or I'll kill you. Just words, a throw-away phrase, but Sigillic Magic was also just words, and power to give their intent form. At times he would start choking when all he'd done was *think* about trying to find a way to explain about Auri. How could he possibly warn the Sentene about the thief, and the hidden exit, without touching on just how he knew?

Feeling heavy as lead, he turned back, but only to fetch his slate book. Then, far less precipitately, he headed for the attic.

It was, at least, not as chilly as it had been in the dream. Autumn in the south was pleasant enough when it wasn't raining. Fallon stopped at the central point where he and Auri had been, then rubbed his temple, feeling a headache coming on. Now what? A trap for when the servant returned? If he claimed that he'd heard a noise, followed the man up here... Or perhaps he could pretend he was up so late in order to win approval by finding the hidden library. They'd believe that of him, and once a divination had revealed this hidden exit, the Sentene would naturally investigate, even though the people involved might be long gone by then.

"What are we doing?" asked an interested voice.

Fallon started and whirled to find a maskless and bare-chested Imperial 'Observer' at the head of the attic steps, with a rather more clothed Sukata just behind him. Both were armed. Kellian hearing would explain Sukata, but Samarin had been asleep. He'd not only woken, but collected a sword and followed?

"I—" The various excuses Fallon had been weighing fled his mind, and already he could feel his throat start to close. "N-noise," he stammered. "Or dream." The choking worsened, and he looked wildly around the attic for some excuse, some reason that would make the pressure go away, then gasped, despairingly: "Nothing! There's nothing here."

As performances went, this one would likely lead to Fallon being accused of theft, once the books were discovered to be missing. Certainly neither Samarin nor Sukata looked for a moment like they believed him.

"Nothing certainly makes you flustered," Samarin said, eyebrows climbing. "Shall we look around, since we're here?"

"I...had a...had a..." Fallon made himself stop, and firm his mind. Better to not try to explain at all.

The same keen hearing that had exposed his hunt now saved him, as Sukata turned her head sharply, then walked swiftly to the end of the attic, blending into the shadows so thoroughly that it looked like her night robe was walking on its own. That robe stopped directly in front of the hidden door. Dezart Samarin, not slow on the uptake, followed to press an ear to the wood.

"Fallon," Sukata said, in her thin voice. "Please ask the Lieutenants and Lord Surclere to join us."

Relieved, Fallon left at a trot. He already knew Lieutenant Faral was on watch on the ground floor, and it was the simplest of things to tell her and then just trail along behind as she woke Lieutenant Meniar and Lord Surclere.

When they reached the attic, Fallon found that Dezart Samarin had collected both a shirt, and his mask, though he didn't do anything at all, just stood in the background with Fallon as the Kellian burst open the hidden door and effortlessly immobilised the people on the far side.

It wasn't until the *other* people in the next house came up to investigate the noise that Fallon understood why Samarin had taken the time to dress. Kolans reacted to that mask. Even Kolans who were convinced that their attic had been broken into in the middle of the night stopped waving fire irons and became meekly obedient as soon as they set eyes on the symbol of their Emperor's authority.

Fallon waited, mentally rehearsing his chosen explanation. But no-one asked for it and eventually, too weary to care, he went back to bed and let Auri watch the last of the fuss, and Dezart Samarin's quiet interventions that ensured that books were returned and conspirators taken away.

Spy. Observer. Trouble.

Chapter Fourteen

"I suppose you'd need to be a pretty good mage to own a place like this."

Unlike Sebastian, Sukata never acted like there was anything wrong with Kendall seeing magic simply as a way to earn a living. "It would require a great deal of wealth," the Kellian girl said. "Mages are usually well paid, but one would need to be out of the ordinary to receive recompense on the scale this house requires. Do you wish for something like it?"

"I want this room." Kendall bounced lightly on the cushiony bed with its cleverly carved headboard and brand new linens, then glanced around at the desk and the shelves containing books, ornaments and curios. The place was spacious and bright, and she had liked it the moment she'd walked into it the previous night. Especially the windows, which looked down over the street and had seats built into their bases. The tall panels of glass squares were currently lit by a cherry-pink dawn, and Kendall privately enjoyed how even this relatively mild light could give Sukata a shimmering rosy glow.

Sukata never looked quite ordinary, for she was tall and ever so slightly out of proportion and had claws, but dawn always made her delicately unreal, and Kendall could only wish those who hated the Kellian could see more of them at this time of day. Rennyn had once told Kendall that Rennyn's great-grandmother had called the Kellian stained glass monsters, and that had made Kendall so annoyed, not least because she couldn't help but admit that it fit.

"It is a rich house, but I think it was a happy one too," Sukata said. "And this branch of the family less insular than the Claires. Daunting to know that all of them died seeking ways to stop Queen Solace."

"Sebastian said that a lot of them were killed trying to do one big joint experiment. By the time he was born there was only one old man living here." Kendall, watching her friend's face narrowly, tried to puzzle out new shadows. "Are you thinking that maybe there was a baby or two they didn't know about? That there might be some of this Surreive part of the family still out there?" More people who could control the Kellian, if Rennyn and Sebastian were out of the way.

"That is a possibility. Given the situation with Prince Helecho, it may even be something we could have reason to be glad of, if we fail to protect the Claires."

Only just preferable to be inherited by some unknown person, instead of a nasty demon prince. Better by far to deal with Rennyn and Sebastian, and that was still fingernails on a chalkboard to the Kellian, for all Rennyn was so careful to never accidentally order any of them about. Even if she got better and could have a Kellian baby with Captain Faille, even if it was one of their own people who inherited the ability to control them, the Kellian would always on some level be property because that was how the spell was structured. They hated it so much.

Kendall washed, and let Sukata catch her up on a drama Kendall had slept through. One of the servants, working for thieves based in the house set flush with theirs, had managed to take books from the Tyrlanders' luggage, and only Sukata's sharp hearing had uncovered them.

"Trying to steal Thought Mage techniques?" Kendall guessed, buttoning her shirt.

"So it seems. This house was linked to Duchess Surclere when she wrote to direct it be prepared for guests, and it seems at least one group moved immediately to search for secrets. Though, interestingly, the mage they work for—Magister Accan—vanished a fortnight ago.

"Bet the ones you caught aren't the only lot in this house keen to sneak a peek," Kendall muttered, as they headed down to see what the specially hired household had produced for breakfast.

"That is not a bet at all," Sukata replied in her extra-neutral voice as they opened the breakfast room door.

Kendall wasn't pleased to find 'Dezart' Rhael Samarin serenely stuffing his face. There weren't many people who could rival Rennyn for being completely full of themselves, but this Samarin was definitely a contender. Probably worse, because he couldn't be more than a few years older than Kendall. This morning, the smug git had put his mask on the table and piled his plate with what must be a bit of everything from the nearly dozen covered dishes lined up on one side of the room.

These smelled good enough for Kendall to set aside an impulse to turn on her heel. Instead, she ignored the spy altogether, filled her own plate, and sat so that the flowers in the centre of the table made it easier not to have to look at him. Samarin just ate, and it seemed they could hope for a quiet breakfast, but then the Pest showed up, looking like death warmed over, but never able to keep his mouth shut for long.

"May I ask you a question, sir?"

"I don't see how to stop you," Samarin said, but not nastily. "Get your breakfast first, though."

"The enchantments on your mask," the Pest went on, the second he sat down. "The most obvious is the one that prevents anyone but you from wearing it. But there's at least one secondary enchantment, and I cannot untangle its purpose. Is it something you can to tell us about?"

Samarin glanced down at the mask. "Can? Yes. Will? No. I'd be interested to hear if you can successfully divine it, though, since it's not designed to announce itself. Do you find Duchess Surclere's methods of casting difficult to learn?"

That wiped the Pest's special keen look from his face. When they left the ship, Rennyn had given him the same exercises Kendall and Sukata had started with, and Kendall knew he practiced them each evening after they'd finished the day's travel. And that he wasn't doing too well with it, was still making his test object twitch and jump, rather than being able to pick it up. It was obvious that he'd hoped to quickly pass Kendall and Sukata, or at least catch up to them.

"I have barely taken the first step of learning Thought," the Pest said, in the super-serious voice he used for anything about magic. "My lessons so far are nothing new, since the basics of what standard instruction calls Force Magic were already well known. Achieving any kind of control is difficult, of course, and I can see why Duchess Surclere insists on focusing on the strictly physical and advancing in degrees toward abstract concepts. But the discussions we have had on Symbolic—" The Pest broke into a rapturous smile that made him look moon-struck. "Symbolic is already considered a perilous artistry, where poor choices have monstrous consequences, but the *combination* of Thought and Symbolic is an enormous step. Words, Sigillics, are so limited. When I first heard of Her Grace's use of Thought Magic, I focused on the immediacy, but the true marvel is that it allows you to cast what words cannot say."

He really talked like that. Almost as stupidly wordy as some of the books Kendall had tried to read.

The Pest had taken a deep breath to calm himself down a little, adding with a quick shrug. "I've only begun to face how difficult it will be."

Samarin had listened attentively, with just the slightest crinkling to the corners of his eyes while the Pest went into his usual raptures. "And you two? Sukata and...Kendall, yes? Do you consider Duchess Surclere's techniques attainable?"

"The techniques, yes." Sukata was being guardedly polite. "The conceptual leap required for Thought to become more than crude, physical manipulation...that I can only hope for and work toward. But even the short time I have spent learning from Her Grace has shown me that I habitually approach magic in a very fixed and inflexible way, and that the thoughts and feelings of even the most rote of Sigillic casters have a greater impact than we are ever taught. And I begin to wonder if the reason that the Claires cast as well as they do is because they regard the rules as negotiable."

"I'd bet thinking the rules don't apply to them is half the reason there's only two of them left," Kendall said bluntly. That or a habit of offering spies bed and breakfast.

"It's just a better level of understanding," the Pest said, still super-seriously. He'd never made the mistake of being directly insulting to Kendall again, but he kept trying to explain things to her, like she was the poor backwards child everyone had to be nice to. It made Kendall even less inclined to do the Sigillic assignments they were all given.

"What were you doing up in the attic last night anyway?" she asked, in hopes of knocking him off his cleverer-than-thou perch.

But the Pest just shrugged and said: "I fell out of bed and thought, since I was up, that I might as well look for the hidden library. Then everyone turned up with swords and half frightened me out of my skin."

The unbelieving smile Samarin produced at this almost reconciled Kendall to being stuck with him, but the Pest was too busy stuffing his face to even notice. The door opened and Lieutenant Meniar came in, also looking like he hadn't slept. He gave them a weary smile and headed straight to mound a plate high with food before settling in the chair opposite Kendall.

"Her Duchessness has been ordered to keep to her bed, and we're not letting her up until after lunch. Hopefully a long rest without travel will let her finally overcome the impact of that light casting." He glanced at Samarin. "Faille would like to review those dossiers, if you have them."

Samarin brushed his fingers against a pile of paper sitting next to his plate. "Your intention was to spend some days in Koletor waiting for the rest of your group?"

"And sorting out the library here," Lieutenant Meniar said, as Lieutenant Faral came in, and took up a plate. "The Duchess says that most of it should be unremarkable—nothing interesting enough to be worth last night's adventures—and everything of note should be in this hidden room. It'll only open to family, but she's not sure where it is, so we can oblige her by locating the door. And there's the divination to cast, to see if we can pick up any further indication of—"

Screaming started.

A girl first, then others, with some plate smashing for good measure. Sukata and Lieutenant Faral were gone before Kendall even had time to turn her head, the door swinging in their wake. Lieutenant Meniar put down his fork and hurried after them and the Pest leapt up and followed. Kendall listened to some more crashing, with added banging, then tried a forkful of some kind of boiled and spiced grain.

"Not going to help?"

Kendall eyed Samarin sourly. "They'd rather you didn't go get in the way while they deal with anything really dangerous. Not that whatever that is will be."

"Why not? The creature you're hunting is capable of breaching circles, after all."

"Because Sukata and Lieutenant Faral would have known before the screaming started." Kendall crunched a piece of flat, toasted bread, and decided there was more chance of him shutting up if she didn't point out that he hadn't gone to help either.

"An Eferum-Get threat anywhere in the house would be known to them?" Samarin waited, but Kendall didn't bother to answer, so he went on: "And are you finding Duchess Surclere's methods easy to learn?"

"Don't you have dossiers for us as well?" Kendall snapped, exasperated by the scut's lazy amusement. "What do you get out of acting like you don't know anything about us?"

"Dossiers aren't inexhaustible," Samarin said. "I know that you had no background in magic before Queen Solace's final return, and that you and Sukata Illuma have been reported moving small objects with Thought Magic. But that does not tell me whether you find it easy."

"Of course it isn't," Kendall snapped. "Why would it be easy? Why does it matter to...Fel, you're not another would-be student, are you?"

"My duties do not permit the time," he said, as if that was something highly ironic. "But I need to evaluate the threat this form of magic poses. Both to would-be Thought Mages, and to the rest of Kole. It matters to an extreme degree if this is something that will injure or kill almost everyone who attempts it. And even more if it is something the majority could achieve."

A world full of mages acting like Rennyn Claire. Or, worse, *not* acting like Rennyn Claire. Acting, instead, like the Elder Mages, who had wrecked everything they were supposed to be looking after, and let the Eferum-Get into the world.

The Pest came back, followed by Sukata, who said: "Something came out of the cellar. An animal, out to steal food, not hostile. Faral and Meniar are attempting to locate it."

"All that screaming for a rat?"

"Something called a varsh," the Pest said. "The staff seem to consider it unclean."

"A reptile the size of a small dog," Samarin told them. "Usually found in the aqueducts and sewers."

Kendall glanced at Sukata, remembering an occasion in the past when Rennyn's obnoxious great-uncle had taken control of an animal and sent it to do his dirty work. Which was probably why the Lieutenants were chasing around the cellars after a kitchen-scrap thief. Sukata was polishing off her breakfast with efficient speed, obviously with a task to do, and Kendall followed her lead so she could trail Sukata when she took a glass of juice and the dossiers upstairs to Rennyn and Captain Faille's room.

Sukata briefly explained what the screaming had been about, and Captain Faille went to check it out in person and go do errands, leaving them charge of Rennyn, still asleep and looking damp and limp. They left the juice on the table beside her bed and moved to the far end of the room, which had another seat built into the windows, though looking out over narrow back gardens.

"I think I like my room better, but they're both really good," Kendall said softly, inspecting a book that had been left face-down on the sill. Stupid Kolan squiggles. "Do you think we could talk her into not selling the place?"

"Perhaps it's necessary to fund the restoration of Surclere. The Duchy is very poor, and it will be a large task to revive it. There is no need—" Sukata paused.

"No need for a house here—except if maybe the Kellian decide not to stay in Tyrland. You know, that Samarin, I think he's here as much to find out more about the Kellian as anything else."

"Yes, the Emperor is interested in the possibility of using us. This Dezart Samarin, there is a sense of...not threat, but the possibility of threat from him. He judges us on several levels, and whatever a Dezart is, it seems a position of considerable authority."

"Could you tell what this other enchantment on his mask was?" Kendall hadn't untangled more than the fact that it was magical.

Sukata shook her head, but then Rennyn, voice croaky, said: "Both of those doors behind the Emperor had recognition wards on them, and that mask felt like it belonged to them. There may be other places in the Empire set so that you can enter only if wearing one of those as a key. Samarin seems to be swimming in a haze of enchantment, however. Let me know if you unravel any more."

Since it was all just magical buzz to Kendall, she shrugged and went to offer Rennyn the juice. "Are you going to try and get rid of him before we go north to the forest?" she asked.

"It would be interesting to try. But I suspect his value as a deterrent is real. Illidian tells me there are at least two more among our hired staff he considers suspect, but are likely spies, not here to thieve, and will lose interest once I've addressed that matter." Rennyn looked across at Sukata. "And while Aurai's Rest is relatively private, it is no secret, and Illidian does not believe it will be harmed by having an agent of the Kolan Emperor visiting it."

"You are intending to deal with the interest in Thought casting?" Sukata asked, not showing any reaction to the mention of the Kellian's forest home.

Rennyn nodded. "Before we leave Koletor I will have a small manual published. I would have preferred more time to draft something in-depth and considered, but the core of Thought is so very basic, after all, that I can put something relatively clear together, and hopefully get some of these watchers out of the way. Perhaps even save some lives."

"You're not starting that this morning," Kendall said, firmly, taking the empty glass. "We'll read to you if you can't sleep."

Rennyn's eyelashes lowered ominously, and it was hard for Kendall not to think of Samarin talking of Thought Mages as a threat. Rennyn Claire, thin, tired and drawn, could still kill annoyances with less effort than it took her to get out of bed. Kendall glowered back at her, not budging an inch.

With a sigh, Rennyn gave in. "Lieutenant Meniar and Illidian are being tiresome. But it's not worth arguing about." Adding a faint grimace of apology, she rearranged her covers and closed her eyes.

It was a sham. Kendall could see from the set of her shoulders, the way one thin hand gripped the sheet, that Lady Once-Powerful was going to lie there and stew in her frustration for a while. There was no help for it, so Kendall soft-footed her way back to the window to practice drawing sigils and wonder what the world would be like when Thought Mages with nastier tempers than Rennyn's were roaming about being cranky with people. Kendall started to wonder if *she'd* end up able to kill people as soon as glower at them. And whether she would.

She thought about that all day, while they hunted for the hidden library, and when Rennyn eventually came down and opened the door the Pest finally found concealed in the cellar, and after Lieutenant Meniar cast the focus detection.

And the divination pointed east.

oOo

After much excitement, Rennyn settled the question of whether her Wicked Uncle was in the city by travelling to an inn at Koletor's eastern edge and having Lieutenant Meniar cast the focus detection again. When it continued to point east, they could at least rule out imminent threat, although Illidian accepted Dezart Samarin's offer of extra guards without even a small hesitation.

"Do you think you have the strength to cast the variation immediately?" Rennyn asked.

Lieutenant Meniar shrugged. "So long as no-one minds me sleeping the rest of the day." He paused. "And needing to be carried back to the house."

No-one objected, so Lieutenant Meniar re-chalked the divination, and added north to their east before sitting down heavily on a chair.

"Will this change your plans?" Dezart Samarin said.

"Until the other Sentene arrive, pursuit is not wise," Illidian said. "After that, the simplest thing to do would be to continue to divine the direction as we travel to Aurai's Rest, since it is both north and a short way east of here."

"Combined with the last divination that indicated west, we've now narrowed the location to this band through Kole, Semarrak, Alisar or Fye," Rennyn said, marking the map Illidian had brought along. "Which is the most progress we've made since my Wicked Uncle left Asentyr."

"I'll request reports on unexplained deaths in that region," Dezart Samarin said. "And arrange for the extra security. I can also arrange for transport north, if you wish it."

He pulled down his mask before leaving, and Rennyn already knew Kole well enough to recognise that this simple adjustment would guarantee that there would be no interference from the more-than-suspicious owner of the inn, who had been most dubious about the use they were making of his best parlour.

"A useful addition," she said, a little amused to have found another person inclined to organise everything around her. "I very much hope our interests continue to run in the same direction."

"His concern regarding the missing mages seems genuine," Illidian said, erasing the few remaining traces of the Sigillic from the floor. "And Prince Helecho too great a potential threat to ignore. The whole of Kole's strength might be needed."

As they replaced furniture shuffled aside to allow Lieutenant Meniar to mark out his circle, Rennyn wondered if their search would truly lead to an all-out battle. If her Wicked Uncle did intend to lead an Eferum-Get army to conquer this world, would he start with Kole? Perhaps he was in those two northern kingdoms—Alisar or Fye—where... Rennyn knew nothing about them, except the likelihood that the places would be cold. At some point her over-protective escorts would start suggesting the hunt would have to wait until after winter. Her Wicked Uncle had already been allowed far too much time to set his schemes in motion.

"Should we worry about the chance he's waiting for us at Aurai's Rest?" Lieutenant Meniar asked, hauling himself reluctantly out of his chair.

"That would be an extremely dangerous place for him," Illidian replied. Then he added reluctantly: "Though a tactically well-chosen one."

For there were few defending mages at the Rest, and the Kellian were weak to magic. While her Wicked Uncle could not command them as Solace had, the Kellian were an extremely dangerous force, and a mage of Helecho Montjuste-Surclere's skill would have a wide range of bindings and enslavement castings to choose from.

Rennyn could not avoid the memory of a net closing around her, a cage of words, and a wash of pain and gloating violation. She forced herself not to turn her thoughts away. This instinctive flinching could be her undoing if she was unfortunate enough to meet her Wicked Uncle again.

Breathing deeply, Rennyn allowed herself once again to admit that he was likely a better mage than she, and that she was afraid. But she would not turn him into her own personal horror, would not accept this paralysis. If she met him again, she would act.

Illidian's hand on her shoulder came as silent reminder that, unlike Solace, this was not a battle she had to face alone. Although there were times when she felt that her increasing collection of friends and allies only gave her more people to worry about.

She smiled up at her husband, then asked: "Shall we allow our Imperial representative to wave his mask and conjure up transport?"

"There is no reason not to make use of him," Illidian said, as Keste Faral solved the problem of an exhausted mage companion by lifting him into her arms.

Lieutenant Meniar, brown skin darkening for several different reasons, said: "I'd like him if I dared trust him. But a gift horse that talented has to have a nasty kick. I don't imagine you get to wear that mask just by smiling all the time."

Keste, who was one of the least talkative Kellian of Rennyn's acquaintance, spoke then, her voice soft and contemplative.

"And yet he wears it as if he hates it."

Chapter Fifteen

The sights, scents and sounds of a sprawling Kolan market would have had Kendall trying to look in every direction at once, except that Sukata was angry. Kendall wasn't entirely certain if the Kellian girl was so furious because of Rennyn, or perhaps Kendall, but she sure made it hard to pay attention to anything else. Angry Kellian were like chained lightning, and a little pool of startled silence followed them wherever they went. It didn't help that Sukata had left behind the hat she usually wore on sunny days, and was lit up like a candle: hair, eyes, and pointed nails all vivid flames announcing that here was something different, dangerous. Even the Pest, who had started out nearly as upset as Sukata, couldn't take his eyes off her.

Nor could his high-and-mightiness Samarin, who had spotted them leaving and followed like a hound on blood scent. He at least had stowed his mask in a big inner pocket of his cloak before prowling along behind them, but he still acted like he thought that the world was there to entertain him, and that Sukata was as good as a play. Kendall hadn't learned nearly enough Kolan to understand what people were murmuring as they passed, but Sukata was getting more attention than Kendall thought smart. And they'd be here all afternoon if she kept stalking past everything without even looking.

Rennyn hadn't even explained why she suddenly wanted musical instruments. Small ones and different from each other was all she would say, gazing off into the distance. And then suddenly Sukata and Fallon were being all white and agonised and tiresome. All over stupid magic lessons too.

Kendall lagged behind, trying to at least *look* for instruments. The market filled a broad square paved with sandstone. The only permanent structure was a central knee-high pool tiled with shiny blue and green, which looked to Kendall like an outsize Kolan bath in the wrong place. The rest of the space was a maze of bulging tents, light wooden stalls with wheels on one side, and blankets spread between them, so you couldn't let your feet wander without risking tramping over glassware or piles of clothes. Everything was so close-packed there was barely room for the heaving crowd.

A jangle of notes cut through the noise. Kendall peered about, and oriented on a pair of boys being chased off from a stall hidden down a narrow corridor formed by the backs of two rows of tents. "Let's try down there," she said, but Sukata was still too busy being angry, disappearing into the crowd ahead.

With an irritated shrug, Kendall let her go. Sukata might be carrying the purse Rennyn had given them, but Kendall had enough Kolan coin to make at least small purchases, and would have no problem finding her way back to the house. Some time alone to think would be a good thing.

You saw a lot more of what a person was like when they lost their temper. Sukata would assuredly get over her snit and go back to acting the way she usually did, but having seen her like this, Kendall had to seriously wonder how much of the way Sukata usually behaved was Sukata. Almost every Sentene mage Kendall had talked to had been obsessed with living up to their Kellian partners, and they'd all in some way or other said that Kellian were very proud, and that while they were extremely polite, they rarely had a high opinion of people. Sukata acted all quiet and obliging, but right now Kendall could easily believe that she thought people who weren't Kellian were little more than bugs.

That was probably the wrong way to look at it. But it was worth thinking about some more. Kendall put it aside for later as she reached the stall, pleased to spot a set of pipes among a mix of scraps of silk and cheap jewellery. And there was a line of fine-cast bells. The stall-keeper, a lanky carrot-top, eyed her like he expected her to act like the kids he'd chased off, so she pointed at the second-smallest bell and said "How much?" in Kolan.

The gabble in response was stupidly fast, but Kendall managed to pick out the price, and countered with something more reasonable. Carrot-top shook his head, but smilingly produced a cowbell from beneath the display-top and clanked it as if it was worth listening to. Kendall firmly pointed back at her first choice, and offered a tiny bit more. She wasn't—

A hand, reeking of perfume, clapped over her mouth. Pulled back against a man where there should only be tent wall, arms trapped, Kendall was lifted and turned so that her lashing boot missed the stall. She tried biting, working to find flesh, but Smelly had his hand cupped and already they were out of the sun, slipping through draping canvas.

Dim space. A second man, stubbled face beneath a tight-tied green scarf. People, girls, on the floor, lying unmoving. Chained to the centre pole.

Green Scarf lifted a chain ending in a cuff. Worked power itched at Kendall even before she spotted the sigils up and down the pole, and she wriggled frantically, then remembered that she was the student of someone who could kill people at a glance, and no-one to be messed with.

But her attempt to push her captors away with Thought was as successful as holding back a river with bare hands. This was bigger than bowls, and it felt as if all the energy she put against them melted away. Kendall tried again, straining to stop Green Scarf coming any nearer. He didn't budge, but the chain could be worked on, springing from his hands to clatter back against the centre pole.

The hand over Kendall's mouth lifted long enough for Smelly to clip her smartly across the ear. He was quick to replace his hand before she could yell, but even with her head reeling, Kendall managed to sink her teeth into flesh and dug in with vicious satisfaction as he grunted and stifled a yell. But the distraction had given Green Scarf time to retrieve his cuff and before she'd more than felt the grip on her foot he'd clapped it around her ankle.

Green Scarf had to hold the cuff closed, fumbling to thread through a bulky padlock, and Kendall kicked again, trying to jam his fingers. The etched Sigillic was active, and filled her legs with jelly while a sheep came to sit on her head. Green Scarf dug his fingers in, clicking the padlock home, then said something in a gabble that didn't sound Kolan. Smelly let Kendall go, and she plonked down on her behind, struggling not to pass out because she really needed to yell, not just sit and let them win.

Smelly moved forward, a barrel of a man grimacing at a hand dripping blood but still looking far too pleased with himself. Kendall longed to wipe the self-satisfied expression off his face, and was astonished when her anger was immediately rewarded, as Smelly glanced at the back wall of the tent and froze, jaw sagging.

It was too much work for Kendall to look. She needed everything she had left to stay awake. It was only after Smelly and Green Scarf had dashed through a second tent flap that she had a glimpse of what they'd seen: a charcoal mask. But by that time Kendall's whole world had tilted and she was preoccupied with the scratchy feel of matting against her cheek. A booted foot came down next to her nose, then went past, and that was it for Kendall until a tugging at her ankle revived her drive to escape and she kicked feebly.

"Not helping."

Kendall cracked her eyelids, and found she was now facing stretched canvas instead of matting. Same tent, same central pole with its chains, but one of the plates holding chain to wood had been pried free. Her feet were propped up on something that shifted beneath them, and fingers...

Opening her eyes properly, Kendall found Samarin sitting on the mat with his mask pushed back and her feet in his lap, wiggling a bit of metal in the padlock holding the cuff in place. It didn't seem to suit, so he reached down to a strip of cloth laid out beside him and exchanged it for another.

"Why do you have all those...keys?" she asked, only just resisting the impulse to kick again. At least until he had the cuff off.

"My role is to go to the places the Emperor cannot, and meddle. I've met a lot of inconvenient locks over the years." He laughed. "This isn't even the first attached to a girl."

So full of himself he was overflowing. And worse, he'd obviously rescued her, though she couldn't quite work out how. The other three—no, two girls and a boy—also lying on the floor didn't stir at all.

"Why did they run away? Did you have the Guard with you?"

He touched the mask covering his hair. "They may have thought I'd a small army right behind me, but even obviously alone, this is often more than enough. The attention of the Emperor. Justice that bribery or threats won't turn aside. And trying to dispose of me would only bring a harsh demonstration of the might of the Kolan throne, since the mask will make the Emperor aware of my death."

His wide mouth twisted, as if he thought all that a bitter joke, then he tried another bit of metal.

"If people are getting snatched right in the middle of the capital's markets, then the might of the Kolan throne isn't all that much."

"Certainly not infallible: someone's being lazy, or deliberately looking the other way. Though I know of no system that will change the nature of those who see a pretty child and covet her."

"I'm not a *child*."

"No? You look about twelve."

"Twelve! I'm sixteen!" she snapped. Then, after a reluctant beat, added: "Nearly."

He lifted his brows, then abruptly pulled on her leg, so that it was no longer her foot sitting in his lap, but most of Kendall. Bending over so that his nose was in danger of poking into hers, he gave her the most obnoxious smirk and said: "Still a child."

Straightening, he dumped her back on the tent's floor and lifted her ankle again. Kendall longed to kick him, but she wanted the chain off more, so she swallowed hard and said instead:

"Better that than a creepy old man pretending he's not even twenty." She hadn't missed that 'over the years' he'd tossed off earlier.

"Oh, I was quite the prodigal," he said, unperturbed. "Indeed, I expect I'm even younger than you think. So what set your tall friend off?"

"None of your business."

"No? Well, I expect she'll tell me herself."

He would ask Sukata too, the scut. And knew Kendall would answer rather than see Sukata be made to talk about a thing that had so severely upset her—

particularly now Kendall had figured out the why of it herself.

"It was our latest Sigillic exercise," Kendall said, reluctantly. "Rennyn's not just showing us how Thought Magic works: she trying to teach us to be devising mages, and she keeps telling us to write Sigillics to do the same thing as whatever she's most recently Thought-cast. Not that she's been casting much at all lately, but the last thing she did was make an apple fall into segments.

"The Sigillic I wrote was just something short, and it was no good—likely to make the entire room fall into segments, according to Herself. The Sigillics Sukata and the Pe—and Fallon wrote worked. But even though they were really long, they were identical. The Pe—Fallon said that of course they were the same, because Fan-Fen..."

"Falzenar's Division and Miktok's Restriction," Samarin said. "The most logical combination of Sigillics to use there."

"That's it," Kendall said, eyeing him doubtfully. "And we could all see that Rennyn was expecting us—them—to realise something, but then she sighed, and made a couple of changes to mine, and told Fallon to cast it, and it worked too. Then she told us to go buy instruments."

"Ah, I see. Your Sukata's upset because, flawed or not, you produced the superior Sigillic."

"No," Kendall said irritably, though this was exactly what she'd thought at first. But Sukata wasn't like that. "Sukata really loves magic. She wants to understand it properly, to be a devising mage, and a Thought Mage, and to use Symbolic properly. And yet for every one of these Sigillic writing exercises, she's done just what she did today—stitched together a couple of existing Sigillics that someone else had come up with. Because that's how she's been taught to do it. Rennyn's never come right out and said Sukata and the Pest aren't doing what she asked them to, but she made it kind of obvious today. Sukata's angry at herself."

"Huh." Samarin picked up another bit of metal. "You can't stand to see her criticised, can you?"

"It's just the truth," Kendall told him crossly.

"Perhaps. But it's entirely unsurprising for a well-studied student mage to be annoyed when shown up by some random sprat who has only been studying magic for a handful of months. How do you think she'll react if you make this next step in Thought you're all aiming for?"

What was he trying to get at? "I expect she'd be glad to know it's not just the Claires who can. She's not the type to be jealous."

"Such devotion," he said. "How long is it you've known her again? No, don't kick me, I've a serious point to make. There's a lot of this blinding and immediate loyalty going around. Sentene mages who would walk over glass to defend those assigned to protect them. Rennyn Claire, marrying the first Kellian she meets, all in haste. Diminutive spitfires who don't have a good word to say about anyone, except one particular fellow student. There's a pattern."

"What in the Hells are you trying to say?"

"Why are you such a friend to Sukata Illuma? How did all this steadfast and true companionship come about? Who gained most from it?"

Kendall boggled at him. She and Sukata were friends because they were friends. Because they'd both been picked on studying at the Arkathan. Because together they'd trailed around after Rennyn, and been exasperated by Sebastian, and looked after the pair of Claires after the Black Queen's death. It wasn't about *gaining*...

Yes, Sukata had ended up as Rennyn's student because of Kendall. But that wasn't because Sukata had angled for it.

"They have an extreme vulnerability to magic, you know," Samarin went on. "An innate lack of resistance. Is it coincidence that their service as Sentene brings with it a supply of companion mages? That those mages often go on to become parents of Kellian? Or is this a logical tactic for a people determined to breed out their greatest weakness?"

"You're cracked."

"I'm asking the questions that need to be answered, before Kole can settle her attitude toward a people whose home settlement is, technically at least, within the Imperial borders. Asset? Ally? Threat? There are more ways to invade than to show up with an army at the border."

"Triple cracked and left out in the sun."

"Be that as it may, I would appreciate you giving the question some thought. Have you observed anything that fits with the theory? Anything to contradict it?"

Kendall proceeded to let Dezart Rhael Samarin, Hand of the Emperor, know exactly what she thought of playing snitch for him, but Samarin only smiled, then glanced briefly away before selecting another bit of metal.

"No doubt you will proceed according to your own wonts," he said. "Just perhaps not alone down hidden by-ways."

The inner flap of the tent tore as it was thrust back, but it was not the two men returning. Sukata, long knife in hand, stepped through and stopped short, the Pest peeking anxiously around her.

Samarin finally produced a satisfying click from the padlock and said: "There we go," as he slipped it loose. "Perhaps you two could find one of the Market

Peacewards. They should be wearing a red quarter-mask."

Ignoring this, Sukata knelt as Kendall sat up and pulled the cuff off her ankle. "Are you hurt?"

"Just wishing I could twist someone's neck," Kendall said, glaring at Samarin because it was strangely hard to look at Sukata, and not because of any Kellian weirdness with light.

"There was someone wearing a quarter-mask following us anyway," the Pest said, and ducked back out the way he'd come.

"If you were roaming the markets with that knife drawn, I'm not surprised," Samarin said, tucking away his collection of bits of metal.

"Aren't you going to unlock these others?" Kendall snapped.

"I'm sure the Peaceward will enjoy doing that." He stood, slipping his mask down over his face again, and went into the adjoining tent just in time to disconcert whatever a Peaceward was.

"I didn't notice," Sukata said, as soon as I they were alone. "I am sorry, Kendall. That was inexcusable."

"Not your job to look after me," Kendall said.

Can't stand to see her criticised.

Kendall pushed the smug, sneaking memory aside. "Nice set-up they had, too—that damn cow bell."

This, of course, meant nothing to Sukata, but Kendall wasted no time pulling open the concealed slit in the tent wall and marching back out the way she'd come. No surprise that the red-headed scut was gone, but he'd left his table of wares behind.

Kendall took the entire line of fine-cast bells, each a different size from each other, and tossed her paltry collection of Kolan coin on the table in return.

"There," she said, handing half the bells to Sukata, and refusing by so much as a dropped glance to acknowledge that anything could have upset her. "Whatever Herself wants with musical instruments, this'll surely be more than enough."

She spared a moment to collect the Pest, then led them effortlessly back to the House, shrugging off any suggestion that the Dezart and the Peaceward might want to ask them questions. The one thing Kendall didn't need, at the moment, was more questions from Samarin.

He'd asked quite enough already.

Chapter Sixteen

Ten bells. They were ideal for her purpose, and Rennyn adapted her new Sigillic around them, coaching Lieutenant Meniar into casting the result in the house's receiving room. Then she tapped a fragment of a tune out on the set of bells suspended over the Sigillic, and nodded when the sound was repeated, and the casting took hold and settled to waiting.

"I can see it's a divination," Fallon said, watching eagerly. "But I don't understand what you're divining."

"A sound only I can hear," Rennyn said. "Which, in this company, is unlikely enough to suggest that what I am hearing is not sound at all, but some expression of a casting. The difficulty has been producing a divination that did not react to every casting in the area, but only to the one I wanted. It took some time to think of a method for that."

Rennyn could see that something about this excited Fallon inordinately. And then, as happened too often to be coincidence, his fascination cut off and he looked sick, then retired behind her other students to stare at the ground. Rennyn exchanged a glance with Lieutenant Meniar, who nodded briefly. They had been discussing the question of Fallon's health, and the Sentene mage had his own subtle divination operating.

None of her students were at their best at that moment. Of course, Rennyn had raised the problem of over-reliance on set forms with Fallon and Sukata yesterday, and both had been predictably crestfallen. Sukata had then compounded her unhappiness by failing in her entirely self-appointed duty to keep her fellow students safe. Not that she showed much if any of this on her face, but her stance was not as upright as usual.

And Kendall...Kendall was all prickles at the best of times. Since the yesterday's unexpectedly dramatic trip to the market, she become something different: less inclined to talk, more a silent, spiky ball radiating 'leave me alone'. Not, apparently, overly frightened by her near escape, nor simply embarrassed, but shut away and withdrawn. The only thing that roused her was opportunities to glare at Dezart Samarin.

"Enough for the morning, I think," Rennyn said, rising from the couch conveniently situated beside the casting. "Today's assignment for you three is to write a Sigillic to stop a holed rowboat from sinking."

"Should I set someone to watch this?" Lieutenant Meniar asked, offering her his arm.

"No need. At this stage all I want from it is confirmation that there really is a casting. I haven't structured a way to identify its purpose. I really can manage these stairs on my own, you know."

"You'd not deny me the opportunity to admire your progress," he said, cheerfully. "Your ribs aren't bothering you at all?"

"Not a twinge," she said, more than pleased by the fact. "Nor has the headache reoccurred, even when I cast." But the climb up the single flight of stairs still brought on a faint dizziness. "I think I'm as recovered as I'm going to get," she added as Illidian, coming down from above, met them on the landing. "Not technically ill, but no physical reserve."

He clasped her hand at this, but only said: "The reinforcement work has finished."

"The nights will be dull without the prospect of attic invasions," Rennyn murmured, though she had, of course, slept through the first one entirely. "What did your divination tell you, Lieutenant Meniar?"

The Sentene mage waited to speak until they were all three inside her bedroom and he had closed the door behind them. Then, uncharacteristically grave, he said: "Fallon's not ill. He's enchanted."

Considerably startled, Rennyn said: "I haven't detected any pattern of intent."

"Nor did I. My divination wasn't set for it anyway. But the boy's throat closed, completely. Some kind of membrane formed across it, I think. I'll refine the divination to get a better idea of the physical impact."

Rennyn glanced at Illidian, and saw that the vertical lines that bracketed his mouth had deepened.

"A casting to prevent speech?" he suggested.

"Possibly," Meniar replied. "It's something that released, at any rate, once he'd stepped back. But that's no simple block to keep him quiet: a few of minutes of that and he'd suffocate."

"Well, there's an explanation for why he occasionally appears outright terrified," Rennyn said. "Some mischief of his uncle's, do you think?"

Illidian shook his head. "He claims to have departed without his uncle's knowledge. Although this casting may pre-date his attempts to become your student."

"And what were we discussing that triggered it today? Divinations? Music? Advanced Sigillics?" Rennyn thought back over all she'd observed of Fallon in the previous weeks. "He's always particularly intense about Thought casting. I hate to imagine that someone's set him to learn my so-called secrets, under threat of death. But my lessons certainly don't all have that impact on him."

"I'll divine further, and then prepare a Sigillic that will unblock his throat if that becomes necessary."

Lieutenant Meniar grimaced. "And hope that the casting does not include contingencies beyond that. I will leave unpicking the intent to you, Your Grace."

He smiled at her, nodded at Illidian, and left.

"Lady Weston was positively superstitious about your instincts," Rennyn said, as Illidian sat beside her on the bed. "Do you think your interest in Fallon was sparked because he poses a threat?"

He gave the idea due consideration. "Unlikely," he said at last. "More likely that I felt that he was threatened."

This last had an ironic note. Illidian claimed that it was pointless for him to dislike the in-built protective instinct of his people, but he was also very aware that part of his own personality was defined by the terms of Solace's casting.

"When I decided to bring students along, I didn't think they'd come with mysteries," she said, slipping off her shoes. "I'll begin looking for a way to define the enchantment without his notice." She paused. "As for Kendall, I'll try a direct approach this afternoon."

"And if her anger at Samarin is due to something more than chagrin at being rescued?"

"Then we will test the Emperor," she said, but sighed and shook her head. "I don't think it's that, any more than I think it's her near-escape. From past remarks, I'm fairly sure this isn't the first time Kendall has encountered trouble related to being small and pretty. If Samarin had added insult to injury, I'd expect more scratches. A black eye, at the very least."

Besides, Rennyn had contrived to get rid of the Dezart temporarily by presenting the larger portion of the house's secret library to the Emperor, and Kendall's mood hadn't noticeably improved. She was unhappy, not angry.

"Well, I'll ask," she said reiterated, and let herself be distracted into expending her energy more thoroughly than a flight of stairs would ever take. So nice to no longer have complaining ribs.

oOo

"What would happen if I just used 'Boat Stop Leaking'?"

"More than likely that would work," Rennyn said, as she crossed from the door of Kendall's chosen bedroom. "An emergency solution that you might use if you were going down rapidly. But an unclear construction, allowing the possibility that the casting would expand the definition of 'stop', fixing the boat in place. And I would expect it to be energy-hungry."

She held out her hand and Kendall handed up a smudged piece of paper. As usual a direct, logical and creative Sigillic, this time dutifully mindful of limitations.

"This comes close to Symbolic," Rennyn said. "You're not ready for that."

"But would it work?"

"It would depend on your control, and your view of trees. Telling a boat it's made from a tree and should grow bark might seal the leaks, but there's every chance you'd gain leaves, branches, roots, or perhaps even enclose the entire boat in bark. If nothing else, there's a risk your boat would become very heavy." She shrugged. "Or it could work exactly as you wish. I don't think it would work successfully for me."

"Why not?"

"A tree crashed through the roof of one of our houses when I was a child," Rennyn said. "And so to me a tree is linked to destruction, to being heavy, and dangerous. One of the reasons Symbolic magic frightens so many people is that it's open to much greater variation from caster to caster, or even from casting to casting. But did you use this because you thought it the best solution, or simply quicker than expressing exactly what you needed to happen in sigils?"

Kendall only shrugged, her dark brows lowering into the suspicion she wore like a shield. But today it failed to hide the clear unhappiness in her eyes. She had been distracted enough by the problem to briefly forget whatever was troubling her, but now radiated 'go away' in a manner that was not entirely safe for someone learning Thought Magic.

Searching for an opening, Rennyn looked about, then said: "This room was my mother's."

The headboard of the bed had triggered a fragment of memory, and Rennyn—who had been standing too long at any rate—sat down beside the pillow and touched the carved wood, counting the feathers of the magnificent wings of an eagle. The correct two had ever-so-faintly more polish, though not yet enough to make the secret obvious.

"It opens!" Kendall pressed forward, but the space was empty, and she settled back, disappointed. "Your mother was one of this Surreive branch of your family?"

"Yes. Because of the danger of outsiders finding out what we were trying to achieve, there was a lot of cousin-marrying between the Claires and the Surreives. We ended having to be very careful who married who, to avoid too much inbreeding. Theoretically my parents' marriage was arranged, but my mother hated the idea, of course, and refused to go along with it."

"Was she a lot like you?"

"I look like her. A little taller. Seb is more like our father."

"I guess they went along with arrangements in the end."

"Oh yes. My father, who had been sent to Kole, obliged my mother by agreeing that he would do better to look for someone unrelated and trustworthy to bring some fresh blood into the family. She began matchmaking him to suitable women of her acquaintance, and found herself pleased when the matches fell through." Rennyn tried to smile, remembering in sharp detail being told this story. "My father always said he loved her from the day they met."

"Sorry. I know you hate talking about them."

That was Kendall: stubborn as a mule, but full of sharp observation and unexpected kindnesses.

Drawing power, Rennyn formed a bubble of silence around them both, and watched the shutter slam back down on her student's face as Kendall recognised the casting's intent.

"Will you tell me what happened, Kendall?" she asked, and when the girl almost visibly settled in for a fight added: "You've been making me wonder if I should have Dezart Samarin arrested. And not only because it would be a salutary experience for him."

Kendall produced an expression of complete disgust. "I think he'd enjoy it if you tried." Her hackles had lowered a little, but she sidestepped. "You won't have a day at all if you run around casting when you've just gotten up."

"The power cost of this is small," Rennyn said, truthfully. "I've been putting far more energy into trying to work out what has hurt you so."

She didn't push further, just waited, and was gratified that she had reached the point with Kendall where the girl did, eventually, speak.

"That prat thinks the Kellian cast some kind of...that part of their magic is making people loyal to them. That we're all just doing what they want."

Thoroughly astonished, Rennyn asked for Samarin's exact words, and then was glad she'd sent the man away, else she'd be tempted to box his ears.

"There's absolutely nothing in the terms of the spell that Solace cast that would give them such an ability, conscious or unconscious," she said firmly. "Nor is the symbology anything that would even suggest that. Solace used cobweb, dew, and dawn because she wanted deceptive strength, transparency, and speed. Just the tiniest hint of spider came along with the cobweb, which is why they are all so long-limbed. But the kind of glamour you are speaking of isn't even touched upon, not to mention being a rather difficult casting even when you try it deliberately. And mages would be the least susceptible to it, since they have the strongest innate resistance."

"Which resistance?" Kendall asked, rather thickly. Having managed a terse but precise account of her conversation with Samarin, the girl now seemed to be trying to reject an accompanying revival of emotion through sheer force of will.

"All living creatures have some resistance to magic worked on them—even beneficial castings. Humans have more than animals, and mages the most of all. That's one of the many reasons healing magic is difficult."

"Is that why it seemed to slip off when I hit Smelly with Thought Magic?"

Briefly wondering if Kendall had a nickname for her, Rennyn nodded. "Especially if he was a minor mage. Thought in particular is difficult to use on living people. Not impossible, but it's like trying to hold a greased dish. It's often simpler to work on the environment around a mage."

"I should have pulled the tent down," Kendall said. "I'll remember that."

She did not look a great deal happier than before, but Rennyn allowed her casting to lapse, knowing that there would be no talking Kendall into a happier state.

"I can't guarantee you that what Samarin suggested isn't true," she said. "But I consider it extremely unlikely. And I don't have a method for measuring feelings and deciding whether they are real. You can only choose how to react to them."

Leaving the girl to chew that over, Rennyn walked back to her bedroom, where Illidian sat cross-legged on the floor, finishing up some maintenance stitching on the leather-reinforced clothing he wore when expecting combat.

Settling in a chair next to him, Rennyn had no qualms re-establishing her minor silence and repeating Samarin's words, finishing up with: "I recognised that the Dezart's purpose in trailing us about was primarily to evaluate the Kellian as a potential asset for the Empire. I didn't realise he might consider such a small group of people a threat."

Illidian, who had set aside his mending, said: "A small group of people commanded by one of the most powerful mages in existence? Or, if he actually credits that theory, a group of people who have bewitched such a mage."

"I'm not sure such a thing could even work on me. Not as current head of the Surclere family. It would go against everything Solace intended of that casting to have her heirs in thrall to her bodyguards. I wish I could have heard Samarin directly, to have a better idea of how seriously he took this theory."

"The idea of breeding for magic resistance is new, but it's far from the first time we have been accused of unnatural influence. It's the primary theme of Earl Harkness' campaign."

Illidian's thin voice was entirely calm, but Rennyn had been learning the man she had so hastily married, and could read the slight shifts in his posture. He disliked this suggestion of the Kolan Dezart's extremely.

"Would you prefer to not allow Samarin near Aurai's Rest?"

Since their purpose in visiting the forest settlement was both a point of great sensitivity to the Kellian, and the only thing that had so far caused significant strain between Rennyn and Illidian, she was not at all surprised when he raised an equivocal hand, and said: "I have yet to form a suitable plan to keep him—or a replacement—away. And the Rest itself is no secret."

Rennyn reached out and brushed her fingertips along the side of the hand he had raised. "Perhaps he could sleep through the visit?" she said, with a smile.

"That is tempting." He sat looking up at her, grave. To enspell someone out of convenience walked the near edge of what could be considered justified.

"We will see what happens, then," she said, putting off the problem of Rhael Samarin, just as they had postponed the question of whether she should end the lingering life of the original Kellian.

But the answer—and the consequences—would have to be faced. All too soon.

Chapter Seventeen

Illidian turned his head, listening. Then he rose, and held his hands down to her. "Sarana's group has arrived."

They emerged into the hall at the same time as Sukata, who had clearly heard as well—a neat demonstration of why a silence casting was necessary for a truly private conversation in a Kellian household. The girl's habitual lack of expression did not hide her excitement, for she was near to bouncing as she headed for the stair.

Sukata had come from Kendall's room, and the shorter girl followed along behind, wearing a consciously blank face. Having now a better understanding of what had so disturbed Kendall, Rennyn was fairly certain that whatever overtures Sukata had made had been received with a determination to pretend that nothing whatsoever was wrong—and that Sukata was probably convinced that her own display of temperament was at fault.

Illidian checked as they reached the head of the stair, then leaned down to murmur to Rennyn: "A deputation from Aurai's Rest has come to meet us, and joined them on the road."

There was relief, and just a note of amusement to his words, and Rennyn blinked up at him, then looked down at the crowd. From this angle, a single stranger came to her eye, but it took only a moment to trace a strong resemblance and translate Illidian's observation into: 'My mother is here.'

Darian Faille. Rennyn knew her to be highly respected among the Kellian, and also strongly of the opinion that it was a mistake to live among humans. But since the Kellian were extremely disinclined to force personal opinion on others, she could not be regarded as a leader of a faction against serving as Sentene in Tyrland, but rather simply someone who chose not to do so herself.

Since Kellian were by nature unsmiling, Rennyn was unsurprised when Illidian's introduction produced only a handshake and a moment of direct study. Sukata provided contrast, first hugging her mother and then a second newcomer, a slender girl not quite her own height.

This last prompted Rennyn to look about for Kendall, spotting her sitting almost out of view at the top of the stair. The new arrivals had come at a bad moment, but not seeing anything to be done about it, Rennyn returned her attention to the crowd, and was introduced to the Kellian girl, Tesin Asaka, pretending not to notice the girl's patent wariness whenever she spoke. At least these two removed the lingering concern that her Wicked Uncle was off attacking Aurai's Rest.

Five Sentene pairs had formed Sarana's party, and Rennyn's hired Kolan servants, though told days ago to prepare for the main arrival, took a flustered and overwhelmed attitude toward the task of adding an extra two to this number. Rennyn sorted mentally through the room arrangements, made a quiet suggestion, and then went to sit in her capacious parlour, knowing that Illidian would effortlessly ensure confusion became order.

The arrival of the rest of the expedition brought forward the item on the journey's itinerary that Rennyn particularly didn't want to face, and she wished they'd caught some nearer trace of her Wicked Uncle, so they could put off the visit to Aurai's Rest. Giving the survivors of the original Ten Kellian a choice about their future might be both right and necessary, but her own discomfort at her role was compounded by the impact it would have on Illidian.

All of the Kellian struggled not to shrink from what she represented. Killing the Ten, no matter how kindly, was not going to improve Rennyn's relationship with the Kellian descendants. Nor Illidian, even though he had raised the possibility in the first place. How could it not place another pressure, another strain on their marriage?

That wasn't each broaching the question of the impact of the death of the original golems on Solace's casting was something she could not approach with any measure of pragmatism. Would it be easier for the Kellian if the enchantment was broken, and they became a more ordinary sort of people? Would their personalities change?

Who would she be married to?

This vexed thought was interrupted by movement at the half-open door, and the arrival of a determinedly-brisk Kendall with a tray.

"Hope you're not planning to keep these numb-suck servants on," the girl said. "They're as useless as a shed-full of hens after you've said 'boo'."

"It is unfortunate that we arrested a person who seems to have been the mainstay of the household," Rennyn agreed, looking over the tray with interest. "But these are only a temporary engagement. Whoever makes these nut cakes can stay—I don't care about the rest of them. It's a bit complicated, since I don't know how long we'll be away."

"You're not going to pay them to kick their heels here while we go north?"

"Perhaps a partial staff. Leaving it unoccupied strikes me as unwise."

"Leave the Pest behind to lord it over them. He can finish cataloguing your library." Kendall's eyes narrowed, and Rennyn realised her own expression must have changed. "Finally sorry you brought him along?"

"I don't think it would be very safe to leave any of our group alone," Rennyn said. "We haven't managed to be very quiet on this trip."

"You think That Monster might have heard?"

"All too likely," Rennyn said, looking up as Illidian came into the room, escorting his mother and Sarana Illuma. "Though I admit to a tendency to see my Wicked Uncle in every shadow, to blame him for encounters with Eferum-Get, and suspect him of taking to kidnapping mages."

"Kidnapping?" Sarana said, nodding acceptance when Rennyn held up an empty cup.

While Rennyn poured tea, Illidian gave Kendall a glance that sent the girl reluctantly from the room, then briefly recounted the Emperor's warning.

"You believe this Helecho Montjuste-Surclere to be responsible for the disappearances?" Darian Faille asked.

"I believe that...it is not wise to underestimate my Wicked Uncle," Rennyn said. "A mage born in the Eferum, a blood-drinker, and inventive. He is capable of posing an enormous threat, and it seems to me that these disappearances constitute the loss of Kole's strongest defenders."

"A prelude to an Eferum-Get invasion?" Sarana said, and almost visibly began to plan defences and counter-attacks.

"Would you know Prince Helecho if he changed his appearance?" Illidian asked, accepting a cup of tea.

Rennyn, turning this over, abruptly remembered Kendall, in an exaggerated imitation of Rhael Samarin's amused confidence, saying: "I expect I'm even younger than you think." Rennyn had repeated that to Illidian and he must be thinking of it in connection to her Wicked Uncle, whose age was a somewhat uncertain matter thanks to the time-distorting nature of the Eferum. She met his eyes, startled, then said:

"No, not necessarily. An illusion I would spot, but features can be altered in the same way a wound is healed, and there would be no trace of that once the initial casting was done. But I'd certainly notice an inability to go outside during the day. I suppose it's possible that my Wicked Uncle will eventually adapt to this world and become more tolerant of sunlight, but I'd be astonished if he had already reached the point where it was not fatal to him."

Still, making himself part of their expedition was the sort of thing Rennyn suspected her uncle would find highly entertaining. Nor should she dismiss the chance that he had found a way to tolerate sunlight, just because she did not think it possible.

"I will ask Lieutenant Meniar to cast the divination more frequently. And think on a shorter-range casting looking specifically for my Wicked Uncle, in case he has abandoned my focus." She could not suppress a faint grimace, since she would not at all like to use the one tangible symbol of him she had at hand. But she refused to shy away from any of the unpleasant necessities in store from her, so let out her breath slowly, then said to Sarana: "When do you want to leave?"

oOo

"I value my life too much to suggest it in the hearing of the Imperial Guard, but this is by far the most well-defended household in Koletor."

Blinking her way out of a light doze, Rennyn frowned at Rhael Samarin, framed in the parlour doorway by two of the recently arrived Sentene: Mede

Lankor and her mage partner, Rundl Hynes, clearly entertaining doubts about letting Samarin near her.

"Would you like us to stay, Your Grace?" Rundl asked.

"No, but thank you," Rennyn said, adding a reassuring smile and hiding her annoyance that two tiny silence castings had made her miss the conclusion of the discussion about the proposed journey north. Illidian must have taken his mother and Sarana upstairs.

"I think this is the first time I've seen you alone," Samarin said, sitting down and studying her with all his usual self-possession.

Rennyn rubbed her eyes before looking him over in turn. She had been half-expecting a private conversation with Illidian's mother—had had a strong impression that there was something Darian wanted to say to her—but she should perhaps be less surprised that Darian Faille, with typical Kellian reticence, had let her be.

"It provides a good opportunity to have words on the subject of teasing my students," she said to Samarin, and was surprised when his faint near-constant smile faded, and he responded gravely.

"Yes, I misjudged there. Instead of minor mischief, a heart's blow. I am sorry for that, though it does not make the question any less valid."

"You take the idea seriously?"

"I take a great many things seriously. You don't feel the possibility is worth consideration?"

"I don't see anything in the spell construction, and if there's any active enchantment of that sort, it's one beyond my ability to detect."

Mindful of Mede Lankor posted just outside the room, Rennyn did not go into the subject further, and asked Samarin, instead, if he had any further information on the disappearances.

"Verisia has missed a mage as well," Samarin said, promptly. "You know of Thyla Hettan?"

"Specialised in mage-wrought bridges?"

"Gone a little under a fortnight ago. The report did not detail whether she was wearing her focus at the time, but I've confirmed that the Kolan mages all were. It is not necessarily an important factor, since it's rare to find a powerful mage not wearing a focus, but a point worth noting."

"Does your Emperor wear a focus?"

A tiny pause, and then Samarin nodded.

Rennyn thought about all the things her inventive Wicked Uncle might do, then said: "Would you be able to tell if Corusar had been replaced? I don't mean the old stories about how he died long ago, and his voice is simply mimicked by hidden Court officials. I mean replaced."

Samarin's wide mouth twitched, but then he went still, and a frown grew on his youthful face.

"I am quite certain he has not been," he said, at last. "As are you, I think, because your sensitivity to worked magic is said to be acute, so it must have been apparent to you that the throne room enchantments have been in place for a very long time. If something occurred while I made an interesting trip into the northern forests, I suspect my discovery of any substitution would be shortly followed by my swift removal from play."

"Could a replacement be achieved without the Court's notice?"

Samarin raised an equivocal hand. "It would take someone of your calibre, but with rather more knowledge of Kole, and extended access. The problem would be that the next powerful mage who sought audience would surely notice the re-set enchantments, especially if they had visited before. And it would be noticed if all the greater mages were suddenly refused audience."

"Unless they had all vanished."

He nodded, but then made a dismissive gesture. "If someone were to try to take Kole's throne, I would be astonished if they did so by assuming the Emperor's Preservation. Few have a taste for such a...rigid definition of immortality."

"No. I am surprised..." she began, and stopped.

Her Imperial audience had been conducted both without notice, and with disconcerting efficiency. Tired and headachy, Rennyn had not given the enchantments surrounding Corusar the attention she would in more propitious circumstances. Glancing back at the Dezart, she found him relaxed but watching her steadily. She knew little about this young man, but the one thing his title made clear was the Emperor's trust. The confidence of a barely-human Emperor whose rule had long been sustained by a casting that surely must be wearing thin.

Was it missing mages, the Kellian, or something else that had seen Samarin joined to her entourage?

"I loathe politics," she said, with a sigh. "But I have a great interest in magic. I hope I can assist the Emperor with the problem you are investigating without becoming too entangled in matters that don't concern me."

Rennyn stood up, and Samarin rose politely as well, and paused as she dealt with the dizziness that standing often chose to inflict on her.

"Some problems have a way of tangling even the most disinterested," he said, and offered her his arm.

Chapter Eighteen

Four days in coaches had taken them far into northern Kole, among the small settlements on the edge of the great forest of Semarrak. Smooth Imperial roads gave way to narrow lanes, and Duchess Surclere and her escort were finally obliged to switch to horses to approach the forest itself. Fallon enjoyed the riding well enough, but found himself firmly wishing they were still in the coaches, where Kendall had been safely sectioned off from Dezart Samarin.

Kendall Stockton was undoubtedly the most cross-grained girl he had ever met, but Fallon had felt sorry she had been so hurt or frightened or whatever had made her spend the past week barely talking. Most of the morning she had continued to hold her tongue, contenting herself with glaring at the Dezart whenever he strayed too close. But after they had set out again following midday break, she waited until the Dezart's horse came alongside hers, then said:

"Why is this Emperor of yours so convinced that only he can look after Kole?"

They were not travelling with the full group—the majority of the Sentene had gone ahead at a faster pace—but Fallon was singularly aware of almost everyone around him suppressing a reaction to the clear intention to attack in Kendall's tone. Not that Dezart Samarin seemed bothered by the question. Fallon, riding behind Kendall's roan, could only glimpse the man's profile, but thought he looked pleased.

"Does the Emperor strike you as conceited?" the Dezart asked. "The Empire was in turmoil at the time of his ascension, you know, and assassination attempts almost inevitable. After the legitimate heirs of the Tashant line fell in the Tysian War, there were many near-equal claimants to the Lion Throne, and the order of inheritance much disputed. Kole proclaimed nearly a dozen Emperors and Empresses in as many years—every precaution failing to protect them. After so much uncertainty, the Preservation was considered a triumph."

"But why be Emperor at all? He can't have wanted to make himself into a statue. To not ever eat or sleep or have any fun. Rennyn said he can't even take it off, without dying."

Duchess Surclere, riding double with Captain Faille, glanced back, then nodded.

"Very unlikely to survive the removal, at any rate," she said, without any hint in her tone that Kendall shouldn't be asking such things of the Emperor's personal representative. Duchess Surclere really was extraordinarily tolerant of Kendall's cheek.

But Dezart Samarin didn't seem to mind either. "I think you'd find the Lion Throne is difficult to run away from."

"If he's so fancy a mage as to think up that lobster shell thing, that means he's a deviser, right? You're not going to tell me that he couldn't find some way to make it look like he died, so someone else was stuck with being Emperor?"

"Lobster..." Dezart Samarin broke off, though it looked to Fallon that he was struggling with laughter, not anger.

"But he stayed," Kendall continued, relentlessly. "And put himself somewhere he can't get down. That's not something you do for yourself—that's what you get when someone thinks it's important, necessary, for them and only them, to do something."

The quick glance she threw forward to Duchess Surclere made clear the comparison Kendall was drawing.

"The Emperor's thoughts on the subject aren't recorded," was all the Dezart said.

"It's widely believed that Corusar had nothing but the Empire left to live for," Fallon offered, then cursed his eager tongue when Dezart Samarin turned to consider him.

But the Dezart simply nodded. "The Emperor's family had been killed some years before, during one of the more extravagant spates of poisonings," he explained to Kendall. "Is it such a mark of pride, to not walk away from your responsibilities?"

"Being born doesn't make you responsible for something," Kendall replied. "No matter what anyone else says, you have to choose to start giving people orders. Your Emperor made it so he can't even step down."

"And the Empire has flourished."

"I'm not certain, even ignoring the preservation casting, that Corusar *could* step down," Fallon said carefully. "Not without starting up the succession wars again. There's an official heir, but I guess even more people now who could claim to be next in line."

"There is a carefully mapped out succession, along with three regional governors who have been directed to manage any transition," Dezart Samarin said. But then he shrugged, and added: "Still, ambition is a snake that turns in the hand."

Kendall sniffed, but before she could launch another sally, Sukata had taken advantage of a widening of the lane to ride between Kendall and Dezart Samarin's horses.

"We are coming to the edge of the Nymery Steading," she said, thin voice determinedly clear. "When we crest this rise, we will see the forest proper."

"You have been through this area before?" Dezart Samarin asked, courteous but with a faintly disappointed air, as if he had wanted to see what Kendall would come up with next.

"I lived here until I was seven," Sukata explained.

Kendall didn't say anything. Since that day in the market, she always either went silent around Sukata, or was carefully polite. It really was quite unfair of Kendall to not forgive her friend for being out of temper over that Sigillic exercise. Fallon hadn't enjoyed that at all either, even though Duchess Surclere hadn't lectured them for relying too much on the standard forms. But it had been painfully embarrassing to realise how far they were falling short of her expectations.

He dropped back a little further, since the mare Sukata was riding had shown herself particularly intolerant of being followed closely, then let himself dwell on expectations for a while.

He had to be careful: whenever he thought too much about the unique divination the Duchess had created, and the possibility that it was Auri the Duchess had detected, his breathing suffered. He'd had years of practice in turning his mind firmly to safe subjects, but his head was too full of possibilities, of imagining what the Duchess would do with the divination, and what he could safely say.

Auri was less hopeful: she thought it coincidence that the tune the Duchess had been hearing was the same as the one she'd been humming the night of the attempted theft. Probably, she said, she had heard the same thing Duchess Surclere had been listening to. Even so, she'd finally agreed to go hum at the divination the next time the Duchess set it—something sadly not likely until they reached the forest settlement of the Kellian.

Fallon had not yet fully worked out why they were even going to this "Rest", other than to give their Kellian escort a chance to visit the place. It was more than that, though, or they wouldn't be risking Duchess Surclere to the trip. A carriage was impossible on this road, and a cart would be a jouncing punishment: even the gentle amble on horseback took its toll, which was why the Duchess rode with Lord Surclere. He would hold her before him when she began to tire.

The slow pace grated, since Fallon was so anxious for the Duchess to re-establish the special divination. He sighed softly, and made himself think of something else, then noticed that the younger Kellian girl, Tesin Asaka, had strayed up beside him. Her direct gaze was assessing, so he hastily groped for something to say.

"Do you have trouble getting Circle Turners to come all the way into the forest?" he asked, referring to the minor mages who travelled through all the small towns and villages renewing their protective circles.

"That was a problem for a time," she replied. "It's not necessary now, since my mother is living there."

"Did you have a mage when the settlement was first established?"

"No. The Ten kept watch, and killed any Eferum-Get that came near."

Fallon blinked at this simple solution. Circles were islands of safety from the night's stalking death, and to sleep outside was suicide. Even in Tyrland, where the Sentene so effectively dealt with emergent Eferum-Get, there were always the filmy, drifting life-stealers: slow and weak and doom to the unwary and unprotected. In the early days of the Eferum-Get invasion, it was said that all people could do was travel by night and sleep during the day, and pray to the departed gods that they did not encounter Eferum-Get they could not outpace.

Kellian, however... Fallon glanced ahead, remembering how Sukata had strode through the market, fuming and ablaze and glorious. Yes, he could readily believe ten Kellian capable of dealing with every Thing nights in the forest had thrown at them.

He wanted to ask more, but decided against it, knowing well that too much interest in Kellian would be a mark against any nephew of his uncle. And then his gelding reached the crest of the rise, and he forgot everything but the forest.

Semarrak was famously dangerous. The few forest settlements had been overrun during the first years of the incursions, and Kole's method of dealing with Eferum-Get using periodic large-scale sweeps had not meshed well with a boundless woodland. The Eferum invaders, left to themselves, had either died or adapted, and now Kole's north had a surfeit of predators quite happy to hunt during the day—and, apparently, more human-like creatures with Eferum origins. Those, though, were said to hide in Semarrak's heart.

At any rate, the forest was famed for the creatures that dwelled within it—not even mentioning Kellian— but staring north, Fallon felt that it should be better-known for its trees.

Dark trunks rose in a wall, disdaining frippery considerations such as undergrowth or bordering woodlands. A herd of cows, placed conveniently close to the forest edge, offered perspective, should it not already be clear that these were trees to make specks of men: wider and taller than any that Fallon had ever seen. Yet they didn't spear directly for the sky, but lolled and sprawled, as if resting on their elbows beneath their glorious autumn crowns.

The road through the forest proved to be wide enough to almost accommodate continuing to ride side-by-side—in part because there was so little undergrowth. It wound through a sea of golden leaves, circling broad trunks, and occasionally picking its way over miniature mountain ranges of root systems. The air was also noticeably cooler and damper, prompting a brief pause to ensure the Duchess was properly wrapped. Above, as distant as the ceiling of a great hall, the canopy glowed brilliant red and yellow in the afternoon light, but little warmth broke through to the ground.

"Do you get many traders coming this way?" Fallon asked Tesin Asaka, who he suspected was keeping to the end of the string of horses to act as rear guard. Even though she must be not more than twelve or thirteen, he had no doubt she was more than capable of fulfilling the role.

"Not to the Rest," Tesin replied. "We travel in to Theal quite regularly, though, and pack back what we need." Her brightly interested eyes were focused on Dezart Samarin, who was in turn studying Sukata. "They do not quite like us in Theal, but they like the trade goods we bring out from the Rest. I cannot yet decide whether the Imperial Army arriving to billet so many horses in readiness for us will have raised or lowered us in the town's estimation."

"Was local distrust the reason the Kellian settled in Semarrak?"

"That and economics." Tesin glanced up alertly as several small birds emerged briefly from the canopy, darting for insects. "There are varieties of fungus and certain trees that only seem to grow in Semarrak. The forest's edge is picked clean of them, but we have little difficulty reaching far better harvesting points. Aurai led the Ten to see the doubled value of settling here."

"*Who*?"

The girl blinked once at Fallon's tone, but answered with unimpeded calm. "It is Aurai that the Rest is named for. She was the Ten's teacher and guide for many years."

"Oh." Someone in the past, who had travelled with the original Kellian golems? Fallon, aware of Sukata glancing back, pushed everything but simple fact out of his head and said in a throat only a little constricted: "That—my sister's name was Aurienne. We called her Auri."

"I see," Tesin said, though plainly she did not fully understand his reaction. "The Ten's Voice was Lenaurai, originally."

This time startled response came from ahead of them. Dezart Samarin had slewed around in his saddle in a rare moment of open surprise. The Dezart's mount's reaction to his distracted grip on the reins postponed an explanation, but soon enough he turned again to Tesin and said:

"Aurai's Rest was founded by Lenaurai Falcy?"

"You know of her?" It was Sukata who asked.

"She's mentioned in the Imperial histories," the Dezart said, resuming his usual light tones. "How interesting to know what happened to her. Did, ah, your Aurai leave any descendants?"

"Not going to turn out to be the lost heir of the Empire or anything is she?" Fallon said, then instantly regretted it. And he had been criticising Kendall for saying incautious things to the Imperial representative!

Fortunately, Dezart Samarin took this with his usual good humour. "Rather the opposite," he said.

"Why does it matter if she had descendants?" Tesin asked.

"If I count my generations correctly, it doesn't," the Dezart said, more than confusingly. "Which makes the question only idle curiosity."

"Aurai had three children," Sukata said, calmly. "There are many among us who can trace our lines to them."

"I shall have to add a footnote," was all Dezart Samarin said to that, which was not at all a satisfying response, but neither Sukata nor Tesin pressed him, and then a glimpse of a small stone building ahead provided a distraction.

This was not the Rest, apparently another day's travel into the forest, but a traveller's shelter surrounded by a circle not large enough to accommodate all their horses.

"Aren't they likely to be attacked?" Fallon asked Tesin, as he helped prepare pickets for the horses in a well-trammelled clearing just outside the circle. "The creatures here hunt more than humans, right?"

"We would sense a predator's approach. And the first group intended to sweep as they travelled, to clear the way."

The Kellian girl, with a stake in one hand and hammer in the other, paused to gaze back at the shelter, and at Duchess Surclere standing with Lord Surclere. Fallon was not yet adept at reading minimal Kellian expressions, but he recognised this as thoughtful evaluation backed by banked intensity, for almost all the Kellian looked at Duchess Surclere like that. He did not doubt he'd have equally complex reactions to someone whose commands he literally could not disobey. In fact, given that he kept trying to will his teacher into producing an answer to a question he dared not ask, his own expression might not be all that dissimilar.

Had she started to guess there was a question? To hear Auri, trapped on the edge of existence?

He let his breath out in a slow hiss, sternly putting these thoughts aside and mentally reciting Verisian verse for all the remainder of the fleeting afternoon.

Then, after evening meal, he curled up in a corner of the small but by that time pleasantly warm hut as early as he could feasibly excuse himself.

He had been thinking about it too much: the conversation he would have with Duchess Surclere once she understood enough to start it. By now he was confident that there was at least a chance she could stop him dying, at that most dangerous point, but her physical weakness remained one of the biggest barriers to his own survival. It would be best if she dealt with this Eferum-Get uncle before learning of Auri.

Sighing, Fallon drifted into the Dream, and watched his sister inspect the well-built but cramped shelter before wandering outside to marvel at the trees. The two lieutenants were removing nose bags from the horses, while Lord Surclere's mother was bringing extra water from a nearby stream.

"Everything's so *huge*," Auri said, bounding lightly up to try to stand on a tree limb arcing over the stream. "You could practically ride along these branches. Were you attacked by anything on the way here?"

Auri addressed questions to Fallon even when she hadn't brought him into the Dream and, if he remembered, he answered them in the daily diary. Hopefully he would have more room at the Kellian settlement so he could leave the book propped open.

"Why is he upset?" Auri asked now, having jumped down to peer up into Lieutenant Meniar's face. "Did he argue with his partner?"

Fallon's dreaming mind did not react quickly enough to do more than note the Lieutenant's distracted frown, as Auri moved restlessly on to circle through the horses, examining them critically, and declaring a long-necked bay her favourite.

"She looks like she has a lot of personality. I bet she nips the other horses, just to make mischief."

Sukata's touchy mare. Fallon wouldn't be surprised at all if she nipped as well as kicked. Auri stroked the mare as best she could, but as usual there was no reaction. Even cats and dogs—and Kellian—failed to sense the bored girl trying to win their attention.

A circuit of the far limits of Auri's reach flushed no hidden predators, but the sprawling immensity of the trees kept her entertained, along with attempts to bound through piles of fallen leaves. They did seem to rustle minutely when she kicked, just as still water would hold a suggestion of a quiver. Back home, Fallon had once set out a big bowl of water, in the hopes that Auri would be able to establish a yes/no communication with their father, but Father had not noticed at all, and Fallon had woken exhausted.

Trailing back to the shelter, Auri straightened abruptly. "Is he in trouble?" she asked, and hurried ahead almost gleefully to make an invisible fourth in a ring around Dezart Samarin.

The others in the circle were Lord Surclere, Darian Faille and Lieutenant Faral: all three adult Kellian in the Duchess' current entourage, trying not to loom. At least, two were: Darian Faille seemed quite inclined to loom, standing directly in front of the Dezart, holding his gaze.

"You'd think he'd look a little nervous," Auri observed. "*I* would be, if anyone stood over me like that. And that's not even counting claws that could cut me open."

But the Dezart, as usual, appeared primarily entertained by the encounter, and was saying: "I've no objection at all. Did Hirel Falcy not tell your forebears anything of her past?"

"Hirel?" Darian Faille repeated.

"An honorific," Lord Surclere said. "It means teacher." He took a step back then, and indicated some handily arranged stones beside the path to the stream. "Please. This sounds a longer story than anticipated."

"Who is this Falcy person?" Auri asked, then made a confused face when Lord Surclere told the Dezart that 'Aurai' had never spoken of her past, beyond that she had been a bond servant who had abandoned her post before completing her contracted period.

"Entirely true," Dezart Samarin said, after they had settled on the stones, his faint smile easing away in the face of so much Kellian gravity. "Lenaurai Falcy was a bond-servant to Emperor Arav, tasked with instructing his children in the sword arts."

"Which one was Emperor Arav?" Auri asked, as the Kellian reacted only with added stillness. "Oh, wait, I know—he was the one who was going to invade Tyrland, back when the Black Queen was in charge."

"Emperor Arav had quite a number of children," Dezart Samarin was saying. "Three by his wife, and a good dozen 'secondary' heirs. Being sent to Hirel Falcy's class was a kind of acknowledgement of parentage, for he expected a great deal of his children, and retained the absolute best to instruct them."

"Didn't Emperor Arav once have an entire town pegged up at night outside their circle, just because a statue of him was allowed to fall over?" Auri said, poking her fingers casually into the Dezart's eyes. "Why are they acting so solemn over ancient history?"

Oblivious, Samarin continued. "The Emperor himself was an excellent swordsman, and once a month he would have his children match him, to gauge how they were progressing. Wooden swords, and many bruises, and further punishment if you wept. He was particularly exacting with his heir, Kyrus." The Dezart shrugged. "They hated each other and, given the Emperor's temperament, it was perhaps inevitable that one day the Emperor would cast aside the practice weapon, draw his sword, and attack Kyrus in earnest."

"And Kyrus defeated him. This is known." There was just a note of uncertainty in Lieutenant Faral's voice.

"So the histories tell us," Dezart Samarin agreed. "And so the more than dozen children who witnessed the fight told the Court: Kyrus had fought with their father and their father had died. After which, Kyrus drew the severed haft of the practice sword from his father's body, and declared 'I did this' most firmly. Since Arav was feared and loathed almost universally by that point, this direct route to taking the throne brought no repercussions, and gave Kyrus a reputation for strength that was most useful in the early days of his rule."

"And he sent Aurai away to protect the lie," Darian Faille said, her words very quiet.

The Dezart's faint smile briefly reappeared. "For protection, at least. He had no guarantee that every one of his many brothers and sisters would always remain silent, and indeed in later years there was more than one who, at least in their cups, hinted heavily that there was a reason their teacher vanished one night soon after Kyrus was declared Emperor.

"If Kyrus had started with a fuller mastery of Imperial bureaucracy, he would have not been so concerned about drawing attention to his teacher, and simply created an excuse to nullify the contract. Sending her away broke bond to the Imperial service, and automatically made Hirel Falcy outlaw. That meant being dragged back and a great deal of whipping, in those days. Not so dramatic as the penalty for killing the Emperor, of course. That would have been Hirel Falcy's death, and death to all her family, and death to her line." He cocked his head to one side, meeting Darian Faille's fixed gaze with unimpaired calm.   "Unto the seventh generation, which is why, even among a rather long-lived people, this discussion is one of curiosity, not consequence. Is it not?"

The Dezart stood then, nodded politely, and walked off to the little stone shelter.

"Wasn't all this three hundred years ago?" Auri said. "Why are they all so grim? Not that they aren't endlessly grim anyway, and, really, I don't think much of your Duchess' taste.   This Kolan's much more interesting."

Kellian often talked in a language of hand signals, so Fallon could not guess what Lieutenant Faral said before she walked off to re-check the horses, but Darian Faille said one thing out loud to her son before following:

"I hope the Rest survives your visitors."

Lord Surclere, expressionless as usual, returned inside, and Auri trailed him, and listened to less interesting conversations until everyone inside went to sleep. Then she again explored that day's bounds of her existence, hunting hidden birds and animals, and making little games trying to jump between branches that barely held any substance for her. And all the while chattering on and on: an eternal, one-sided conversation, heard only in a dream.

Chapter Nineteen

After determinedly avoiding all discussion of Aurai's Rest, Rennyn had not known whether to expect a crude collection of shacks or a fortress. Instead, the road opened upon a garden-festooned hill: an uneven oval narrower and lower to the east, while the west rose to a high, bare crest above steep terraces. Although there were smaller trees, the space was clear of the vast Semarrak oaks, with the hill rising like an island above a sea of gold.

"Glorious," she murmured.

Rennyn felt more than saw Illidian's approval. "Spring and autumn at the Rest are incomparable. I have missed seeing this."

He had been born here. All of the Kellian had been born at the Rest. Even after the majority had chosen to dwell in Tyrland, they travelled to the forest settlement to bear their children, and raise them away from the pressure of people who were afraid of even half-grown Kellian.

It was certainly not a hand-to-mouth childhood. The buildings—finely crafted in stone and wood—clustered down at the eastern end of the hill, and were surrounded not only by crops, but by areas of garden and lawn bounded by the inlaid path of stone that marked a well-maintained protective circle. A river curved close, but of course did not cross the circle, and there was even a water wheel turning lazily.

"How many families live here?" Dezart Samarin asked, drawing his horse level with Illidian's.

"There are eighteen adults and four children," Illidian said, evenly. "But the Rest supported more than thirty families when permission to serve Tyrland was sought from King Theum."

"And you simply keep watch and kill any predators that stray close?"

"If necessary. There are caves beneath the hill, and we bring all the animals into them at night. The buildings are sturdy, and it is only in years where food is particularly low that the slashers or keenwolves will attempt direct assaults."

"How very interesting," Samarin said. "The surveyors who continue to insist that Semarrak is uninhabitable are perhaps broaching a less civilised part of the forest."

He did enjoy fomenting mischief, this peculiar Kolan, who could not be anything but fully aware of how little he was wanted in this placc. Illidian had once told her that Tyrland was home to the Kellian, but it had long been clear that Aurai's Rest held an equal claim. Here alone in all the world was a place made by and for them, where no-one would say they did not belong. Why remind them of the Empire's technical claim over the forest?

The tingle of a clear and strong protection distracted Rennyn as they crossed into the settlement circle, and another piece of mischief surfaced in her memory. Breeding for magic.

She set that aside. If she was going to expend her energy on doubt over the reasons for her marriage, her ability to control the Kellian would trump all other factors. Her bloodline had been an unseen keystone since the Kellian had first become a people rather than tools. The Kellian had recoiled from that knowledge, but then adapted and forced themselves to face the ramifications of the Symbolic Magic that defined their core. But Illidian had been drawn to her before he had known what she had inherited, and had not let it keep him from her.

What would become of this place, dependent as it was on Kellian speed and instinct, when they tested the boundaries of their existence?

As the inhabitants of Aurai's Rest emerged to greet their arrival, Rennyn leaned back against Illidian's chest, and dropped one hand to the arm curled lightly around her waist. He shifted so he could briefly lace his fingers through hers, squeezing in silent reassurance before they dismounted and faced the business of greetings, and the wary regard of those who had not met her before, and who were trying to be polite, and to hide their horror. There were three non-Kellian among them, working especially hard to keep their expressions welcoming.

After Rennyn had been fully overwhelmed by names and faces, the travellers were shown to rooms, and paused in the business of settling in for Lieutenant Meniar to cast the focus divination yet again, and establish that her Wicked Uncle was still north and east of their location. But certainly not at Aurai's Rest itself.

"How is your strength?" Darian Faille asked, having observed this process without comment. "Do you wish to sleep?"

"I think I'll last until dinner," Rennyn said, taking stock of herself. She had dozed a little on the highly undemanding ride, and at least did not feel like she would drop.

"Then I will show you the Rest."

Was Darian, Rennyn wondered, creating an opportunity for the other Kellian to do much the same thing as the Sentene mages had: talk to Illidian away from the Montjuste-Surclere heir he had so hastily married, to reassure themselves that it was something he had truly chosen? Given that there were many among the Sentene mages yet to be convinced, Rennyn resigned herself to the continuing distrust, and followed her mother by marriage.

Not unexpectedly, Darian was considerate and polite, taking Rennyn on an undemanding tour of the central buildings of Aurai's Rest. The settlement was tidy, most of it arranged around the eastern base of the hill, but while the shared kitchens and dining areas reminded Rennyn of the Kellian barracks back in Asentyr, the creators of Aurai's Rest had imbued everything with an elegance of form and a regard for craftsmanship that elevated the settlement to a precious object in itself.

There continued to be a sense of restraint about Darian, the shadow of words unsaid. Rennyn, aware of unfamiliar awkwardness, sought for a neutral topic.

"Who designed the Rest?"

"The Ten." Darian surveyed the roofs of the main buildings as she led the way up a bricked path. "Veya and Tio in particular."

Rennyn blinked, then counted from one to five in Verisian: "Ala, Tio, Seya, Nal, Veya?"

"Yes. Aurai's response to ten near-identical women who had no names for themselves."

"Was Aurai Verisian?"

"She came from the border country," Darian said, keeping her pace slow as Rennyn followed her up another section of the gently winding path. "Though we still know almost nothing of her family."

Having had Dezart Samarin's revelations passed on to her, Rennyn suspected she understood the troubled note in this last remark. Nor was she surprised when Darian added:

"Illidian looks worn."

"Yes." Pointless to deny such an obvious fact. "Nightmares. And caring for me has been a great deal of work." Rennyn concentrated on walking, as the gentle climb began to take its toll. "I think that the threat Prince Helecho poses is also weighing on him. There's so little we can do to find him, and yet we cannot be sure he is not hunting us."

"From what I understand, this Eferum-Get Prince's most logical course is to avoid anyone who knows his identity. Is he not more likely to keep safely away from you?"

"He seemed the sort to spend several years looking forward to surprising me at an unprotected moment," Rennyn said judiciously. "But not, perhaps, if he cannot do so without risk. Tyrland was his mother's obsession, and I just entertainment along the way. Though that's perhaps wishful thinking. I don't relish meeting him again, even to put an end to him."

Darian accepted this admission of cowardice without comment, and they walked on for several steps before the Kellian woman, unhurried and unsparing, said:

"I was concerned at the haste of your marriage. Illidian has explained the reason for it. Do you truly believe that Tyrland's Queen would have forced you to wed her heir to gain control of us?"

"I believe it inevitable that the advantages of such a marriage would have occurred to Tyrland's Court, if not the Queen. How Queen Astranelle would have acted, I cannot say. From what I've seen of her, she is firm on matters of importance, but stays aloof from what she considers minor issues."

Darian fell silent, and did not attempt to continue the uncomfortable and stilted conversation until their path ended at a door framed by an arch set into the hill, the finely-wrought stone shaped into a series of interconnecting leaves. An entrance to one of the caves?

"And yet you left your brother in their control."

Rennyn blinked, and worked to bring her mind to order, resenting the sapping weariness that the short walk had produced. "Seb is far less tractable than he appears."

Darian did not argue the point, instead pulling the door open to reveal a smooth-sided tunnel.

"This is the heart of the Rest," the Kellian woman said, her faint voice thinning further, as if the tunnel was stealing it away. "Ordinarily I would not bring one not of our blood here, but there are more reasons than marriage to make an exception. Will you greet them?"

"If you wish it," Rennyn said, not succeeding in hiding a certain tightness that had crept into her throat. Clearly Darian had a reason for bringing her unprepared to face the women Rennyn's family had abandoned.

The tunnel curved downward, and soon opened out into a much larger space. There was no need to conjure light: a combination of mageglows and braziers picked out the edges of a fan-shaped cave wide enough to hold dozens. It was warm and dry, and the walls had been hung with geometrically patterned cloth, but it was still unmistakably a tomb.

Eleven stone coffins. They were arranged in a semi-circle in the centre of the cave, their stone bases patterned with twists of vine, sprays of blossom, birds. Two were sealed.

Rennyn, overwhelmingly aware of the reason the Kellian had asked her to come Aurai's Rest, stepped forward until she stood at the foot of the seventh coffin in the curve. Creamy linen covered the occupant to the waist and one long, sharp-nailed hand rested on its edge while the second curled against the cheek of its owner in an attitude of deep sleep. A bed of white sand glimmered beneath those fingers, making the container no less a coffin, but at least more comfortable than an uncushioned box of stone.

Looking left, past the sealed central coffin, Rennyn studied with some difficulty faces that seemed to fade in the gentle light. Identical, with only slight variations in hair, and in the positions in which they lay. Not mirrors of Solace: the faces were longer, with a spare and lean aspect that their creator had not owned. But the resemblance was unmistakeable and entirely expected, for these women had been an extension of Queen Solace's body, copies of her, but with Symbolic Magic altering more than just colouring.

"Dew, dawn and cobweb," Rennyn said aloud.

Darian Faille ignored this, filling a small bowl from a bronze jug by the door, and moving to the first of the sleeping women. Dipping her fingers into the bowl, which contained what Rennyn guessed to be honey-water, she transferred a tiny amount. Like Illidian before Solace's attack, Darian did not trim the pointed nails of either hand, and the drops fell from their tips to the woman's mouth.

Rennyn neither spoke again, nor moved to assist, watching instead for any hint of reaction to demonstrate that these women were alive. If they breathed, they did so imperceptibly, but Rennyn noticed a small shift of a head, and a flicker of eyelid. Dreaming?

What would the Ten dream of? Not Tyrland, surely. More likely of raising children in a dangerous and beautiful forest, or even of Aurai, whose centrally-positioned tomb declared her role in the lives of these Kellian.

Darian Faille, returning the bowl to a nook by the entrance, moved to the exit, and Rennyn followed her outside, shivering a little at the late afternoon chill. Darian closed the door, and they stood looking down at the settlement the Ten had created.

"I suspect I would have enjoyed knowing Aurai," Rennyn said. "I am glad the Ten found a friend in her."

"A fortunate encounter," Darian agreed. "There are many who would have used them as tools, but Aurai was by nature a teacher, and became the Ten's guide, never more than suggesting paths. In all the history of the Kellian, we have never elected or acknowledged a leader."

"It seems to me there are some among you who are more inclined to...organise than others," Rennyn said, as neutrally as she could manage.

"Yes," Darian said. "And in the structures of Tyrland's Sentene some of us are set above the others, but only in the matter of directing the activities of defence, and strictly on the understanding that Kellian can leave the Sentene at any time. Have you considered what a child of your marriage will bring?"

So this was what had been preoccupying the Kellian woman. Rennyn had thought that passing her inherited control to a child born to a Kellian would ease some of their dismay, but it was clear that the idea of a Kellian Surclere dismayed Illidian's mother.

"I am not a leader of the Kellian," she said. "Nor would inherited power make a child of mine the leader of the Kellian."

"But what could be more natural than for other outsiders to treat a Montjuste-Surclere Kellian as pre-eminent? To expect leadership. To be dragged into making decisions on behalf of others. What will that do to the child?"

Rennyn had been standing for too long. Or perhaps she simply had no energy for contemplating problems she could not possibly solve. She looked about, and found a long, flat stone to perch upon.

"Are you suggesting I should not have children?"

"I cannot make such choices for you. But I would be lax not to bring the consequences to your attention."

Which was as close as a Kellian would come to pushing. Rennyn suspected it hadn't been easy for Darian to do.

"Thank you for telling me," she said. "It's not a present concern, since the healers tell me I shouldn't risk trying to have a child unless my health improves, but it's something I'll need to keep in mind." Looking down, she saw that Illidian was approaching, and let out her breath in quiet relief.

"My initial plan was to have nothing to do with the Kellian after Solace had been dealt with," she added. "Thus avoiding a great many complications."

"But perhaps creating new ones," Illidian said, sitting down beside her. "You have been greeting the Ten?"

Rennyn had made no greetings, and did not feel she had conducted herself anything but awkwardly before the sleepers. But she bobbed her head noncommittally, and smiled at Darian as her mother-by-marriage excused herself and walked down the hill.

"Would you want to raise our variously-possible children here?" she asked, knowing Illidian would have heard the discussion as he approached, just as she was aware that Darian would still be in a Kellian's range of easy hearing.

"No. I want to make a home of Surclere. And I am of the opposite view to my mother: I feel that we as a people are still growing, and that contact with humans expands us. While there will undoubtedly be a weight of expectation placed on a child of yours and mine, it will be unlikely to come close to the pressure you and Sebastian suffered."

This was a most unusual speech for Illidian, and Rennyn leaned into his side, appreciating the intended comfort.

"Tonight all of the Ten's descendants present will sit in vigil at the Heart," Illidian went on. "We will not ask you to wake them until tomorrow."

And perhaps discover that her ability to command Kellian was not enough to wake the Ten. Or learn that the golems did not wish to end their half-life. But most likely tomorrow would be the day that she took nine innocent lives, and faced whatever consequences that brought.

"Do you—if the Ten ask for release, and that breaks the casting that makes you Kellian—do you think you will be able to maintain Aurai's Rest?"

"No. We could defend against most attacks, but there would inevitably be losses, a slow attrition of our numbers. And we could not risk children here. The lesser stalkers cannot bring down an adult, but they hunt from concealment, and we are only able to live here because we can sense when they are nearby."

"A high cost." Not just Aurai's Rest, but a people's sense of self. Rennyn doubted there was a single Kellian who was not dismayed by the possibility of Solace's casting failing, but they would not cling to it at the expense of the nine remaining golems.

"It would uncomplicate other matters."

Rennyn looked up at Illidian, startled. He surely did not think it preferable for the Kellian to cease to be, no matter what the situation in Tyrland—or in their marriage.

"Like uncomplicating a knot by cutting through it?" she asked. "Do we then celebrate the pieces?"

He didn't answer, gazing down at the settlement.

"I've been trying to look at the control ability from different angles," Rennyn said, restively. "That casting on Fallon made me wonder if I could devise something that would stop me from giving any form of command."

Illidian shifted. "That does not seem to me a safe thing."

"Perhaps not. But how safe is it for me to be around Kellian, truly? Especially young children. I've managed to guard my tongue so far, but inevitably my attention will slip."

She felt his hesitation, a palpable thing, and straightened, studying his expressionless face. Her weariness contracted into a fist.

"When?"

He met her gaze, reluctant but not attempting to lie.

"After you were injured, and were not fully conscious. Several times."

"Times..."

Rennyn's throat was tight. More than once. Careless words that, with a Kellian, became iron command. She could have killed him.

"A demonstration of Surclere arrogance. I was entirely sure, certain, that I had at least not commanded you by accident. If I'm in that bad a state again, I had better have only human attendants."

Rennyn's attempt to keep a pragmatic focus on solutions was severely undercut by a wavering voice, and she gave up pretence, hiding her face in his side. He wrapped his arms around her, squeezing far more tightly than he usually permitted himself. No words, however, no arguments to mitigate distress. He had kept this failure from her because he could not pretend to absolve her, could not tell her that the occasional lapse was forgivable, and could offer no solution.

"I don't want our marriage to be something you endure, Illidian."

"And I will not follow a path that leads me away from you."

Absolute, unwavering. But he was a man who had endless nightmares, and it was becoming harder to believe that they were not about her.

Chapter Twenty

The Sentene mages were upset. Kendall didn't know why, but she'd noticed it first the previous night, when Lieutenant Meniar had forgotten his smile and spent all his time staring at his feet.

Before, Kendall would just have asked Sukata. There was no reason she couldn't go do that now: it's not as if they weren't speaking to each other. But Sukata would be so careful in replying, walking on eggshells that weren't there, and Kendall would feel lumpish and full of angles and out of place.

And maybe Sukata wouldn't even tell Kendall what was going on. It was plain that everybody else knew, except perhaps the Pest and His Smugness. Kellian business, probably linked to why they'd dragged themselves off to this forest instead of chasing down the Black Queen's monster son. Rennyn no doubt would explain if asked, but she'd eaten in her room and was almost certainly asleep.

Opportunity gloomed past in the form of Lieutenant Meniar, hands in pockets and head down as he wandered into the garden beds east of the hill. Kendall hesitated only a moment before following him along the unlit path. The circle only kept Eferum-Get out, and wasn't proof against things that had adapted to the flesh-and-blood world, but no doubt the Kellian had cleared out anything resembling a predator for miles around. Lieutenant Meniar certainly wasn't taking any care, and didn't seem to notice her following him as he walked all the way up to the inlaid stones that marked the protective circle, and stood staring over the stream that ran just outside.

"What's going on?"

He straightened with a jerk, and gave her a reproachful glance.

"Spill."

Lieutenant Meniar shook his head, but it wasn't a refusal. "You know about the Ten, right?"

"That most of the first Kellian are still alive? Yeah. I figured one of the reasons we were coming here was to introduce Herself to them."

He laughed, a sour cough of sound. "Yes. And to ask them their views on life—and other options."

"What do you..." Kendall stopped, remembering talking to Sebastian, just after Rennyn had been made a Duchess. "You mean...what do you mean?"

"They've asked Her Duchessness to give the Ten permission to die, should that be what they want."

That made sense: just the sort of thing that the Kellian would do, once they properly understood the spell that had made them. Still...

"That might make the Kellian unhappy—probably back when they decided to do this, before we left Tyrland. Doesn't explain you."

He tipped his head back, gazing up at stars rather than forest. "The Kellian we work with are an entirely unplanned consequence of Symbolic Magic, side-effects of the creation of the Ten. Duchess Surclere proved the casting was ongoing. We don't know what will happen to its side-effects if the Ten are removed from the picture."

Kendall felt as sick as Lieutenant Meniar looked. "Die?"

"Even that is possible. Or Queen Solace's casting will unravel, and only their human heritage will remain. Or perhaps nothing at all will happen. That's Symbolic Magic for you—it is as imprecise as it is powerful."

He glanced at her, then dredged up an attempt at a smile.

"It's not a complete throw of the dice. We know what happened to the descendants of the one of the Ten who was killed about fifty years ago: absolutely nothing. But it's hard to set aside the less probable consequences."

For Lieutenant Meniar—and half the other Sentene mages—in love with their Kellian partners. For Rennyn, married to Captain Faille. For...

Muttering something that might pass as thanks, Kendall turned on her heel and headed to the bedroom she had been assigned to share. Sukata had gone there after the dinner clean-up, so Kendall had figured she'd kill an hour or two until the need for awkward silences had passed. She barely caught Sukata, freshly dressed, on her way out.

"Are you going to tell them?"

Sukata's fingers closed on the hem of her coat—a tiny giveaway to make up for not being able to look nervous.

"We are to spend the night in vigil in the resting place of the Ten," she said, her thin voice even more muted than usual.

"Are you going to tell the Ten that letting them die could make you stop being Kellian—maybe even kill you?"

"To do so would be to influence their answer."

"You think they wouldn't want to know?"

"To protect ourselves by prolonging their cruel state is not possible, Kendall. Who we are...we cannot buy our existence at the expense of the Ten."

"And what's it going to do to Herself? Even if absolutely nothing happens to you, you're asking her to kill your...your grandmothers! And if—!"

Kendall made herself stop, an immense consciousness that she was hurting Sukata washing over her. Now wasn't the time to pick an argument. All it did was make it harder to find a way back to the time when there was nothing more natural than ranging herself at Sukata's side, because the pair of them were allies in dealing with a full-of-herself mage too powerful for her own good.

"Sorry," she said. "You go do your...whatever."

She was saved from the temptation to add a barbed "Since it's nothing to do with me," by Captain Faille, coming out of the room he shared with Rennyn. He gave Kendall one of his Looks, easily translated as "You're on duty," before going off up the hill. Sukata, after a moment's hesitation, followed without another word.

"Bugs and rot," Kendall muttered, but so low even a Kellian probably wouldn't have heard, then went and scratched on Rennyn's door, and opened it.

Kellian mightn't hold much with ranks, but Duchesses—or Captain Faille—still warranted what was probably one of the prime rooms, with windows looking out over the fields and gardens. Pointless, since they'd straight away been firmly shuttered and barred, and a heavy curtain pulled over them against any hint of autumn chill, with a brazier added to make sure the room kept toasty. Herself was still up, dressed for bed, but sitting cross-legged on it, not doing anything noticeable with the hairbrush she held.

Kendall had only once seen Rennyn Claire cry: right after she'd told the Kellian that she technically-not-really owned them, and they'd all gone from sort of liking her to flinching. In the months since then her slow recovery from the broken ribs and the hole in her side had led to plenty of fits of black sullens, and some days of sheer had-it-up-to-hereness, but even at her worst she'd mainly responded with gritted teeth and thinning patience. The Kellian asking her to kill their grandmothers, back around when she'd been made Duchess, must have been the cause of those days when she'd been all withdrawn and distracted.

Head tangled in her own concerns, it took Kendall an entire handful of moments to study the still profile of the most powerful mage in the world and read devastation.

What? Why? Rennyn had to have known about the Kellian plans for the Ten before they'd even started the trip. But this almost waxen stillness, the grey pallor, the exhausted set of her shoulders...

"Give me that," Kendall said, and took the brush because there was no way Rennyn was going to be this unhappy and want to admit it. Kendall began working on Rennyn's hair with deliberate vigour, dealing with tangles briskly enough to smart. Minor distraction, but that had long been part of the reason Herself kept Kendall around.

Had Rennyn and Captain Faille had their first really bad argument? No, Sukata would have been able to hear that, and would have leaked distress from every pore. And there was no hint of the faint metallic tang of worked magic in the room, so Rennyn hadn't been using one of the silence castings she occasionally put up. Nor had the Captain looked at all angry. Not that Kendall could ever tell much of what Captain Faille was feeling.

There weren't a whole lot of things that Rennyn Claire cared about enough to knock her this hard. Only Sebastian, really, and there's no way word of any hurt to him could have beat them here. The introduction to the people living at Aurai's Rest had been awkward, but there'd been no suggestion of stone throwing. And, really, Rennyn could probably put up with all the Kellian cold-shouldering her so long as Captain Faille stuck around.

Kendall worked on braiding, waiting until she was close to the end before speaking.

"What would happen if you ordered the Kellian to not obey your orders?"

The jerk of Rennyn's head told Kendall she'd guessed right. An accidental order, and a descent into a blather of guilt and doubt. Probably a whole self-sacrificial thing telling herself she couldn't stay married to Captain Faille

"The next order cancels it out," Rennyn said, after a long moment. "You really can be astonishingly observant, Kendall."

Kendall sniffed. If seeing noses on faces was being observant.

"The family that lived next to me, back in Falk, there were so many of them they were three-a-bed," she observed to the air. "One day, Nina Lippon showed up with a black eye, and it turned out Jessamy—that was the youngest—had elbowed her in the face when she was asleep. Nina's face was really sore, and Jessa felt a bit bad about it, but no-one was acting like Jessa had gone after Nina with a knife or anything."

Kendall twined one of Rennyn's ribbons through the end of the braid, and tied it off firmly.

"I'd tell you not to sit in here digging your own pit of gloom, but I know you're going to pass out before you get more than a foot down. I want to know, instead, whether you think the Kellian should tell the Ten what might happen if they all die."

That got no response at all, so Kendall busied herself making sure there was a jug of water, and a few sweet biscuits within reach. But Captain Faille had already set everything up before leaving, so Kendall had nothing left to do but set the brush on top of Rennyn's small case of toiletries and head for the door.

"No, I don't," Rennyn said, just as Kendall gripped the door handle. "I also don't truly believe Solace's casting will break—the chance is only remote, and nothing compared to the likelihood that Solace's line ending will cause it to unravel. Faint possibilities should not be a factor in deciding whether nine women endure a half-life."

Those possibilities were still going to keep everyone up half the night—and if the original Kellian chose to die then there was nothing faint about how Rennyn would feel about what came next.

Too worked up for an early night, Kendall left Rennyn to her stewing and wandered about the settlement, avoiding the library-sitting room-hall where most of the mages had congregated. No-one seemed to have a house to themselves here: it was all laid out in large buildings with lots of rooms, one big central kitchen, and even something resembling a Kolan bath-house. Kendall spent some time there, not comfortable enough to strip off, but giving herself a more thorough wipe-down than she'd managed before dinner.

Emerging into the chill night air, Kendall narrowly avoided running right into Dezart Samarin, obviously getting himself a good look around while there were no Kellian to keep an ear out for him. Stepping back, Kendall waited until he had more of a lead on her before following.

The Sentene mages should have thought to put a proper watch on him. Maybe it was true that there was nothing particularly secret about Aurai's Rest, but there was sure plenty dubious about His Imperial Smugness. And while he wasn't actively breaking into anything, he more than once stopped to make a very particular survey of places that didn't look at all interesting to Kendall. At the third of these he pulled a little book out of an inner pocket, and made a note with a stub of a pencil.

As if he'd found what he'd been looking for, he abruptly turned and walked briskly back to the building where Rennyn's group had been given rooms. Kendall stayed as close as she dared, turning over schemes to get hold of that book and...but it would be written in Kolan. She'd have to show it to someone, and how would it be if it were in code as well, and looked like a laundry list?

He seemed to have had enough skulking about for now, at least, heading inside and straight for the room he'd been assigned. But then, just as he opened the door, he turned his head and looked directly at her peering around the corner. He was smiling— *smirking*—completely full up with smug on smug as he met her eye and she knew, just knew, that he'd seen her from the very start, as soon as she stepped out of the bath-house.

If Kendall had been holding anything she would have thrown it at the door that closed behind him. Of all the jumped-up, snot-nosed—! Making a game of her! She'd...she'd...

A picture of how silly she must look, practically stamping her foot in an empty corridor, punctured Kendall's fury, and she let out her breath, then snorted.

"Don't think that's going to make me let my guard down, scut. None of us are fool enough to trust you."

About to turn and head back outside, a loud thud stopped Kendall in her tracks. That hadn't come from Samarin or Rennyn's room, but—

A crash pinpointed the Pest's room, though before Kendall could do anything about it, Samarin flung open his door and dashed out into the corridor, a sword in one hand.

"Where—?" he started to say, but had his answer in the Pest, trailing a sheet and staggering like he was drunk.

"The music!" the Pest gasped, clutching Samarin's arm. "The music!"

Maybe he was drunk. Before His Smugness could respond, the Pest ducked past him and threw himself at Rennyn's door, so frantic and off-balance that he seemed to have forgotten how handles worked, fumbling and scrabbling before finally getting it open, and almost falling over again.

Kendall stared. At a rumpled and very empty bed. At curtains pulled back, shutters unbarred...and the Pest, staggering but still headlong, scrambling out the window.

Chapter Twenty-One

"Sukata!" Kendall shouted it, so loud her throat hurt as she turned to face toward the entrance of the building, and up the hill to where all the Kellian had gone. "Sukata, *HELP!*"

Then she was running, shoulder-to-shoulder with Samarin, so that they almost jammed in doorway and then window. The drop was short, and the flowerbed beneath already mangled. Samarin had gotten ahead of her, but slowed as he hunted out direction. There was noise—the Pest seemed determined to trip over *everything*—and then Kendall saw something a good deal further out. Just a sliver of white off toward the edge of the circle, and she pelted toward it, wishing the moon was out, or she could enchant herself to see in the dark, or knew a single useful Sigillic.

Ahead, magic twisted, shifting from beyond her hearing to a strong knot of force. Kendall couldn't guess at intent at all, felt it more as a shape, something stretching away from her, away from the figure directly ahead of her. And it *was* Rennyn, walking unhurriedly, and entirely alone. Casting? Had the damn-fool woman climbed out her own window and gone for a walk without a word to anyone, and not even wearing a coat? Kendall would kill her herself.

"What—?" A cry from Kendall's right and behind her—Lieutenant Meniar, pounding into the chase from the direction of the stream. "Your Grace!"

"Stop her!" the Pest shouted. "She's not awake!"

A tunnel. It felt like a tunnel. Kendall didn't understand at all, but she wasn't close enough to stop Rennyn from continuing her steady walk forward, and somehow each step seemed to take Herself dozens of feet: already she was once again no more than a smudge of white in the distance, and the tunnel was narrowing behind her, as if the roof was dropping down.

Fearing that she would bounce right off whatever it was, Kendall reached out, trying to push the roof back up. She couldn't see it at all, could make no sense of what it even was, but she could grip it, a slippery nothingness, and somehow lighter even than necklaces and bowls and all the things she had practiced holding.

"Keep moving!"

Samarin grabbed her arm and hustled her forward, and Kendall tried to walk and hold the roof up at the same time and felt it sliding.

"Carry her!" Samarin somehow tucked himself beneath Kendall's shoulder, and Lieutenant Meniar was on her other side. They lifted her like a doll and ran and Kendall let them because all her attention had to go to the tunnel, and it was rocks now, boulders, a mountain trying to close down on them.

"A travel casting," Lieutenant Meniar said, turning his head, and Kendall realised he was talking to someone in the tunnel behind them, more than one person, breathing harsh, though she couldn't hear any footsteps. None of them were standing on anything, they were running on air and she'd lost track of the slip of white ahead, and the mountain narrowed down into a knife-hammer of pain behind her left eye, and she lost her hold. They fell.

Kendall shuddered, and rolled off a lump of person into a rustle of dry leaves. She clutched her head, glad for the velvet of darkness, but equally glad when a skitter of worked power became a glow of green light clinging to the ring Lieutenant Meniar wore. And she was intensely relieved to see Sukata. Sukata, Captain

Faille and his mother, looking like they'd been running a week as they picked themselves up. And even that Tesin Asaka, all tangled up with the Pest. Kendall hadn't been sure any of the Kellian would even hear her, let alone be able to reach them before the tunnel thing closed. Kellian could move lightning-fast, but they couldn't keep it up over distance, though obviously they'd tried, and now could barely stand.

"Before everyone starts shuffling about," Samarin said, "try to mark the exact direction we were travelling."

Kendall had no idea, so didn't bother to try, but she was not surprised at all when the Kellian immediately agreed on the same direction, and arranged an arrow using branches. Even as they did so, they were searching the blackness, trying to spot any hint of white, any trace of movement.

"How far ahead?" Captain Faille asked, and his voice told them all the things his shadowy face did not.

"I suspect miles. Probably more." Lieutenant Meniar sounded as apologetic as he was frustrated. "That was a major working, the kind of magic thought lost. And I didn't even sense it forming."

Kendall was staring at the Pest, who had sat up only to curl forward, arms wrapped around his knees, looking straight-out terrified. As if he'd been captured by bandits and they were debating which bit to slice off first.

"How did you *know*?" she asked.

The Pest flinched, and couldn't have looked guiltier if he tried.

"He knew she was gone," Kendall added, as everyone turned to stare at the Pest. "Shot out of his room squawking about music and ran after Rennyn."

"Similar to the incident with the thieves," Samarin said. "Are you some kind of dreaming oracle?"

The Pest's mouth flapped uselessly, and he clutched at his throat.

"Hells." Lieutenant Meniar thrust a hand into his coat, and brought out his folded slate book. He flipped to a Sigillic already written out and began casting it.

"What's wrong with him?" Tesin asked, putting a sympathetic hand to the Pest's back.

"He is under enchantment," Captain Faille said, shifting as if in response to something he could see out in the dark forest. "Something to prevent him speaking on certain subjects—one of which appears to be how he knows what is happening while he sleeps."

The person who looked most surprised by this was the Pest himself, who stared at Captain Faille, but then looked marginally less despairing, even though he was starting to turn blue. Then Lieutenant Meniar finished casting his Sigillic, and the strangest popping noise came from the Pest's mouth. He gulped a great, heaving breath.

"Good," Lieutenant Meniar said, smiling his relief. "We're not going to ask how you know, Fallon, not at all. Only tell us what's safe for you to talk about."

"The music!" the Pest gasped immediately. "The music the Duchess has been hearing. Her eyes were closed. It—"

He broke off again, hands already at his throat, and looked like he was trying to calm himself down, and not getting very far at all. Lieutenant Meniar, mouth set, began hurriedly writing out the Sigillic again, which didn't do much for the Pest's calm.

"You don't have to speak," Sukata said. "We will not ask at all."

But the Pest couldn't seem to believe her, or maybe what he believed made no difference, and it became a race between how quickly Lieutenant Meniar could write out a Sigillic against how fast a boy could turn blue. Until Samarin stepped up behind the Pest, and brought the hilt of his sword down in one quick, sharp blow.

Fallon crumpled, and Samarin bent over him, joined by Tesin, who said with quiet certainty: "He is breathing now."

"Whatever this Ban is, it's likely to rely on his own awareness," Samarin explained. "Since he knows that we know he has a secret..."

He shrugged then glanced out into the darkness, before handing Captain Faille his sword. The Captain, with the briefest of nods, took it and walked away from the glow of Lieutenant Meniar's light. The noises that followed were a reminder that they were in a famously dangerous forest, and obviously no longer the part of it made safe by a clutch of Kellian.

There wasn't much that Kendall could see of their surroundings, but she had noticed a couple of differences. "The trees are nearly bare," she said. "And it's colder. Is it—how long did we..."

"This would match the forest many days' travel north," Darian Faille said. "I do not believe it is later in the year."

Lieutenant Meniar finished writing his Sigillic, then flipped to the other side of the slate and began another. "If it's a true recreation of Nameen's Walk—Fals Nameen, one of the best-known of the Elder Mages—then it is said to allow the traveller to move miles in seconds, but to arrive hours later. So the subjective time of the traveller is very short, and the true travel time hours. I think this is the same night, but I can't tell how much further ahead Her Grace might be."

"We have a direction," Darian Faille said.

"Yes. Nameen's Walk was said to be entirely straightforward in that respect. But..." Lieutenant Meniar turned to Captain Faille as he walked back into the dim light. "If we are too far behind, then the slightest deviation of our own path would mean missing the destination entirely. And we have no way of knowing if we're even past the halfway point."

"She was walking and we were running," Kendall said, before anyone could think to suggest they do anything but follow Rennyn as soon as possible, even though Kendall personally felt as if a thousand rocks were tied to her, dragging her down.

"Even halfway toward my primary mission is progress for me," Samarin added lightly, but had enough sense not to sound as if he was enjoying himself half as much as usual.

"I'll set a ward," Lieutenant Meniar said, still writing. "And try to remember a directional Sigillic I read once, so we can keep to our course. Sukata, can you arrange a fire that won't set the entire forest floor alight?"

Darian Faille, very indistinct at the edge of Lieutenant Meniar's light, seemed to be breaking off part of a fallen branch to create a rough staff. "We will secure the area," she said, and led Captain Faille off.

Kendall sighed, took off her jacket and folded it into a pad to stick under the Pest's head. She wouldn't want to be out in a forest in her night-clothes, without even shoes. At least the week had been dry, though there was damp enough if you dug down into these layers of leaves.

"Won't he just wake up and choke again?" she asked, turning to help Sukata and Tesin find rocks for a camp fire.

"Probably," Lieutenant Meniar said, tersely. "I'll put a Sleep casting on him, for now. Her Grace and I have been trying to divine the enchantment for days now, but I don't yet understand it well enough to try to unpick it."

And didn't want to try without Rennyn, he did not add, any more than any of them were talking about Rennyn, who was also in her nightclothes somewhere, and all too probably with a monster who had made very clear what he wanted to do with her.

They'd gone and delivered her right to him.

Chapter Twenty-Two

"Wake up, cousin."

Rennyn jerked violently, and found herself upright, arms spread to either side. Her skin stung as she struggled against restraint, as if the tiny hairs on her arms, shoulders and back were being pulled out. Sunlight stabbed at her eyes as she tried to gain some sense of her situation, twisting in the bindings, but she saw only greenery, and the occasional flash of orange.

Tumbling forward, Rennyn realised that she'd been roped quite loosely to a wall only as she fell from it, and then there was nothing but the knives in her feet.

She might have shrieked. She heard the sound as if it had come from someone else, rising above the jolt of white fire lancing up through her. She crumpled onto a soft, uneven surface, curling in on herself in an excess of hurt, and then forcing herself past the haze of pain to urgent examination of bare feet, finding blood and...glass? Blue-green glass among crusted cuts. One thick shard had been driven so deeply into her instep it was almost lost to view among the sudden flood of bright blood welling around it.

Lieutenant Meniar's lessons had given her some useful medical techniques, but Rennyn had not spent a great deal of time on the structure of feet. It was a simple matter to block the pain, and removing the glass a mere flicker of Thought, but beyond that came less obvious territory. Not certain of her options, she clamped down on the flow of blood so she could spare another look for the room.

A ruin. Dazzling shafts of light descended from a stone grid of ceiling. The air was thick and warm, and everything festooned with vine, but there was no sign of movement, of any immediate threat. Besides, this much daylight would be protection enough against any Eferum-Get. That voice had been just another nightmare then, combined with the shock of whatever this place was, and however she had reached it.

Not in the least reassured, Rennyn turned back to the dilemma of her feet. Accelerated healing would sap her physical strength disastrously, and she could not afford to pass out. So, small repairs, using the least amount of power possible. A tiny divination, to identify what was leaking so much blood and then fusing together the largest vein. For the moment the rest of the damage would simply have to be held closed with a variation of a caulding. On top of this she added one of the infection-preventatives, though Lieutenant Meniar would surely shake his head at her failure to properly clean the wounds first. The pain suppression would make it possible to walk, at least until she had some idea of where and how and what next.

"You might want to move."

Rennyn flung herself backward, landing directly in the nearest beam of sunlight. But her Wicked Uncle didn't appear. There was nothing moving, nothing but a room covered in vines.

"This is truly gratifying. Have I haunted your dreams, little cousin?"

She stared, orienting on the voice. The furthest wall, shadowed but still exposed to far more light than the Eferum-Get prince should be able to tolerate, was as covered in vines as all the rest, and dotted with a handful of orange flowers. But a fixed gaze revealed a figure beneath the vine's heart-shaped leaves.

"You do not find me at my best, I fear."

Understatement. A creature of rags, of sunken cheeks and hollow eyes. Helecho Montjuste-Surclere, monster, blood-drinker, cause of so many of her ills, strung up like some kind of fleshy trellis, with a brilliant orange-gold flower tucked over one ear. Rennyn's galloping heart slowed, and she pushed nausea away with all the other dismay and upset she could not deal with just now.

"Shouldn't you be shrivelling into a blackened lump or something?"

"Master your disappointment."

Rennyn straightened, not quite ready to trust even as she wondered whether he had been placed on a north-facing wall to prevent direct exposure to sunlight. Placed...

There were other people-shaped lumps. Picking her way on numb feet across the uneven ground, Rennyn approached the nearest. A woman, one with dark curling hair and a vivid scattering of freckles. Pressing fingers to a bare patch of neck, Rennyn found a slow but steady beat. The woman did not seem to be in nearly so bad a condition as Prince Helecho. The vines themselves...they thrummed with power, but she could not feel intent from them.

A room with four people suspended on the walls, and Rennyn to make a fifth. Dezart Samarin's missing mages, without a doubt. There would be almost twenty others.

"Don't stand in one place for too long, little cousin, or you'll be useless to me."

Looking down, Rennyn saw tiny filaments of white reaching from the vines nearest to her feet. She stepped away, snapping one strand that had reached her ankle and attached itself firmly. No, dug its way in, she realised, stooping to pluck it out. Remembering stinging pain, she swept her hands over her arms and shoulders, dislodging a little shower of hair-fine tendrils. Roots? They had gone straight through the thin cloth of her lounging suit.

"Remarkable that you imagine I have any interest in being of use to you," she said, as calmly as she could manage.

"Few lack self-interest."

Still not looking back at him, Rennyn continued her examination of the sleeper. Beneath every vine the white filaments dug into the woman's skin, but did not appear to penetrate deeply. Not wanting to spend more energy than strictly necessary, Rennyn did not leap to a divination, and instead shifted the woman minutely forward, craning to see...yes, two larger tendrils, thick as fingers, positioned just below the shoulder blades.

Rennyn turned from the woman to her prison. Solid walls, grey with the faintest traces of old paint. A door of heavy stone that did not respond to a tentative push. Nothing she could not cut, though it would be easier, perhaps, to break through the ceiling. She only need levitate a short way and she would be on the roof of wherever this was. She narrowed her eyes, concentrating on the 'feel' of the place. All around her, a background hum pricked at her senses. That was possibly the vine, which undoubtedly was more than an ordinary plant, even if she still could not detect intent.

Throughout her investigation, her Wicked Uncle remained a silent audience, making no more comments. Perhaps he truly was as powerless as he seemed, and she had been given a great gift of chance. An opportunity to deal with him without any difficulty at all, and finally weaken the miscasting that robbed her of her physical strength.

All she had to do was kill a hateful, horrible, and completely helpless man.

"How long have you been here?" she asked at last, because there was no point ignoring a source of information just because he gave her the shudders.

"A month or so. There are periods of unconsciousness, so I can't be more exact."

"Have you met whoever is behind this? Or remember how you arrived here?"

"No. I've watched these others be brought in, however, including yourself. Around every five days or so. I broke free, the first time I woke, before the...infestation was complete. From that I can tell you that too much damage to the vines will bring the guards, and the guards are extremely magic-resistant, though not quite so fast as I was then. I made it all the way to the front entrance that time, and bounced most impressively off the shield about this place. The vines themselves draw off Efera, and I presume keep humans unconscious, since these others haven't woken. That doesn't quite work on me."

"Guards?"

"Some kind of glasswork construct. Numerous. Difficult to kill."

Rennyn glanced at the blue-green shards she'd pulled from her feet, and then finally, inevitably, she turned back to the monster pinned to the wall.

The family resemblance was strong. The same colouring, the same mild curl to his hair as her father and brother, and a similar shape to his face. Even at such an extreme, he seemed to be enjoying her predicament. She met his gaze, refusing to flinch away from it again. He had mishandled her, captured her, tried to chain her soul, had put his teeth in her throat, and then nearly killed her. But she had survived it all.

"You're being very obliging," she said at last. "But if you imagine I'll release you, prepare for disappointment."

"No?" Prince Helecho didn't look perturbed, perhaps simply didn't believe her. "And yet I heard you were liable to collapse after even a little casting. Do you think you can bring the shield about this place down? I had trouble even detecting the pattern of the thing, at first, though I've had plenty of time to make a study of it since. What will you do when the need to rest overwhelms you? Even now you've stood in place for too long."

Rennyn moved, not bothering to glance down to see the cause of the faint tension and release, though noting that the roots did not hurt until you pulled them away. She looked instead at the ceiling. Was there a shield there? There was certainly something, but it was hard to distinguish it from the hum of the vines. And then she shook her head, not denying her Wicked Uncle's point, but emphasising the only decision she could make.

"You're a killer. A true monster. I won't exchange my life for the lives of however many people you might attack in the future. By any measure of common good sense, I should cut your throat now."

He laughed. It was a tired sound, but held a note of genuine amusement. "You won't do that."

"No," she agreed. "Not being a killer—at least not of someone so defenceless. But nor am I going to release you."

"Giving up? How dull."

Rennyn had expected desperate anger, even pleading, but he seemed almost unmoved, studying her flatly. She felt that his gaze dwelt on her throat, on the scar he had left there, but she refused to allow herself to hide it.

"Here is a question for you, then," he said at last. "What is the goal of this place? Are all these humans in the walls still people, or just hanging sacks of meat? How many more will it take? And who might join you, beneath the leaves?"

The strongest of mages. Would Sebastian's distance protect him? And what of the Sentene mages, certainly within reach at Aurai's Rest? Sukata and

Sarana, Lieutenant Meniar: were any of them as strong as those already taken?

But that did not alter the simple fact that exchanging one threat for another was not a solution. Whatever she did, it could not involve leaving her Wicked Uncle free to kill.

Without his help, however, escape was unlikely if there really was a shield about the whole of the building. She did not currently have the strength to overcome one by sheer force, and even if she could, she would almost certainly collapse immediately after bringing it down.

"Do you still have my focus?"

"Feel free to search me."

Rennyn chose not to notice the smirk, answering her own question by seeking the echo that would betray the near presence of her focus. Nothing. But it could be in the building, reachable without needing to pass through this supposed shield. Once she had it...well, she could be truly destructive, perhaps enough to at least ensure that this place could steal no more mages. That would mean sacrificing the current captives...would it be better to attempt rescue? Pulling one of them off the wall without killing them— without alerting the guards—might be the larger challenge.

Her other option was to learn as much as she could before she was pinned to a wall, and then hope that she could somehow be found, and that whatever those vines were doing to the captive mages really could be reversed. Illidian would not spare a moment in searching, of course, and she could not let herself think about how he would be feeling now, about the poor timing of their last conversation.

She gazed around at leaf litter and vine, pushing herself past unpleasant obstacles, searching for practical measures, a way to maximise her chances.

Then she crossed to where she had originally fallen, and picked up the largest piece of glass.

"What's this?" her Wicked Uncle asked. "Have you found some dramatic and unexpected solution?"

"You could say that", Rennyn replied, advancing on him. "I'm going to take out your teeth."

Chapter Twenty-Three

For the first time in her experience of him, Rennyn's Wicked Uncle looked disconcerted, his gaze fixing on the glass in her hand. But then an eyebrow quirked, and his features relaxed as he decided she could not mean her words in their most literal sense. The mocking expression he produced after that was deliberately assembled, an assumption of unassailable calm entirely familiar to Rennyn. He shared one of her weaknesses: pride.

"You think you can control me?" he said. "Well, I suppose you've already demonstrated your taste for very obedient men."

Ignoring this jab, Rennyn stopped in the nearest beam of sunlight and held up the piece of blood-smeared glass so that it glittered. The power-sapping vines were a factor she could not compensate for, only hope that they would not weaken the casting of someone they weren't actually attached to.

"You're not going to give me the option to choose death over chains?"

Rennyn did not lower the piece of glass, turning it to find the angle that would capture the most light.

"Those are the only two options," she said. "I can't leave the problem of you for someone else to deal with. Though if death really is your preference, let me know now before I waste energy casting."

"And then collapse into a self-righteous heap?"

"I'll have to take that chance. If I manage to stay awake, what will I need to do to get you off that wall?"

This time his smile was cold, and not at all pleased. "After you've served me revenge flavoured with hypocrisy and collected another dog at your heel playing protector?"

She had found the brightest point of sunlight, and held the piece of glass motionless as she surveyed her distant uncle. "I'm defanging you, not making you into a pet. What you tried with me—let alone the situation I'm in with the Kellian—are nothing I wish to repeat. Your choice is to be killed, or to never kill. Which is it?"

His face, the only part of him he seemed able to move, went very still: a statue of a starving man, covered in ivy. This was not a small decision: Eferum-Get were killers at their very core, hungry for the lives of others. Being bound against killing would diminish him, force him to adapt to the living world, if a month bound to a wall in this sunlit room had not already done so.

It seemed silence was to be the whole of her Wicked Uncle's answer. Sunlight shimmered as Rennyn began to draw power. Only a Symbolic casting had any chance of producing a binding he could not break—especially with her limited energy stores. There was little enough at hand that she could choose to represent her intent, but what she wanted was simple enough.

The shard of glass was hot between her fingers as she lifted it and drew it across the scar that she hated, and could not erase. A representation not just of death, but of blood, and all the pain, the multiple injuries her Wicked Uncle had dealt her. Then she stepped forward, and cut his throat.

oOo

"Well, at least you didn't fall over."

Rennyn, leaning temporarily against the nearest wall, didn't look at him. Her body was already crying for sleep, and it seemed particularly cruel to be in a place where she could not risk sitting down. She was at least fairly certain that the casting had taken, despite the presence of those vines. She had chosen "do no harm" rather than "do not kill", weakening the injunction by broadening it, but given her Wicked Uncle's apparent enjoyment of inflicting pain, it would not have been enough to bind him only from death.

"How much damage will taking you off that wall do?" she asked, forcing herself to shift a few feet. "Are you going to start dying if I get you down?"

"I shouldn't think so. I don't need to breathe."

Rennyn blinked, and glanced at the nearest unconscious mage. "It's in your lungs?"

"That seems the major focus of the infestation. From this angle. Are you ready to leave now? Am I sufficiently diminished?"

His voice was dry, all hint of his reaction to her casting locked under a surface layer of sarcasm. The diagonal slash she'd made across his throat had already healed, leaving a thin white line. Her own neck stung, not so easily mended, though at least she'd managed only a shallow wound.

"I get you down, you get me outside this shield?"

"That's the idea. Or do you feel a need for another layer or two of injunctions?"

"I don't have the energy for that. I shall have to discover the value of your word."

He made a noise she did not mistake for laughter. "This is going to be educational for both of us, then."

She surveyed him flatly. "I presume you have some semblance of a plan."

"A sketch. The guards are the problem. When you get me down, they will come. I won't be able to move immediately, and you have as much chance of fighting them as of developing a sense of humour. You need to get me off the wall, then hobble to where they put you up, and look suitably bag-like until they're gone. If they follow the previous pattern they'll knock me out and string me back up. Get me down again, before the infestation is re-established."

"How intelligent are these guards?"

"Well, they've not treated me to any sparkling repartee. Functional."

Few constructs—golems—were as capable of decision-making as the Kellian: one of the reasons constructs were not in more common use. They would not necessarily make a connection between her introduction to the room, and a near-escape of an older captive. But they might check her.

"I am very tired of limited options," Rennyn said, and pulled away from the white strands that were reaching to bind her to the wall.

Blocking out distaste, she first approached the problem of freeing her Wicked Uncle by moving anything not firmly stuck to him. Then she studied the major points of connection, the sections she would have to pull aside when she switched to fast movement. And that could not begin until she had dealt with those two thick spikes into the back.

She could not pull him forward as far as the woman, and barely managed to crane up far enough to catch a glimpse and confirm the spikes were there. Her legs trembled, and she moved away a few feet to break the ever-eager roots that had taken the opportunity to fasten to her ankles.

"One chance," her Wicked Uncle murmured. "And you are not filling me with confidence."

Leaning against the wall, Rennyn took slow deep breaths in preparation and reflected that, if she failed, she at least would not have to listen to him. It was bad enough that she was going to have to touch him. Best to do that without looking at his face.

Gripping her useful piece of glass, she wished she could trade it for intact feet, and started forward.

The narrow gap between his back and the wall would only just fit her hand. Rennyn felt for the first of the spikes, plotted once again every move necessary, and then sawed. Her main fear had been that the spikes would be too tough, tree roots in comparison to the tendrils, but the first parted like butter, surprising her into nearly jerking back. She cut her palm in her effort to keep hold of the glass, then poked the shard wildly to where the second spike was barely within her reach. There...no. She jabbed again, urgently.

Her Wicked Uncle sagged several inches, and she dropped the glass, tearing at the vines that crossed his chest, lifting the largest above his head. Then she pulled his arms inward, as if she were trying to remove a shirt. When most of his upper body was exposed, she grasped him by the shoulders and used her weight to drag him forward.

Numb feet stole her balance and she fell, thumping down onto her back. Her Wicked Uncle had sprawled face down, no longer attached, though bleeding from a cut across his back between the stubs of the two spikes. He was only inches short of the nearest beam of sunlight, but did not so much as twitch—or sizzle.

The thought of getting up again was almost unbearable. Rennyn groaned, and compromised by twisting onto to her hands and knees. She had to move. Move!

The weight of the stone door worked in her favour. A low grating noise gave her bare warning, and she flung herself upright, well short of her original position, but at least in a patch without other occupants, where she could twine her arms through vine. Trying to control her breathing, she dropped her head, closed her eyes, and went limp.

Rustling. Rennyn's shoulders tensed, and she worked on relaxing them, on being unconscious and uninteresting and nothing that needed attending to. This was not the kind of thing she was good at: she had too much curiosity, and was far from a natural actress. But, though the faint noises scraped along her nerves, she would not risk even a glance to see what she was up against.

More than one. They were not loud, these glass guards, but she was able to track their swift progress across the room to where her Wicked Uncle lay. A faint Efera discharge followed, accompanied by a muted grunt, as if someone had been struck hard enough to hurt. And then...yes, they were lifting him now, the noise increasing, leaves shaking.

Something touched her head. Rennyn did not flinch, not quite, but she could not help clenching her jaw and screwing her eyes more tightly closed. The touch came again, cool against her cheek, and then multiple...fingers lifted her.

The way she stiffened would be obvious to any half-competent observer, but the guards simply raised her higher on the wall, tucking more of the vines around her. And then the contact was gone.

They could not be overly intelligent. Almost, Rennyn risked a slit-lidded glance as the faint sounds suggested movement toward the door, but she held the impulse back, waiting for the grating that signalled the door had been closed.

It did not come.

Had they all gone, and simply left the door open? Or had one remained, suspicious, watching? Rennyn breathed. She would count to ten. Ten breaths.

Twenty breaths.

Thirty.

She pictured a thousand tiny roots sprouting, everywhere the vines touched her. Imagined something pressing into her back, below the shoulder blades. One or the other would paralyse her.

Was this exhaustion the weariness her casting had brought on her, or the sleep of the vines? The pain of her cut palm distracted her and she lost track of the number of breaths she had waited. Still there came no sound, no suggestion that anything had remained behind. It would be stupid to lose herself out of pure over-caution, and surely whatever these guards were they would not notice a stolen glance beneath barely-cracked lids.

Stone grated. Rennyn jerked involuntarily, but she was safe, had waited long enough—and was not inclined to waste a moment more, immediately wriggling free of her nest of vines and stinging threads, conscious of a need not to 'disturb' anything more than necessary. And then she forced herself into a tottering shuffle, wasting no time in pulling her Wicked Uncle down a second time. And then, every inch of her groaning, she had to return to her own place against the wall, just in case the guards had been alerted.

After a stretched pause where the door remained firmly shut, Rennyn quivered and curled down. She had to rest, at least temporarily. The pain suppression on her feet was not fully hiding a dull throbbing, and her left knee had developed an odd tendency to give way. All of her was shaking, though she could not tell if that was the aftermath of urgency, or a sign that she had pushed herself beyond physical limits. Surely she had not done so very much. Tiny castings—and one big lump of Symbolic because she could not have allowed that knot to be anything less than firm.

Frustration welled. She had chosen this, had chosen not to kill him, to not take the best chance she would ever have of regaining her physical strength. But she pushed aside those thoughts. She was awake. Her magical strength was still there, and unless she misjudged entirely she could cast without blacking out as she had when she'd put too much into that light casting, back during the encounter with the Kentatsuki swarm.

A tiny thread attaching itself to one bare toe reminded Rennyn that remaining awake was not the only vital concern. She shifted several inches, then let out an aggrieved sigh and gazed at the enormous distance that lay between her and her Wicked Uncle, face down in the vines. If she had to move him every minute or two...

Would it be possible to clear a safe spot on the floor? She examined the possibilities as she crawled back, keeping her still-bleeding palm clenched in a fist because she did not have the time to attend to it yet. The dirt and leaf litter meant the thicker vines that covered the ground were not nearly so thoroughly attached, though firmly anchored every so often by roots more substantial than the white threads.

Reaching her Wicked Uncle, she rolled him over, and then did her best to shift vines about so that there was a gap for her feet and a gap for her behind: a place for her to sit for more than a few moments.

Her palm wasn't too bad. The bleeding seemed to be stopping on its own, though the ragged skin didn't look very pleasant. She daren't cast anything to try to deal with it, and perhaps that was as well, since the pain helped with her struggle to stay awake. But she had learned too well the limits of her physical condition, these past few months: there was no winning against this dragging weariness. If she were going to risk more magic at this stage, she would not be using it on herself.

Lieutenant Meniar had not provided convenient lessons on waking the unconscious, but it was simple enough for Rennyn to follow her Wicked Uncle's lead, for he must have gathered what little Efera that had not been drained from him and pushed it into a straightforward command of will.

"Wake up, monster."

His eyes opened. Even ten minutes ago Rennyn would have greeted that development with a mixture of relief and trepidation, unsure whether her Symbolic casting would keep him from tormenting her. But Rennyn had reached a point where she felt no more than a technical interest in the complex changes to his expression, the attempt to look in her direction, and then the slow—achingly slow—attempts to move.

She watched him as if he were at the end of a long tunnel. A monster she had set out to kill. A man? Perhaps. She had no illusions about the likelihood of him becoming someone worthy of trust. The chances of him helping her escape were slim to vanishing, but still marginally better than her hopes of breaking through a shield on her own. Had binding him been the right decision? She wished she'd been able to ask Illidian's opinion, since there were large potential consequences for the Kellian.

Illidian...

"You're becoming part of the furniture, little cousin."

She had—inevitably—dozed off, and the root tendrils had crept into the space she'd cleared. They tore, stinging, from her ankles and rump as she was lifted.

Too close. Too close! The de-fanging had not banished everything, did not prevent swooping distress as she found herself in a monster's arms. She squirmed involuntarily, then tried to hold back further reaction.

"What a wonderful expression," her Wicked Uncle murmured. "As if you were covered in slime. Would you like me to put you down? I have my doubts on avoiding guards if we're kept to the pace you walk."

He was casting, something intended to cloak their presence. Rennyn clenched her jaw, then forged a path through the situation with a tight focus on the practical.

"Any measure of their level of hearing?" she asked in a similarly low voice, turning her head toward the door and finding that he'd already opened it.

"Not so acute they responded to our discussion, or the noise that door makes," he said, his shrug bringing her momentarily even closer to his face. "But, yes, shut up now. I'm not minded to test the question."

A flat note to that last. She pictured him waking here a month ago. He had run, and fought, and woken again pinned to a wall in a sunlit room. Had the light burned him, those first days? There had been experiments, long ago, testing the reaction of Eferum-Get to sunlight. Some scorched, some crumbled, and some faded like shadows. The strongest and the weakest were the most sensitive, and her Wicked Uncle was very very strong. The vine must have kept him alive even as it held him in place.

How many days had it taken before he did not flinch at the dawn?

However much he had adapted, he still took pains to avoid the now sharply-slanting beams of the light as he crossed the room. Rennyn noted this, along with the thickness of door, storing information for when it might be needed and ignoring as much as she was able the part of her that kept muttering *teeth, teeth, teeth.*

Beyond the stone door was a courtyard with a dry fountain in the centre and archways leading in four different directions. Their prison was clearly not a small building. A crumbling, ivy-festooned...what? She would think it a temple or a palace, but all the ceilings she could see were stone grids allowing glimpses of the sky. No other more decorative carving, though she spotted more faint traces of paint. Sky blue and vivid green. She had never seen anything like the place. But her knowledge of architecture, like most non-essential matters, was minimal.

Her Wicked Uncle, balancing effortlessly, pushed the stone door of their room shut with one foot and then waited, back pressed against it. Of everything she could see, only the door was entirely clear of vine, but Rennyn could detect nothing that would prevent growth. Perhaps the guards kept them clear.

She was struggling once again with the interminable task of keeping her eyes open, and clenched her injured hand to jolt herself back to alertness, then froze as something moved on the far side of the courtyard.

A person? An ant? A creature of many limbs of vivid turquoise, and all along its back...wings? Or antennae like a moth's. The head reminded her of a wasp's. It moved in their direction—not quickly—and the casting Rennyn's Wicked Uncle was maintaining intensified.

He really wasn't breathing. Rennyn noticed that because she held her breath, and recognised an absence from him. But his heart was beating faster. She hated that she could tell.

More movement. Glass constructs, some turquoise, others of deep blue, ranging in size from a small cat to a half-grown person. Their joints made no sound as they picked their way across the vine-covered ground, moving purposefully—but not toward the two escapees.

Rennyn relaxed marginally as the strange procession vanished through another of the archways leading out of the courtyard. So the things were resistant to magic, but not immune to casting effects. Or perhaps were simply not very observant.

Whatever the case, her Wicked Uncle wasted no time debating the possibilities. As soon as the last of the constructs had passed from sight, he skirted the edge of the courtyard and slid around the corner of one of the arches.

A short corridor to a second courtyard, and this time her Wicked Uncle chose speed over caution while picking a circuitous course so that he never stepped from shadow. The next corridor, however, ended not in a doorway, but a ramp leading up to a square of sunlight.

Helecho walked as far forward as he was able, so that Rennyn could glimpse paving, the remnant of an archway, and—further away—a glitter of water. And, just before the end of the ramp, shards of glass. Here was the shield that had stopped him last time, now doubly impassable to an Eferum-Get prince.

Biting her lip, Rennyn did not ask why he had not waited for evening. She would not risk drawing the guard with an incautious word, especially since—after a long pause gazing intently back the way they'd come—he allowed the concealment casting he'd been using to lapse.

Beyond the shield, paving stones began to lift. Shedding showers of litter and sand, they tilted until they were vertical, and then settled neatly back down, one by one. A curving wall to solve the problem of sunlight, with dirt and leaves lifting in turn to plug any gaps, and help hold the stones in place.

Rennyn, her attention divided between this practical solution and the way they'd come, stiffened. "Movement," she murmured, in the softest of whispers.

Her Wicked Uncle didn't look back, but his casting shifted to a complex twist that was not immediately comprehensible to Rennyn. She attempted to decipher it while watching a new procession of guards—or possibly the same one—patrolling busily around the nearby courtyard. They were less than fifty feet away, moving at the same unhurried but businesslike pace, and gave no sign of having noticed the escapees.

If they came in the direction of the exit, she would pull the ceiling and walls down to block the corridor. That was unlikely to hold them for long, and would risk her hold on consciousness, but delay was a better option than combat.

Her Wicked Uncle's casting took on a familiar pattern, echoing notes she had half-heard more than once. He was not using sheer power to force his way through the shield—perhaps he did not have the strength for that, without a focus—but was matching and subtly altering the casting itself, sliding a gap into the shield.

Then he walked forward, and they were outside.

Immediately, he stepped right, moving from the shadow of his already-crumbling temporary wall into a narrow band cast by the remains of a pillar. From there he could go no further for the moment, trapped in a sliver of shadow. Behind them, the paving stone wall collapsed.

In the wake of that clatter, neither Rennyn nor her Wicked Uncle moved, listening intently. Rustling. The sound of dozens of delicate footsteps, approaching rapidly. And, then, retreating. It seemed the constructs were bound to the building's interior.

Her Wicked Uncle promptly set Rennyn back on her feet, and contrived to plaster a smug and obnoxious expression over clear exhaustion.

"And now you say thank you, little cousin."

He would never be anything less than hateful to her, but he had been true to his word, and it would be petty not to acknowledge that.

"Thank you," she said. "You surprised me."

His smile widened. "Did I? Reflect that the absolute worst thing that I could do to you—outside returning to mutual self-destruction—was to keep to our bargain, leaving you not one thing to complain of. How will you hate me now, little cousin?"

"I think I'll manage," she said, and turned to conceal her annoyance, surveying the terrain.

A lake, or very wide river, dotted with small islands and crumbled buildings, linked by bridges in various states of repair. Directly ahead was a single arch of stone, probably formed using magic. One side had been shattered, leaving only a narrow path intact. Excessively tall statues in various states of disrepair lined the far bank and beyond...more tumbled walls and the remains of a road winding through familiar trees. Semarrak oaks, looking rather bare.

"This is an island as well?" she said, looking back over the corridors they had just exited. A cellar, swimming with magic, with very little sign of whatever building had been aboveground.

"The second prison you've broken me from, little cousin. I wonder if that balances your other handiwork."

He began drawing power as Rennyn turned to stare at him. Second? What... But of course he meant Solace. For all his power, Helecho Montjuste-Surclere had been, like the Kellian, a tool created by Queen Solace.

His casting this time was shadow. It reached out toward the bridge like a dark finger. He followed it unhesitatingly, tossing parting words over his shoulder.

"If we meet again...let us hope that we do not."

Rennyn did not move, or respond, until he had crossed the narrow point of the bridge. This man she had travelled so far to kill, the key to her recovery, walking away

"Goodbye, monster," she said, with a shake of her head.

With her back to the problem she could not similarly abandon, Rennyn considered the wilderness before her. Famously dangerous Semarrak, and obviously not a part near the Kellian settlement—or any place frequented by people. The wind was rising and, outside the ivy-covered cellar the temperature was less than pleasant.

No food, no shelter, no allies.

No shoes.

It should be overwhelming, but Rennyn did not let herself be caught up in guessing her chances. She would start with a place out of this wind.

Chapter Twenty-Four

Being under a sleep spell might mean Fallon was getting plenty of rest, but missing breakfast and then lunch was a big problem. As the day wore on and he remained awkward baggage, a dim ache of hunger began to tug at him. But, despite needing to conserve his energy as much as possible, Fallon couldn't help but be relieved when Auri drew him into the Dream for a second time since he'd been knocked out.

"Does it hurt, being carried like that? Does all the blood rush to your head?"

"Not much," he said, considering his body slung over Darian Faille's shoulder. "I can feel how much I need to eat, and I need to go to the bathroom, but I just sort of feel uncomfortable otherwise. If my head hurts, I think it's because Dezart Samarin hit me." And saved his life.

"I wonder if healer-mages have spells to use for when sick people need to pee?" Auri hopped along a ridge of rock, grinning. "Or if they just won't think about it until you go all over this lady's shoulder."

"*Auri.*"

"She'd probably drop you. I would. How many days do you think they'll keep walking vaguely in this direction before giving up?"

"I don't know." Fallon glanced nervously at Lord Surclere, whose expression was much the same as it ever was, yet somehow gave the impression of a strung wire being wound tighter with every step. "I think most likely some would continue looking, and the rest would try to get out of the forest. Depending on exactly where we are in Semarrak, continuing north might be the shortest route out, anyway, though then there'd be mountains to get through."

And then what? Permanent unconsciousness? Years as a sleeping magical puzzle for student mages to try their hand at? No, this pit in his stomach would swallow him up long before then. This was absolutely the worst time for the revelation he'd been hoping and fearing for so long. Duchess Surclere absolutely had to take priority, but there would be a point where the energy cost of maintaining the Dream would eat away at him so severely that nothing could pull him out of the downward spiral.

Auri poked him in the shoulder. "Stop fretting yourself into the ground, worry-wort. You should be celebrating! They know! They knew you were enchanted and they were trying to figure it out, even. Your Duchess turned out not to be useless after all. Let's hope she's not dead."

"Don't be so callous, Auri."

"Blah." Before Fallon say anything more, Auri pointed: "That's why I pulled you in. What do you think that is?"

Something was glowing, far off among the trees. At first Fallon thought it might be one of Semarrak's legendary inhabitants, those that supposedly dwelt at its heart and had descended from powerful, humanoid Eferum-Get. But when he followed Auri to the limits of her range and peered through the widely-spaced tree-trunks, he could make out a squat stone obelisk, about half the height of a man.

"Looks like a road marker. They enchant them to glow along the Imperial Ways."

"But it's not really glowing, or someone else would be pointing at it."

"It's obviously old. Perhaps we're just seeing the dying dregs of the enchantment. I didn't know there were once Imperial roads through Semarrak, but I guess the Empire does claim the forest as part of its territory."

"Roads go places," Auri pointed out, but there was nothing Fallon could do with the information, and the stone was slowly lost to sight as the group moved on.

For eight people thrust into the depths of a dangerous forest without any preparation, and with only one weapon, they were doing remarkably well. Anything actively stalking them was noticed by the Kellian long before it reached them, and Captain Faille or his mother would leave the group to take care of it. Only twice had anything dangerous even come close enough for Fallon to see.

Some of these hunters had been edible, and Tesin had supplemented the meat with mushrooms and nuts that she seemed able to spot with the merest glance. She'd even located gourds that could be hollowed out to carry only slightly odd-flavoured water. And everyone except Fallon was dressed well enough for a fine day in autumn, though the wind had picked up after midday.

In fact, Fallon thought the biggest problem most of Duchess Surclere's rescuers had was—ironically—a lack of sleep, since dawn had arrived only a couple of hours after they'd emerged from the transportation casting. Kendall was the worst, struggling with the cost of whatever she'd done to hold open the travel casting. Had that really been a recreation of Nameen's Walk, just as Lieutenant Meniar guessed? *Elder Mage* magic! Which was not a good sign at all, since there was only one person around other than Rennyn likely to know how to manage such an amazing work.

Ahead and to the right, Fallon spotted the glow of what must be another of the road markers—even further away this time. Since there was still nothing he could do about it, he followed Auri who, with an instinct for drama, had strayed over to where Sukata trailed the group with Kendall.

"It would be very easy for me to carry you," Sukata was saying. "It will not tire me."

"Yes, it would. Don't be silly. And I don't need carrying."

Kendall made a far from convincing attempt to walk normally, picking her feet up instead of shuffling through the leaves, and promptly staggered, snagged by some hidden obstacle. Sukata caught her, hesitated, and formally offered her arm, which Kendall pretended not to see for another few steps, then took with her usual lack of grace.

"The headache is the problem," Kendall mumbled. "The pain muffling wore off too quick."

"They are designed to have a short duration. The pain is your body's warning that you pushed your limits, to keep you from casting again."

"Last thing I want to do is play pick up right now," Kendall muttered. "Just rest. Guess we're going to have to stop soon anyway."

"Another hour at least until sunset," Auri put in helpfully, but Kendall and Sukata just looked grimly at the sky, and then in unison at Lord Surclere. They walked together in silence, clearly thinking about where Duchess Surclere might be at that moment, and what could be happening to her.

"I am glad you called for me, Kendall," Sukata said carefully.

The shorter girl made a face. "Why in the Hells wouldn't I? We're all supposed to be looking after Herself. I should have stayed in the damn room." Then she hunched her shoulders, adding: "I'm glad you heard me. Can you imagine me and the Lieutenant trying to cart the Pest about while that Imperial pain-in-the-neck played at being in charge?"

Sukata looked at her feet, and Fallon could tell that she was pleased. But then she said very softly: "He is a pain-in-the-neck with very good hearing."

Fallon, Auri and Kendall all stared forward to where Dezart Samarin was keeping pace with Lord Surclere at the front of the group. Well out of normal earshot.

"Good as yours?" Kendall muttered.

"Possibly. He hides it well, but he reacts to noises as you do not."

"Have you seen him casting?" Kendall glowered at the Kolan man's back. "Or could it be something that's been cast on him?"

"I have never seen him cast. But his mask is layered with enchantment, and he never strays any distance from it. It may lend him more than authority."

"Or he's a sneaky lying mage. Not that anyone here was planning on trusting him any further than we could throw him."

Sukata's attention had strayed to something to their left, and then her hand flickered in one of the signals that the Kellian used to talk to each other. Fallon turned to see both Darian Faille and Lord Surclere heading west. Something must be stalking them, and whatever it was required a more than usual response.

With the two older Kellian gone, Sukata hustled Kendall up to join the rest of the group, where Fallon himself had been propped neatly against a rock, and Lieutenant Meniar was using the pause to check him over.

"His colour's not good," the Lieutenant said. "I don't think this is sustainable."

"Borrow your slate?" Dezart Samarin asked.

Lieutenant Meniar raised his eyebrows, then wordlessly handed over his slate book, along with a stick of chalk. He'd already removed one of its 'pages' and given it to Sukata, ready for emergencies, and three sides of the remaining two were written up with Sigillics. Dezart Samarin began writing rapidly on the remaining blank.

"Still going to say you're not a mage?" Kendall asked acidly, while Fallon tried to peer at what the man was writing.

"Still entirely without the strength to cast usefully," Dezart Samarin replied, and handed the slate back to Lieutenant Meniar.

"A muting spell?" Lieutenant Meniar looked from the slate to Fallon's body. "This won't necessarily stop whatever chokes him from activating."

"In which case you can knock him out again," Dezart Samarin said. "But if that casting interacts with his awareness of not being permitted to speak on certain matters, preventing speech—and keeping him away from slates and the like—may be enough to prevent the choke from triggering."

"This one's clever," Auri commented. "Think it will work?"

Fallon didn't reply, watching tensely as Lieutenant Meniar decided to go ahead with the experiment, and cast the mute before lifting the sleep spell that had sat on Fallon's head the entire day.

"Bet I miss all the interesting stuff again," Auri grumbled, as Fallon settled cautiously down where his body sat, and he lifted his head to respond, but was out of the Dream, sitting surrounded by people.

He tried to speak, lifting a hand cautiously to his throat, and waiting tensely for that familiar tightening. Nothing happened. He let out his breath in relief, reassured that he couldn't possibly explain a problem as complex as Auri without words.

"Looking good," Lieutenant Meniar said, pleased. "I expect you'll be wanting something to eat."

Fallon did. He also wanted to do something about his bladder, but fortunately Lieutenant Meniar seemed to understand that without Fallon needing to attempt any embarrassing pantomime. By the time the two Failles returned, Fallon was feeling almost cheerful, munching on nuts while Lieutenant Meniar wrote out a Sigillic that would make his heavy bed socks think they were waterproof.

"Not exactly what this waterproofing casting was intended for," the Lieutenant said, after explaining the two Sigillics to the Failles. "But it should serve in the short term. Sukata, will you cast it?"

As Sukata obeyed, Darian Faille took off her jacket and, ignoring Fallon's silent protest, dropped it around his shoulders.

"Do you believe this proof against further attacks?" she asked. "Or should we avoid addressing any kind of question or speculation to him?"

"Hard to say whether yes/no questions would trigger it, but it's better not to take the risk. In the short term, I don't think he knows much more about the Duchess' disappearance than he's already told us." When Fallon tried to shrug in a way that expressed agreement, the Lieutenant patted his head, then turned to Lord Surclere. "Next water source we get near, we'd better think about camp."

Lord Surclere nodded, then paused when Fallon— remembering those two glowing road markers— straightened and peered off to the east, trying to spot the second one. All the Kellian immediately shifted into alert defensive postures.

"Not a threat," Lord Surclere murmured, after a moment. "Something you saw in your dreams?"

Fallon nodded and, finding that his throat gave no sign of tightening, jumped to his feet and took a few steps in what he hoped was the right direction, beckoning.

"Wait here," Lord Surclere told Lieutenant Meniar, "but mark our current heading." Then he followed Fallon until they had, with only a little difficulty, located a stone almost as tall as Fallon, worn and unreadable, but definitely not a natural rock. There was a road, too, or the remains of one, almost entirely buried. It stretched off to the north, then hooked to the right.

Fallon thought at first that Lord Surclere simply couldn't decide what to do. He stared down the curve of the road for an uncomfortably long time, not moving at all, while Fallon gazed up into a face that had always looked grim to him, but now seemed chipped from ice, locked into harsh, unyielding lines. But then Lord Surclere turned, and gestured for the others to come join them.

"A structure ahead," he said, when they arrived. "We will scout."

He and Darian Faille took Sukata with them, which surprised Fallon until he realised that they would be thinking of wards and magical defences: all the things they could not detect. But it was not long at all before Sukata came trotting back.

"Old, ruined and empty," she said. "But there is water, so we will camp either here or just outside it."

The road had been a false trail, then. Fallon tried not to sag as they continued forward and it became clear that this was no likely lair for whoever had stolen Duchess Surclere. Remnants of buildings, few with any intact walls, let alone roofs or an appearance of being habitable. They were dotted among the trees at the edge of a lake, and on a number of small, flat islands joined by bridges. A row of impressively large statues were evenly spaced along the lake's edge, all of women facing out over the lake. Twenty-one statues, several of them broken and tumbled, and the rest so worn that Fallon couldn't guess if they were meant to be the same person.

"Deserted, perhaps, but no less confusing," Dezart Samarin murmured. "I am learning a great deal about Semarrak this week."

"Nothing in the secret Imperial records?" Lieutenant Meniar asked lightly.

"Not that I've encountered." The Kolan man circled the square base of the nearest statue: a massive block of stone supporting a statue nearly thirty feet in height. "No markings, or distinctive style. Palace or temple complex would be my guess. I think, in other circumstances, I would like to follow that road back, to see what it connects to."

"Somewhere less windy, it's to be hoped," Lieutenant Meniar said, turning as the two Failles joined him. "I can't sense anything obvious, but the place feels odd. I'd like to go over the complex just briefly, before the sun sets. Do you have a preference for where we camp?"

"Better away from the water's edge," Darian Faille said

Lord Surclere surveyed the high banks of the western reach of the lake—back toward where their path would have taken them without Fallon's detour—then said: "In the lea of that rise."

They started along the bank, but Fallon noticed Tesin Asaka lagging behind, peering at the leaf-littered ground. She started walking in the opposite direction, and Fallon naturally followed her, wondering what she was looking at. Then he saw it: a red-brown crescent curving across two leaves.

"Blood," Fallon said, or tried to, but his throat made no noise and so he just hurried to catch Tesin, spotting another crescent and another as he did so.

Fallon had no sooner guessed that they were following the outline of a heel when he saw a patchy mosaic of splotches that made a whole footprint: a string of them, left and right foot both, curving around the base of one of the less intact statues. Faintly, a trickle of power, of intent, touched his senses, and he started running as Tesin circled the rubble around the statue.

Too slow. Fallon hurled himself frantically forward, and if she had not been a Kellian he would have knocked the slender girl into the lake. As it was, she dodged backward, and then caught his arm to arrest his headlong dive.

"What is it?" she asked, setting him aside.

"A ward! A ward!" Fallon tried to shout, and when her puzzlement did not keep her from taking another step, he snatched up a handful of leaves and tossed them over the ring of bloody footprints, even as he got his first good look at the neat hollow that had been scooped out of the statue's base, leaving a domelike rock sitting on the ground, partially hiding a neat little person-sized space. Occupied.

The leaves flared to flame and ash, which promptly blew back into their faces, accompanied by the most transitory surge of power from the woman curled into a tight ball beneath the statue. Duchess Surclere. Against all odds, they had found her.

"Ward?" Lieutenant Meniar asked, hurrying up, and then stopping and letting out all his breath, though whether in relief or dismay Fallon couldn't guess. With only the curve of her back and her draggling braid presented toward them, it was impossible to fully assess her condition, but the bloody handprint on the leg of her pants could hardly be a good sign, and the skin visible between waistband and shirt was blotched red and purple.

"Definitely a ward, though I've never encountered its like," Lieutenant Meniar went on, voice rapid and a little high. "A Symbolic casting, perhaps designed to minimise the energy cost of its maintenance, barely drawing on her unless something crosses the circle. I can't gauge the details of the exclusion, but it would have been simplest for her to set a blanket ban."

The Lieutenant was talking to Lord Surclere, who was somehow behind Fallon. Kellian speed. Fallon didn't even need to turn to see that he was there, could feel the tangible thunderstorm presence. How would Lord Surclere feel, to have come so far, to have the Duchess right before them, so plainly injured and exhausted—and locked behind a barrier whose energy cost might even kill her if they tried to cross it.

Lord Surclere walked into the circle. He didn't even test the ward with a hand first, just stepped forward, leaned down, and picked up the Duchess. No doubt, no hesitation. Or perhaps he would rather burn than—but, no, Fallon thought it was simply utter certainty that the Duchess would not make a barrier that would keep him out.

The ward dissipated when Lord Surclere stepped back out of the ring of footprints, so they at least would not have to worry about the impact of its maintenance. He stopped as soon as he was outside, and just stood there, looking down at Duchess Surclere as if he could not believe that they had really found her. And everyone else stood in a circle before him, staring just as fixedly at the woman whose health had been the central concern of their journey. A single day alone.

"Throat," Kendall said, in a strangled whisper. She tugged at the blood-stained collar of the Duchess' shirt, then let out her breath on discovering not a fresh bite, but a sharp slash, dried to tacky stickiness.

This in turn broke Lieutenant Meniar out of his frozen dismay and he became all business, moving Kendall aside so he could check the Duchess over.

"Only the feet are bad," he murmured. "And I don't like this rash. But her heartbeat's strong." He picked what might be some rope fibres out of the red blotches that spread up her ankles, puzzled.

"Should have known she'd rescue herself." Kendall was frowning blackly. "She got out, escaped. But where from? There's nothing here."

"Obviously more than we can see," Lieutenant Meniar said, crisply. "For now, we need to get her out of this wind, and work on cleaning up these cuts."

After which, Fallon privately hoped, they would return to Aurai's Rest. But somehow he doubted it would be that simple.

Chapter Twenty-Five

Rennyn woke to a new experience. Her husband, asleep, with his arms around her. Lying in a nest of leaves beneath a fragile pre-dawn sky, Rennyn set aside the mystery of how he came to be there at all, and allowed herself to enjoy this gift. Illidian's heartbeat. Illidian's steady breathing. Illidian's warmth.

He was having a nightmare. Muscles shifted, and fingers twitched against her back. His face was barely visible in this light, but she thought that in sleep it was more expressive than his waking mask, revealing hints of anger and pain and fear.

Moving with infinite care, Rennyn lifted her hand and touched his cheek, tracing one of the grim lines that bracketed his mouth. It woke him, as she had expected, and she knew he would remember the first time she had touched him so, and the night that had followed.

His arms tightened, and for the longest time there was nothing but an embrace without need for more. Then a low grumbling interrupted, and Rennyn stifled a laugh.

"My stomach is not romantic."

"But it is here."

With him. The most important consideration, and one she had almost overlooked when she had been castigating herself for accidental commands.

Sitting up, she discovered a collection of sleepers, and blinked at Fallon, curled between two divinations and with...was that a spell to keep him silent? Sukata, sleeping propped upright, was maintaining the wards around their little camp: low-level things that would keep out life-stealers but not do more than delay stronger predators. Lieutenant Meniar, Kendall, the girl Tesin Asaka, Dezart Samarin...and there, keeping watch, Illidian's mother, who met her gaze and nodded.

Illidian handed her what looked like a small pumpkin, which proved to be a makeshift cup. Taking it, she found that her hand had been neatly bandaged, along with her feet, with a visible buttonhole to reveal the bandages had been someone's shirt. She was also wearing Illidian's coat, though still with her sadly stained lounging suit beneath it.

"I see there is an exceptionally interesting story behind how you managed to find me."

"A complete absence of organisation," Illidian said, offering her a large leaf curled around several slices of cold cooked meat. "We forgot even the honey cakes."

His voice did not quite shake. A day not knowing what was happening to her had taken its toll. She leaned against his side as she ate, and they watched the sky grow lighter. Then he picked her up and took her off to a neatly dug latrine with two stripped branches suspended over it as a rough seat.

"And here I thought we'd moved past the need for you to carry me to privies," she said, after she had finished and he was taking her down to the lake to wash her hands.

"You are light-hearted today," he said, sounding pleased.

Rennyn blinked. "I suppose I am. Glad to be alive, of course, but I think it's that...I have been trying so hard not to hate being consistently tired, and yet all the time convinced it was keeping me from solving all these other problems. But this place—I have no idea what this place is, but being tired only meant I needed to rest before starting work on rescuing the other mages." She smiled. "Though I am exceedingly glad to no longer need to tackle it alone."

He bent his head and pressed his lips to her temple and then, after she had washed in the chilly water, found a convenient tumbled wall to sit on with her snug in his lap. They had an excellent view over the lake—ethereal and still in the early morning—and were far enough from camp to not worry too much about sleepers.

"Other problems such as Earl Harkness, and preventing accidental commands?"

"Accidental commands, and removing the inherited controls. Things I theoretically could fix, if only I could devise a way to it. Earl Harkness is a different sort of matter: he's not something for which I can produce a magical solution—not without being rather immoral." She sighed. "My supposedly carefree post-Solace life is a little full of complications like Harkness. While I'm looking forward to seeing what kind of home we can make in Surclere, I've never cultivated the sort of skills I'll need to be its Duchess. I am not a negotiator or even passably diplomatic. I am not good with compromises or weighing fine moral points. So I've been pushing those type of problems away and trying not to think about them."

"The Ten," he said, fully aware of her reluctance in relation to their trip to Aurai's Rest, for all she hadn't discussed it with him.

"Yes," Rennyn admitted. "I don't want to command the Ten to die. And yet how can I just ignore them in their half-life? And I do want—eventually—to have children with you, but that is absolutely a choice that will impact dozens of other people, and should I not take their views into account? And, oh, it's not like I needed that blasted play to point out that perhaps it was unconscionable of me to marry you. How can I continue to put you at risk of careless commands?"

"That is a choice between the possibility and the certainty of pain. And does not take into account what I gain from you."

He said this so warmly, curling a strand of her hair around his fingers, that she was lost to words for a moment, and then recovered herself with a few long kisses. None of which would make the problem of accidental commands go away, but certainly reminded her that he had reasons for facing that risk.

"I was very glad to wake with you this morning."

Illidian knew, of course, what she meant. "And perhaps it is time for me to stop running from the merest possibility of hurting you?"

"I think it's useful to remember that *you* have never hurt me." She curled her fingers through his, and kissed one blunted fingertip. "You know your own limits better than I. I was just glad to wake with you." She glanced up at him, smiled a little grimly, and added: "Yesterday I had a very different waking. It perhaps should have occurred to me that if someone or something was kidnapping powerful mages, my Wicked Uncle was very much a likely target. He'd been trapped here for at least a month."

The husband holding her so carefully became a man of steel and wire, then took a steadying breath and listened without comment as she told him of the decisions she had made. Choices that complicated the Kellian's future, especially if Rennyn and Sebastian died without children.

But, typically of Illidian, his response was only: "Do you feel that you have put him behind you now?"

"I...don't know. But I think I've changed the shape of how I feel into something more manageable. Do you—what choice would you have made?"

"I would prefer him dead. But I, too, would not have killed a man bound and helpless. Much as I would like to pretend he is not a man. I most certainly prefer you free."

"How did you manage to find me?"

He told her, at least up to the point where he said: "We would not have reached it in time if Kendall had not held it open—"

"What?"

"I wondered if that was an issue. Meniar is certain that Kendall extended the duration of this Walk. Having read your guide on learning to cast Thought Magic, it seemed to me this was a step beyond the exercises you had permitted."

"Abstract casting, yes. A travel casting like that isn't something you just...hold, although it may have felt like that to her."

"And so Kendall has now entered the stage of becoming a Thought Mage where you recommend days of quiet meditation and rigorously controlled exercises?"

"That's certainly the ideal. I presume Fallon has had a crisis of his own?"

Illidian explained reason for the muting spell. "When Meniar set divinations to monitor his sleep, the boy did not hide his relief."

"An enchantment only active while he's sleeping might explain it isn't obvious to me. I'll have to sit by him without the noise of the wards and divinations and so forth, to see what I can sense. But since he appears to be stable, I think this morning had better be devoted to rescuing mages. Or at least stopping further abductions."

He nodded, finished relating the details of their rediscovery of her, and then took her back to the small camp. Nothing had changed whatsoever about the fact that she had accidentally commanded him, and was all too likely to do so again during their life together.

She would continue to hate the thought, to try to find a way of preventing her control...and yet, perhaps no longer blame herself quite so much.

Only Lieutenant Meniar and Dezart Samarin had joined the waking world, and she smiled a greeting, then noticed the bare skin visible above the top button of the Kolan's coat.

"Do I owe you a shirt, Dezart Samarin?"

"A small exchange, if you happen to be able to point me to my missing mages."

"Point, yes. Extricating them is going to be a formidable challenge, however, though the ones I saw were at least still alive."

Whatever this place was, it was time to start dealing with it.

Chapter Twenty-Six

Kendall, tramping through endless dream forests, heard a familiar voice and woke with a start, then bit her lip on the little noise that burst out of her at the sight of Rennyn, awake and wearing a long-suffering expression as she was poked and prodded by Lieutenant Meniar. She looked as calmly herself as if it was any other morning, and just smiled at Kendall, and then at Sukata and the Pest. It was still early, barely past dawn, and cold enough to be glad someone had built up the fire.

"The immediate concern is infection in the feet," Lieutenant Meniar was saying. "I used the strongest scours and cleanses I know on them, and I think I've arrested what was present—along with giving them the tiniest hurry-along in the healing process. Since we've limited supplies, and I'm not seeing discharge, for now I just want you to stay off them."

"I think I've done enough walking for a while," Rennyn said. "You're not generous with your pain suppression, Lieutenant."

"Full relief just encourages people to damage themselves more," he said. "I remember when Keste broke an arm..." He trailed off, glancing south unhappily.

"I expect Lieutenant Faral will be at the forefront of any search party," Rennyn said, which was an easy bet. None of the Kellian liked when they didn't know where their mages were, even if they didn't have a high opinion of them generally. And Kendall was fairly sure Lieutenant Faral liked her partner a bit more than that.

"I've tried communicating, of course," Lieutenant Meniar went on. "But I'm guessing we're four to eight days' travel from the Rest, so chances are high that my message-waft won't reach them—not to mention I had to write it on a dried leaf. I didn't want to try one of the more power-hungry workings until I knew what I'd need here." He shrugged, then prodded at one of the purplish patches on Rennyn's wrists. "Do these hurt? The only thing I've seen like them are spider bites, but I couldn't divine a poison and...well, I certainly hope you weren't bitten as often as this suggests."

"Not bites," Rennyn said. "It does hurt, but only a little, and it's part of the larger problem we have to overcome."

"So stop just sitting there and get on with explanations," Kendall put in irritably.

Rennyn only laughed at the interruption, but then she did explain, and Kendall could only listen in complete disbelief to a story that started with waking imprisoned in the same room as the demon prince. And instead of sensibly killing him, exactly as they'd all set out to do, Rennyn had wasted her energy putting a spell on him. And then just let him walk off.

"But..." Kendall said, trying not to sputter. "But you had to kill him to break the miscasting! How...why?!"

Rennyn shrugged. "I found I would rather spend my time tired than be a person who kills helpless prisoners. Even hateful ones. Besides, to be strictly pragmatic, I doubt I would have managed to get out of that place without putting him to use." She glanced up at Captain Faille. "I can still work on trying to rid myself of the miscasting, which I certainly couldn't do while dead or pinned to a wall."

Captain Faille didn't say anything. He had probably been really looking forward to killing Rennyn's monster uncle.

His Imperial Smugness Samarin had been staring out over the little islands where there was supposedly some hidden cellar, but turned back to ask: "Do you believe you've neutralised Prince Helecho as a threat?"

"For the moment. He will find it very hard to break the Ban I put on him—harder even than what he did to me, since mine was no miscasting, and the symbol I used very powerful." Rennyn absently touched the red line cut into her neck. "He remains a superlative mage, and 'do no harm' is broad enough that he might manage considerable mischief about the edges, but I think the rapid adaptation forced on him during his captivity is as much a force as my casting. The Eferum may well have become dangerous to him as a result."

"We will judge him by his future actions, then," Samarin said, in the pompous tone he slipped into occasionally—when he was reminding them he spoke for his Emperor. "The situation with the stolen mages is the more immediate concern."

"I thought a straightforward reconnaissance to start with. Given its sunken aspect and partially open ceilings, I planned to simply walk around the outside of the thing, to see if there was anything more illuminating than mage-studded ivy."

They paused then for breakfast and privy visits, and quibbling over whether they'd all go, or send an advance group. All the Kellian were clearly being extra-alert—even more so than they had during the walk north. Just because Herself seemed to think her monster uncle had been dealt with, and wasn't lurking about waiting for a chance to attack, didn't mean anyone else was going to be so silly.

Had Herself really given up her best chance of recovery? Kendall didn't know whether to be angry, or to try to understand why being pinned to a wall made a monster any less a monster. And what did Rennyn's choice mean for Kendall's plans? She'd been going to stay until Rennyn was better, and had expected that to happen almost immediately after Rennyn's obnoxious uncle had been killed, maybe even bringing forward their return trip to Tyrland. And what about the whole 'Tyrian winters would probably kill me' thing that was a big part of why they'd gone to Kole in the first place?

Kendall noticed the Pest gaping at her, but he turned his head quickly away when she shot him a glare. She'd make a remark about how good an idea a muting spell had been, except that now she knew the Pest had spent the entire journey trying not to die she couldn't help but feel a little sorry for him, rot him. Getting that strangling enchantment off him was probably the main reason he wanted to be Rennyn's student in the first place—along with being the sort of person who was almost as much in love with magic theory as Sebastian.

And that was the answer to Kendall's question. Rennyn was surrounded by people who thought the sun shone out of her whatsie, and it wouldn't make any difference if Kendall wasn't around. Kendall could go get the sort of training she wanted without having to worry whether Herself was being looked after. Though best to put off leaving until they were back in Tyrland, or she'd end up having to learn Foreign before she got to the useful stuff.

Lieutenant Meniar and the Imperial Smugness were talking glass golems now, listing off historic instances where mages had thought glass of all things was just the stuff to build servants out of. A lot more than Kendall had expected because apparently glass worked symbolically for animating constructs. Someone called Dia Dessal had ridden around on a glass stag. The founder of Kole had met the Dawnbringer in a palace whose inhabitants were all glass. Some mage who couldn't walk had had a pet glass golem that fetched him anything he pointed at. Another had a little army of glass warriors. Some of the stories, like the one about Dia Dessal, were even set in Semarrak.

The debate about who should go look at cellars ended with Darian Faille and Sukata trotting off first, to make sure nothing would attack them just for making a circuit of the island, and everyone else trailing along in a slower second group, so they would at least *see* if the scouts got eaten by vine-monsters or glass golems.

Rennyn, riding along in Captain Faille's arms, was looking about all interested and relaxed, even though golems meant a mage, and a pretty powerful one to have stolen all these others and made shields and walk-things and whatever. Typical of Herself to behave as if they were visiting a fair and not in deadly danger.

Captain Faille, after a murmur from Rennyn, turned so Rennyn could more easily talk to the Pest as they walked.

"If I observe you later while you sleep," Rennyn asked, "do you believe that will trigger the Ban that has been set on you?"

The Pest shook his head firmly, looking stupid-happy. He really did want nothing more than for Rennyn to work out his enchantment.

"I'm sorry it took me so long to realise there was something wrong, Fallon. I offer you no guarantees, but I am certainly going to try to help."

Was the Pest going to cry? He looked like he was biting the inside of his cheek to stop himself, while making a feeble sort of gesture to acknowledge Rennyn's promise. Would it be a bad idea if the Kellian taught him their hand signs? Would trying to write or sign an explanation make him choke, or would something happen to his hands instead?

"How is your head, Kendall?"

Kendall started, then muttered: "Fine. Hardly feel it."

"All those exercises lifting things weren't such a waste after all," Herself said, with one of her more irritating sorts of smiles. "I'm very glad you managed it."

Kendall shrugged. There was no need to make a big deal out of that.

"You can have a break from your exercises, at least for today. Tell me tomorrow if the headache hasn't gone."

Kendall refrained from pointing out that she'd had no intention whatsoever of spending her time turning leaves or bowls—or even grand necklaces—over and over just for the sake of it. Instead she pointedly looked ahead over the series of small interconnecting bridges to where Sukata and Captain Faille's mother had reached the island that had supposedly been planted with vine-covered mages.

That island looked almost empty, with just a low rim of foundation stones marking the edge of whatever had been there long ago. A biggish building, that took a few minutes to circle, but there was so little of the structure left above-ground that the scouting party weren't blocked from view at all during the circuit. They mostly kept back from the edge, but after completing the circle, Darian Faille walked right up and stood on the very rim, staring inward. When nothing boiled out to attack her, she turned and walked back with Sukata, alert but unhurried.

"The shield makes it difficult to untangle any other enchantments," Sukata said evenly. "But I located no detects, or any sign that the active mass of casting responded to our presence. There are at least two groups of constructs. Approximately twenty individuals. They did not appear to notice us, and I sensed no directed threat from them."

"Very well," Captain Faille said, and they walked on.

The whole thing felt unreal to Kendall as they continued over the small bridges, having trouble with the last because one side of the smooth arch had cracked and fallen away into the lake, so they needed to go single file. They must look a sight, with the Kellian picked out in a delicate glow by the early morning light, and Rennyn and the Pest swamped by too-large coats over nightclothes, and all of them a good deal mussed and crumpled after sleeping in piles of leaves. They looked more like they needed help themselves, rather than being rescuers.

Two tumbled pillars marked the ramp of the entrance. They passed it by, circling left, but only for a quarter turn about the island before Rennyn indicated that she wanted a better look and they walked right up to the edge of the exposed cellar, all the Kellian alert but detecting no imminent attack. Kendall couldn't sort out anything from the swirl of magic that had become increasingly clear as they approached the island: a shield, yes, but even that felt tangled and complicated.

Craning on tiptoe, Kendall gazed over a cellar that was an even square in shape, a patchwork of open spaces and areas where ivy twined through ceiling grids of stone. Other than being everywhere, the ivy didn't stand out particularly, but Kendall still shivered to look at it, imagining roots trying to burrow beneath her skin.

"I do not believe there was ever an upper building," Captain Faille said. "This has been constructed to be precisely what we see."

"A sunken garden?" Samarin asked, but nodded as he said it. "The other buildings have far more fallen stone—and there's no sign that anyone has been here to salvage it. Nor any hint of movement beyond the glass constructs."

Kendall had spotted one of the mages. Or a person-shaped lump, at least, in the room directly beneath them. That was an ear, and there a hand. She traced the bumps on the walls, struggling to see clearly through the stone grid, and decided there were six. Six people, just below her, with roots burrowing beneath their skin, and spikes in their backs.

"The flowers only grow where people are," she said, in a voice almost as thin and thready as Sukata's. "And they're the wrong sort of flowers for ivy anyway—ivy gets tiny green nubby sorts of flowers, not blowsy big orange ones."

"I still see only two patrols of the constructs," Sukata added. "They do not appear to enter the room below us—perhaps not any of the rooms containing mages."

"Except to put them on the walls, and respond to disturbances," Rennyn agreed, and then no-one spoke for a while because one of the little swarms of glass...caterpillar-ants was moving in their direction.

In a way they were almost pretty, all blue or blue-green, like a collection of glass vases that had been stacked together. With legs and little waving antenna. There weren't any spikes or barbs or teeth or anything that looked like a weapon, but if they'd fought Rennyn's monster uncle and won, they were nothing to sniff at.

Once the patrol had moved away, Darian Faille pointed to the scouting party's left. "They enter this room, even though it appears identical to the one directly below us—with a ceiling grid and a stone door."

"Not yet occupied," Lieutenant Meniar muttered. He was looking a bit sick—probably because he was the healer mage who was going to have to figure out how to get a couple of dozen people 'unpinned' without killing them.

"They also groom the ivy of dead leaves," Dezart Samarin said. "Gardeners, guards or both? In either case, a limited range of function, and clearly not much scope for reacting to events outside their area of duty."

"I would like to see how they respond to a shield across the door of a room," Captain Faille said.

"You think they could simply be bottled up?" Samarin moved a little further along the wall. "Is it a shield that can be cast through? I can't tell."

A little surge of magic from Rennyn was all of her response, and the stone blocking the doorway of the room below rolled to one side. They waited, tense, but no swarm of glass guardians responded, and Kendall couldn't feel any change to the thrum of set casting.

"Block the guards off, break the shield, rescue the mages?" Lieutenant Meniar suggested.

"I can't break this shield," Rennyn said. "Perhaps with my focus, but not otherwise. I could create a temporary door, as my Wicked Uncle did, but then I would go to sleep. I am going to have to compose a Sigillic that one of you can cast...and can't quite see a method to use. I'll need to think it over."

"There is no guarantee that these patrols are the only defenders," Captain Faille said. "I would like a view of the central courtyard: it seems larger than the others."

"Block the guards, open a door, investigate the centre," Dezart Samarin said. "There is no point rescuing the mages only to have them stolen again in a month's time."

"We could risk a short flight over the top," Rennyn said, but only shrugged when no-one else seemed to think this a sensible idea, and suggested instead they find a spot to sit for a while so that she could concentrate on untangling the layers of magic.

Captain Faille found a rock near the cellar and sat with Rennyn on his lap. Kendall could see that

Lieutenant Meniar and Sukata were also concentrating hard, trying to work out how all the enchantments had been constructed by listening to the vibrations they made. It was all just humming to Kendall, so she stuck with trying to spot the Mystery Mage behind it all. The Pest, though, sat down and went to sleep. Maybe he was trying to see something with the enchantment he could use while sleeping, but if that was the case he mustn't have found anything, since he only looked vaguely disappointed when he woke up right after Rennyn had finally had enough and said they could go.

They continued on around the strange cellar, trying to confirm the number of glass constructs and spot all the lumps concealing mages, all while discussing ways of getting them unpinned alive. Then it was Rennyn's turn to fall asleep, almost mid-sentence. Lieutenant Meniar shook his head over her and said that the cuts meant she'd need even more rest than usual for a few days.

Walking back, Kendall decided that Rennyn's good mood was not just because she thought she'd taken care of her uncle, but also because she'd postponed having to probably kill the Ten. But she wouldn't manage to stay cheery next time she dropped a cup of soup down her front.

Lagging at the end of the scouting party with Sukata, Kendall muttered: "She's swapped that monster's life for hers—but the wrong way around."

The squinch of Sukata's mouth told Kendall that was exactly what Sukata thought as well. But then the Kellian girl said: "Would you have killed him?"

Kendall was about to say 'of course!', but hesitated, thinking about what it would be like to kill anyone.

"He enjoyed hurting Rennyn so much."

"I know. And to have to deal with him for the sake of survival...that is not a decision I would have enjoyed. But the Duchess' reasoning is true. What Prince Helecho did in Tyrland—excepting the injury to the Duchess herself—was at the orders of Queen Solace. Very probably controlled almost as much as we."

Sukata's voice, already barely audible, slipped away, and Kendall gripped her hand, knowing her friend was remembering being pressed to the back of her own head, her body used as a tool by someone who didn't care one speck about her. Kendall needed to remember that Sukata—like all the Kellian—had had a horrible experience only a few months ago. Just because she was always so quiet and prepared didn't mean the aftermath of the Black Queen's return had been any easier for her than it had been for Rennyn with her more obvious injuries.

Glancing up, Kendall saw that the Imperial Smugness was watching, and without even meaning to, she dropped Sukata's hand. Then, trying to look only at her feet, Kendall saw from the corner of her eye Sukata's long, pointed fingers curl and then straighten. And hated herself.

Every time she thought they had worked their way back to a comfortable place, Samarin's stupid questions would pop into her head, and Kendall would do something to make everything even more awkward and wrong. How could she put them out of her thoughts, or find an answer that could begin to be believable? How could she stop hurting the best person she'd ever known?

Chapter Twenty-Seven

After the scouting trip, the remainder of the morning was spent on practicalities. Shelter first and foremost, utilising the foundation of one of the ruined buildings, with a combination of Sigillics and Kellian strength compensating for their lack of useful tools. A little basic, but enough to fit all inside, and keep out wind and rain.

Fallon was groggy-headed from his nap by the cellar, but since he wanted to be able to sleep as soon as the Duchess woke up, he freely expended his energy, while struggling to clamp down on his expectations. There would be no miracle solutions. The Duchess was going to sit with him, and they would take the first step on what would undoubtedly be a long road.

But she knew! She knew! SHE KNEW! The foremost expert on the Eferum in all the world would guide Auri out of wherever it was that she was trapped, and Fallon would finally be able sleep without watching his sister in the Dream, and would wake up rested and without any need to worry.

"Why can't we just magic up a few beds and blankets?" Kendall was asking Sukata, as the Duchess' three students scouted among the scattered ruins for the withered remains of vines.

Once again forgetting his mute spell, Fallon started to answer, then sighed. Not being able to speak was definitely safer, but it was very irritating.

"Conjuration impermanency," Sukata said, with the briefest of glances at Fallon. "To create something from pure Efera—from raw magical power—takes a heavy investment of energy, and does not hold. Conjurations fade quickly, and are rarely worth the energy cost."

"But..." Kendall looked down, then back at Sukata. "Didn't the Black Queen conjure the Kellian?"

"That was Symbolic Transformation. Queen Solace used a Symbolic casting to create the Ten from her own flesh. Symbolic castings are always far stronger than those that rely purely on Sigillics, and Queen Solace must have poured an enormous amount of power into them for...for the Ten to have endured as long as they have. When the Efera invested into them fades, Transformation castings usually revert to their former state, but with a Symbolic casting where the former state is so very different, it is difficult to predict what will occur when the casting unwinds completely."

Kendall's expression made clear that she was picturing the Kellian forebears abruptly melting to goo, or something equally dramatic. Since the Kellian transformation had obviously already run through the original energy invested into it, and the Ten had not been unmade, that was far from likely. Symbolic castings had a tendency to continue on in some way, even when you would rather they would stop—just like the miscasting that sapped Duchess Surclere's health. And perhaps whatever Auri had done to herself.

The relief at no longer being alone, of definite help unravelling Auri's miscasting, made him feel light-headed. More than light-headed: he needed a break. Sitting on the nearest tumbled wall, he watched the two girls hunt for vines and worried about his energy use. He'd managed some Sigillic casting—a transformation to weld stones and packed earth together—but shouldn't be this near to dropping. It had been a mistake to go into the Dream by the cellar. Auri had tried to walk over the top of the shield to the cellar's centre, but immediately complained that it felt sticky and given up. Her interest was fixed on the results of Lieutenant Meniar's divinations, and what the Duchess was planning to do about Fallon, and not at all on cellars. Fallon had made the mistake of arguing, which was never the right way to get around Auri, and so he'd wasted even more energy.

He was so sick of being tired.

"There's one," Kendall said, and a still-glossy sassflower vine detached itself from the branches of a nearby tree.

Fortunately she wasn't facing Fallon, who hadn't been able to hide a flash of panic. Self-immolation. Drowning on dry land. Explosions. Fallon couldn't remember all of the cautionary tales that warned mages away from attempting Thought Magic, but he knew he didn't want to learn a new one.

"You will bring your headache back," Sukata said, quite as if that was the only concern.

"I feel fine, now," Kendall said, coiling the vine into her collection.

"You over-extended yourself and now you must rest," Sukata said firmly, which told Fallon that the Kellian girl did, after all, know how Kendall had progressed. Perhaps Lord Surclere had told her.

For a moment Fallon allowed himself to be sheerly and meanly jealous. Kendall made no bones about her lack of interest in magical theory, and openly admitted she was studying with Duchess Surclere simply to learn a profession. Of all the people to make the transition to abstract Thought casting! But still, he hardly wanted her to accidentally kill herself—or any of them—as a consequence. And she had made a very large difference in finding the Duchess.

At least Sukata and Kendall seemed to have worked their way through their disagreement, at least to the point where Kendall had reverted to doing whatever Sukata suggested. She made no more attempts at

Thought Magic, and they returned with a considerable haul of vines to watch with interest as Darian Faille and Tesin Asaka used them as binding and hinges for a door. Lieutenant Meniar, who was pacing his use of magic in case of emergency, had risked a few Sigillics to carpet the floor of their new building with a thick cushiony grey stuff transformed from the lining of his coat pocket. That would only last a few days, but with heat castings and a door they would be relatively comfortable if the weather turned bad.

The clear midday sky kept it pleasant enough outside for the moment. Fallon raided their growing stock of food, and settled down not far from where Duchess Surclere lay curled before a tumbled wall. The scene—with the ruins, the lake, and the most powerful mage in all the world sleeping in a pile of leaves—scarcely seemed real.

They had started out to hunt a monster and now faced a hopeless muddle of escapes and mysteries, but they had the Duchess back again, and so at least Fallon could continue to hope. She knew, and she would...well, she knew. He had to haul back on his expectations, keep them in hand. She had promised to investigate.

Not at all inclined to get up again, Fallon watched Lieutenant Meniar stretch out inside their new house to test his matting with a nap. Lady Rennyn woke up almost immediately after, and was taken off to the new privy by Lord Surclere, but settled down next to Fallon when she returned. He couldn't hide his excitement, and she smiled at him.

"Don't worry about trying to go to sleep immediately," she said. "I want to get a proper feel for what, if any, emanations you produce while awake first."

Fallon wished he could talk, could begin to say what it meant to him that she was even looking. He started to pantomime this, but perhaps it was fortunate that Lord Surclere distracted the Duchess, returning with two of the pages of Lieutenant Meniar's book of slates, and his chalk box.

Duchess Surclere settled down to some meditative Sigillic drafting, plainly still trying to think of a way they could open a door in the shield. But her occasional glances at him told Fallon her mind was not entirely on devising. He wished he had a view of the slate, but decided not to risk distracting her by moving, even though the sun had shifted so he was in shadow and a bit too cool.

Dezart Samarin was less circumspect, strolling over to sit on the wall behind the Duchess. He watched silently until she glanced up at him, then said: "What about a variation of a Fingalese Reflection?"

The Duchess lifted her eyebrows, and turned back to consider her Sigillic draft. "A distinct possibility." She picked up the second slate and began writing, before adding: "If you're going to start openly collaborating instead of just dropping hints, perhaps you'd like to assist Lieutenant Meniar in the 'unpinning' issue. Healing is really not my area of expertise."

"You think it's mine?"

"I gather you're famous for it," Duchess Surclere said, and smiled as if she could see the Dezart's momentary shift of expression behind her. "The price of teasing Kendall is her excellent memory. Too many dropped hints, I'm afraid."

The Dezart now appeared entirely unruffled, but Fallon thought he wasn't overly pleased. "I wonder what leaps of imagination you've made?"

"It's also because you remind me rather of my Wicked Uncle."

That startled the Kolan. "Of an Eferum-Get monster? How very complimentary you are, Duchess Surclere."

"And you remind me of myself, as well. All three of us, we are very powerful and we have been set to an overwhelming task. Solace created Prince Helecho to help her regain Tyrland. My whole family devoted itself her defeat, to the point where I know so little outside Eferum theory that I'm frequently embarrassed by the gaps in my education. And you...Prince Helecho is a good deal more vicious than you seem to be, Dezart, but he's entertained by people in a similar way. Perhaps because he was so separate from our world, but I think also because so much of this is new to him. You are much more widely experienced, but you frequently give me the same impression. A great deal has been denied to you, but for now you are out of your cage, and enjoying the freedom."

Fallon had absolutely no idea what the Duchess was talking about, but her comments were obviously hitting home. The Dezart's expression had become ominously still.

"I seem to have vastly underestimated your ear for intent, Your Grace."

"I also met you when the transformation—it's a Symbolic Transformation, isn't it?—must have been very recent."

So Dezart Samarin really was a shapeshifted mage? But why did he insist he couldn't cast? And what was the point of pretending to be someone else when no-one in Duchess Surclere's entourage had any tie to Kolan society? Really, the only person they'd likely have objected to was Prince Helecho.

Deeply interested, Fallon was sorry when the Duchess glanced back at him, frowning. Perhaps she had forgotten he was listening.

"Sukata, could you please wake Lieutenant Meniar?" she said, then added: "I'm presuming you can hear me, Fallon. Your energy use is worryingly high, far higher than the amounts Lieutenant Meniar divined last night. I don't know if such variation is usual for you, but I don't think it's safe. Are you able to stop?"

Fallon goggled. Or didn't. He didn't move, watching with the same fixed regard that he'd maintained since...since...

Since he'd gone into the Dream. He was asleep. Had been asleep for...surely a large portion of the time the Duchess had been sitting with him. Without Auri.

Chapter Twenty-Eight

Fallon's sudden leap to wakefulness prompted an immediate flurry of weapons-readiness from all four Kellian. The boy swayed on his feet, then took off at a run toward the lake, only to be effortlessly collected by Darian.

"A threat?" Illidian asked, then added to Rennyn: "I feel nothing."

"Is this something to do with the enchantment on you, Fallon?" Rennyn asked, starting to climb to her feet and then hastily changing her mind, perching on Samarin's wall instead.

The boy allowed the barest dip of his chin, and flinched as he did so, no doubt expecting retaliation from his Ban. When that did not happen, he nodded more firmly, and then gestured at the cellar island, tugging at Darian's hold.

"Very well. What I'm going to do is speculate on what is happening to you, and you will confirm that as far as you are able. If this triggers your Ban, I will make you sleep." Seeing his reaction, she added: "And then take you back to that island, perhaps."

This produced clear relief. He *had* done something, then, when he'd gone to sleep during their morning reconnaissance.

"First, however," she said, "I would very much like to know what you have attached to your right ankle. Perhaps someone could check?"

It was like a game of hot and cold, with Fallon's reactions her guide. He didn't even need to nod: merely looked both pleased and fearful as Sukata bent to investigate the chunky, artificially-stiffened bed socks. The girl produced a thin leather anklet and tiny pouch, which she opened to reveal a ball a little larger than a marble.

"Looks like your focus," Kendall said. "But not quite as dark."

"Not a focus at all," Rennyn said, since focus echoes were entirely different to what had drawn her attention to Fallon's ankle.

This produced astonishment. Interesting.

"You thought it was? Certainly not your focus, for its failure to amplify your casting strength would be obvious."

"The sister."

Fallon didn't even have to nod, turning eagerly to Illidian, naked hope writ large.

"Lost a sister three years ago during an attempt to summon a focus," Lieutenant Meniar said, rubbing sleep from his eyes. "The miscasting warped the entire room about her. Did your sister return with the focus?"

From Fallon's reaction, his tentative shake of the head had been accompanied by the punitive impact of his Ban. Fortunately it did not seem to last, but they needed to take better care.

"Phrase everything as statements," Illidian said, putting a hand on the boy's shoulder. "This object was the result of your sister's miscasting."

Fallon nodded.

"Your sister did not return."

This produced an expression combining 'no' with something more complicated. Rennyn, running short on sure guesses, turned her attention to the sphere Sukata handed her.

A dark red-brown stone. Most definitely not a focus, but still with an elusive trace of power about it, though less than she'd felt when he'd been asleep. It was tied in some way to whatever allowed Fallon to observe those around him. Was he able to see all the way to the island cellar? But, no, if that was the case he would not have needed to sleep during their reconnaissance.

Postponing the risk of more questions, Rennyn cast several divinations, trying to amplify intent. There was nothing clear, no purpose that she could untangle. The stone didn't seem to do anything except draw power from Fallon. She pressed it to her temple.

Keep this a secret or I'll kill you.

Blinking, Rennyn lowered the stone. That was the Ban then—probably not even deliberate, and thus entirely unpredictable. Confirming their guesses was definitely not 'keeping a secret', and if Fallon was not clearly facing some urgent crisis she'd abandon this game of hot and cold.

Casting a physical divination, a broad and simple 'what is this', Rennyn considered the object she held. Then she tried very hard not to drop it. Dezart Samarin, beside her, reached over and took the sphere from her hand, giving Rennyn a chance to regain her composure. From the exceptionally blank expression he wore, she suspected he had caught the results of her divination.

"Does the Ban prevent you from talking about your sister entirely?" Rennyn asked.

Fallon shook his head, firmly this time.

"So your sister—she was called Auri...?"

"Aurienne," Dezart Samarin said, neatly demonstrating that Rennyn had not been paying nearly enough attention to her students.

"Aurienne created an Eferum-gate in order to summon a focus. She miscast, and...you weren't home at the time, I understand. So you returned home, and found this...stone."

Fallon shook his head. Rennyn frowned at him, and then at the stone Dezart Samarin handed back to her.

"Still, for you to be caught in the miscasting, even though you were absent, there would have had to be something to draw you in. If that wasn't triggered by finding...I suppose she left a note? Telling you to not talk. You read the note, and were caught by this Ban." At his eager nod, she continued: "And then, when you went to sleep you found yourself able to see everything immediately around you—a casting not of your design, but fuelled by your energy."

This produced both a nod, and an expansive gesture to indicate something more than just seeing.

"Your sister was there," Illidian said. "When you sleep you meet your sister."

Rennyn hid her surprise, both at the idea, and at Fallon's positive response. She looked down at the sphere she held, then around at her ramshackle collection of rescuers. Darian, Illidian and Tesin: excellent against physical attacks but vulnerable to magic. Lieutenant Meniar: more tired than she'd like given how much they would need him. Sukata: full of quiet determination, but without the strength of a focus. Kendall, who she should warn not to—no, if it came to a point where Kendall tried to cast, then the risk would probably be worth it. The 'Dezart', who probably genuinely couldn't cast. And Fallon, who she rather suspected would die in the night if she did not find a way to relieve his current power drain.

"Well," she said. "I think I have a way through the shield, and perhaps on the way we can decide on a first attempt for separating plant and mage. At the least, I think we need to get Fallon closer to whatever...whoever he left back on the island.

She glanced down at the stone again, and closed her fingers about it. Now was not the moment to tell her puzzle-box student the result of her physical divination. This was not a focus. This had once been bone and blood and flesh.

This was Fallon's sister.

Chapter Twenty-Nine

No-one argued with Rennyn's decision to troop back to the garden of mages. A feeling of urgency had descended, all muddled with a sense that they were hurrying off to get themselves killed. And all for a bunch of people they'd never met. By far the smartest thing to do would be to head south, have His Smugness report the find, and set a few hundred people at the problem. The mages had all been there weeks—even months—and so no-one could say it was necessary that Rennyn personally poke that nest of glass hornets.

The Pest was a different matter. He always looked a bit peaky, but now wore a spun-sugar air, as if one good knock would see him in pieces. His expression kept bouncing between bubbling-over and worried sick, and he obviously ached to explain properly what was wrong with him. His sister had tried to summon a focus and instead got herself stuck in Fallon's dreams? Somewhere that didn't sound like the Eferum, but certainly wasn't anywhere even Rennyn had been able to spot. And this sister was now trapped on the mage island, while still being maintained by Fallon. Maybe.

It was a pity they hadn't brought Sebastian along after all. Some whole new place that wasn't the Eferum or maybe was, and sisters who only came out at night, would be just the sort of thing he'd love to dig into. And bore everyone for hours warbling on about how it all worked.

While everyone else was agreeing that the first thing they'd have to do would be to see if they could section off the glass golems, Kendall privately admitted that if they marched off south, Rennyn would probably only get vanished again. Fixing this problem was a thing Rennyn Claire couldn't walk away from, any more than facing down Solace had been. All of the most powerful mages that Kendall had met had either been complete monsters, or stuck sacrificing themselves for noble causes.

Like the stupid Emperor of Kole.

Rennyn asked, in the mild tone Kendall knew to distrust: "Have you any further recommendations regarding separating the mages from the vine, Dezart Samarin?"

"I may," he said, equally mild. "I want to see them personally first."

Kendall was fairly certain that the Imperial Smugness couldn't be the Emperor of Kole. The Kolans would sure as shine have kicked up a fuss if their Emperor had taken off on a jaunt to the Forest of Semarrak. But what else could Rennyn be suggesting, with her talk of transformations, and mages famous for healing lore. Had the Emperor traded places with someone? Who was ruling Kole while he was gone? Who would get up on that throne, put on that mask, and... No. It couldn't be the Emperor, because Rennyn had been totally clear that the Emperor couldn't leave that throne room, could never take off that mask. Not without dying.

Shaking her head, Kendall tossed the question to the back of her mind for later. Even though she wasn't going to be casting, let alone fighting, she needed to focus. Anything might be a clue or a warning of an attack. Kellian instinct meant they could anticipate almost anything coming at them, but that didn't mean it wouldn't help to watch Sukata's back, and keep an eye on Rennyn and the Pest.

They marched all the way back to where they'd first stopped to peer into the cellar, with Rennyn writing Sigillics all the while. She handed one of the slates to Sukata, then looked at the Pest.

"Do you need to sleep to address whatever has changed? If so, I'll put sleep on you briefly while we're re-establishing the pattern of the constructs' patrols, but I don't want you asleep while we're making our attempt." She smiled faintly. "In case we need to run."

The Pest just nodded, and sat down with his back against the nearest rock. A tiny flicker of magic sent him off right away.

"His energy use has dropped with the relocation," Rennyn said, after a short pause. "If we can't untangle this problem this afternoon, I think we're going to have to sleep here."

Lieutenant Meniar grimaced. "Could we keep him awake all night and then bring him back here to sleep tomorrow morning?"

"Possibly. But even awake he's likely being drained at a higher rate than normal." Rennyn handed a second slate to Lieutenant Meniar. "This is a guise-shield. It's power-hungry, so I'd rather you didn't have to use it, but if the constructs refuse to stay where we put them, I'd rather avoid combat if at all possible. For one thing, we don't know precisely how they're linked to the vine."

"They might be powered by it," Captain Faille said.

"Logical," Rennyn agreed, looking up at him. "Do you think we should try to simultaneously trap both patrols?"

Captain Faille and his mother exchanged glances, then Darian Faille said: "If we divide into two groups, then we have far less chance of withstanding an attack."

"Very well—we're already gambling on their simplicity, after all. I'll close the door to the room below as soon as the first patrol is in. Sukata can cast the binding. Unless Fallon has something to report."

Rennyn woke him as she spoke, and they all looked down at worry, disappointment, and frustration. After a pause, Rennyn simply handed him the last leaf from Lieutenant Meniar's slate book.

"I don't want to risk you casting unless it's absolutely critical, Fallon. This is a variant guise shield—less powerful, but something we can try if the first fails. If trapping the constructs works, we'll head to the centre of the garden and attempt to resolve this snare, and you can try sleeping again there if we see no other way forward."

The Pest nodded, though he was clearly now fretting his head off. He took the slate, chewing on his lip as if it was breakfast, and moved to stand a little to one side. Sukata, gripping her own slate very tight, moved to the very rim of the cellar, above the empty room they had experimented with before. They all waited without further conversation, watching the progress of the nearest patrol.

Ants. Bees. Constructs. Tools. A set of instructions given form. Kendall wondered if they ever rested. If they had nests somewhere in the vine-covered rooms, and got to sit down occasionally. Whether they had names, and if, looking down at them, the Kellian thought about the Ten.

The glass golems certainly didn't seem to be looking up, going about their vine-grooming business without any hint they noticed or cared that a bunch of people were standing just outside their garden. They didn't even react when Rennyn closed the door on them, after they'd entered the nearest empty room. They only tried to open it after they'd finished their short combing circuit of the room, and by that time Sukata had cast the binding Sigillic that made the stone of the door hold fast to the walls.

The first glass ant-thing that tried to leave was a small one, and when it reached the closed door it climbed up it, did a funny little waggle, then pattered off to one side and started around the room again. Another did the same, and then a third. It wasn't until one of the largest of the constructs found the door closed that there was any difference: that one reared up and pushed at the door.

Nothing.

It made a little circle before the door, reared up again and pushed.

Nothing.

The third time, with the door still stubborn, it started around the room again, and Kendall heard Rennyn let out her breath.

The rescue party waited, still wordlessly, until the constructs had followed the same pattern three times over. Finally, Captain Faille said: "Next patrol."

They moved, repeated the exercise with all the same knotted-stomach tension, and then circled back to the entrance.

"Now we get to the guesswork and luck?" Kendall said, as Lieutenant Meniar flipped the slate and read over, for the half-thousandth time, the apparently tricky Sigillic Rennyn had come up with to get through the shield.

"I should think the Sigillic will work," Rennyn said.

"I wasn't talking about getting *in*. What do we do once we're in, when something goes wrong?"

"Well, don't sit in one place for an extended period of time, for a start. But that's why I've written the shield Sigillic on the reverse of each slate—any mage should be able to cast it, including you, Kendall, should it be necessary to run."

Kendall stared at Rennyn, then let her face show exactly what she thought of that. But there was no use pointing out that it might have helped if Kendall had even once been allowed to practice casting Sigillics before they stepped on the ant's nest.

"I agree that it's best to investigate the heart of the garden before working on freeing the mages," Rennyn was saying. "I've too many guesses on what we might find there to suggest an ideal approach."

"We will avoid conflict if we can," Darian Faille said. "But at this stage I would recommend responding to a direct attack decisively. We will attempt to take attackers alive, however."

Wondering if Captain Faille would try to fight while holding Rennyn, Kendall let herself be shuffled into a Sentene defensive formation, with Darian Faille and Sukata taking lead, and Tesin in the rear to catch any attackers coming up behind them. Unable to think of anything more useful, Kendall picked up a rock to throw if they did get to fighting.

She listened to the way the sound of the shield changed as Lieutenant Meniar cast, and made sure to step forward with everyone else when he was done, since the longer he held open the shield, the more tired he'd get. Her shoes crunched over something, and Kendall looked down to see glass, and had to push away a vision of Sukata, shattered into pieces and trampled upon. Even the first Kellian had been nothing like these bug-caterpillar-things. So far as Kendall could make out, once the Black Queen wasn't around to give them commands, the first Kellian had been a lot like babies—deadly, six-foot, clawed babies—who just needed some time to start wanting more than to be told what to do next.

They walked down the entry ramp and then paused, listening. The play of magic was distracting, making it harder to focus on ordinary noise, and the whole place felt heavy and a bit wet. A lot warmer than it had been outside the shield, too. It smelt like a hothouse.

"An experiment first, please," the Imperial Smugness said, and pressed his hand against a relatively clear spot on the nearest wall. "And you as well, Lieutenant, and perhaps Sukata and young Tesin."

No surprise that the ivy didn't even seem to notice Tesin, while almost immediately reaching out tiny little white threads toward Lieutenant Meniar and Sukata. Kendall stared hardest at the last hand, Samarin's, and saw that the ivy did react to him, but only after a much longer pause.

"You might want to mind your ankles," Rennyn said.

Kendall looked down and saw that the little filaments were reaching toward her feet. In one mutual shudder, everyone moved, even those who didn't have any mage ability. Even Captain Faille. It was like the place was trying to eat them.

"Let's not linger," Samarin said. "Direct to the centre."

'Direct' didn't mean all that fast, and Kendall's headache started back up with the thrum, thrum, thrum of the place. Corridor, fountain courtyard, corridor. The 'garden' wasn't really all that big, and with the glass bugs shut away like the mages, there wasn't anything but ivy and old stone. As they slowed near the open central space, everything felt like it was pressing down.

The last time Kendall had felt like this, it had been when the Black Queen had succeeded in her Grand Summoning, and a whole mountain of power had squashed down into the one place. This wasn't even a tenth so bad, but it was the strongest casting Kendall had felt since that time.

"Not an attack," Captain Faille said.

"Around what I'd expect of twenty or thirty strong mages in a joined casting," Rennyn said, sounding more interested than anything else. "I'm still not clear on the intent, though, yes, definitely not an attack. The focal point is directly ahead. Is that...?"

"Statue, not person," Darian Faille said briefly.

Another step or two made this less cryptic. In the middle of the next courtyard was a statue instead of a fountain. It wasn't nearly as worn as the ones out by the lake, though it seemed a similar enough shape. A tall woman with long braided hair, wearing a robe. She held her hands out before her, cupped together, as if praying to the Dawnbringer.

And nothing much else. A lot less ivy. The walls were almost clear of it, revealing swirling patterns etched in the stone, but there were roots growing neatly in channels leading directly to the base of the statue.

Rennyn murmured something to Captain Faille, and he took her up close to one of the walls.

"I shall be most impressed if you're able to read proto-Efanian, Duchess Surclere," the Imperial Smugness said.

"Unfortunately not," Rennyn replied. "But this, I think, is Nameen's Walk. It is strong enough, and has been used often enough recently, for me to make out the shape of the casting.

"What in the Hells is proto-Efanian?" Kendall asked.

"The name given to the casting language used by the Elder Mages," Sukata said, her whispery voice making clear she was impressed. "No-one knows how to read its written form."

"I could reconstruct this, I think," Rennyn added, sounding pleased. "Well, with a lot more strength I could." She paused. "I think my focus is somewhere in this room. I can feel it."

The Imperial Smugness fished his mask out from its big inner pocket, and put it on before surveying the room again. If he really couldn't cast, maybe the mask was the reason he seemed able to hear as well as a Kellian. Whatever the case, Kendall would still bet he was a liar.

He glanced her way, so she glared at him, then concentrated on finding Rennyn's focus. Not on a chain around the statue's neck, which would have been too convenient—and worrying. There were precious few places to put things in the open courtyard, unless there was a hidden cache beneath the paving stones.

They all looked a little ridiculous, pacing about while still acting like they expected the jaws of some trap to swing shut at any moment. It was the Pest, entirely out of place in his grubby bedclothes, who stooped and plucked a chain out from among the roots that filled the channels leading to the statue. From the chain, in a little wire holder, was a clear stone almost the size of a hen's egg.

"Belonging to one of the other mages?" Rennyn said. "Can this casting actually be able to make use of our focuses?"

While Darian Faille stood guard, and Rennyn continued to study the decorated walls, everyone else scrabbled about pulling focus after focus from among the roots. The first was joined by another, and another, and became a pile. Kendall shrugged off her jacket and they used it as a makeshift bag.

"How many mages did you say were missing?" Lieutenant Meniar asked, adding a medium-sized focus to the others.

"From Kole, twenty-two. Two verified as gone from Verisia. Another from Dunnesan, and that possible case from Fel Sparo. The numbers are rather complicated by false reports, the increasing panic, and those whose location is simply unknown. But these extras may be from the northern kingdoms—they rarely share information with Kole, particularly since the loss of certain of their mages would leave critical holes in regional defences."

"Or they could have been here a real long time," Kendall pointed out. "It's not like this place is new-built."

She had paused in her poking her way along one of the channels, and flinched when she discovered a little root-hair had burrowed into the back of her hand. She picked the thing out, grimacing at the red dot left behind, but then forced herself to keep working. Next time she started thinking Rennyn was soft, she'd have to remember that she'd actually climbed back into the vines and let them stick her all over. Kendall wasn't sure she'd have been able to do the same.

Kendall's persistence was rewarded by another focus. She slid it out, drew her breath for a pleased exclamation, and then paused. Standing, she trotted over to where Captain Faille was patiently holding Rennyn by yet another wall, and held out not one but two smoky-dark focuses bound to the same leather cord.

Rennyn's eyebrows lifted. "It seems my Wicked Uncle approves of my focus-summoning methods," she said, taking the cord. "And now we have a neat reversal of circumstances."

"Is he likely to come looking for it?" Lieutenant Meniar asked. He helped Rennyn work her focus free of the binding, and then pocketed the smaller focus and cord.

"He has invested far less time into that than I had in mine," Rennyn said, gripping her own focus tightly for a moment before slipping it into the little pocket on the front of her shirt. "Everything else being equal, he's likely to simply start again."

Rennyn had gone into the Eferum nearly three hundred times to summon her focus—and at the moment wasn't likely to survive a single transition. Getting that little black stone back was probably worth the entire trip.

"Now that you have your focus back, can we use it to remove the miscasting from you?" Kendall asked.

"It doesn't quite fit, symbolically," Rennyn said, with a faint sigh. "If I had the false focus that caused the miscasting...but that was crushed in the aftermath of the Grand Summoning. This, at least, may mean a little less fainting when casting. Unless of course it leads me to be over-ambitious."

Rennyn looked up at the sky then, and they all copied her. Clear blue, but the shadows cast by the walls marked the progress of the afternoon.

"There's a Sigillic divination I want to try," Rennyn said, after a moment. "While Fallon and Kendall mark it out for me, Lieutenant Meniar, perhaps you and the Dezart can make an examination of one of the trapped mages?"

Her voice sounded odd. Lieutenant Meniar frowned, then put a hand on Rennyn's forehead. She shook him off impatiently.

"No fever that I can tell. But yes, my throat is a trifle sore. Which, at this juncture, is simply another reason not to delay."

Along with being straightforward disaster. In the best of conditions Lieutenant Meniar would be able to nurse Rennyn through a cold, but stuck out in the middle of nowhere trying to rescue a whole bunch of other people, and it would be just the thing to push Rennyn onto the downward spiral of illness and exhaustion that they'd been at such pains to avoid.

No-one argued the point. After the briefest discussion Lieutenant Meniar, Samarin, Sukata and Darian Faille went off to look at the nearest flowering mage, while Rennyn dictated an endless Sigillic which became a double ring of squiggles around the statue. Tesin continued to search out focuses, and Captain Faille succeeded in being stonier than the statue at the centre of it all.

They'd reached the point of making tiny corrections to individual sigils by the time the second group returned—and Rennyn's voice had definitely gone croaky. Kendall could have kicked herself for not thinking to bring along something to drink.

"Any hope?" Rennyn asked, as Samarin paused to look over their chalk work.

He was still wearing the mask, so Kendall couldn't see his face, but his voice was crisp and businesslike.

"Two options seem viable. The first will take at minimum two casters—one to remove the growth into the lungs, and the other to cauld the holes left behind. And then immediate, more substantive repair work would need to be carried out. With the resources at hand, this approach would allow us to get one or even two down by nightfall. If we chose healer-mages—and they survived and recovered with sufficient speed—they could in turn assist us tomorrow. In...between five to eight days we could have them all down, though given the conditions of operation, we're likely to have a series of secondary issues. Infection. Blood clots. Collapsed lungs if the caulding doesn't hold."

"I do hope you're leading with the less desirable approach."

Samarin went on as if Rennyn hadn't spoken. "The second option will greatly depend on what this vine is doing, and whether we are free to interfere with it. A Symbolic casting—with all the consequent risks of imprecise symbolism—could be used. Instead of removing the mages individually and repairing the damage, we could treat the separation as a natural process and...ripen them, if you will."

It wasn't often that Herself looked startled by magic, but she gaped a little at that.

"I'd have to cast it," Lieutenant Meniar said, with the gloomiest expression Kendall had ever seen him wear as he looked down at a slate full of tiny Sigillic writing. "The survival chances of pulling these spikes out of them and patching the holes is not high. The...the possible results of option two scarcely bear thinking about, and it will require a very thorough knowledge of anatomy to manage."

"Anatomy or botany?" Rennyn said, and then offered an apologetic little grimace at Lieutenant Meniar's pained response. "Well, we can't make any decisions until we know more about the vine itself, and what all this power is being drawn off to do." She looked around at them, hesitated, then said: "And now we reach the point where we start hitting casting limits. I think this one is best left to you, Sukata. It's not so power-hungry I think it will put you at risk, and I've structured it to allow you to cut it off at any time, but it will leave you very tired. Please don't maintain it to the point of collapse."

Sukata, typically, went all very straight and upright, and keen to show that she would be responsible and reliable. Everyone else drew back to the archway they'd entered through, and watched her try.

The circle of sigils was so large Sukata had to walk around it—twice—to complete the casting, her attention never wavering from the chalk figures as they began to glow from the power she pushed into them. She staggered back a couple of steps as the thing completed and it began to draw on her in earnest. Kendall watched her worriedly, and then almost managed to forget her altogether as a bloom of green lifted from the circle like a curtain rising on a stage.

Instead of a paved stone courtyard they were standing on the lip of a pit—no, a whirlpool. A dim, distant sound, a muffled gale, made Kendall's headache pound all the more. It came from the green light pouring into the room from four rivers where the root channels were marked: an endless flow that swirled and was sucked down and away.

The statue was still there, an island rising from the centre, and another tiny thin green trail of light dripped from its cupped palms. Chained to its legs was the outline of a woman who looked very much the same as the statue, except thin and insubstantial and worn. The chains were a bright white, and looked like they had to be painful, and even if they weren't, there was a horrid, barbed mahogany-red thing—lichen with...with little mouths of champing teeth—that seemed to have grown out of the whirlpool, all up one of the trapped person's legs and the right side of their body.

Clutching the other leg as if it was the only thing stopping her being sucked down was a weeping, terrified, and transparent girl.

Chapter Thirty

"Auri!" Fallon shouted, or tried to. He started forward, and was almost hauled off his feet by Tesin catching at his collar.

"Help me!" Auri shouted, sobbing with anger and fear. "You've been so slow!"

Had she been like that all this time? Ever since this morning? Had she watched them play hunt-the-focus, and write out all of that enormous Sigillic, calling and calling, and ignored by Fallon along with everyone else?

"We'll certainly try," Duchess Surclere said, and Fallon turned to look at her sharply, because it surely wasn't just the Duchess' sore throat that brought that ambiguous note to her voice. She noticed, and gave him an unhappy smile. "Your sister, Fallon?"

He nodded, then started when she made a faint gesture, releasing the silence casting on him. "Auri," he said, tentatively.

"I'm going to leave you free to speak, but to be safe don't assume that you are able to tell us anything about the miscasting." Duchess Surclere's attention had already moved from him, and she was frowning now at the person chained to the statue, who looked as if she was unconscious, head sagging forward. Captain Faille moved forward so that he stood only two feet from the outer edge of the doubled circle. Fallon followed, and hoped he only imagined the faint tugging that seemed to try to draw him closer.

"Aurienne," Duchess Surclere said, speaking in a firm, flat tone. "Tell me very quickly and clearly the circumstances of your miscasting, and what has happened to you afterwards."

Though she was frantic, and obviously tired, Auri managed this in a way that could only make Fallon proud. All the things they had spent years trying to find a way to tell, delivered in short, gasping sentences. While she spoke, the woman she clung to shifted in her chains, seeming to properly notice her.

"If you put me to sleep I might be able to pull her out," Fallon suggested, once Auri had told everything he thought important, and was surprised when Auri immediately shook her head.

"You'd just get sucked in, Fal. The Dream's all wrong here, like it is in my bedroom. Everything sticky."

The chained woman had raised an apparently heavy head to gaze in a vague way in their direction. She didn't seem to be quite able to see them.

"Are you by any chance Nameen?" Duchess Surclere asked.

The woman moved her head from side to side, not in negation, but as if working to hear more clearly. After an extremely long pause a rustling sound lifted over the distant roar: "*Once. A fragment, a remnant. No more.*"

The words were not audible—her mouth didn't move. She didn't even seem to be speaking Tyrian, but Fallon understood her.

Duchess Surclere continued: "Will you tell us the purpose of this casting?"

For several long breaths it seemed the woman would not answer, but perhaps she was only gathering strength, because her answer, when it came, was far more audible, and she looked directly at the Duchess.

"*A repair. Necessitated...increased tearing, apertures, after war.*"

Looking exceedingly puzzled, Duchess Surclere touched her hand to the pocket that held her recovered focus: a gesture that meant she was attempting to increase her sensitivity to worked magic. Then she straightened, almost knocking her head into Lord Surclere's chin.

"You're repairing the tears in the walls of the Eferum?"

"*Failed,*" the woman—could she truly be an Elder Mage?—replied. "*Flawed premise. Fading...then control lost. Collection process corrupted.*"

"Is this some form of Eferum-Get?" Dezart Samarin asked, indicating the...thing growing up the woman's leg. "Can we help you remove it?"

"*End me,*" the non-voice whispered. "*End this.*"

A wave of unspeakable weariness rocked them, as if wind could be exhausted, as if the air longed to be done. Sukata staggered, and Kendall hurried across to slip a supporting arm around the Kellian girl.

"There's no other way?" Dezart Samarin asked urgently.

"HURRY UP!" Auri had screamed it, her voice harsh, tearing. "I can't—I can't hold on much longer!"

"We have to get her out of there before anything else," Fallon insisted. "We don't know what will happen if you interfere with the casting while she's trapped like that."

But the sagging figure chained to the statue had shifted her gaze to Auri.

"*Child, you too...remnant.*"

"What?" Fallon said, when everyone else seemed to catch their breath. "What does that mean?"

"Fallon..." Duchess Surclere sounded as tired as the Elder Mage. "The stone you gave me. It's not a focus. It's all that remains of your sister's body."

"Are you saying I'm dead?" Auri asked, voice cracking as it scaled up on the final word. "That's not true! It's not!"

"You're wrong," Fallon said, breathless, sick. "She's alive in the Dream! She got taller. She aged. She's not dead."

"You said you would help me!" Auri's hold slipped, and she shrieked and slid several inches before regaining her grip.

"I said I'd try," the Duchess replied, barely audible, and it did not help that she clearly felt awful, because she still wasn't *doing* anything.

Dezart Samarin took off his mask. Fallon would not have even noticed if the movement had not been accompanied by a swirl of highly complex worked magic. Handing thc mask to the Duchess, he said: "Do you think you can reproduce that?"

Duchess Surclere stared at him, then at the mask she gripped awkwardly through the eyeholes. "Are you..." She stopped, then nodded. "Yes, I see the mechanism. How are you still able to function?"

"I leave a small part of myself behind with each transfer. A fragment of a fragment, but over time that makes for a very large cost, and is the reason there aren't dozens of me." The Dezart glanced at his highly confused audience. "I'll need rope, string, even a shirt. Something I can reach her with."

"What are you going to do?" Fallon demanded, as Darian Faille offered the Dezart's own sword.

"The construct only lasts five or so months," the Dezart added as he shook his head at the sword and accepted a length of coiled vine from Tesin. "Bring her to me, and we'll see about a more permanent solution."

"I'll send the mask ahead, so you know to expect us," Duchess Surclere replied, on an oddly dry note.

"Do that," the Dezart said, and for a moment resumed the entertained expression that was his usual attitude. "Though in the interest of making that meeting sooner, and more certain, don't you think that crushing Prince Helecho's focus would hold a certain symmetry?"

The Duchess blinked, stared at nothing for a moment, and then laughed. "It may at that. I will try it. Thank you very much indeed for deciding on direct collaboration."

"Thank you for your future restraint," he said, and turned back to Auri. "Don't let go of your grip there," he ordered. "This is just a symbol of connection."

"I don't *understand*," Auri said.

Whipping the end of the vine in a small circle, he tossed it so that it arced across the swirling vortex. As the end of the vine touched Auri, Duchess Surclere cast, but whatever she did broke Auri's grip, so that as the vine fell away it pulled Auri with it.

"Auri!" Fallon cried out, and thought she turned to look directly at him.

Then the vortex caught the sagging middle of the vine, and Dezart Samarin dropped the end he'd been holding. Both vine and Auri disappeared in a moment, leaving only the Kolan man, alone and empty-handed.

oOo

The Imperial Smugness was staring at his hands as if he couldn't believe he'd dropped his end of the vine. Kendall had no idea what he thought he'd been doing, but was glad when Rennyn finally remembered what this little show was doing to Sukata, and told the Kellian girl she was free to drop the divination.

Feeling Sukata's hesitation, Kendall said firmly: "Do it. Nothing will be helped if you collapse."

With a soft exhalation, Sukata obeyed, and much of the visible weirdness went away, though the endless pulsing that was giving Kendall such a headache still filled the otherwise quiet courtyard. Sukata sagged. She really had been near her limit, and would probably have just kept casting and then what would have happened?

"It's not true," the Pest was muttering. "She can't be...I did this. I brought her here. Auri."

"*Fel,*" Samarin said. He ran his fingers over his face, then did it again. Then he spun around and told the Pest. "You didn't do anything, idiot."

"This is going to get confusing," Lieutenant Meniar said, while the Pest gaped. "Ah, Aurienne, is it? Or...it is just Aurienne in there, yes? It's not both, is it? That would be..."

"Just me," Samarin said. "I think." He turned back to the Pest, and suddenly hugged him, lifting him a few inches off the ground. "Don't you see? She put me in him." He dropped the goggling Pest and turned to shoot a narrow look at Rennyn. "Though you weren't going to help me, were you? You were going to stand there and watch me get sucked up by that thing."

"Yes, I had no idea what to do," Rennyn said, calmly. "This is very much not my area of expertise. Perhaps we should all sit down for a while? I'd like to look over the Sigillic Corusar proposed for the captive mages, and I think we need some recovery time."

"So he *was* the Emperor?" Kendall said, blankly. "But..." She shared a glance with Sukata, and found the same combination of astonishment and horror. "He...died?"

"No," Captain Faille said, and Kendall had a strong feeling he was upset, though as usual it was hard to be sure. He moved to a spot as far as possible from any ivy, and carefully folded himself down cross-legged, settling Rennyn at his side.

Slowly, they joined him, with the exception of Darian Faille, who remained on guard—not by the entrance, but between them and the statue. Remembering the thing of barbs and teeth, Kendall thought that a smart choice. She tried not to stare at Samarin—Aurienne—who was holding the Pest by one elbow and frowning at him. The Pest was sheet white and wobbling worse than Sukata.

"Is the miscasting still drawing on him?" Aurienne asked.

"With this amount of background wash, I can't tell," Rennyn said. "But I think this is as much the shock he's had, on top of the growing exhaustion. To be safe, we'd best assume that distance will continue to increase draw on him, and that the Ban is still active. We apparently have a few months to investigate further."

She looked down at the mask she held, grimaced minutely, and set it on her knee.

"He transferred himself to that?" Captain Faille asked.

"In a way, Samarin was the mask all along. A—a kind of shared occupation between body and mask." Rennyn glanced up at Captain Faille, and Kendall guessed the mighty Duchess Surclere was just a little unsure how he'd be feeling. "His memory constantly copied back to it, and at the last he transferred the fragment of motive will residing in the body. When we return this, the Emperor will experience everything that Samarin did."

"Can he *hear* us?" Kendall asked.

"No. Or, I don't think so. If the mask was all that was required, it would cost him far less in energy to produce than a functioning living construct." She eyed Samarin-Aurienne thoughtfully. "As it is, the construct is a short-lived one. I doubt he could produce a—a long-lived golem without starving the casting that maintains his life on that throne. Mask and golem combined allows him to personally investigate important issues, while overcoming the no doubt not-infrequent tendency for people to decide to murder his Dezarts."

"This could explain why he has retained some semblance of humanity," Captain Faille said.

"While at the same time costing him fragments of self?" Rennyn touched the mask again, then sighed. "At any rate, this is a rather large secret that he chose to confirm in order to save you, Aurienne. You will need to keep up a pretence of being Samarin, even at Aurai's Rest. To which point, since your coat has a pocket for it, I'll return this mask to you on the condition of your absolute word that you will never try to put it on."

"I'm not that silly," Aurienne said, with a spurt of heat. She seemed to be bouncing back quickly for someone who had been crying and screaming only a minute ago.

"You *are* that silly," said the Pest, who had revived only a little. "And she can't pretend to be Samarin. Her Kolan is terrible."

"Then she will be a very reserved and quiet Samarin who has caught my cold," Rennyn replied, promptly. "Your word, Aurienne?"

"I absolutely promise not to put on a mask that has a spell on it that will kill...wait, why would it kill me? This 'me' is allowed to wear it."

"I suspect it's a little more complex than that," Rennyn said, and handed the mask to Sukata.

Aurienne sniffed, and it was so strange to see Samarin's face with such a clearly different personality behind it that Kendall felt the need to move matters along.

"Are we still in a rush?" she asked. "Do we try to get the mages out of this place today, or should we rest and come back tomorrow?"

"Today," Rennyn said immediately. "We don't know how much that Eferum-Get understood, or even if it was aware of us..."

"It was," Darian Faille put in. "There has been a shift, an increase in the sense of threat in this room."

"Possibly it's hindered by the time distortion of the Eferum. That casting..." Rennyn paused, held out her hand for Lieutenant Meniar's slate, and read it over quickly.

"If we follow that concept, we can't risk interfering with Nameen or that Eferum-Get until we've freed the mages," Lieutenant Meniar said unhappily.

"I agree." Rennyn briefly pressed the base of her palms to her eyes. "As best I understand it, when the wall to the Eferum was torn during the war of the Elder Mages, Nameen created this place in an attempt to heal the breaches. Its heart is a Grand Working set over a tear: a casting so large that it requires far more power than even one of the Elder Mages could supply. So she created this vine, which draws ambient magic and channels it into the Working—along with fuelling the protection shield and the glass maintenance golems. Nameen must have been fatally wounded at some point after this, and bound a fragment of herself here in order to ensure the spell would eventually be completed."

"But that spiky thing came along and stopped her?" Kendall asked.

Rennyn shook her head. "That's far more recent— possibly even a result of the surges in the Eferum during Solace's Grand Summoning. The repair...well, I wish I could risk a prolonged and extensive study, since I would be very glad to know what she was trying to do. Whatever it was, it failed, and the part of her that she bound to the casting's completion has been trapped here, unable to end or progress the casting. And then that...I haven't heard of an Eferum-Get of that type before."

Rennyn glanced up at Captain Faille, who shook his head.

"It seems to be projecting out of the Eferum, and drawing off the Efera," she continued. "I think it was able to interfere with the constructs, just enough to include mages in their duties, and to activate Nameen's Walk, since the structure of the spell is already here, though finding—" She paused, lifting her head. "Oh, that's what feels strange. I can hear that music again. Perhaps it's—"

Everyone except Rennyn clambered to their feet, looking panicked. She blinked up at them, then nodded. "Yes, we'd best get started. Lieutenant Meniar, if you will do what's necessary to prepare to, ah, ripen the mages, I'll think over a way to end Nameen's last Great Working."

Chapter Thirty-One

"Do you think this is what the Emperor of Kole used to look like?" Auri asked, peering down at him—her—himself.

"Maybe," Fallon said, glancing uncomfortably at his sister, then concentrating on sorting gingerly through ivy leaves to find a patch of exposed flesh. "He'd need some kind of template or physical sample to create a human construct."

"Wouldn't people recognise him?" Kendall asked. "Aren't there pictures? And he's on the money!"

"There is a resemblance to the profile," Sukata said, pausing in her own search to study Auri. "I do not think it is the same, though perhaps that is a matter of age. Emperor Corusar was nearly fifty when he gained the throne."

"Knew he was really an old man," Kendall muttered. "Just didn't realise how old."

Fallon delicately carved a small cross into the back of the wrist of the woman suspended on the wall in front of him. "I think that's the last one here," he said. "Let's hurry."

"I'll open the next room!" Auri said, but thankfully Sukata caught her before she bounded ahead.

"We must remain cautious," Sukata said firmly.

"I—yes, sorry, I know that," Auri said, in Samarin's too-deep voice. "It's just...I feel so *real*. I can *touch* things, and *move* things, and you all can *hear* me. And everything's sharp with clear edges—I think that part's this body. It can see and hear much better than I could, and it's so *strong*. Did you know he was so strong?"

"That is not surprising with a construct," Sukata said. "He would give himself every advantage."

"Do you think that I'm stronger than you?" Auri asked. "We could arm wrestle later to find out."

"Auri..." Fallon began, then stopped himself. Who could blame his sister for giddy excitement after three years of not-quite-death?

"And you complain about me not being focused," he said instead. "Let's get the last of these done before Lieutenant Meniar comes looking for us."

Even if they hadn't been told to hurry, the fact that the four of them had been sent alone to locate all the mages on the eastern half of the sunken garden would have made the urgency entirely clear. Sukata was obviously exhausted, Fallon wasn't much better, and neither Kendall nor Auri could cast. But there simply wasn't time to do this with due caution.

Trying to restrain the bounce in her stride, Auri led them at a more decorous pace to the next of the rooms sealed by a stone door, and moved it aside with evident enjoyment.

"This should be the last on our side," Fallon said. "We're lucky this place has such a simple layout."

"Four in here," Sukata said, and they separated, each sorting through the particularly thick mass of vines for the people underneath, using the flowers as a starting point.

"Think maybe this lot have been here the longest?" Kendall said, wrinkling her nose. "They're pretty ripe already."

"They're definitely going to want a bath," Fallon agreed. The vine had obviously been feeding the mages in some way, and elimination had probably been minimal, but this set of captives were particularly ragged and filthy and rank.

"It's really more hatching butterflies than ripening fruit, though, isn't it?" Auri chattered on. "And the problem with that symbology is it almost obliges them to be changed, to be transformed. I wonder if they'll come out of this with wings?"

"Please don't say that around Lieutenant Meniar," Fallon begged. "He needs an absolute focus on what he wants to happen, not all the things that *might*."

"That's exactly the reason everyone stays away from big, Symbolic magic." Auri had already found and marked her mage, and was now checking other lumps, in case there was one not marked by flowers. "I'd bet we'll be learning about this casting at the Arkathan next year, or...what's that noise?"

Sukata, who had been puzzling over a particularly overgrown mage, turned her head with a start, then said: "Finish. Now."

Obeying her own command, she dragged ivy down to expose a man's shoulder and quickly scratched a neat marking with her pointed nails. Fallon hastily scrabbled, found the lower vines were loosest, and scored a man's knee far deeper than he'd intended. Mouthing a silent apology, he rushed with the others out the door and let Sukata herd them back to the central courtyard, not wasting breath on explanations until they burst into the open.

"The glass constructs are breaking free," Sukata said, but the news clearly came as no surprise to Lord Surclere, who was standing protectively over Duchess Surclere while she rapidly chalked a Sigillic.

"It's unfortunate this room is all entrances and no doors," Duchess Surclere said. "We have a few minutes, at most. If they get out before we've freed the other mages, I'm going to cast a shield." She glanced up as Lieutenant Meniar and Tesin came hurrying in. "I should be able to maintain that long enough for you to finish, Lieutenant, but if we're under attack I might not be able to activate what I've prepared to close off Nameen's Working. It's not very power hungry, but we're running short of casters who are not nearing a danger point. If you hit your limit, I think you might have to coach Kendall through her first Sigillic."

"Darian is finishing the last room," was all Lieutenant Meniar said, while Fallon—and, he noticed, Kendall—tried not to look appalled.

The Lieutenant began rapidly walking around the room, reviewing the several sets of Sigillics that had been prepared, and most particularly those that bracketed each of the four channels filled by the vine's roots.

"A few months ago I would have run from the thought of casting this," he told Duchess Surclere. "When we're back in Tyrland, I'm going to do my best to talk you into at least doing a few guest lectures at the Arkathan. You've widened my view of magic enormously."

"You're feeling confident?" the Duchess asked, smiling as Lord Surclere lifted her from her finished Sigillic.

"I'm sick to my stomach and one more set-back from vomiting. But not running yet."

"Then I think we'd best begin," Duchess Surclere said, as a light, rapid step warned them of the only runner at that moment—Darian Faille.

"Complete," she said, and without any further delay Lieutenant Meniar began to power Emperor Corusar's Sigillic.

Fallon, unsure where to put himself, started when Auri moved him briskly to the wall directly opposite the statue. Kendall and Sukata joined them, while Lord Surclere stood with Duchess Surclere by the shield Sigillic, and Darian Faille, sword in hand, chose the entrance nearest to the penned constructs, with Tesin at her side.

"Can you hear them still?" Fallon whispered to Auri.

"Chip, chip, chip, chip. I can't tell how the doors are holding up. If they get in here, what do we do?"

"Prevent them from reaching Lieutenant Meniar," Sukata told them. "There is no reason to believe we can't kill the constructs, but the risk is that they will distract him."

"And all the fruit spoils," Auri said, but thankfully too low for Lieutenant Meniar to possibly have that image enter his intent. Then she added: "That was a different noise."

"Part of one of the doors has given way, I think," Sukata agreed.

The Kellian girl moved so she was standing closer to the central statue, where Lieutenant Meniar was now cutting a deep x across one of his palms with a piece of glass. Letting the blood well freely and drip from his fingers, he made a splattery circle around the statue, crossing all four of the root-filled channels. Then came the critical act of the casting: he took a single leaf of ivy and placed it over the bleeding wound like a bandage, commanding it to make his hand whole. An enormous outflow of power roared away from him, following the ivy roots through the whole of the garden.

"They're coming," Auri whispered. "Just the little ones, I think."

With a glance at Lieutenant Meniar, Darian Faille stepped out of the room, leaving Tesin standing uncertain. After a moment's consultation, Lord Surclere put Duchess Surclere on her unshaky feet and strode quickly after his mother, Tesin trotting at his heels. Sukata stayed where she was.

"I thought we were going to use a shield?" Auri said.

"If only the smaller constructs are coming, then we might be able to forego the need for a shield," Sukata replied. Her gaze rested briefly on Kendall, and she added: "It is best to reserve our options."

"I could help," Auri offered eagerly. "I'm very strong."

"We are the second line of defence," Sukata said calmly, but the whole of her body was tense, and she twitched at a ring of steel on glass.

"How long does this stupid spell take to cast?" Kendall asked, shifting from foot to foot in that silence that followed that single, shattering sound.

"Impossible to say," Fallon told her. "Thirty subjects over quite a large area, and—" He couldn't help but flinch at further noise, and cast a worried glance at Lieutenant Meniar, who was holding his hand directly above his head now, palm turned to the sky.

Sukata whirled and leaped upward—a streak impossible to track until she was on the downward arc, hurling something as she landed. It shattered against the wall, and Tesin, who had been chasing it, reversed course and returned to the corridor, only to reappear a moment later with Lord Surclere and Darian Faille.

"The rest are still trying to get out," Auri said. "Is the casting even progressing?"

"Look at the walls," Tesin said.

A tinge of rust. There were far fewer leaves in the central courtyard, so the shift had probably been more noticeable out in the corridor. All the leaves had dark rims, and even as Fallon peered more closely the colour spread, flushing darker and darker until it seemed the room dripped with blood.

"Sounds like a whole door's gone now!" Auri gasped, and Lord Surclere gave the Duchess a nod to indicate it was time for the shield.

She turned, but even as she looked toward her Sigillic, Lieutenant Meniar let out a loud gasp, and crumpled in a heap, the now red-black leaf falling to the ground. Immediately, Duchess Surclere limped to the tight cluster of sigils she'd marked on the statue itself, and filled them with power.

"Lots of them coming, fast," Auri said, her hand closing painfully on Fallon's shoulder.

"And how long is this one going to take?" Kendall asked, but the answer to that was no time at all, as the chained woman, the swirling vortex, and the thing of barbs and teeth swam back into visible existence, only to become painful to look at as the bright chains flared, then shattered. The statue tilted forward.

Duchess Surclere hopped hastily back, stumbled, and was caught by Sukata, who bounded clear. Darian Faille blurred to snatch Lieutenant Meniar out of the throat of a roaring gale. Fallen leaves, pieces of glass, and dropped bits of chalk slid forward to be swallowed by nothingness, and Fallon hastily put his foot on Kendall's coat before it and its collection of focuses followed.

For the briefest moment, Fallon thought he saw the woman again. The fragment of an Elder Mage, a creation of the gods themselves, tasked to shepherd the world in their stead. She stood tall and free, unmarked by chains or the creeping blight of the Eferum-Get. Possibly she nodded. And then she, too, was gone.

oOo

As if a door had slammed shut, all the noise went away. Even, Kendall noticed with immense relief, the endless pulsing of the shield and the too-clever-by-half ivy. No more spell.

Unlike everything lying about loose, and the muggy warmth of the room, the vine hadn't vanished, but most of its leaves had fallen, and it looked withered and dry.

"Are the bugs still coming?" she asked.

"The casting should have removed much of their motive power," Rennyn said. "But there may be a remnant."

They all listened intently, and then Fallon's sister said: "I can hear noise, but I don't think it's bugs."

"Thirty mages." Lord Surclere crossed to take Rennyn from Sukata.

"Thirty confused, dirty, scared, cross mages," Kendall predicted.

"Hungry, too, I expect," Aurienne said. "And most of them weren't dressed for the cold, and some didn't have shoes."

They shared a mutual glance of 'what a headache', which became very odd for Kendall thanks to the Imperial Smugness' insufferable face getting in the way.

"How is Lieutenant Meniar?" Rennyn asked.

"Breathing," Darian Faille said.

"That was closer to his limit than I care to think about." Rennyn shut her eyes, but seemingly out of relief, not tiredness.

"Look at his hand," the Pest said, and then lifted Lieutenant Meniar's hand so that they could see the cut he'd given himself, neatly healed, and surrounded by a deep imprint of an ivy leaf.

"Thirty cross mages with leaves for hair," Aurienne said, brightly.

That made Rennyn laugh. "I hope not. As for the other concerns...I am going to attempt to reverse Nameen's Walk. It's a very energy-hungry casting, and I don't understand it enough to change the departure or destination points, but I think I can hold it for the amount of time it apparently took me to walk here in the first place." She glanced up at Captain Faille. "I think it's the best choice in the circumstances."

All Captain Faille did was nod, but there was no doubt he didn't like the idea. Not because he didn't trust Rennyn's casting, but because she was injured, sick, and a really big spell was guaranteed to lay her out. Though that was probably the exact same reason he didn't object. Back at Aurai's Rest there would be all the Sentene mages and the other Kellian to deal with whatever problems came up. The longer they stayed here, the less time and energy could be devoted to making sure Rennyn woke up tomorrow.

"They will find us frightening," Captain Faille said, frankly. "Fallon and Aurienne, do you feel you can act as less unnerving intermediaries?"

"Of course!" Aurienne said, and shot at her brother: "My Kolan's not *that* bad."

"Do you wish them brought to the entrance, or here?" Captain Faille asked Rennyn.

"I came out at the entrance, but I think this is the origin point. Perhaps the shield interfered? Anyway, yes, here would be best."

Kendall had never been more pleased not to know any Kolan than when she and Sukata were told to stay and look after Rennyn and Lieutenant Meniar, while everyone else went to herd mages. Since Rennyn simply sat herself before the wall where this 'Walk' was supposedly written down, Kendall turned to the little matter of broken golems. The one Sukata had smashed had vanished, but the south-facing corridor was all over glass.

Months of practice hadn't made Kendall as strong as Sukata yet, but she had definitely made leaps and bounds in the tidying things with her mind stakes. She swept all the big chunks to one side with a satisfactory clatter, and began work on the shards.

"You will bring back your headache," Sukata said, standing under the arched entrance to the central courtyard.

"Don't think I could make my head hurt worse than it already is," Kendall said, shrugging. "You just watch—you need to rest."

Sukata produced an uncharacteristically visible frown. "You will make yourself ill," she said.

"I suspect it's fine, Sukata," Rennyn said, from around the corner. "Come talk to me a moment, Kendall."

Suspicious. Kendall had had a sense all day that she'd missed part of a conversation, but she wasn't going to show her confusion, walking back to stand, arms folded, over Rennyn,

"Sit down," Rennyn said, and once Kendall had obeyed added cheerfully: "You don't lack for pigheadedness."

"Thanks heaps." What the Hells had she done to earn a lecture?

"It's a valuable trait in a Thought Mage. What you don't seem to have noticed is you made a transition, holding open Nameen's Walk. There is absolutely no way you could have achieved that without abstract Thought casting."

"What?" Kendall stared from Rennyn to Sukata, then shook her head. "I was just propping the roof up."

"Ideally, your day today would have involved a lot of meditation and carefully controlled exercises. Though I doubt you would have been much impressed by the meditation. On the whole I don't hold a great deal of concern about you accidentally setting things alight: your control is very good. However, I would prefer you didn't cast unnecessarily over the next few days while I am busy being unconscious."

Hot all over, Kendall started to speak, threw away a half dozen things she wanted to shout on the subject of important information that should be mentioned sooner, and finally said: "And if you kill yourself with this Nameen's Walk stunt?"

"Then I have most conveniently written a little manual on how to become a Thought Mage in six simple steps," Rennyn said, and obviously thought herself funny. "Seb can take over your training—he truly is capable of focusing on the practical aspects instead of the theory—but I'd recommend not waiting until you get back to Tyrland before going through the exercises I outlined."

The roaring sound had come back, but it seemed to be all inside Kendall's head. She glared at the source of her anger, snapped: "Shouldn't you be concentrating on figuring out that spell?" and went back to clearing away glass. And not thinking about setting things on fire.

Sukata had followed her, but was being all hesitant, so Kendall made herself cool down a little and asked in an even sort of voice: "You knew?"

"I was not told," Sukata said, which meant Kellian hearing.

"And you didn't tell me because—?"

That made Sukata turn particularly grave. "Because I do not repeat private conversations."

There was no answer to that which wouldn't make Sukata feel all tied up, so Kendall dropped the point. "It should have been you," she said instead.

"Why?" Sukata started to hold out her hand, then lowered it. "I know I made it seem like we were in competition, that I was angry that you—"

"No you didn't," Kendall said, sharply. "I never thought you were—well, not for more than five minutes. That's not how you work. I've *told* you that."

"And avoided me. Stopped talking to me. Wouldn't meet my eyes."

"That's because of that stupid Emperor!" Kendall snapped, and then regretted it because she couldn't just leave it there. "He—he went on at me about how people just go around doing what the Kellian want, and asked what you get out of me and...and..." Kendall had made it worse, and hurried on frantically. "I didn't believe him, told him he was an idiot. I'm sorry. I didn't believe him, but I kept remembering what he said. And I couldn't answer his question. I couldn't say why you were my friend and..." She hung her head, feeling worse than she ever had in her life because whatever she tried she just seemed to keep hurting Sukata.

And Sukata laughed. Kendall hadn't even known that she could. It was a strange little muted sound, but definitely a laugh and though Sukata wasn't smiling when Kendall's head shot up, her eyes were blazing bright.

"Have you noticed," Sukata said, in her thin, broken voice, "that the best parts of being alive don't need an explanation?"

Kendall had never been kissed before. She did not know what to do when Sukata bent her head. She felt clumsy and awkward and confused and resentful.

And happy.

"I am so proud of you, Kendall," Sukata said, and squeezed her tight, then kissed her again.

Someone cleared their throat. Kendall hastily let go and turned to find a woman standing watching with an air of patience, as if she'd been there for a while. One of the mages.

She didn't have leaves for hair—it was braided in an elaborate style, though with strands sticking out all over the place—and dressed in what had once been a very nice dress and now...was not. But that was not the thing that made Kendall struggle not to stare. The deep brown skin of the woman's cheeks was ever-so-faintly indented by the unmistakeable outline of a leaf, of an entire, interconnected pattern of leaves, as if she was a puzzle put together from ivy pieces.

She talked in Kolan gabble, of course, but didn't fire up at whatever Sukata said in response, and followed without fuss when Sukata led her to the central courtyard. Kendall was not quite glad about the interruption, but it gave her a moment to try to put what had just happened into some sort of recognisable state. She felt as if she was Rennyn: as likely to fall down as to take the next step.

"Rennyn Claire!" the leafy woman repeated, when Sukata had made introductions, and then when Rennyn indicated the faint carvings on the wall, the name 'Nameen' came up in all the gabble that followed—gabble that grew and grew as Captain Faille and the Pest escorted in four more mages, and Darian Faille and Aurienne brought five more, and left almost right away. Not all of these wanted to talk about Nameen, and one was shouting more than gabbling, and Kendall could see that Rennyn was going to be left with no voice at all if she tried explaining the same things over and over. She'd already moved past croaky on to hoarse.

Remembering she had a coat full of distractions, Kendall handily drew off almost all of the mages by offering the collection of focuses. And then the first woman they'd met, who seemed to be called Maja Keshkant, took charge. She shooed everyone away from Rennyn, and made them stand in line to take a turn scuffling through the collection in Kendall's coat. She sent Sukata off for water. She examined Lieutenant Meniar, then snaffled his slate and chalk box and cast something on Rennyn to help with her throat.

'Maja' was Kolan for 'Magister', and since everyone in the room was an upper-reaches sort of mage, and they were all talking at each other, it was Maja, Maja, Maja all over the place. They sounded like a herd of cranky goats. But, Kendall had to admit, most of them soon shifted to quiet listening, explaining things to the next group of arrivals, and organising a hunt about for any focuses that had been missed among the roots of the vine.

When Sukata came back carrying a lot of water in a segment of golem, one mage figured out a way to smooth the edges of other collected pieces so they had some useable glasses. Another filched all the slates and made detailed sketches of the readable sections of the carving Rennyn had been studying.

"Do you think maybe we should try and talk Herself out of casting this Walk?" Kendall murmured to Sukata, when the Kellian girl had finally been freed of water duty, and Kendall couldn't find any other way to shut up the argument in her head about whether to take hold of Sukata's hand. "This lot can cast all the spells we need."

"Look at the Duchess' feet."

Kendall looked, and grimaced. Although Captain Faille had been carrying Rennyn about most of the time, the bottom of the makeshift bandages was dusty-black, and damp in patches. Oozing. Even with all the advantages of a couple of dozen mages, they were still out in the middle of nowhere having to make their supplies from scratch, and were already close to running out of spare shirts.

"We spent all morning building a house for nothing."

"I was not looking forward to sleeping in it."

"I suppose we would have all caught Herself's cold, too."

"Perhaps." Sukata reached out and took Kendall's hand, and squeezed it. "She will come through this. She has her own brand of pigheadedness."

"Bah," Kendall said, and squeezed back. The air was decidedly nippy now, but she felt hot all over.

Captain Faille had returned once again, and the mages clustered closest to Rennyn parted like magic to let him through to pick her up. Kendall guessed that he told her that there were no more mages to come, for she nodded briskly, and said something to Maja Keshkant, who promptly clapped her hands together like a teacher bringing a class to order.

"We are to line up in pairs," Sukata translated, as the Kolan woman began speaking. "It is important that we stay as close as possible together, and move briskly. If anyone lags or stumbles, those around must do what they can to keep them moving. It is important to not prolong the casting time."

Darian Faille had Lieutenant Meniar slung over her shoulder. The Pest and his sister-Samarin linked elbows. The more squabbly of the mages reluctantly found someone to hang on to. Tesin, toting the Imperial Smugness' sword, trotted down to play rear guard—and perhaps gee up anyone who started to lag.

Invisible, intangible, loudly there, a tunnel opened. Kendall clutched Sukata's hand, remembering the headache she'd earned last time, and how that had apparently let her in for accidentally doing all sorts of things. That was probably important not to think about right now, so she kept her head down, and trooped forward with the rest.

It seemed like no time at all before the feeling of a tunnel went away, along with the last trace of late afternoon. They were somewhere dark and cold, and Kendall briefly wondered if Rennyn had managed to send them altogether wrong, but then she turned and saw the lights of Aurai's Rest. And there came

Lieutenant Faral, bounding at the head of a crowd to find Lieutenant Meniar in the confusion and snatch him into her arms.

She must have squeezed him tight, because he woke up with a gasp, and then said: "Keste," in a pleased little voice, before going straight back to sleep.

Rennyn had actually managed to keep her eyes open. Too many people were crowding around her for Kendall to get a proper look, even when they started conjuring little lights, and moving toward the nearest buildings. But she'd got them here, and there would be a warm bath, clean clothes, and probably half a dozen healers to fuss over her. Rennyn would be all right.

She would.

Chapter Thirty-Two

Rennyn woke, and celebrated that fact. Then she groaned, coughed, and croaked: "Illidian?"

"Off at a Kellian meeting."

Rubbing grit from her eyes, Rennyn blinked at late afternoon light drifting through open windows, then shifted in time to see Kendall closing a Sigillic dictionary. The girl stood up, arms folded.

"How do you feel?"

The question sounded portentous, but the answer surely unsurprising. Rennyn's skin itched, her feet throbbed, and the inside of her throat was raw. Her bladder ached—though she was at least far less grimy than on her last waking. She...

Rennyn lifted her hand to her throat, found a thin chain, and traced it to a wire pendant holding her focus. On the way, her fingers brushed the tender line she'd cut into her own skin, scored across the bite mark. Then she levitated.

It was the kind of self-indulgent Thought Magic she had not dared for months, and her attention was all for how her aching body reacted to a sustained flow of Efera. She drifted up to the ceiling.

"Enjoying yourself?" Kendall asked, with the particularly fierce glower Rennyn had learned to recognise as an attempt to hide pleasure.

"Yes, rather," Rennyn said, but allowed herself to sink back down to a sitting position. "So they got the miscasting off me?" She felt dizzy, but it was from sudden, violent relief, not the bone-deep physical weakness that had dogged her for so long.

"This morning. They decided they had to try, because...it was something about your heartbeat going too slow. And also, I think, because a whole bunch of them wanted to show each other up and be the one to do something that even you couldn't manage."

"There are advantages to rescuing a few dozen mages. Did they use my Wicked Uncle's focus?"

"Yes—they got Captain Faille to crush it. I think he liked that. You're still sick, though, and run down and all that stuff, and are supposed to stay warm and not do anything much."

"I think I'll take myself to the privy," Rennyn said, with a level of pleasure that a year ago she would never have associated with such a statement.

"I'll get you something hot to eat," Kendall said. "Don't go wandering I'm not supposed to be letting you out of my sight."

It felt like no effort at all for Rennyn to whisk herself down the corridor and back, but by the time she regained the bed the tremor she hated had come back to her hands. Run down, too many weeks without regular casting exercises, or a physical weakness she would never escape? Destroying her Wicked Uncle's focus made for appropriate symbology, but undoubtedly killing him would have been a better choice to rid her of all trace of the miscasting.

She coughed for a while, numbed the pain in her feet, and decided that whatever the case it was still an improvement on yesterday. The great hurdle had been overcome. She could move on to other concerns.

The tremor had mostly gone by the time Kendall returned, and she managed, under the girl's critical eye, to eat without dropping spiced mince all over herself.

"What is the meeting about?" Rennyn asked, once the edge had been taken off her hunger.

"You think they tell me stuff like that?"

"That depends on the meeting. And whether you picked up enough to make a few educated guesses."

Kendall shrugged. "Your stupid uncle, mostly. A bit about that smug-ass Emperor as well."

That made sense. Two major potential threats to the future of the Kellian.

"Are any of the mages we rescued still here?"

"Most of them. You've only been asleep a day. They're still all covered in leaf patterns, and they never shut up."

This had been delivered with a particularly aggrieved note. "And how have they been annoying you?"

"That blabbermouth told them I can Thought cast. Talking of people who never shut up."

"Fallon? Aurienne?"

"Auri," Kendall confirmed. "You've given Fallon your cold, and he's already sicker than you are."

Rennyn frowned. "I hope they're staying close together. I think Fallon is still sustaining her."

"He still dreams of her all the time he sleeps, so yes. Captain Faille told her to stay in the so-called Dezart's room, and put Fallon in with her. Last I checked, she was trying on all his clothes." A pause. "Are you going to take her on as a student? She seems to think you will."

"Not for Thought Magic," Rennyn said firmly. "Unless she demonstrates considerably more focus than I've seen so far. But I don't have a problem trying to teach her devising—if only to keep her in check. Unless something comes up, I'll start you on the exercises for abstract casting tomorrow. And what is that expression about?"

After a very long pause indeed, Kendall muttered: "It should have been Sukata."

"Should it? Why should it have been Sukata?"

"Because she's the one who wants to be a real mage!"

Rennyn summoned her hairbrush from a far bench, and considered the girl curiously. Kendall had clearly spent the day brooding over Sukata's feelings instead of celebrating her own progression—or the satisfactory-sounding conversation the two girls had had before Maja Keshkant arrived.

"And so?" Rennyn said at last. "Your progress won't impede Sukata's. Are you not even a little bit pleased with your own achievements? Ignoring that it's a terrible term to use, don't you want to be a 'real' mage?"

"No," Kendall said, screwing up her nose. "I already told you that! It's so boring. I'm never going to wrap my head around what makes the Eferum work the way it does, and why it makes monsters, and all that. When your brother starts on about it, it just sounds like blah blah blah to me. I can't make myself care about it. What's wrong with just casting these standard forms?"

Highly entertained, Rennyn said: "There is some space in between taking on Seb's love of Eferum theory and only memorising established Sigillics. My family specialised in Eferum theory because they thought it necessary to defeat Solace, but the plan that ended up being used was nothing to do with the Eferum. You can be a devising mage, and a good one, while ignoring Eferum theory altogether."

"And I don't want to kill people!" Kendall burst out. "Look at Auri! Not only did she make a mess of herself, she almost took the Pest with her. And that wasn't even with some new spell she made up, or all the guesswork that seems to go into this Symbolic rot. It's just not worth it."

This was fascinating. Rennyn had put Kendall's reluctant approach to the Sigillic exercises down to being so far behind Sukata and Fallon, not because the known forms represented safety. There was still a great deal she didn't know about Kendall, and why she was so insistent that people didn't "mind each other's business". Had she been wrong to respect the girl's privacy, to not have her past investigated?

"Aurienne is not who you should be comparing yourself to," Rennyn said mildly. "If the past few years haven't cured her of hasty overconfidence, I'll certainly work to do so, for it's the worst trait for a mage. As for devising Sigillics that work, and only do the things that you want them to: it's really not the great mystery you seem to consider it. First you learn the basics, then the accepted forms, and then apply what you know to a problem, and compose the solution that *doesn't* kill people."

Kendall's expressions were wonderful. All that disdain and disgust packed into a single glare.

"You say that like it's *simple*. But every second mage I've met is terrified of what you do."

"Every second mage you've met has been taught that copying is the best approach," Rennyn said. "Think of it as cooking soup. No, don't roll your eyes at me. You're saying you only ever want to cook by using an exact recipe someone else has made up, without even adding a tiny extra bit of salt, because you can kill people with soup."

"You can if you put in the wrong mushrooms."

"Exactly. The first step is learning how to identify mushrooms."

"Do you ever cook?" Kendall asked irrelevantly. "I've never seen you."

Rennyn laughed, then took a sip of water to soothe her throat. "I have a basic competence. I haven't put the time in for more, since it's always been easier to buy someone else's expertise. Seb knows how to cook the three or so things he likes most, but nothing else."

"You really think I could write spells that don't hurt people? I don't understand half the reasons you cast the way you do."

"Kendall, you've only been learning Efanian for a handful of months. I fully expect you to compose workable Sigillics, and at least understand the fundamentals of Symbolic casting as well. You have both a good memory and a strong will, which will help considerably, and beyond that it really is going to depend both on your basic feel for casting, and on what you're trying to do. Isn't there anything you've ever wanted to do with magic that people can't currently do?"

That produced a blank stare and then a withdrawal. The girl muttered something too low for Rennyn to make out, but then lifted her chin and said: "I sure as shine don't want to end up chained to any statues. Or to turn myself into one."

"No, nor hung up in a garden to dry," Rennyn agreed. "I certainly can't predict whether becoming a mage will lead to such a fate, or merely make you better able to protect yourself. Corusar's problem, at least, is one of rule, and becoming a devising mage will not inevitably put you in charge of an Empire."

From Kendall's expression it appeared Rennyn must too clearly have shown how enjoyable she found the idea of 'Empress Kendall', but the door opened and Illidian came in before Rennyn could entertain herself further.

"I'll go check on the Pest," Kendall said hastily, and took Rennyn's tray away.

When the door had closed behind the girl, Rennyn put down her water glass and considered her husband. Had she imagined the tension in him when she'd transferred Aurienne to Corusar's golem?

He banished any immediate concerns by sitting beside her and kissing her thoroughly.

"You'll catch my cold," she protested, at the first pause.

"Unlikely." He tangled his fingers in her hair, but restrained himself to only another brief kiss before saying: "It is not simple wishful thinking to say that I can see at a glance that the miscasting truly is gone. It's in the very way you hold yourself."

"I do feel like several anchors have been cut loose," she said agreeably. "Fel, it's been a complicated couple of days. I suspect we'll need to take ourselves back to Koletor rather quickly, too, to get Fallon and Aurienne untangled. If he's maintaining her waking and sleeping now, he's going to struggle."

"Meniar and Sarana have come to the same conclusion. They do not expect an immediate decline, but it does not help that you have shared your cold. You don't feel you can solve the issue without Corusar?"

"It would be a risk. Golems..." She paused, then laughed softly. "Golems really are out of my area of expertise, and I've not encountered the idea of copying memory at all before." She glanced up at him. "Those transfers bothered you, didn't they?"

"The question of how separate he is from his copies does. I felt very distinctly that the person we knew as Samarin hated the mask he carried. Is that because the Emperor, trapped as he is, finds all masks intolerable, or is it because the Emperor-become-Samarin is a person with a five month lifespan?"

"The mask a symbol of servitude to his other self?"

"Something in that order."

Rennyn followed this philosophical thread to the point of making herself dizzy again, then said: "I have no idea whether there is an answer to that. I don't think he limits the lifespan to prevent himself—his copy self—from abandoning whatever Imperial task he's been set and making for the nearest border. Most of Corusar's casting power is taken up with the enchantments set on the throne room, so creating a copy at all is quite a feat. I think it was important to him—Samarin, I mean—that we recovered the missing mages."

"And asking Corusar for Samarin's opinion of the use made of him would gain little."

Rennyn hesitated. "I don't know that the copy's identity would necessarily be lost or subsumed," she said. "To a certain degree, it may even be dominant. Though...no, it would have to take some form of merging, or Corusar would have a reputation for occasionally forgetting several months of state business. Has that mask been sent on already?"

"This morning. Depending on your condition, we will follow tomorrow morning."

She felt her own momentary withdrawal.

"We will not force you to wake the Ten," he murmured, after a pause. "It is a request, not a duty."

"No, I think it is exactly that," she said. "A duty of my family to people who are, substantially, a branch of that family. I keep shying away from the idea, but I think eventually I would have asked to see the Ten even if I had not stayed with you."

Illidian twined a strand of her hair around his fingers, watching it slip and fall. He was wearing another of her ribbons around his wrist: his own form of Symbolic Magic. Their marriage had been a series of challenges, but they met each one with—she would not even call it a determination not to be parted, but instead a mutual drawing together. Staying together was not work because she was as much home to him as he was to her.

Touching the tip of one of his fingers, she traced the shape of the nail: not a sharp point, but it was longer than he had allowed himself for months.

"I no longer see blood beneath them," he murmured. "But the nightmares have not stopped."

Rennyn did not waste breath on platitudes, admitting instead: "I still don't think I could sit through the end of that play. Even after watching him flinch as I took a piece of broken glass to his throat. I'm not altogether sure even killing him would have...maybe eventually."

"We have chosen to end our hunt for Prince Helecho." His tone was resigned. "Unless we discover he has found a way to cause harm. It is far from ideal for us, but we cannot justify killing him merely to protect ourselves from the possibility of inheritance."

Rennyn curled her fingers through his, thinking of the Kellian under the command of her Wicked Uncle. Her decisions had tied their hands, and so the possible ascendency of Helecho Montjuste-Surclere would haunt them for years to come. Not so complete a nightmare as Solace, but a thing to dread.

She wondered whether the Ten also had nightmares about Solace's return. Endlessly, without waking. The idea made it feel like pure cowardice to postpone any longer, so she dressed and Illidian carried her through the drowsing shadows of late afternoon to where the Ten slept. Only Darian Faille joined them, falling silently into step with her son as they walked up the gentle slope to the Ten's resting place. It was a beautiful afternoon, with southern light picking out points of colour on the hillside. Rennyn felt none of the reluctance she had experienced on their previous visit, merely an acceptance that this task belonged to her, as much as any magical puzzle.

But she could not help but remember the conversation she had had with Darian after her first visit to the Ten. Children. Kellian leadership. An endless reel of complications that brought her back to the possibility that the Symbolic casting that maintained the Kellian could unravel. She would certainly be glad to no longer be able to command them inadvertently, but she knew very well that it was not a solution Illidian—that any of the Kellian—would choose.

Autumn had come to the fan-shaped cave. Vivid leaves and berries, arranged in wreaths and garlands, decorated the walls and the stone coffins. Did the Kellian bring flowers in spring, and layer symbols of renewal on this place that spoke so strongly of death? Or had this been done in preparation for Rennyn's visit, so that the original Kellian constructs would wake to a celebration of colour?

With an effort of will, Rennyn focused on the nine still-living constructs. When Solace's control had been withdrawn, they had learned to protect each other, had found a friend and guide, and then discovered joy in creation. Had lived long lives, and now...

Imbuing into her voice all the command she tried to avoid around the Kellian, Rennyn said: "Wake up."

There was no immediate response, no alteration to the steady hush of sleepers' breath. Rennyn did not allow herself to hope this continued, for a non-response would only make matters more complicated. A minute shift in Illidian's stance warned her of change, and her ear more than her eye detected a series of tiny movements among the sleepers. Then larger alterations: a hand raised to a face, a turn, a lifted head.

"I give you welcome," Darian Faille said, and her voice seemed firmer than usual, deep with added emotion. "I am glad."

Two of the sleepers sat up, and both moved their hands in response. Rennyn had only begun to learn Kellian hand-speaking, and could not follow.

"Thank you, child of Faille's line," Illidian murmured, translating. "I give you thanks, Darian."

Then, the one third from the left—Seya—rose, and Illidian added: "You have brought us a child of the Queen."

"This is Rennyn, eldest child of Tiandel's line," Darian said. "In her lies the ability to command all descended from the Ten."

"We saw this one when the Queen returned," Seya responded. Her gaze had shifted to Rennyn, and her hands moved swiftly. "You asked if the Queen could separate herself from us. And yet your intention was the Queen's death."

"Yes," Rennyn agreed, as more of the shadowy, attenuated women sat up. "I—in truth, I was not very eager to kill her. I was hoping she would answer differently, that she would show some sign of remorse."

"And what is it that you ask of us now?"

Rennyn realised her heart was beating faster. Was she imagining a palpable sense of threat? Before her were nine women who had been created to protect Solace Montjuste-Surclere, who had been used and abandoned, and who were far from likely to accept a replacement for Solace. Who had just been told that Rennyn could command their children.

"Tiandel exiled you from Tyrland," she said carefully. "Abandoned you. I came to apologise for that, and to revoke that exile. You are free to..." She hesitated, then repeated definitively. "You are free. Come and go as you please. Live and...live and die as you wish. I will aid you and yours if you ask that of me, but the line of Montjuste-Surclere claims only kinship with you, not ownership."

Nine pairs of grey eyes studied her, occasionally catching a flicker of torchlight. Nine heads turned as the Kellian forebears looked at each other. Rennyn took a long breath, and realised that her jumping pulse marked more than nerves. A steady flow of power was being drawn from her. In waking the Kellian constructs she had begun to actively feed the Symbolic casting that sustained them.

Two days ago, this would have killed me.

"We give you thanks, Rennyn of Tiandel's line," Illidian translated, when Seya's hands moved again. "And we give you welcome. To our home. To our family."

They rose then, from their coffins, and walked down to greet the children of their children. They admired the changes to their settlement, met the youngest of their grandchildren, and shared silent words and gentle embraces.

Then, one by one, they returned to the cave decked in crimson and gold, and died.

Epilogue

In the throne room of the Emperor of Kole, Fallon DeVries lay in one of four inter-connected Sigillic circles, contemplating his phlegm-clogged chest, his aching bones, and the awful grey weariness that had him longing for sleep, and yet somehow made it impossible to rest.

"Nearly there, Fallon," Duchess Surclere said, looking down at him. "Try to stay awake."

He nodded, and she moved on, reviewing the immensely complex Sigillic one last time. Her feet had healed to the point where she could wear shoes again, but Fallon noticed a faint hesitation whenever her weight came down on her right foot. At least the Duchess had avoided a truly serious cold, with only a mild cough lingering.

Spotting something she wanted to change, she pointed it out to Sukata, who had been taking turns with Kendall to do the writing-out. Fallon watched the Kellian girl covertly, trying to spot any sign of change in the centuries-old Symbolic casting that made her so different. There had been no sign so far, but Duchess Surclere had not been able to rule out a slow unravelling.

"Has anyone ever sat on you?"

Fallon winced, but didn't do more than glance at his Samarin-sister standing before the throne. One thing travelling with the disguised Emperor had taught them was that Yscaren Corusar was inclined to be amused rather than annoyed by impertinence.

~I have set it about that touching me involves instant, ugly death,~ replied the Emperor's directionless, unemotional voice.

"But your armour isn't at all cobwebby."

~A very, very long-handled duster.~

"Really?" Auri asked. "No, I don't believe...really?"

~The energy running through the armour appears to prevent dust from settling,~ the Emperor said. ~Which is fortunate because grime is not something I planned for.~

"Can I—"

"It's time, Aurienne," Duchess Surclere said, firmly.

Auri immediately ran across to the larger central circle, hopped neatly over the sigils, and lay down.

"How are you feeling?" she asked Fallon.

"The same," he said, and coughed. "Except horrified by the things you say."

"He likes it," Auri insisted. "The Dawnbringer knows it must be boring as spit to sit there all day and night doing Court business." She sighed luxuriantly. "I'm going to miss being him, though, especially being so strong and hearing conversations in the next room. I don't see why—"

"Because this is complicated enough without fancy touches," Duchess Surclere said, as she bent to place the sphere they'd thought was Auri's focus into the little circle that just intersected with her larger one. "Now, I want you both to look only at the ceiling, and to start counting together. That won't contribute to the transfer, but I am hoping it will limit the impact of your thoughts and feelings on the casting."

Because, despite the involvement of two mages of enormous power and knowledge, there was a more than slight chance that everything would go wrong. The Duchess had to create a body for Auri, give it enough power to last for a reasonable lifespan, transfer

Auri into it and—most complicated of all—untangle Auri's existence from Fallon's.

"One," Auri said eagerly, and Fallon joined her in at 'two', staring at the ceiling and trying not to think of all the things that could go wrong. There would be no going back, no second chances, from this casting.

"Three," he said, trying to ignore the inflow as the Duchess began to power the Sigillic. "Four."

At long last it would be over, whatever the result. And, though it had not been as straightforward as they had hoped, he had actually succeeded in what he'd set out to do. Won the Duchess' attention, gained her assistance. He hadn't rushed ahead or done any wild casting, but he'd still found a way through.

And he'd witnessed such interesting magic! He had even met a fragment of one of the Elder Mages. Him! Slow-and-steady DeVries!

"Ten," he murmured, the ceiling wavering. Someone had put a brick on his chest.

Then his face hurt. A lot of him hurt, as if he'd gone through a wine-press, but the face was freshest, stinging.

"Fallon! Fallon, rot you, wake up! Don't do this now!"

He stared up at his own face, red-eyed and furious. Did he feel so raw because his face had been peeled off and put on someone else?

"Prop him up," said Lieutenant Meniar's voice.

It became a little easier to breathe. If only the person who'd stolen his face would stop shaking him...

"Auri?"

"Yes!"

He'd known that was how Auri would look, but it was so disconcerting. Even the voice was his own. He blinked and blinked again as Auri flung her arms around him and squeezed.

"Your heart stopped beating. I'm so glad!"

"That we were able to start it again, I presume," Duchess Surclere said. She was sitting by Fallon's feet, looking tired and relieved. "I'm glad too," she said, smiling at him.

"Let him go for a little while," Lieutenant Meniar said, and gave Fallon a businesslike examination before casting a divination to confirm there was no major damage to his heart.

Duchess Surclere cast her own divinations, then said: "It looks like the separation worked. I can't find any sign of the energy draw, at least."

Fallon let out a long breath. Finally! He thanked the Duchess, and then gazed up at his sister, who was studying her new body critically while she waited.

They had needed a 'template' for Auri's permanent body. The Emperor had said he could find a volunteer from his Court and Kendall had even—very reluctantly—said they could use her, but Auri had been firm on wanting to still be a DeVries, to be properly related to their father. So Fallon's twin had become...Fallon's twin.

"Hey!" Fallon shot to his feet, and then swayed as the room turned dramatically around him. He clutched Auri's shoulder and stared...up into her eyes. "Why is she taller than me!?" He started to totter, but Sukata caught him before he fell, and scooped him effortlessly into her arms.

~Three years of energy draw is likely to have limited physical growth,~ the Emperor said.

Auri looked guilty, but failed to stifle a giggle. "Maybe you'll catch up."

"I could strangle you Auri."

"What a waste that would be." Auri turned about, trying to look all over herself. "People will think I'm your older brother!"

"Great," Fallon sighed. "Just great."

"A cousin," Duchess Surclere said. "This is far too complicated to be publicly known."

"So long as I can explain to father, I don't care about anyone else," Auri assured her.

"You have a month or so to decide whether you want to go through the physical changes we discussed," Lieutenant Meniar said. "It will take all of winter to complete a full shift. Altering only your face is quicker, of course, but still best done over several weeks."

"I'll have to pick a name!" Auri said, and turned toward the Emperor. "Can I call myself Rhael? If I decide to stay a boy?"

~Be my guest.~

Auri strode abruptly toward him, and Fallon felt Sukata twitch, but his sister stopped well short of the throne, and then bowed deeply.

"Thank you," she said, in a very subdued voice for Auri. "I'll have years to thank Fallon, and he's my brother so he had to help me. You chose to just because."

~Primarily because very upset mages are unlikely to succeed with complicated Symbolic castings. But it was my pleasure.~

Captain Faille crossed to where a tall, warm-skinned young man lay forgotten in the central circle. Duchess Surclere followed him as he gently raised the unmoving figure and carried him through the door that led to the room behind the throne. No-one else had been permitted back there, and Fallon was tremendously curious, but not even mildly tempted to try to follow—even if he'd been on his own two feet.

Tired, he let his head drop to Sukata's shoulder, and closed his eyes. He couldn't exactly say he felt better physically, but the idea of sleeping without dreaming—or at least dreaming of something other than Auri—filled him with such vast and incalculable pleasure that all the dragging weariness meant nothing.

He'd won his race.

oOo

The Pest wasn't doing it on purpose. In fact, Kendall was fairly certain he'd gone to sleep. But did he have to *nuzzle* into Sukata's neck like that?

Trying not to show her impatience, Kendall kept her mouth buttoned when Rennyn finally came back only to stand blah-blah-blah-ing with the Imperial Statue about working together again. Kendall hated this throne room, so full of little magics designed to tie its Emperor in place. She couldn't look at that thing on the throne without remembering how much Smug-Samarin had seemed to enjoy eating, and riding, and everything that didn't involve sitting in the same room for centuries.

Kendall found she'd moved so close to Sukata that she was almost pressed into her friend's side, and had to curl her hands into fists because she couldn't slip one into Sukata's. She knew Sukata hated the throne room too.

They had kissed each other five times now. They hadn't talked about that. Kendall hadn't wanted to talk. It felt like words would make fences, box her up and confuse everything. More than it already was. She edged a little closer to Sukata.

Auri bounced up, but sobered as she checked over her brother. "He'll start getting better now," she said, almost to herself. "Poor Fal. He's had to put up with so much. I wouldn't want to dream of me all night every night, and I'm me!"

"Do you feel..." Kendall started, hesitated, and then pushed on: "Do you think you'll stay like that?"

"I don't know. I never thought I wanted to be a boy, but I liked being Dezart Samarin, except sometimes I'd look down and I wasn't me, and that was like falling down a pit I'd forgotten was there. I was never as much interested in dresses and poetry and the things my mother cared about, but I quite liked myself generally. I never thought I'd come back as anything but me." A darting smile turned her copy-Fallon's face impish. "Though some boy-parts are *fun*, let me tell you."

"Spare us," Kendall said hastily.

"At the same time, I'm not half so interested in kissing girls as *you*," Auri said, laughed, and then took a quick step back with her hands held up to signal truce, even though Kendall hadn't moved at all. "I'm just so glad to be able to eat and sleep and talk to people and pick things up and...*everything.* I think I'll start caring more about what I look like later."

Rennyn had finally made enough plans to return to discuss 'other matters', and managed to get around to goodbye, and even sketched a curtsey before heading for the door. Sukata nodded, quite grandly, and Auri waved. Kendall, not quite sure how polite she wanted to be, hesitated, then gave the horrible prison of a throne the briefest of nods before quickening her step to catch the back of the group.

~A moment.~

The big double doors closed in her face. Kendall gaped at them, then turned and glared at the statue-Emperor.

"What now?"

~You still haven't answered my question, Kendall.~

The horrible, hollow voice was even worse when there was no-one else in the room. Talking walls, and a not-a-corpse on a throne, and magic to chain it all together.

"I don't give a rat's ass about your stupid questions," Kendall told him, extra clear.

~But I do. I must. I have seen enough of the Kellian now to know they could be an enormous asset to the Empire. At the least they would be useful allies, ones who could open up Semarrak to us. And yet, should they truly become part of the Empire, how much of Kole will end in thrall to them, blindingly loyal?~

"Would that even be such a bad thing? All the Kellian ever seem to want to do is protect people."

"When the Montjuste-Surcleres—especially Helecho Montjuste-Surclere—can inherit command of them? Most certainly.~

"I'm going to fix that."

Kendall hadn't meant to tell him—to tell anyone—that. Definitely not so soon, when she'd barely decided it was her goal. The long pause told her she'd surprised Smug-Ass as well.

~Are you indeed?~

Well, now that she'd said it, there was no point backing down.

"See, I kept not wanting to be the sort of mage that goes around treating people like toys. Or one who ends up like you or that Nameen woman or even Rennyn: so powerful that you seem to think you're obliged to do awful things to yourself, because you're the only ones who can. But Rennyn asked me if there wasn't anything I wanted to do with magic, that no-one else could."

~You believe you will surpass your teacher?~

Kendall shrugged. "Who knows? Probably not. But then, it's a bit like how Rennyn had Lieutenant Meniar cast the spell that got all your mages out of the ivy. Rennyn is hung up on the fact that she can tell the Kellian what to do, and that makes her the wrong person to try to fix being able to command them. She ties herself up in knots about feeling responsible for them but not having the right to interfere, and that stops her thinking about it properly."

~You do not fear chaining yourself to a statue?~

"I'm not silly enough to ever come up with that as a solution," Kendall said. "Besides, Sukata is..." She shrugged and eyed him without favour. A piece of furniture. An old man chained to a chair. "I might even think of a way to fix you."

~Mine is a political problem. There is no fixing politics with magic.~

"Listen to yourself," Kendall retorted.

There was a little pause. Then the door opened, and Kendall left him to his living nightmare. She probably wasn't the right person to fix his problem anyway, though she'd help him if he wanted it. Meanwhile there was Sukata, and the whole idea that Kendall would start minding Sukata's business. Politely, of course. Asking properly first, and not making decisions just because she could. But definitely poking her nose in.

Sukata was worth it.